CURSEBOUND

Also by Saara El-Arifi

The Ending Fire Trilogy
The Final Strife
The Battle Drum
The Ending Fire

The Faebound Trilogy
Faebound

CURSEBOUND

SAARA EL-ARIFI

HARPER
Voyager

Harper*Voyager*
An imprint of HarperCollins*Publishers* Ltd
1 London Bridge Street
London SE1 9GF

www.harpercollins.co.uk

HarperCollins*Publishers*
Macken House
39/40 Mayor Street Upper
Dublin 1
DOI C9W8
Ireland

First published by HarperCollins*Publishers* Ltd 2025
1

Map and chapter illustrations © Nicolette Caven 2025
Notes on Mosima illustrations: Shutterstock.com

Saara Eldin asserts the moral right to
be identified as the author of this work.

A catalogue record for this book is available from the British Library.

ISBN: 978-0-00-859701-6 (HB)
ISBN: 978-0-00-859702-3 (TPB)

This novel is entirely a work of fiction.
The names, characters and incidents portrayed in it are
the work of the author's imagination. Any resemblance to
actual persons, living or dead, events or localities is
entirely coincidental.

Typeset in Scala Pro by Palimpsest Book Production Ltd, Falkirk, Stirlingshire

Printed and bound in the UK using 100%
Renewable Electricity by CPI Group (UK) Ltd

This book contains FSC™ certified paper and other controlled
sources to ensure responsible forest management.

For more information visit: www.harpercollins.co.uk/green

For Rachel

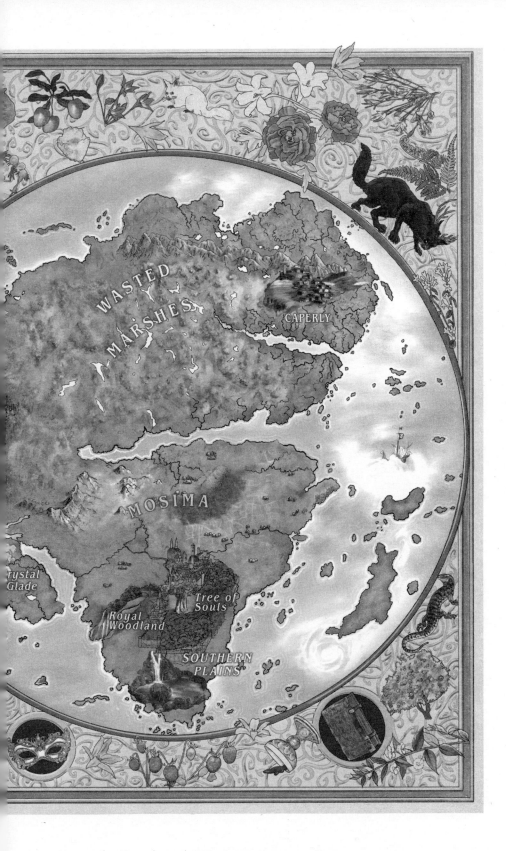

LETTLE'S JOURNAL

Notes
Chronicling Recent Events

Five months ago, I was a diviner in the Elven Lands, namely that of the Waning district – my sister Yeeran would want me to stress that, as she's *ever* proud of our heritage and has remained so even after she got exiled to the Wasted Marshes by her own lover, Chieftain Salawa. And though Yeeran and I have had our arguments, I was not about to leave her to the horrors of the wilderness.

Intent on bringing her back home, I followed her path into the lands beyond the Elven borders. Rayan, Yeeran's former second-in-command, came too – though I could have rescued her on my own, I hasten to add – and together we sought out my sister.

It was while I was on this journey that I foretold the words that haunt me to this day:

The one born of a storm's mist shall be your beloved. But when the waning moon turns, you will grant them their death.

Little did I know that I had foretold the love I now have for Rayan. My heart belonged to him even then.

Yeeran meanwhile was hunting an obeah – creatures whose skin is used by Waning to create drumfire, a weapon of war. With feline bodies coated in onyx-black fur and wide pearlescent branching antlers, obeah have both the speed of a leopard, and the stealth of a stag. Yeeran had hoped to return to Chieftain Salawa with the gift of the pelt from the largest obeah she'd ever seen, a trophy precious enough to grant her impunity from her crimes.

It was the day after we'd been reunited when Yeeran killed her prize. But the beast's death didn't grant Yeeran her freedom, instead we all became prisoners to the fae: unbeknownst to us, obeah and fae are bound together, in killing one you kill the other. And what Yeeran had done was the gravest of all crimes in the eyes of our capturers.

Perhaps I should pause here. Yes, *fae exist*. We had not known it, as there had been no reported sightings of them for a thousand years. And our histories . . . well, they failed to document the truth, speculating that the fae and humans went extinct long ago. But as the fae lore tells it, they were cursed to dwell in an underground cavern, a beautiful prison called Mosima, ruled by two queens of the Jani dynasty, the sisters Chall and Vyce.

Yeeran was held prisoner in a cell next to an older elf, known only as Komi. But her fate wasn't to remain imprisoned like him, for her crime was too severe: she was sentenced to death by the queens, for the obeah she had killed had been bound to the prince of Mosima.

I will not linger on the pain of the moment when I found out Yeeran was to be killed. But know that it is a wound that will never heal. A memory that will never scar.

But then she found the obeah Pila, or rather Pila found her, I'm not sure how it works. Either way, Yeeran became faebound, tying her soul to an obeah.

And no, I did not bond to one. No one knows why Yeeran, an elf, became faebound but it happened and thankfully it saved her life. Komi's too, as part of Yeeran's negotiations with the queens was to free him as well.

The four of us lived together in a quiet corner of the palace. Months dragged on beneath the ground, but I was given a semblance of freedom. I spent my days learning the fae language from Golan, a stylist who proved to be my only friend among the fae. Equipped with this new knowledge I tried to understand the curse that sealed the boundary between the fae's realm and our own.

My research led me to an old fable, *The Story of the Wheat, the Bat, and the Water*, which spoke of the three gods and the three beings they made. It was there that I found an ancient prophecy, first spoken over a thousand years ago:

> *Forever the war will rage, until united, the three shall die.*
> *Humans made low, then fae made lower,*
> *Then elves in ignorance, gone is their power,*
> *Cursed to endure, cursed to survive.*
> *All shall perish lest all three thrive.*

Don't ask me what it's about, I haven't figured it out yet. But I will, and when I do, the world will be peaceful once more.

Yeeran on the other hand was forced to train under Furi, the commander of the faeguard and the sister of the prince she'd killed. It wasn't long before their blows turned to kisses.

I too, found solace in the arms of a lover, Rayan, but not before disaster struck the Jani dynasty: Queens Vyce and Chall were found murdered.

I had foretold their deaths many months ago, but I'd been too blind to recognise the prophecy until it came to fruition. I vowed not to do that again.

Over the next few days the Tree of Souls – a giant baobab tree that connects the curse to the Jani dynasty – began to bind with the new rulers.

Everyone expected the successors to the throne to be Nerad and Furi, the only remaining children of Vyce and Chall.

Furi, yes, the tree chose her, that much came true. But the other to be crowned king was none other than Rayan. My beloved, whose fae heritage was unknown even to him.

For he had discovered the true tragedy: his father was Najma, the prince Yeeran had murdered. Rayan's life had always been pock-marked with pain. His mother had also been killed when he was young, slaughtered by the tyrannical Chieftain Akomido.

And Akomido . . . was secretly Komi all along. How we didn't see it I'll never know. But it had been prophesied that Komi would die by Rayan's hand and so Chieftain Akomido left this life for the next, entombed in the stone that Rayan summoned from the earth.

Komi wasn't the only one to die. Nerad had also laid his betrayal bare – it turns out he was the one behind the queens' murder, his political alliances having swayed so drastically from his family's.

We're nearing the end of the tale, and my hand is starting to ache as I write this. I'm not sure whether it's from writing, or because of what I have to say next.

The last thread to unravel was knotted the moment Yeeran was exiled. On that day, she'd been on the battlefield in a war zone when her archers had fired on the Crescent army, but her soldiers' arrows glanced off them as if the enemy were encased in glass.

But it wasn't glass – it was fae magic.

The fae had made an alliance with Waning's greatest adversary, the Crescent district. In exchange for fae soldiers, Crescent would grant the fae their old territory back. For the fraedia crystal beneath the Bleeding Field was not a mine to be pillaged but the former Fae Lands.

Yeeran, upon learning the news, left Mosima.

Left Furi.

And left me.

All to warn her old lover, Chieftain Salawa, of the fae's involvement.

Will she be successful? I have cast my talismans time and time again to ask the Fates.

But all I get is silence.

PART ONE

❧

Afa's Grimoire

I leave these words for the future to find. Within these pages you will understand the steps that we were forced to take, and why you must continue the path we forged.

The elders claim that the world was once a peaceful place before the gods chose to create their children. The god Asase made my brethren – the humans – out of the seeds of the forest and granted us the magic to speak the language of the trees and animals. It is said that our power was once so great that we used it to create all things of beauty in this world – the colours on a peacock's tail, the heart of a lotus flower, the majesty of the blue whales in the open sea.

But then the god Ewia spun the fae out of rays of sunlight, and the god Bosome moulded the elves from the waters of the earth. The humans' power, great as it was, was then coveted, revered – and fought over by the fae and the elves.

And so we withdrew from the great wars of the world as our numbers diminished, as our power dwindled, and as more and more of our knowledge was stolen or lost.

I have made it my life's work to bring together all the remnants of the human magic and have bound those secrets within the pages of this grimoire.

May it be your salvation.

CHAPTER ONE

Yeeran

Yeeran wasn't alone in the forest. Though she saw nothing and no one, she felt her skin prickle like she was being watched.

It had been five days since Yeeran and Pila had left Mosima. Five days since she'd learned of the fae's involvement with Crescent district.

And as each day passes more and more of my tribe die by their hand. The thought was for her alone, but Pila answered her.

Furi said they were recalling the fae soldiers from Crescent.

What if we're too late?

Her obeah didn't reply and Yeeran was glad of it because she could no longer think about the death that was sure to meet her in Waning.

They pushed further into the forest, Yeeran's feeling of unease increasing.

Though the journey across the Wasted Marshes had been arduous, she'd been thankful that she hadn't crossed paths with anyone else. Yet.

Pila, can you sense anyone nearby?

Pila raised her snout to the lilac sky and sniffed. *I don't smell anything.*

To Yeeran the air smelled like moss and swamp water but she knew Pila's nose could detect far more than hers.

Are you sure? Yeeran asked. *I feel like someone is watching us.*

Only the animals and plants, Pila confirmed.

The Wasted Marshes was a harsh landscape with as many poisonous plants as there were animals. The soil was boggy and often turned into quicksand beneath your feet before you knew it.

They entered a clearing where the earth was more solid. Circled by cypress and eucalyptus trees, it would provide some element of shelter from the weather. And with the sky darkening around them it was sure to rain come sunset. A perfect place to camp.

Yeeran slipped from Pila's back and looked around. Despite Pila's assurance, she still felt unsettled.

There'd been rumours of a tribe of violent nomadic elves, but those stories were unsubstantiated, and had likely just been invented to scare away skin traders who tried to operate in these lawless lands.

What are skin traders? Pila asked.

You know how obeah skin is coveted in the Elven Lands for its magic?

Pila shivered beside her. *Yes.*

Dark skin like mine can be passed as obeah leather to the unsuspecting. It's easier to catch an elf than an obeah.

Pila whined. *I like your skin.*

Yeeran patted Pila's fur. *Don't worry, I won't let anyone hurt me.*

Despite her lingering concerns, Yeeran knew they wouldn't find a better place to rest. She removed her pack and began to lay down her bedroll.

A sudden breeze swirled around the trees and ruffled the eucalyptus and cypress leaves. Yeeran closed her eyes and breathed in the scent, trying to calm her nerves.

Pila pinned her ears back and craned her neck upwards.

What is it? Yeeran asked.

I thought I smelled something, but it's gone.

Any serenity that Yeeran had conjured fled in that moment.

She dipped into a low crouch and swung her drum in front of her. Her fingers danced along the surface as she scanned the trees.

Caw-waw, caw-waw, caw-waw.

The bird's call rang out eerily in the clearing. Yeeran didn't recognise it and she knew it must be a signal from one elf to another.

Hunters.

It was the only explanation. Why else would a group of elves travel to the border of the Wasted Marshes? The forests in the Elven Lands had become sparse with obeah due to over-hunting and so hunters were forced to travel further afield for their prey.

Pila shifted her paws with nervous energy. Yeeran reached over and scratched the gap between Pila's horns. *No one will hurt us,* she said.

Because what the elves didn't know was that the obeah were linked to a fae's soul – you kill an obeah and the fae dies too. To become faebound was a condition unique to fae. That was until Yeeran and Pila bonded and she became the first elf with fae magic.

Caw-waw, caw-waw, caw-waw. The sound was getting louder, Yeeran was sure of it.

You need to run, Pila, Yeeran said.

Pila huffed out her nose. *I'm not leaving you.*

We're more agile apart. If they see me, there's nothing they will do. If they see you, they'll kill you.

Pila growled low in her throat as if to say, 'They could *try*.'

Yeeran leaned forward and pressed her forehead against the obeah's. Her hands slipped into her scruff as she embraced Pila. It was a strange feeling, holding onto a part of your soul. It was as if she was reaching into a mirror but instead of glass her fingers brushed fur and warmth.

I can't breathe, Pila said.

Yeeran released Pila's neck with a smile. *Go now. Make sure you give the clearing a wide berth. I'll see you on the other side.*

The obeah slipped away into the undergrowth, her black fur a flicker of shadows on the fern leaves before she was gone.

It was easy to forget Pila was a creature of the forest. But so too was Yeeran, her father had made sure of it.

As they'd got closer to the Crescent district border the terrain had grown less boggy, but it was still wetter than she would have liked – drier ground could minimise sound.

She moved through the bush at a steady pace, her footfalls silent.

'With each step, roll from the ball of your foot to your heel,' her father had once said. 'And move quickly. The faster the cadence, the easier it is to keep the rhythm.'

Yeeran had adored her father, but he had disagreed with her choice to join the Waning army and they had parted in anger. *Then Lettle killed him . . .* The thought caused her to stumble and she tripped over an overgrown root. She landed heavily on her back.

Birds scattered from the bough above. Yeeran winced at the noise she must have made. She felt a surge of concern down her connection with Pila.

I'm all right, just took a fall.

Next time, don't fall, Pila replied matter-of-factly.

Yeeran lay there listening carefully to the forest, but its rhythms were unchanged, except for the bird calls having fallen silent.

The sun was setting and the darkness of night was gathering in the shadows of the trees. Yeeran wanted to put distance between her and the hunters before sleeping for the night.

She waited a little longer before standing, but then something moved in the canopy above her and she paused.

It looked too big to be a creature of the Wasted Marshes – the fauna here were mainly birds and reptiles. But this beast had long arms and legs that spread wide as it pranced from tree to tree. Yeeran watched the shape move, mesmerised by its agility. Then, without warning, it began to spiral down the nearest trunk towards her.

She sat up, her hands moving to her drum, but it was too late. The figure was already standing above her.

With the light of the sunset at his back all she could see were the whites of the man's teeth as he spoke. 'Hello, there.'

Yeeran froze. It took a moment for her eyes to adjust to the man standing above her. His grin, which she had initially thought was sinister, spread up his cheek in a lopsided, boyish way, ageing him down from the forty years she estimated.

'Hello,' she said uncertainly.

'You seem lost,' the man said, offering her his hand to help her up.

Yeeran wasn't sure why she grabbed it but there was something about him that seemed non-threatening.

Those are the people you should be wary of the most, Pila said across the distance.

True, she replied.

Yeeran stood and brushed herself off.

'Did I see you climb down from a tree?'

The man bobbed his head, causing his blond hair to flop over his eyes. He pushed it away with a calloused hand.

'Yes, us Nomads make our camp among the tree line.'

'Nomads?' she said with just a hint of doubt.

His eyes flickered to hers before looking away. 'Yes, Nomads,' he repeated with just a hint of mettle.

He went to pick up Yeeran's drum that had fallen from her shoulder when she had tripped. Her eyes narrowed as his fingers lightly brushed the skin. She wondered if he recognised that it wasn't made from obeah leather.

For a second she thought he wasn't going to pass it back to her, and she tensed, ready to fight for it.

Then he said softly, 'I'm always amazed at how something so beautiful could reap such violence.' He held out the drum to her.

His words disarmed her for a moment, but she snatched the drum back and swung the strap over her head before replying, 'Anything beautiful can be a weapon, it all depends on who wields it.'

The man cocked his head, looking thoughtful. 'Yes, some of the loveliest plants make the most poisonous tinctures.'

They stood in silence for a moment, the sky darkening around them.

Then the man smiled once more and said, 'I'm Alder, and it is the Nomad way to invite every elf we meet in the wilderness to join us for a hot meal.'

'You are truly nomadic elves?' Yeeran asked. He didn't look like the primitive cannibals she'd heard of in stories.

His grin grew. 'We are. No rules but the forest's.'

Though she was curious, she did not trust Alder. She shook her head. 'I'm sorry, I have to be on my way.'

Alder's face fell in disappointment. 'Are you sure? The feast tonight will be the best of the year, as some of the Nomads have just returned from trading in Crescent. They always stop by the market to get a collection of spices.'

Yeeran's interest was piqued, not because of the food, but because of the intelligence these traders could bring from Crescent.

Yeeran, you cannot be considering this, Pila said from afar.

It is better to be prepared for what awaits us in the Elven Lands. This small delay might help us in the long run.

I don't like it. Why would they invite a stranger for food? Pila replied.

Yeeran voiced the obeah's question.

Alder laughed. 'It is how our community grows, for so many elves choose not to leave.'

You'll leave though, right? Pila asked.

Yes, of course, Pila, I would never abandon you.

Yeeran turned back to Alder. 'Lead the way.'

When Alder had said that the Nomads made their camp in the tree line, Yeeran hadn't truly believed it. But then Alder loped up the nearest tree.

'You expect me to climb up there?'

'It's easy, just follow my footsteps,' Alder said, crouching on a tree branch above her. He wore no shoes and his clothing was made from loosely woven hemp, all of which made him blend in perfectly with the forest.

Perfect for hunting, she thought. *Perhaps he lies and lures me to my death.*

You think he could be a skin trader? Pila asked, her concern down their connection making Yeeran wince.

No, Pila. I don't think he is, it was just an errant thought.

Somewhere to the south Pila unsheathed her claws.

'Are you coming?' Alder called.

After some false starts she made her way up the eucalyptus tree. When they were some twenty feet from the ground, Alder launched himself into the air. She called out, expecting to see his body plummet, but something caught him.

She inched closer, scrutinising what she was seeing in the fading sunlight. Silver threads, like a spider's web, ran in knots from one tree to another. As she looked further, she caught the glint of more latticed thread spreading across many of the trees around them.

'Silkvine. We harvest it in the north and use it to build our canopies,' he said, beckoning her towards him.

No wonder you couldn't smell them, Pila. They were above us the whole time.

Yeeran crawled her way across the nets to a large central canopy where glittering eyes watched her approach.

'Everyone, this is . . .' Alder paused, grasping for the name she hadn't yet given him.

'Yeeran,' she said a little breathlessly. Her heart was pounding in her throat as the silkvine moved beneath her.

A few of the Nomads smiled and nodded in her direction. There were about fifty elves, of all ages and genders. Only one thing tied them together – they all had slices in their ears to indicate dismissal from their respective armies. Even Alder's ears had been cut clean through the tips, a practice carried out by the Crescent army.

'How long have you been up here?' Yeeran asked as she carefully crossed her legs beneath her.

Alder lowered himself next to her. 'A few days, longest we've stayed in a place for a while.'

A young elf of ten or eleven skipped over with two clay cups in his hand. Yeeran's knuckles went white as she gripped onto the silkvine.

'Nettle wine?' the boy said, offering Yeeran a cup.

She peeled her fingers off the canopy and reached for the glass. The drink was sweet and warming.

'Thank you,' she said to the boy as he handed Alder the other cup with a respectful bow.

Once he'd left, Yeeran asked Alder, 'You're the leader of the Nomads?'

There were some titters from the group and a few laughs. Alder smiled. 'We abide by no rules nor ruler. But I am the Nomads' Wayfarer. I guide our steps.'

'And where are your steps taking you?'

Alder's eyes glinted in the moonlight. 'Where the currents glide and the winds blow.'

The Nomads raised their cups to the sky and called back to him, 'The Nomads walk no path.'

It was clearly a frequent tribute, and it gave Yeeran a sense for who these people were. And they were not hunters.

'What are you doing in the Wasted Marshes, Yeeran?' Alder asked once he'd sipped from his own cup.

'Searching for a flower,' Yeeran said smoothly. 'To help cure my friend's illness.'

She borrowed the lie from Lettle. Her sister had used the story to get past the border in Crescent back when Lettle and Rayan had followed Yeeran into exile.

It felt like a lifetime ago.

Alder leant back on the silkvine net and crossed his ankles. He was one of those people who seemed unaware of his own beauty. His face was so symmetrically shaped it appeared to be chiselled out of marble.

'Ah, Mia,' he called out. A woman with obsidian black hair walked across the swaying silkvine as if it were as stable as bricks. In her hands she held a large crockpot. The smell emanating from it had Yeeran's stomach growling.

'Food's up,' Mia called across the canopies. There was a slight hesitation from the group and she added with a scowl, 'Don't worry, I didn't cook it, I just brought it over. Baked yams stuffed with hazelnuts and crispy moss—Oh!' Mia noticed Yeeran. 'Who are you?'

'Yeeran,' she said before Alder could reply on her behalf. 'I was in the Wasted Marshes searching for a flower to cure my friend. Alder found me and invited me for food.'

The repeated lie sounded wooden on Yeeran's tongue but Mia simply raised an eyebrow and looked at Alder fondly before saying, 'Of course he did. Here, grab a yam before you get left with the mushy ones at the bottom.' She handed her the bowl.

Yeeran reached for the leathery vegetable. Its brown skin served both as a form of sustenance but also as a vessel for the stuffing and seasoning, so she could easily eat it with her hands.

She suppressed a groan as she chewed. The yam was delicious, buttery and nutty but with a hint of spice that set her tongue alight.

Alder watched her with a knowing smile. 'I told you, we feast well after trading with Crescent.'

The net beneath them swayed as more Nomads rushed forward to grab dinner.

Mia saw Yeeran freeze and said, 'Don't worry, the silkvine never fails. Well, except once, but that was a while ago, and it hadn't been knotted properly.'

Mia wasn't as reassuring as she thought she was.

Yeeran dared to move and reached for another one of the yams. 'How do you cook up here?' she asked before taking another bite.

'We don't,' Alder replied. 'We bake all our food in the ground using hot coals so as not to disturb the animals with fire smoke.'

These people were *definitely* not hunters. But neither were they the uncivilised nomadic elves she'd heard of in stories. The world they'd built above the tree line, though terrifying, was ingenious.

'So what flower are you looking for exactly? Maybe we can help?' Mia asked, sitting next to her. 'Alder here knows every plant and rock and creature in the forest.'

'It's . . . it's . . . purple with a yellow centre . . .' Yeeran tried to summon a more specific answer, but she'd never been the one with the vivid imagination. That had always been Lettle.

Mia looked to Alder, who shook his head. Yeeran wasn't sure if the gesture meant, 'I don't know it,' or 'Stop asking questions.'

Either way, Yeeran was grateful that Mia stopped prying.

After finishing her food Yeeran asked, 'What news of the Forever War? It has been some time since I have been away from my tribe.'

Once, the Forever War had been Yeeran's only purpose. The fraedia crystal beneath the battlefield had fuelled a war that had lasted centuries. The crystal was a precious commodity, creating the ideal conditions to grow plants and warm homes, no matter the weather or environment. The perfect fuel and fertiliser.

As a Colonel in the Waning Army, Yeeran had believed in their right to the fraedia and had waged war with the three other elven tribes in order to claim it. Despite being exiled, her allegiance still lay with her tribe.

An elf on Yeeran's left answered. They introduced themselves as Damal, and their voice crackled like fire but without the warmth. 'Crescent has gained ground. Their new magic is proving difficult to overcome.'

'New magic?' Yeeran asked carefully.

Damal's thick brows pulled together. 'You *have* been travelling a long time then.'

'Nearly four months.'

'Ah, right about the time that Waning saw Crescent's latest trick for the first time. A colonel in the Waning army was dismissed because of it. But it took a few more events for them to finally realise Crescent had a new form of magical defence – invisible shields.'

Yeeran schooled her face into an expression of shock. 'Invisible shields, how?'

Damal shrugged. 'No one knows.'

Yeeran knew: it was fae magic.

'Apparently a third of all the Waning army has been wiped out completely,' Damal said. 'The citizens are protesting. But civil unrest is rampant across Eclipse and Waxing too. Surprisingly Crescent is the only stable district right now.'

Nettle wine got clogged in Yeeran's throat and she began to choke. A *third* of the Waning army? They had been her family, her friends. Her *tribe*.

Mia thumped her on the back, a little harder than was perhaps necessary. 'Better?' she asked, hitting her one more time for good measure.

'Yes, thank you,' Yeeran croaked back.

Alder was watching Yeeran, and she tried to keep her expression neutral. But the truth was she was devastated to learn of the Waning army's fate.

She fortified her resolve. *I can still stop more death. Perhaps even end the war with the news I bring.*

Otherwise, breaking Furi's heart had all been for nothing.

Yeeran tried to push Furi from her mind. But when she shut her eyes she couldn't help but conjure the image of the fae bathed in sunlight, her hair a golden halo around her. Yeeran pressed the heels of her hands into her eyes, trying to ease the pain that blossomed there.

Mia took it as a sign of tiredness. 'I'm exhausted too, I think I'll retire.'

'Would you care to stay with us, Yeeran?' Alder asked. 'There is space on Mia's canopy. Her partner is away tonight.'

Pila? Are you safe at the border?

Yes.

I think I will stay the night here. I do not think they mean me ill and it would be nice to sleep the whole night through.

Pila yawned somewhere off in the distance. *All right, sleep well, as will I.*

'Yeeran?' Alder prompted.

'Oh sorry, yes, I would like that very much, thank you.'

Mia led her further into the web of canopies. She pranced ahead of Yeeran, her long hair running in waves down to the backs of her knees. Like Alder, she too was an ex-soldier of Crescent, and so the points of her ears had been shorn, though a little more crookedly than Alder's.

She couldn't have been in the military for many years to have grown her hair that long, but she was still young. Like Waning, Crescent utilised child soldiers. The thought left a bitter taste in Yeeran's mouth as she inched her way across the nets after Mia.

'Here we are,' Mia chimed as she stopped under a sheltered canopy beneath the bough of a eucalyptus tree. 'If it rains, you won't even know it,' she said.

'I have my own blankets, and a tarp just in case,' Yeeran said.

'You probably won't need it,' Mia said as she lay down on the silkvine. 'I wove the net so tightly that it cradles the whole body, it's very warm.'

Yeeran lay down beside her and realised Mia was right.

Sleep came easily.

Yeeran woke with a start. She had rolled right to the edge of the canopy, and her face was pressed against the bark of a eucalyptus tree.

Her heart hammered in her chest as she moved carefully away from the edge.

It was still the dead of night, and she couldn't have slept more than one or two hours. She felt the soft presence of Pila's dreams in her mind as the obeah slumbered somewhere to the south. Meanwhile, Mia snored softly beside Yeeran, her hair draped over one shoulder like a shroud.

Yeeran's drum was still strapped to her side and the barrel dug in painfully. She tried to rearrange it, but stopped when she felt the canopy pulsate as if someone was walking across it.

She turned to see a shadow moving towards her. The features of the apparition came into focus as it came to stand over her.

'Alder? What is it?' she asked him.

His grey eyes glistened in the moonlight. 'Hudhni iilaa qabri wadeni artaj,' he said, before his mouth hung slack-jawed.

'What?'

'Hudhni iilaa qabri wadeni artaj,' he repeated.

The words were nonsense to Yeeran and she felt a prickle of unease ripple through her. She reached for her drum, but as she did Alder took another step towards her, his hands held up as if to strike.

'Get away from me!' she shouted.

Mia immediately woke. 'What's going on?'

But Yeeran wasn't prepared to take on two people, so she reached for her magic and shot at Alder's legs.

Though she used threads of fae magic, she had the ability to use it differently than the fae did. Her experience in drumfire allowed her to create short bullet-like threads, but unlike the fae she had to use a drum to access her magic.

Alder cried out and fell to his knees as the bullets struck him.

'What are you doing?' Mia shrieked, running towards Alder.

Other Nomads were waking up from the commotion, but Yeeran didn't intend to stick around to fight any more people than she had to.

Whatever Alder's intentions, she knew now they weren't good. *If only I had trusted my gut in the first place*, she chided herself.

Climbing up the tree had been hard, but climbing down was easier. All she had to do was unspool a longer thread of magic.

Bada-dum, bada-dum, bada-dum.

In the Elven Lands, magic was derived from obeah skin stretched across a drum. The tone of the drumbeat produced different bullets, weaponising the sound waves. Yeeran used the same concept when she reached for her magic now, but instead of the magic coming from obeah skin, it came from within her. She used the intention of drumfire to focus her mind.

Bada-dum, bada-dum, bada-dum.

Yeeran drew out a continuous beat with a sharp, staccato rhythm, unravelling the magic within her. Then she concentrated on manipulating the thread to twist around a branch before she launched herself into nothingness.

For a second she felt like she was flying, but then the ground came rushing up to meet her. She rattled her fingers across her drum, directing the thread of magic to reel inwards before she hit the ground. It held her weight an inch from death.

Yeeran? Pila's thoughts were groggy from sleep before crystallising in alarm. *What happened?*

Yeeran recounted the attack in a few seconds.

I'll be waiting east of the stream that runs south of the camp, Pila confirmed. Then Yeeran felt the echo of the obeah's paws as they struck the ground resonating in her mind.

Fly fast, Pila.

It was Yeeran's turn to do the same.

There was no use trying to hide her footfalls. She needed speed, not surprise.

She dashed out into the night, her drum swinging in front of her for easy reach. Combat was the last thing she wanted. There were many more of them than her, despite her fae magic.

So instead she ran, and didn't look back.

To her surprise no arrows followed her flight, no shouts came from her back. But either way, it was still a relief to be reunited with Pila.

She jumped onto the obeah's back and Pila lurched through the forest, faster and faster until the Nomads took on the blurred shape of a nightmare from long ago.

CHAPTER TWO

Lettle

Lettle threw her prophecy tokens across the room. One of them struck a mirror on the wall, showering glass shards onto the ground.

It was the second mirror she had broken that week. The first time the glass had been cleaned away and replaced during the night. It had been a stark reminder of how many servants attended the royal chambers.

She let out a sigh and collapsed backwards on the bed. The ample bedding cushioned her fall but did nothing to comfort her frustrations.

Lettle had been throwing the talismans hourly ever since Yeeran had left eight days ago. But the Fates refused to share any news of her sister.

The door to her bedroom opened and Golan's face appeared in the crack, one eyebrow raised. He tipped his head to the broken mirror. 'If you didn't like what you looked like, you should have called me to do your make-up earlier.'

Lettle pushed herself to her elbows. 'What?'

Golan stepped into the room and pointed to the glass shards on the ground. 'The mirror? It's broken?'

'Oh that. I threw my tokens at it.'

Golan swept away some of the glass with his cane before crossing the room and lowering himself onto the edge of her four-poster bed.

'Still haven't managed a prophecy?' he asked gently.

Lettle released a hot breath. 'No. Nothing, absolutely nothing.'

'What does Sahar say about it?' Golan asked.

Lettle hadn't seen the previous seer of Mosima – a title that had now been bestowed on Lettle – since she'd gone to his apothecary the day after Yeeran left. She cast her thoughts back to that moment over a week ago now.

'I harvested more owen tree sap for you on that shelf,' Sahar had said, not looking up as she came in. He was staring at a notebook in front of him. She recognised it as his prophecy journal.

'New prophecy?' she asked as she picked up the vial of owen tree sap. The sticky liquid helped ease the pain in her atrophied arm.

Sahar closed the notebook as she came over. For a minute his brown eyes looked full of sorrow, but then he shook his head. 'Nothing of interest.'

Lettle knew the heartache that could come with foretelling what was to pass, so she didn't press him. If he wanted his privacy, she would grant him it.

She pulled out her own prophecy tokens from her pocket to replace them with the jar of owen tree sap, causing the talismans to spill out from their little pouch.

Sahar helped gather them up. As he did, he held one of the tokens up to the light. 'These could do with a little oiling, helps the wood from cracking. Here, let me get some.'

When he had returned the talismans were slick with oil. That was the last time they had spoken.

'I haven't seen Sahar for a little while,' Lettle said to Golan now. 'Though I hear he's moving into the palace at Furi's behest.' As well as being the previous seer, Sahar was also Furi's father.

Golan nodded, his long dark braids swaying. 'Yes, I heard so too. He might even be at dinner tonight and you can ask him then.'

Lettle tried to rally her hopes but she must have still looked miserable because Golan laid a manicured hand on her arm. 'The Fates will speak to you again,' he said gently.

'How do you know that?' she replied, far more angrily than she'd intended. But by now Golan was used to her temper and knew her ire wasn't directed at him.

Golan shrugged. 'I don't.'

Lettle stood up at his words and went to the window. She opened the glass shutter, which was wide enough for a fully grown obeah to fit its horns through. As she was unbound to an obeah, the hatch's sole use was admitting a welcome respite of cool air.

Not that there was much breeze in Mosima. The underground cavern was temperate though a little too humid for Lettle's tastes. But plants thrived in that atmosphere, and so the landscape ahead of her was a vibrant green. Even the red rock of the cave's ceiling was covered in moss and trailing ivy.

Hanging in the centre was the one thing keeping everything alive – the fray, the largest deposit of fraedia crystal Lettle had ever seen.

Right now the fray was dimming to a deep red with the oncoming sunset.

'It's nearly dinner time,' she said.

'Yes, that's why I'm here.' Golan tapped the satchel by his waist which Lettle knew was full of potions and lotions to make her look beautiful.

'You know you don't need to do my make-up anymore. Rayan has named you as my advisor.'

Golan smiled his perfect smile. 'I know, but I like to. Plus, King Rayan always appreciates my efforts.' He winked and Lettle rolled her eyes.

King Rayan. It was still so strange. She ran her hand along the windowsill. The windowsill of the royal chambers – her chambers.

First she'd been a prisoner in this forgotten land. Then she'd been a guest. And now she was the consort to the king: an elf who was part of the fae royal court.

It was almost too unbelievable to believe. And yet, here she was. With plush carpet beneath her feet and down pillows to rest her head. She'd come a long way from the poverty she'd grown up in.

Golan got up from the bed and made his way to the wardrobe.

Lettle pointed to the plum-coloured dress hanging on the handle of the cupboard. 'I already picked out an outfit for tonight,' she said.

Golan let out a low whistle between his teeth. 'I do not believe I have much more to teach you—'

'And also the fuchsia sandals there.' Lettle went to pull out the slippers she'd chosen earlier.

Golan's face fell. 'You were so close. Perhaps there's more for you to learn yet.'

That tugged a smile onto Lettle's lips.

'There she is,' Golan said, crossing the room again. 'I know it's been difficult with Yeeran' – Lettle inhaled sharply at her name – 'gone, but you'll see, soon enough life here will take on a steady rhythm and your troubles will seem smaller and smaller each day.'

Lettle didn't like the sound of that. She didn't want to *forget* Yeeran, or how she'd abandoned Lettle in Mosima.

She didn't abandon you – she left to warn the Waning tribe of the fae's involvement with Crescent. She went to save lives. But Lettle's conscience wasn't something she wanted to grapple with that day, so she squashed the thought and clung tighter to her anger.

Her gaze lingered on the shattered glass where her tokens lay.

'Let me speak to the Fates one more time.'

Lettle gathered up the carved pieces representing major organs in the body: lungs, heart, stomach, kidneys, liver and intestines. The final organ, and the most important, was the brain, signified by Lettle herself.

Carved from the Tree of Souls, the wood held residual magic from the curse that bound the fae. It was this magical potency that fuelled her connection to the Fates. Before carving her talismans Lettle would have had to slaughter an obeah to practise divination, but now she had these.

She threw the pieces against her dressing table and slipped into magesight.

Magesight allowed a diviner to read the Fates clearly. It also enabled a person to see fae magic too. Her gaze slid past Golan.

He didn't glow with the unique shine attributed to the faebound. *Lightless*, the fae called the affliction.

But Lettle knew the truth. Golan had a hidden light that shone much brighter than every other fae she'd ever met. Just because they couldn't see it in the same way didn't mean he was lesser.

As if sensing her thoughts he reached over and squeezed her shoulder. 'You can do this,' he said.

She turned her magesight back to the tokens. But there was not one flicker of silver. Not even a wisp.

'Enough of this,' she said dismissively. 'I need some mead. Let's get ready.'

The royal dining hall was on the top floor of the palace. Lettle made her way up the stairs with heavy steps.

The staircase had once been made of glass, built by the former queens. But when they had been killed the panes of glass had fallen and shattered. It had been Rayan who had replaced them, calling on the rocks from the earth to form a staircase of stone.

Just like Rayan, it was sturdy, and carried her to new heights. The thought lifted her spirits.

Her breathing came out in short uneven puffs. Over a week ago, she'd been in the hospital with a collapsed lung, an injury caused by the fae prince, Nerad. Though his betrayal had caused deeper wounds than the ones inflicted on her. Those who had suffered most were his mother and aunt – the queens – who had died by his hand. Lettle had been left with her life, though she got more out of breath than she once had.

This dress isn't helping. The train of the skirt was balled up in her fist as she ascended the stairs. She hated how she was expected to dress up for every meal. But she was *consort* now as well as the royal seer.

Consort to King Rayan. His name brought a soft smile to her lips, parting the tacky gloss that glistened on them.

The door to the dining hall was open, and as she crossed the threshold her stomach sank. She was late: dinner had already been served.

The stone table was large enough to seat fifty people, which Lettle thought was ridiculous considering there were only ever three of them: Furi, herself, Rayan – and tonight Sahar too. That was the extent of the royal family.

Queen Vyce, Queen Chall, and Nerad's ghosts lingered in the empty seats, making Lettle shiver as she strode past.

The others didn't seem to notice the vacant space where the dead had once sat and were talking jovially to each other, though the chatter stopped as Lettle walked in.

The table was laden with vegetables of all kinds: carrots roasted in honey, potatoes seasoned with sage, cauliflower fried in butter. The latter was Lettle's favourite, and though she missed meat, the dish was a good replacement. The fae did not eat animals, a consequence of them bonding with obeah.

Lettle shot Rayan an apologetic glance for her lateness and pulled out a chair to his right.

'Let me get that, seer.' A servant dashed forward from the shadows of the room where candles wept red wax in alcoves.

The servant reached for the chair, brushing his knuckles with Lettle's. For a second Lettle saw disgust cross the servant's face. Then it was smoothed away into polite uninterest.

Lettle scowled at him. She'd grown used to the fae's blatant disregard for elves, but this new covert hatred was almost worse. They were pretending to accept her, and she loathed it.

She made sure to remember the servant's face. There were over a hundred fae who worked in the palace, and it had only been in the last few days that she'd started to take notice of their comings and goings.

'Sorry I'm late,' she said to the room while reaching for the mead.

'No bother,' Rayan said, his eyes crinkling. Sahar smiled politely and dipped his head in her direction.

Furi set her jaw and didn't reply. Over this last week the fae's temper had been shorter than Lettle's. And she knew why – Yeeran.

Lettle downed her glass of mead before smacking her lips and pouring another.

Rayan raised an eyebrow but had enough tact not to ask her how her divination was going.

Furi did not. 'So I take it you weren't able to glean anything of our future today?' she drawled in fae before stabbing a carrot with her fork. The language, gifted only to those bound to an obeah, had been difficult for Lettle to learn to read let alone speak, but Furi refused to talk to her in anything else. It was yet another way Lettle was made to feel like a stranger in this strange land.

'No,' was Lettle's curt reply in elvish.

'Pity.' Furi's lips turned up into a smirk. Furi's mother had banned divination during her reign, so it was no surprise that Furi didn't find the skill remarkable.

Yet, it was powerful enough to predict her mother's death.

The thought was bitter and full of malice. Lettle took another sip of mead.

'Daughter,' Sahar chastised Furi. 'You cannot expect the Fates to answer to Lettle's every call. We must have patience. They will tell us what we need to know when we need to know it.'

Sahar's response extinguished any hope that he might be able to help.

Furi looked ready to roll her eyes, and for a moment Lettle could see who she had been as a teenager. It was like looking into a reflection of Lettle's own past and it startled her to think of having anything in common with Furi.

Lettle shifted in her seat and changed the topic. 'How fares the retreat from Crescent? Have you managed to make contact with the last squadron of soldiers?' She directed the question at Rayan. She avoided talking to Furi as much as she could, but it was still Furi who answered.

'No, Berro has been sent to recall them.'

'Berro?' Another fae that Lettle despised. Berro's blatant lust for Rayan grated on Lettle.

'Yes, it will be a difficult diplomatic negotiation. As we have to convey the news of the death of Akomido . . .' Furi flashed her gaze towards Rayan, who shrugged. 'And try and prevent another war.'

Komi's death was still a raw wound for Lettle. His true identity had been that of Chieftain Akomido, also known as the Two-Bladed Tyrant, infamous for his inhumane dictatorship in Crescent. It was still difficult to entirely disengage from the memories she had of him during her time here. Happy memories, that were now tainted by the truth of who he really was.

'You think Berro will be able to prevent Crescent from retaliating?' Lettle asked doubtfully.

Furi gave her a withering look. 'Berro has been my second-in-command for years, she is as capable as I am in navigating politics.'

Which is not very. Though Lettle didn't speak the words, Furi must have seen them written on her face.

'Perhaps you should stick to throwing your dice, and I will handle the politics of *my* land,' Furi said.

Lettle prickled at the reminder that she was an outsider. Even Rayan was half-fae, and the fae had accepted him like one of their own. Without Yeeran here Lettle was truly the only outlander.

Rayan cleared his throat, drawing attention to him in the hopes of defusing the sparks of tension that crackled between Furi and Lettle. But Furi's words had cut deeper than Lettle cared to admit, and her fervour had already fizzled out.

'I've been going through my father's research,' Rayan said, changing the subject. 'Including everything that Nerad had stolen from his collection, but there isn't much.'

Furi swallowed her mouthful and said, 'What are you expecting to find?'

Rayan's gaze turned troubled. 'I'm not sure. Something about the curse that binds us down here. My father didn't share all he knew.'

Lettle and Rayan shared a look. There was more Rayan wasn't

telling Furi, but they'd decided to keep the truth hidden from her for now. In his final letter to his son, Najma had warned Rayan of the untrustworthiness of his family.

Yeeran may stand by Furi's morals, but I do not.

Furi's gaze had drifted to the window towards the Royal Woodland beyond. But Lettle could tell she wasn't really seeing the forest – she was traversing her memories of her older brother.

Furi jerked back into the moment, her fork clattering against her plate.

'Daughter?' Sahar asked, concerned.

To Lettle's horror, Furi's eyes turned glassy. The queen rarely showed much raw emotion. But when she spoke her voice was lifeless, raising the hairs on Lettle's neck.

'It doesn't matter, none of it does. We're stuck down here. And perhaps that's a good thing. We're protected from the Crescent soldiers who will surely wage war against us out of vengeance for killing our ally.' Furi lay the blame of Akomido's death at Rayan's feet but he didn't seem to be affected by her attitude. The Two-Bladed Tyrant may have been the fae's ally, but his death by Rayan's hand had been foretold since he'd been a boy.

And there was no stopping prophecy.

The one born of a storm's mist shall be your beloved. But when the waning moon turns, you will grant them their death.

Lettle flinched as the old prophecy seared its way across her mind. Foretold by the Shaman Imna, it had haunted her since she'd left Waning. It was her greatest secret, and the source of all her guilt: one day she would kill Rayan.

But not today.

She reached under the table with her left arm. Though she had little grip and limited movement in the elbow – a legacy of the Wasting Pox she had as a child – she found Rayan's thigh and rested her hand there. He instantly slipped his own hand under the table and cradled her left hand gently in his.

Lettle felt herself relax at his touch. Rayan turned back to Furi.

'I don't think accepting our fate is the solution, Furi. I know I can find a way out by using my father's research.'

Furi's nostrils flared but she didn't contradict him. She could never hold onto her anger towards Rayan, perhaps because of the blood they shared.

'Rayan's right,' Lettle added. 'We need to keep trying.'

Because Lettle wanted to go home someday. And while the curse was in place Rayan was tied to the land, unable to leave Mosima without dire consequences, and Lettle could not leave without Rayan.

Furi stood abruptly. 'I think I'll take my leave, I have a splitting headache.'

Lettle didn't watch Furi go, but she felt the temperature in the room grow immeasurably warmer once the door closed behind her.

'I too will retire to my new chambers. Thankfully they're only a few doors away,' Sahar said, patting his stomach. Then he looked at Lettle with kind eyes. 'Do not worry that the Fates have not spoken. You are a proficient seer, we know that. Be kind to yourself.'

Sahar's words touched Lettle deeply. The old man turned to Rayan.

'Goodnight, grandson. May you dream well.'

There was a moment of silence once Rayan and Lettle were alone. Then Rayan pulled his chair closer to hers and ran his hand along her cheek before lowering a kiss onto her lips.

'I've been waiting to do that since you arrived.' He pressed a smile to her cheek.

She wrapped her hand around the nape of his neck and with one scoop he pulled her onto his lap.

'Why can't we eat dinner like this every night?' she said into his neck.

Rayan's laugh rumbled up his throat. 'I don't think Furi would like it.'

'Who cares about Furi.'

Rayan's laugh deepened and he brought his smiling lips down on hers once more.

He tasted of honey and lemon rind. It unfurled a coil of desire from deep within her core and she arched into him.

'Oh – sorry!'

They broke apart and turned towards the voice that had so rudely interrupted them. Lettle narrowed her eyes when she saw it was the servant who had been there earlier.

'I was just going to clear away the p-plates,' he said, stuttering.

Rayan waved him in but didn't make a move to lift Lettle from his lap. 'It's fine we were about to leave for our bedchamber anyway,' he said.

Lettle raised an eyebrow. 'Were we? I don't think I was quite done with my mead.'

The servant hesitated over the table. 'Should I return later?'

Rayan shook his head. 'No, no, it's fine, just leave the mead please.'

Lettle muffled her laugh against the stubble of his cheek. The silence stretched as the servant moved in and out clearing the table of all the dishes.

Eventually just her glass was left.

'Here you are, consort.' The servant dipped his head as he handed her the glass. Something akin to revulsion flickered in his eyes. Curious, she turned to magesight.

If you looked at the core of those faebound, the spark – for all living things had a spark – swirled with something a little darker, almost coppery.

The servant was not faebound. She'd suspected as much when he didn't speak to her in fae. Though some of the Lightless, like Golan, had learned to speak it fluently, the vowels were difficult to master so few did.

The servant straightened, his long hair fluttering behind his back, before almost running out the door.

'I think we scared him off,' Lettle said.

'Yes,' Rayan replied while nuzzling her neck.

'Careful! You're going to spill my mead.'

Rayan reached for the goblet and brought it to his own mouth. 'My mead.' He took a deep drink, his brown eyes twinkling. When he pulled the glass away, his lips were shimmering with the honey wine.

Lettle leaned forward to lick it off, but before her lips could touch his he coughed.

'Cover your mouth,' she scolded him.

But then he coughed again, more frantic this time.

'Rayan?'

His breath was coming out in rasping puffs as if his throat was closing up.

The wine glass fell to the floor.

No, Rayan *threw* it.

His eyes went wide and he turned to Lettle and gasped out one word: 'Poison.'

Then his eyes rolled to the back of his head and he fell limp.

CHAPTER THREE

Alder

For many years, Alder had lived in the Elven Lands. But he only knew that from the cuts on his ears. He had no memories of his time in the war there, an affliction that a few in his party suffered from.

'A blessing,' Mia called it. 'Your brain protecting itself from the horrors of the world.'

He took Mia's word for it and tried not to dwell on the absence of memories. He had no need to wonder what his rank was or who his parents had been. The Nomads were all the family he needed.

And yet, I still cannot shake the feeling that something is missing.

The thought had gained ground over the last few months, consuming his waking mind and tainting his usual sunny disposition.

Lack of sleep isn't helping either. He rubbed his hands over his eyes and swung his legs over the edge of his silkvine net. The pink rays of dawn were breaking through the canopy like the glittering skin of a sockeye salmon in the shallows. This time of the morning was always his favourite, filling him with all the possibilities that a new day could bring.

Alder felt his canopy move behind him.

'Morning, den-dweller,' Mia said as she sat down next to him.

Alder had earned his nickname the day the Nomads found him over a decade ago. He'd been sheltering in an obeah den on the western plains of the continent. He'd been filthy and incoherent, a family of obeah his only companions.

But the Nomads had cleaned him up and welcomed him home.

Home, he thought. *It is as changeable as the seasons and as cyclical as the harvest.*

Today 'home' was the Wasted Marshes, closer than he liked to get to the Elven Lands, but every five years the elves were required to travel into Crescent to trade. Though the forest was fruitful, items like rope and hemp were easier to buy from the city rather than weaving them.

'Did you not go back to sleep after Yeeran left?' Mia asked. Her words let out a breath of fog into the cool morning air.

Alder shook his head. 'I couldn't.' He massaged the spots above his knees where Yeeran's magic had struck him.

'How are your legs?' Mia asked, noticing him wince.

'Just bruised. She didn't puncture the skin.'

Mia snorted. 'I guess we can thank her for that.'

He ran his hand through his hair and thought back to the haze of the night before.

'She must have been so scared. I should have warned her,' he said.

'How were you to know that it would happen last night?' Mia said soothingly.

Alder looked out into the distance. 'I wonder what I did, or what I said.'

'Who cares, you were just sleepwalking. You are not responsible for your actions,' Mia said with a dismissive wave of her hand, then jostled his shoulder. 'Don't worry about it. Yeeran seemed unlikely to stay anyway.'

It was true that Yeeran had been distrustful of the group from the moment she'd met him. But something about her had interested him – and it wasn't because he'd seen her ride an obeah.

He looked sidelong at Mia. He hadn't told her that particular detail, sure that she would claim he was seeing things. It wasn't the first time Alder had seen someone riding an obeah. The last time the Nomads had been in the Wasted Marshes five years ago he had sworn that he'd seen a whole group of riders.

Alder had watched them from the trees, following their trail at a distance. They'd worn cloaks with a sun embossed on the back in gold thread. Alder knew of the districts in the Elven Lands even if he couldn't recollect all their cities and traditions, and he knew none of their insignia had a sun.

Who were these figures and where had they come from?

In all his time with the Nomads they had never met another civilisation out in the wilderness. Lone travellers – exiled or otherwise – weren't common either, but those they did come across often joined the Nomads' community. Because it was that or be alone forever.

And yet here was a group of people *riding obeah*?

Alder still remembered the yearning to be among them, to ride upon the obeah's sturdy backs and feel the forest flash past. Ever since he'd been found sheltering in an obeah den, he'd felt a kinship to the beasts.

Perhaps that is what is missing from my life. An obeah steed. He laughed to himself and Mia gave him a strange look.

He shook his head, refusing to elaborate. Though it had been years since he'd first brought the tale of the riders back to camp, the teasing he'd endured was still fresh. No one had believed him then, so why would anyone believe him now?

'The sleepwalking, it's getting more frequent,' Mia said. Her words felt like a cold dip in the ocean, and all thoughts of obeah were rinsed from his mind.

'Yes, it is,' he admitted.

His sleepwalking scared him. It had started a few months earlier; he'd wake up in a different canopy, or he'd startle someone awake with sounds or shouts. The next day would bring with it a pounding headache and the type of uneasiness that accompanied the morning after a heavy night of drinking.

What had he done? What had he said?

Something moved in the bushes below them and they both jumped, but it was just a hare and it sprang away into the undergrowth.

'I hate being this close to the Elven Lands,' Alder said, trying to bring his breathing back to normal.

'Me too. Dart should be back from Crescent today. Then we can move on.' Mia seemed unaware that a smile had spread across her face when she spoke Dart's name.

'Five days is a long time for you to be apart,' Alder said.

Mia's grin fell away. 'The longest we haven't seen each other in all our time together.'

Though the Nomads were a solitary group with no affiliations to other tribes, their five-yearly trading was their one opportunity to learn of all the happenings in the Elven Lands. While the Forever War was something all the Nomads had turned their backs on, some of their party found the allure of news too intriguing to pass up. It was why Dart had stayed in Crescent longer than the others who had gone to trade.

Alder patted her hand. 'When Dart returns, we'll start the march south. I'd like to winter as far away from the Elven Lands as possible.'

Mia's back rippled up in a feline stretch. 'Yes, I miss the sea and the warm sand.'

Alder smiled. He knew within a day of being at the beach she'd complain about sand getting everywhere and start asking when they were ready to leave.

'Yes, a sun-soaked beach is exactly what I think we all need,' Alder said.

It wasn't long after their conversation that Dart appeared in the clearing below. With surprising agility for a man of his size, he climbed the tree attached to Alder's canopy.

'Wayfarer,' he greeted Alder with a nod before turning to Mia.

Alder looked away as they kissed and embraced. He loved Mia and Dart dearly and was glad when they finally acknowledged their feelings for each other two summers past. They were the type of couple who made each other better. But sometimes it was hard to watch their happiness, as it shone so brightly upon lonely eyes.

'I bring news from Crescent,' Dart said once he had thoroughly greeted Mia.

'And more supplies, too, I hope,' Alder replied.

Dart sat next to Mia, holding her hand between both of his large ones. 'Of course, Alli brings them now.'

Then Dart let out a long sigh.

'Was it that bad?' Alder asked. He had only viewed the capital city, Shah, from a distance, and the smoke and noise it had emanated had been enough to put him off forever.

'Yes, the war has ravaged the population, though morale was higher than I've seen it in some time. Did Reeta return with my message?'

'She did. What is this new magic Crescent are using?' Alder asked.

'A few people were whispering about . . .' Dart dropped his voice '. . . *fae* magic.'

Alder and Mia exchanged a look then burst out laughing.

Dart pursed his lips before releasing them into a small smile. 'I suppose it does sound a little implausible.'

'Yes,' Mia said, patting Dart on the arm. 'If there were fae in the world, we of all people would know it.'

Dart nodded, but then he added quietly, 'You know in the Elven Lands they tell tales of nomadic elves and think of them as mere stories. I heard one while I was there – apparently, we only eat the ground-up bones of the dead.'

'Your point?' Mia said. She always hated to hear about the rumours that swirled around the Nomads. She had once admitted to Alder that was why she no longer joined the trading group who went into Crescent.

'Well, think of the tales the elders spin of the fae. Teeth so sharp to rip out throats, and all they drink is blood,' Dart said with a shrug.

Alder ruminated on Dart's words and his thoughts went back to the cloaked riders he'd seen all those years ago. His laughing petered to a stop.

'Did I miss anything while I was gone?' Dart asked.

'Alder invited a traveller for dinner – I think he took a shine to her to be honest – but then he sleepwalked and scared her away,' Mia summarised bluntly.

Dart let out a sigh. 'Another one?'

'Yes,' Alder said more sharply than he intended. His lack of sleep was making him more irritable than usual. He rubbed his hands over his sore knees. 'I think I'm going to go bathe in the stream.'

Dart raised an eyebrow at the change of subject, but he knew Alder well enough not to push the topic.

Alder slipped down the nearest tree. He didn't use a map to navigate his way to the stream. He'd always been good at knowing exactly where he needed to go.

He removed his clothes and lay down in the running water. The current wasn't strong but it soothed his fatigued muscles. Though cold, the water invigorated him, easing some of his worries.

Soon he found himself drifting into a peaceful slumber, but then he stopped himself. Not because he was afraid of drowning, but because he was afraid of what he'd do in his sleep.

He sat up and something in the nearby bushes jumped up, startled. Alder spotted the obeah and called to it.

'Hello, friend,' Alder greeted it. 'Do you want to be my steed?'

The obeah sniffed the air and cocked his head and for a moment Alder thought it could understand him. But when he waded towards it, the beast dashed away.

'Goodbye, friend,' Alder said with a touch of moroseness.

He lay back in the stream to try to lift his mood, but the water's healing properties had seemingly abated.

So he dressed again and made his way back to the Nomads. It was time to leave the Wasted Marshes and all thoughts of obeah.

Even if deep down he felt the cavern of loneliness widen each day.

CHAPTER FOUR

Lettle

Rayan was dying right in front of her.

Was this what the Fates foretold? That he would die drinking poisoned mead intended for her?

No. She couldn't let him go, not yet.

'Hold on, Rayan, hold on.'

His lips were turning blue.

Lettle picked up the remnants of the overturned wine glass before dashing out of the dining hall.

'Sahar!' She banged on every door on the corridor. She wasn't sure which was his, but her screaming must have penetrated the wood, because before she could knock on the final door, it opened to Sahar's face.

He was dressed in a floor-length nightgown, clearly about to go to bed.

'Lettle?' He seemed shocked to see her.

'Rayan's been poisoned. It's in the mead. Can you fix an antidote?' She thrust the goblet towards him.

Sahar's eyes went wide in horror before he took the vessel from her and examined the liquid inside. 'Where is he?'

'The dining room still.'

'Return to him, make sure he doesn't swallow his tongue. I'm on my way.'

Lettle ran back the way she had come. Rayan's breathing had

turned ragged and he was still unconscious. She moved his head onto her lap and spoke soothingly.

'Sahar is coming, he'll know what to give you. Don't worry, you'll be up and ready to go by the morning. Just don't leave me, you hear? You cannot leave me, Rayan.' Her words gave way to sobs.

'Lettle?' Sahar's voice called out as he entered.

'Over here. We're over here.'

The fae held a bag of medicines.

'Do you have an antidote?' Lettle asked.

'I'm not sure what the poison is. It's entirely untraceable from smell, texture or viscosity. I'll have to give him a few blanket antidotes and hope one of them does the job. Though of course they could just make it worse . . .'

Rayan wheezed and for an awful second Lettle thought he wasn't going to breathe again.

'Sahar, do something!' Lettle shouted.

'Yes . . . well . . . all right.'

Sahar removed two vials from his bag and pressed them to Rayan's lips. 'Let us start with these. The side effects are less . . . worrisome.'

They waited to see any change in Rayan. But after a few minutes his lips just went bluer.

'Is it supposed to have worked by now?' Lettle asked, panic lifting her voice an octave higher than usual.

'Hmm.'

'Hmm is not an answer, Sahar!'

The fae reached back into his bag and pulled out a vial of reddish liquid.

'The only other poison that has these properties is teqan root. If they used it, then this is the antidote. If they didn't then the antidote might just well kill him.'

'Any other ideas?'

Sahar's lips flattened. 'No.'

'Then do it.'

He poured the liquid into Rayan's mouth and they waited. After a few minutes Rayan's lips went from blue to puce, then to a flushed pink.

Sahar whistled low. 'So teqan root it was . . .'

Lettle collapsed over Rayan's head, resting her lips on his forehead.

'Lettle?' Rayan whispered.

'You're safe,' she replied. 'Sahar healed you. Rest now.'

Furi flew into the dining room. 'I heard Lettle scream.'

Lettle was surprised she'd come to her aid so readily.

Furi spotted Rayan and ran to his side in time to see his eyes shutter closed again. Her eyes narrowed and her words came out cold and deadly. 'What happened?'

Once Lettle had explained, Furi let out a short exhale and strode from the room. Lettle watched her shadow stretch down the corridor beyond as she started barking orders.

I hope they catch the culprit. And kill him, Lettle thought bitterly.

Something moved by the window hatch to her left and she turned to gaze into the wide eyes of Ajax: Rayan's obeah. He tilted his head to dip his horns under the window frame and stepped into the room.

He looked at Rayan and whined.

'It's all right, Ajax, Rayan will be OK.' Lettle looked to Sahar for reassurance.

'Yes, he needs rest now. We need to get him to his chambers.'

Lettle turned to Ajax. 'Will you help?'

The obeah lowered his front paws and dropped his head. Sahar and Lettle pulled Rayan onto Ajax's back. Together, with Lettle supporting Rayan's torso, they made their way to their chambers.

The royal physician was waiting for them when they arrived.

'Queen Furi sent me. She said Rayan has been poisoned.' The doctor had three assistants with him who helped Lettle situate Rayan in the bed while Sahar told the tale.

'Quick thinking getting Sahar's aid, Seer Lettle,' the physician said in Lettle's direction. 'Teqan root, very rare indeed. Few would have thought of it, Sahar.'

'Owning an apothecary shop perhaps puts me in good stead.'

'But even then, few apothecarists would know of it . . .'

Lettle drowned them out, her attention wholly consumed by the rise and fall of Rayan's chest.

He looked so small cradled between the pillows and blankets of the bed. She had so nearly lost him. If only she hadn't been there. If only he hadn't drunk from her cup.

Rage surged like lava through her veins.

'I'll be back,' Lettle announced to the room. 'Please, someone stay with him, I don't want him to wake up alone.'

Furi wasn't in her rooms when Lettle got there. After persistent questioning and a reminder of her status, the guard outside Furi's rooms suggested she might find the queen in the war room in the lower levels of the palace.

Lettle had only been seer for less than a month and she was already exhausted by how differently she was treated compared to Furi, or even Rayan. The authority she thought she'd have as part of the royal court seemed only to work in the presence of the king or queen.

Lettle gave the guard her meanest scowl before making her way to the war room.

The quickest way to the bottom floor was to exit the palace via the stone staircase and re-enter behind the Tree of Souls. The fray was still dimmed with the darkness of night, so the only things lighting her way were the star gliders who amassed wherever the Jani dynasty were. The flying lizards had large bulbous heads that glowed with bioluminescence. Which was helpful because they lit the pathway to Furi.

Up ahead, the Tree of Souls loomed tall and wide. It wasn't just the largest baobab tree Lettle had ever seen, it was the largest tree she'd ever seen full stop. The leaves shifted in the soft breeze, no more forceful than a sigh, it whispered through the canopy.

Lettle quickened her pace. The Tree of Souls was the centre point of the curse on Mosima. It tied the Jani dynasty to the land, and each leaf that grew represented the life of an ancestor.

Cursed to endure, cursed to survive: the words were scoured into the bark of the baobab.

Lettle felt her blood chill as she crossed its thick roots. Like knots, they bound Rayan to Mosima.

She was practically running when she arrived in the war room. Furi looked up as she came in, her eyes bloodshot.

'We located the servant,' the queen said with finality. She was leaning against the map in the centre of the table. The room was empty.

'That was quick.'

Furi let out a sharp laugh. 'That's the thing with being stuck in a cavern – nowhere to hide.'

'Did he admit his guilt?'

Furi shook her head. 'No, he claims he didn't poison the mead.'

Lettle bared her teeth. 'He was the only one who touched my goblet. And the rest of you weren't poisoned.'

Furi raised her hands in a shrug. 'He still says it wasn't him.'

Doing the deed was one thing but the fact he'd lied after being caught in the act made Lettle's veins hum with anger.

'What will you do with him?' she asked.

'He'll be punished.'

That wasn't enough for Lettle. 'Kill him.'

'You know we can't, Lettle. Fae do not kill other fae.'

'Sure, and Nerad jumped from the steps, right?'

Furi flinched. Lettle hadn't been sure about Furi's hand in her cousin's death, but she was now.

'Lettle,' she said, her voice like a warning call.

'Well, if you can't kill him, then I can,' Lettle said.

Furi's laugh this time was full of mirth. She rounded the table and stepped towards her, pulling herself to her full height – a foot above Lettle.

'Oh, little Lettle. You think you can kill? You think you can take a life? He has a family, you know. Two children. Can you take a father away from his sons?'

Lettle smiled, showing all her teeth. 'I've done it before, and I can do it again.'

It was true, she'd killed a father. Her own.

Some may have thought Lettle's actions were merciful – her father had suffered from an illness of the mind and was unaware of who and where he was. But she knew the truth in her heart. She had killed him out of selfishness as she could no longer bear to see him suffer. A simple overdose of snowmallow flower had eased that burden.

And just like that, he was dead.

A flicker of respect sparked in Furi's eyes. Then she said simply, 'No.'

'Furi—'

'No. You will not approach him and you will certainly not attempt to murder him. Lest I remind you it was *you* he was trying to kill?'

There it was – the blame. It seared like a hot poker into Lettle's side and she sat heavily into one of the chairs.

All her anger guttered out in an instant. 'They'll never accept me, will they?'

'No,' Furi said, turning emotionless eyes to Lettle. 'But we don't need them to accept you, only respect you. Respect your authority. Coming after you is a slight against the Jani dynasty.'

She flicked her gaze back to the table where the whole world was spread out before her. 'And now we have not only a battle brewing with Crescent, but a battle within as well.'

Lettle watched as Furi's eyes lingered on a point on the map. It wasn't Crescent, but Waning. Where Yeeran was.

'She'll come back, you know,' Lettle said with conviction.

Furi's gaze snapped up. 'That's what I'm worried about . . .'

They lingered in the silence of their own thoughts. Until Furi said, 'Go to bed, Lettle, rest with the king. We can debrief in the morning.'

Bed. It was exactly what she needed.

Lettle barely remembered getting back to her rooms. But the physician told her the next day that she'd unceremoniously thrown him and his assistants out. Which didn't sound like her at all.

When her head hit the pillow next to Rayan's sleeping face, all memory was lost to dreams.

CHAPTER FIVE

Yeeran

Three days later and Yeeran and Pila arrived at the border of Shah, the capital of the Crescent district.

They stood at the top of a hill shrouded by the edge of the forest. Chimneys puffed out smoke filling their view with a thick haze. Soldiers patrolled the streets and even at a distance Yeeran could see the Crescent emblem shining on their backs. It instantly made her feel apprehensive.

For so long they had been her enemy.

Pila shifted beneath her. *It smells like excrement and sour grapes,* she noted.

Yes, I can imagine it smells very different to Mosima.

It looked different too. The city was built out of white stonework, instead of the deep red brick in the fae realm. Where Mosima was plush with flora, Shah had little greenery; even the forests that surrounded it were sparse. With so little cover, Yeeran was worried about being spotted.

We'll move through at midnight. I'm not sure how yet, but we'll need to cross the border into Waning.

And it's guarded? Pila asked.

Yes. Though less heavily on the way out than on the way in.

Let's fight our way through, Pila said simply.

I don't think we can, Pila. We'll be outnumbered.

Pila stiffened and looked to her left.

What is it? Yeeran asked.

Fae.

Yeeran felt her blood lurch in her veins as her heart began to beat faster.

Then she saw them in the distance. Four of them in total. They rode upon their obeah's backs through the centre of town.

'Three gods,' Yeeran breathed. 'They're just walking through the city in the middle of the day.'

Yeeran watched as the fae passed by a platoon of soldiers who saluted to them.

They're not even trying to hide their involvement in the war, anymore. Nerad's meddling with Crescent before his death had clearly changed the dynamics in the war, putting the fae in more danger. It wouldn't be long before the whole of the Elven Lands knew exactly who was behind Crescent's new magic.

The four fae crossed the town square and went towards the border. As they turned Yeeran saw the Crescent uniform on their backs and hissed a breath out through her teeth.

After a brief exchange with the soldiers, the fae crossed the border onto the path towards the Bleeding Field.

Yeeran bunched her hands into Pila's scruff. *Furi had promised that she would call the retreat on her soldiers out here. Why are they still heading towards the battlefield?*

And in her mind, she wondered . . . *How many of my comrades have died at their hands?*

Pila growled low in her throat. The rumble was soothing beneath Yeeran's palms.

At least they have given us a means to cross. All we need to do is get a set of Crescent uniforms.

Yeeran left Pila by the forest and made her way into the city. The Crescent army's barracks were situated south of the border. Yeeran had scrutinised the route on a map many times, but it was a different experience navigating feet instead of tokens on a board.

'Watch out!' The shout took her unawares and Yeeran crashed into a cart of vegetables moving through the streets.

Her hands tried to break her fall, but instead they squished through the bruised skin of the tomatoes in the back of the cart.

'Oh, oh! You've ruined my stock!' the merchant cried.

Yeeran wiped the tomato juice off her hands and turned to the man.

He had a reed-like frame draped in strips of mix-matched cloth. His cart, now that she looked at it, was full of vegetables far past their turn. One courgette she was sure had a bite taken out of it.

'You're going to have to pay for my ruined vegetables now, I can't sell them,' he whined.

She noted his palms, though dirty, held no calluses one might expect of a farmer.

She knew this ruse. She and Lettle had done it more than once.

'You pushed the cart in my path,' Yeeran said calmly.

'I did not – what an insinuation! I ought to call the soldiers down on you,' he spluttered. Impressively he also managed to go a deep shade of red. He was a true artist.

'You did,' Yeeran continued. 'And you hope that my guilt will encourage me to empty my pockets to you.'

'How dare you question my integrity!'

'You can stop with the tomfoolery. I have attempted this gambit more than once. You cannot cheat a thief. Besides, I have an alternative proposition for you.'

The man's demeanour subtly changed and his skin flushed back to his more neutral pale pink.

'What do you want?' His voice had changed too. Less sour, like it had been sweetened with honey.

'You can have everything I'm wearing in exchange for a Crescent uniform. I imagine they aren't hard to come by. In fact you might have a set yourself from conscription days—'

'They took it away from me when I was dismissed. Didn't they do the same to you?' He tipped his head to her sliced ears.

Damn, forgot about those.

'And a hat. Crescent uniform and a hat. Then you can have everything I'm wearing. It's fine quality. Finer than you'll find anywhere in the city.'

The thief frowned. 'You want me to get you a Crescent uniform and a hat, for everything you're wearing?'

'Yes.'

'And the drum?'

'Not the drum.'

'But the boots?'

'You can have the boots.'

He thrust out his hand. 'Deal.'

'I'll need it quickly though, as soon as possible,' Yeeran said as she shook the thief's hand.

The smile he gave her was sly. 'Watch my cart.'

Then he dashed into a nearby cottage and sauntered out five minutes later whistling.

Yeeran raised an eyebrow. 'That was quick.'

He threw her a bundle of clothes. 'That's the army's launderers.'

Yeeran couldn't help but laugh. Of course it could have been that easy.

'Go on, give me your clothes,' he said.

Yeeran inspected the uniform he had brought.

'You could have picked a clean set,' she grumbled as she began to change.

'You didn't specify,' he said, smiling wolfishly.

'And the hat?'

'Oh yes,' he said and reached into his cart. He pulled out a raggedy bit of cloth with a moth-bitten cap. 'I'll be sad to part with it if I'm honest.'

'I bet,' Yeeran grunted before pulling the hat low over her ears.

The thief whistled as he inspected the fae clothes she'd discarded.

'Fine, very fine. Well, I'm off to pawn these. Good day to you.'

'And you,' Yeeran said.

Pila, I'm on my way back.

I know, I can smell you. Did you have to put on clothes a person died in?

Yeeran tried not to retch. *Did you have to tell me that? And how can you tell anyway?*

She felt the flicker of Pila's response and cut her off. *In fact, don't tell me. I don't want to know.*

Fine, I'm to your right, by the way.

Yeeran had sensed the obeah before she saw her. It was like knowing exactly where your shadow would be.

She lunged towards Pila and jumped onto her back in a fluid, well-practised motion. But she was still never quite as graceful at mounting an obeah as Furi.

Furi . . .

Sunlight burst across her memories, flushing her skin and making her heart race. For a second, she could smell her, mango juice and the spice of the perfume she wore. Her senses lingered in her memories until she could taste her on her tongue . . .

Are you all right? Pila asked.

Yes.

No.

She would never be all right again. Furi had set something alight in her that she never wanted to go out.

But Furi was in Mosima, and Yeeran was here. She thought back to the last time they had spoken. Furi had been framed so beautifully by the setting fray-light on Conch Shore.

'You're leaving,' Furi had said.

'Yes.'

'To warn your chieftain.'

'Yes.'

'Who is this chieftain to you?'

No one. Not anymore, Yeeran thought. Then she turned her mind to Pila. *Are you ready? We're going to move through the town square now. We have to pretend to know where we're going.*

I can do that, Pila said. *If you tell me where to go.*

Straight ahead, towards the border where those guards are.

The few people who were in the streets went quiet as Yeeran and Pila passed. A soldier saluted and for a second Yeeran felt queasy at the thought of being perceived as a Crescent soldier, their rivalry with her own tribe was so deeply rooted. She pulled the hat more tightly over her ears and hoped no one would notice.

Pila loped towards the border.

'Name and orders?' the soldier at the gate asked.

Pila huffed out her nose and the elf looked up. She had startling purple eyes, the same tone as Lettle's, and Yeeran felt a pang of misery.

'Oh, sorry. I thought all of your party had already passed through,' the soldier said, visibly shaken by their presence.

'No, I have different orders,' Yeeran replied. She tried to keep her upper lip lowered to hide her flattened teeth. It gave her a slight speech impediment but Yeeran hoped it came across as a thick accent instead.

'I – I'll still have to take down your name, if that's not a problem.' The soldier's voice broke at the end.

'Berro O'Sanq,' Yeeran lied smoothly.

The soldier frowned and for a moment Yeeran thought the ruse was up.

Then she opened the gate.

'Thank you,' Yeeran said, and the soldier's frown deepened. She suspected something, but not enough to stop her.

Pila, go through the gate. But as soon as we're out of sight start running.

The obeah moved past the iron bars that made up the Crescent border. The forest grew denser to their left, and as soon as they were shielded from view Pila began to run.

With her every footfall Yeeran got closer to her old home. And her old love.

CHAPTER SIX

Lettle

L ettle woke before the fray heralded the light of dawn. Rayan was snoring softly beside her, his breath even and steady.

She let out a slow sigh of relief. He was alive.

After tracing his jawline with her gaze for a little while, she pulled back the sheets and padded across the room. She sank slowly into the armchair behind her dressing table.

She was about to pour herself a glass of water from the jug on the desk but then thought better of it. What if it too had been poisoned?

Her prophecy tokens lay in their pouch where she had left them. Though the shattered mirror from her earlier attempts to speak to the Fates had been cleaned away, her determination hadn't waned.

She tipped the tokens out of their pouch with a violent motion, scattering the pieces around her. She was as used to slipping into magesight as she was by the disappointment that no prophecy would bring.

'Argh.' She clawed the tokens back into their pouch and tied them on her waist.

'Still nothing?' Rayan said from the bed.

'Oh, did I wake you? I'm sorry.'

'No, it wasn't you.' He ran a hand over his haggard face.

Lettle went to sit beside him on the bed. 'How are you feeling?'

'Like I downed two bottles of whiskey. What happened?'

Lettle slipped her hand around his waist and rested her head on his warm torso. The beat of his heart was soothing beneath her ear.

'Poison,' she whispered. 'Meant for me.'

She felt tears slip from her eyes onto his chest. Rayan's hands wrapped around her like a shield.

'I'm all right now,' he said.

'You nearly died. Sahar saved you.' Her tears had turned to sobs.

Rayan's hand moved to her face. He gently cupped her cheek, tilting her gaze up until she met his. 'I'm OK now, I'm alive and well.'

Lettle let out a small laugh. 'I'm the one meant to be comforting you.'

'There'll be time for that later,' he said, his voice dropping to a husky whisper. Despite the tiredness written across his face, he was still trying to make her laugh. Then he looked to the window and all mirth fled his brown eyes.

'The poisoner – did we catch them?'

'Furi has the servant in custody.'

He nodded, his hands balling into fists by his sides.

Lettle gently pulled the bedcovers up around him. 'You should rest today, I'll call for some breakfast.'

The fact that he didn't protest made her realise how exhausted he must still be feeling.

'That sounds like a good idea. But Lettle, don't go anywhere without Ajax.'

After last night their trust in the fae had been fractured.

'I'll be right back,' she said as Rayan's eyes began once again to flutter closed.

Ajax appeared in the doorway to the bedroom.

Lettle went to him. She'd always felt comfortable around the obeah, even before she'd known he was bonded to Rayan.

She stroked the tip of his broken horn. 'Good morning, Ajax.'

The obeah dipped his head in greeting.

Lettle couldn't deny she felt safer walking through the palace with the beast by her side. Though the servants nodded to her as she passed, she knew their respect was feigned.

Lettle waved forward a young maid. She couldn't have been older than nineteen, young to have been condemned to servitude at the palace. The maid wore her brown hair cropped close to her chin, emphasising the severity of her jaw.

'Could you run to the kitchens and have someone bring breakfast to our rooms?' Lettle asked.

'Of course, it would be my pleasure, seer,' the maid replied in a tone devoid of any pleasure. Lettle noted a slight gap between her front teeth, an endearing feature that soothed the harshness of her pointed canines.

As she whisked away down the corridor, Lettle turned to make her way back to the safety of the royal chambers.

'Lettle!' The call came from behind her and she looked over her shoulder to find Golan.

'Early morning for everyone, I see,' Lettle said by way of greeting.

'I heard the news just now. Is it true what they're saying? Rayan was poisoned?'

Lettle hesitated for less than a second. Golan had been the one to source the poison that had led to the queens' deaths.

He could see in her eyes what she was thinking and she instantly regretted her own traitorous thoughts.

'It wasn't me, Lettle.'

She looked deep into his blue eyes willing her words to sink in as she said, 'You would never do anything to hurt me, Golan. I know that.'

He smiled, but it seemed a little tired. 'Is Rayan fully recovered?'

'He's exhausted, but it's nothing food and sleep can't fix.' Then she added, eager to mend any distrust between them, 'Would you like to join us for breakfast?'

Golan looked surprised.

'Please join me, Rayan isn't going to be much company, and I need a distraction after last night.'

Then Golan gave her a truer smile. 'All right, lead the way.'

Rayan was still asleep when Lettle returned. She closed the door to the bedroom softly so their talking wouldn't wake him, then joined Golan in the living room.

She sank into one of the velvet sofas with a sigh, but before she could relax there was a knock at the door.

'I'll get it,' Golan said, rising before she could even protest.

A moment later Golan returned with a servant carrying a tray of food. It was the maid Lettle had sent to the kitchens earlier.

Lettle's mouth watered as pancakes glistening with honey were set down on the table in front of her. Two bowls of fruit and a platter of warm raspberry tarts followed. Once the food was set and the cutlery laid, Lettle leaned in to begin serving herself.

But a prickle at the back of her neck made her turn. The maid was waiting patiently behind Lettle's chair, her gaze expectant.

'Oh, you may go,' Lettle said with a wave of her hand.

'Seer, I'm to taste every plate of food before you consume it,' she said.

'What?' Lettle said.

'The queen has ordered it. Every meal consumed by the royal court must be tested before being eaten. A precaution, seer.' The maid's lips quirked at the corner and Lettle wondered what she really thought of her new duty as food taster.

'What is your name?' Lettle asked.

The maid's teeth clenched as if the question was bothersome. 'Anyah, seer.'

Lettle set her jaw. 'Well, Anyah, please taste the food and get out.'

Anyah's eyes widened for a second before she nodded and got to work.

Once she'd left, Golan turned to Lettle. 'Was that really necessary?'

Lettle set down the fork that hovered by her mouth. 'I'm tired,

Golan, they all hate me, and resent serving me. Why should I bother being kind in return? You saw how she was.'

'Still, you'll never change their minds if you treat them like that. You don't want the rest of your life to be plagued by assassination attempts.'

'The rest of my life? I'm leaving as soon as the curse is broken.' Lettle couldn't wait any longer, she shoved a mouthful of pancakes into her mouth then scowled. 'Cold.'

But Golan wasn't finished. 'You really think the curse can be broken, Lettle?'

'Yes,' she said with her mouth full. 'The human magic exists, and we know that because Rayan's father was able to parse some of it in order to leave the boundary.'

'But how?'

Lettle took a while to answer. Though she trusted Golan completely, this wasn't her secret to tell.

'Rayan believes his father's research will lead us to the answer,' she said slowly.

There was a sound from the bedroom and Rayan appeared bleary-eyed in the doorway.

'Morning, Golan. Is that breakfast?' he said through a yawn.

'Yes,' Lettle replied. 'And, don't worry, it's been taste tested by a delightful servant called Anyah.'

Rayan raised his eyebrows. 'Furi's instructions, I take it?'

'Yes.' Lettle tried not to roll her eyes.

'It's a good idea, after yesterday,' Rayan said, shovelling food onto his plate. 'What were you talking about before I arrived?'

Lettle looked to Golan, then said tentatively, 'Your father's research.'

Rayan's eyes shuttered, then he sighed and disappeared into their bedroom.

Lettle had thought she'd gone too far with sharing Rayan's work, until he returned and placed a well-worn letter in front of Golan.

'You might as well read it. Lettle and I cannot figure out where he hid his work. Perhaps you might.'

Golan leant over the handwritten note. Lettle had read it enough times to memorise the most important parts: Najma had recovered Afa's – the last human's – grimoire and hidden it along with his research 'where the earth's teeth grow once a river flowed'. Golan put down the letter once he'd read it.

'Lettle and I have been researching every valley and river within Mosima and the surrounding area. So far we've come up with nothing that links his words to a particular place,' Rayan said.

Golan frowned. 'It doesn't strike a chime in my memory . . .'

'He could have given us a bit more to go on than "where the earth's teeth grow",' Lettle said.

'Wait, say that again,' Golan prompted, and Lettle did.

Golan's eyes widened. 'Tyr ertees groh,' he murmured the words together.

Lettle gave him a concerned look. 'Are you feeling quite all right?'

Golan flapped the letter excitedly. 'Tyr ertees groh!'

'We're going to need more than that, Golan,' Rayan said dryly.

'Don't you think it was strange that your father wrote his letter in the universal tongue? What you call elvish?' Golan said.

'Not really. He couldn't have known for certain I would bond with an obeah.'

'But he probably thought it likely you would one day learn to speak fae. We've been reading this in the universal tongue, but when you say it out loud it has another meaning in fae.'

Rayan nodded, understanding.

'What?' Lettle said, completely lost.

'Tyr ertees groh sounds like "the earth's teeth grow" in elvish,' Rayan replied.

'But what does tyr ertees groh even mean? I don't understand it.'

'We didn't exactly concentrate on geographical landmarks in your language training. Tyr though, you should know,' Golan said.

'Tree,' Lettle said with triumph.

'Actually forest, or more like a glade,' Rayan gently corrected her.

Golan flicked away a braid that had fallen over his face in his excitement. 'Exactly, and ertees groh is a unique phrase related to water. It means dew drops, but in this context it translates to the Crystal Glade, or the "water forest".'

'And that's a place?' Lettle asked.

'Yes, south-west of Mosima towards the coast. Let me see the rest of this sentence. Hmm, "Once a river flowed . . ." I cannot figure out that meaning in fae.'

'Perhaps he combined a fae phrase with that of elvish. So the work is in a valley in the Crystal Glade?' Lettle said hopefully.

'Well it's more than we had a few minutes ago,' Rayan said with a bit of colour on his cheeks.

'How far is it to the Crystal Glade, Golan?' Lettle asked.

'Five days. Though I've never been there myself, the Crystal Glade is featured in a lot of our older stories.'

Lettle reached for Rayan's hand. 'We have to go.'

'I can't, Lettle. Leaving for that long could bring untold damage to Mosima.'

Lettle cursed. The invisible ropes that tied Rayan to the land were beginning to chafe her.

'You two should go—' Rayan started.

'No,' Lettle said before he could continue on. She wasn't leaving Rayan, not after she'd seen him come so close to dying.

'Lettle, you must. Someone needs to find my father's research. We don't know who else saw that letter.'

'Exactly, it's probably not even there. We don't know if Nerad figured out the clue, he had the letter last and might have unpicked the riddle.'

'But it's worth exploring,' Rayan said.

Golan was watching Lettle and Rayan's exchange.

'I think Rayan's right, Lettle. Someone needs to check this out. And if we don't want more people knowing, then it has to be us.'

Lettle ground her teeth. She wanted to find a way out of Mosima, but equally she didn't want to be parted from Rayan.

'I would also be more at ease knowing you were out there where fewer people are trying to kill you,' Rayan added.

Lettle's head dipped low and Rayan lifted her chin with gentle fingers.

'Ajax will go, so though I won't be able to talk to you, he'll be my eyes and ears, and you won't be alone.' He ran his thumb over Lettle's bottom lip and if Golan hadn't been there, she would have bitten down on his finger with a mischievous smile.

'Fine. Let us go to this Crystal Glade.'

Her words started a chain of events that happened faster than she had expected. Rayan called for supplies to be brought and Golan began to pack her clothing.

Lettle stood on the periphery of the room rolling her talismans in her hand as people swirled in and out to make ready the final preparations. The day disappeared in an instant and soon it was evening and time to depart beneath the cloak of darkness.

But before they left, they met with Sahar and Furi in the Royal Woodland. Rayan had been insistent on keeping the details of their excursion a secret so Lettle let him do the talking.

'Lettle and Golan are leaving Mosima? Why?' Furi asked, confused. She was sitting on her throne, Sahar resting on the step below, his grey-whiskered obeah threaded between his feet.

'I think it's best that Lettle leaves the city for a little while. Until we have rooted out the extent of those who wish her ill,' Rayan said. His eyes were still tired around the corners and Lettle knew he hated lying to his family.

'We've caught the culprit. You think there are more assassins?' Furi asked.

'Yes, I do, and I'd be more comfortable with Lettle out there than here while we investigate.'

'Where will you go?' Sahar asked.

'South-west,' Lettle said quickly. 'I'd like to see the ocean, not just the small piece of it that *your* land has to offer.'

Furi's gaze met Lettle's, recognising the subtle jibe. Lettle might have been an outlander here, but up top she was free.

Sahar nodded. 'You're going to go with Golan and Ajax?'

'Yes,' Lettle replied.

Furi took a moment, then shrugged. 'Fine with me.'

Lettle wondered if she imagined the relief she saw in Furi's expression. But then again it was a relief to Lettle as well that she wouldn't have to dine with Furi every day.

'I'll escort them to the boundary and return for dinner,' Rayan said.

Golan, Ajax, Rayan and Lettle travelled silently to the cavern's edge. It felt like only moments ago they were breakfasting in the warmth of the royal chambers, and now the weight of expectation lay heavy on her shoulders.

As they reached the outskirts of Mosima the streets grew quieter. So when they rounded a corner and heard the cacophony of revellers, Lettle was surprised.

'The Honeypot Tavern,' Golan said, his eyes downcast.

As they drew level with the merry-makers, Lettle slipped into magesight to see the people better. It was then that she realised everyone in the tavern was Lightless.

She lingered by the open window.

'Who are they to rule over us?' someone in the centre of the room called out.

'No one!' the crowd called back.

'Who are they to tell us we are lesser?'

'No one!' the gathering repeated again.

Hands wrapped around Lettle's wrist and she jumped back, startled. But it was only Rayan.

'We should go, Lettle.' His face was shrouded with concern as he too had heard the treasonous words.

Golan had walked ahead some, so when Lettle joined him, she said, 'Everyone in that tavern is Lightless.'

He dipped his head. 'Yes, there are few places where the Lightless feel welcome. The Honeypot Tavern on the edge of town has always been a solace for my kind.'

She didn't ask him if he'd heard the rebellious cries of the crowd. She could tell from the way his gaze shifted to Rayan's that he had.

Something was simmering in Mosima.

Change, Lettle thought. For the last thousand years little had altered in the fae's prison. That was until Najma had found a way out of the boundary and that in turn led to Yeeran and Lettle entering Mosima.

Lettle wondered how much of her presence here had contributed to the dissent that now rippled across the Lightless. To see an elf in the royal court when they still struggled to be accepted among their own kind. For the first time Lettle understood the servant's motives in wanting her dead.

'Come on,' Rayan called to them both, having quickly overtaken them. 'The sooner you're out of Mosima, the better I'll feel.'

They made their way to the cavern's walls at a much quicker pace.

When they reached the boundary, Rayan spoke the word that parted the human magic that kept them trapped here. 'Aiftarri.'

Golan slipped through with a nod to Rayan. 'I'll look after her,' he said.

'I know,' Rayan replied, waving him off.

Ajax was next. Brushing his side along Rayan's legs, he made his way to true freedom.

Then it was just Rayan and Lettle.

Her hands brushed her pouch of prophecy talismans. This trip was important, because without her divination she felt useless in Mosima. At least if she wasn't able to talk to the Fates, she could do this one thing to contribute to her and Rayan's future.

Rayan's hand slid around her lower back and pulled her into a kiss.

She took her time tasting him, enjoying the warmth of his mouth on hers before they broke apart.

'I have something for you,' Rayan said, reaching into his pocket. 'I found it on Conch Shore. I thought you could add it to your necklace.'

He placed a smooth green stone in her hand. It looked just like the green of Ajax's eyes. Her hand went to her throat where the other trinkets Rayan had given her had been woven onto a chain, each one a treasured memory.

'Thank you,' she said, her voice thick with emotion. She didn't need to say the three words that burned in her chest, he knew she felt them. But she said them anyway. 'I love you.'

'I love you too, Lettle.'

Then she turned her back on him and all of Mosima before striding out into the world beyond.

CHAPTER SEVEN

Yeeran

Yeeran scratched at the collar of her jacket. She'd turned the Crescent uniform inside out and the stitching was irritating her skin. But it was important the Crescent emblem wasn't noticeable or she'd be flayed before reaching the palace gates.

She and Pila lingered on the edge of the tree line as the sun set over Gural, the capital city of Waning.

Home. The thought brought with it a ripple of apprehension as she took in the chieftain's residence.

The edges of the palace shone amber as if set alight by the sun's rays. The fountains that danced in front of the entranceway shed a fine mist on the palm trees that lined the walkway.

Yeeran had once found the palace beautiful, but now she couldn't ignore the ostentatious sight it cut across the landscape. Pale blue hexagon tiles lined the brickwork, so jarring next to the squat stone houses beside it. Salawa had insisted on the colour – 'To look like a morning sky,' she'd said. Dead birds littered the ground at the base of the walls where their little wings had been crushed from the unexpected impact.

The fountains were circled by guards just in case someone thirsty stumbled towards clear water for a drink. No, the fountain wasn't for drinking. Even if clean drinking water was scarce during the summer months.

It was all so artificial. Even the palm trees had been brought from the southern island of the continent and cultivated here.

This isn't like Mosima at all. Pila voiced exactly what Yeeran was feeling.

She thought of the Royal Woodland and the red-brick palace that seemed a part of the cavern that surrounded it.

Yes, this is different indeed, Yeeran replied. *So too is the woman who reigns here.*

All Yeeran had to do next was walk towards the entranceway and announce herself.

One of two things would happen after that: Yeeran would be immediately killed for breaching her exile, or she would be granted mercy long enough to talk to Salawa.

Then take me with you, Pila insisted. *You said that obeah are revered here—*

'For their skin, Pila! I will not let you come to harm.' Yeeran was so concerned, she voiced her words out loud.

But if you entered the palace riding me, then you'll get their attention.

No, I will not put us both at risk.

One at risk is the same as both at risk, Yeeran. You know I'm right. At least this way their intrigue might stay their hand and guarantee you an audience with the queen.

Chieftain, not queen.

Same thing.

Yeeran thought of Furi and her connection to the very soil of Mosima, to the people, the plants. Then she flickered through her memories of Salawa. And she realised she couldn't recollect the last time Salawa had visited the soldiers on the Bleeding Field.

Not the same thing, Yeeran insisted.

Come now, let us get this over with. If we intend to save more of my brethren with this news, then it is better it is shared.

Yeeran hesitated. She knew Pila was right, but it was different going together into danger. She felt more vulnerable, despite knowing if one died then the other perished too, no matter where they were.

Fine, let's go. Pila loped towards the palace before Yeeran had finished the thought.

The streets were emptier than Yeeran expected for that time of the day, but she was glad of it. The closer they got to the centre of town, the louder the drumbeats from the Bleeding Field became. They had once been a familiar rhythm that had comforted her, now they sickened her. Countless obeah killed for the weapons used in the Forever War.

And countless fae.

But no more. The first guard to stop them at the palace gates didn't recognise Yeeran and it surprised her. She'd been the most decorated colonel in the Waning army.

He must be a new soldier. New meant inexperienced. New meant volatile.

'Are you *riding* an obeah?' the soldier said, his expression stupefied. His drum lay forgotten by his waist.

Not quite the dramatic arrest you expected, Pila said.

'I'm here to request an audience with the chieftain,' Yeeran said.

The soldier's gaping mouth curved into a smirk. 'You can't just request an audience with the chieftain. Obeah or not.'

'Tell her my name is Colonel Yeeran, with news about Crescent. She'll want to see me.'

'Colonel Yeeran?' Realisation overtook the soldier slowly, his expression ticking towards understanding like the mechanisms of a clock as it struck the hour.

'But you're exiled on pain of death.' He fumbled for his drum.

Yeeran, he's going to shoot.

Pila crouched ready to spring, but Yeeran was already one step ahead.

Yeeran moved her own drum to the front of her waist and played two low notes with the flat of her palm. Threads of fae magic unwound from her fingertips towards the soldier, tying his hands by his waist.

To him, it would look as if an invisible restraint had been spelled upon him. But for Yeeran, the golden threads glowed bright while using her magesight.

'I didn't want to have to do that. And I can see that some of your comrades are on their way. Now, I will not hurt anyone. All I need is an audience with Chieftain Salawa. I'm happy to wait here until the message is delivered. Trust me – she'll want to hear what I have to say.'

The soldier's blue eyes had gone wide.

'I'm going to release your hands now,' Yeeran continued. 'Tell the approaching soldiers to stay at a distance. I do not want there to be bloodshed.'

The guards all but ran as soon as Yeeran released the threads.

I think you should create a threaded shield, just in case, Pila said.

Good idea.

Yeeran wasn't as skilled at using fae magic as she would have liked, having only just learned how to master a threaded cage in her last few weeks in Mosima. So she focused her mind as she began to beat her drum once more, using intention and the music to weave together strand after strand in front of her face. She tried to do it subtly, without the guards ahead of her noticing. She couldn't afford retaliation.

After several minutes she'd woven a shield of threads big enough to protect her and Pila. It wouldn't last long, half an hour at the most. But it was good enough for now.

Furi would be disappointed to see how long that took me.

I think Furi would have other things to be disappointed about in this scenario, Yeeran. Pila wasn't chastising her, the obeah didn't have it in her nature; she was merely stating fact.

Furi would have many words to say to Yeeran and her choice to share the fae's secrets with the world. But Yeeran didn't want to conjure the imaginary argument that would one day come to fruition. The anticipation of it was hard enough.

Twenty minutes went past and Yeeran felt her concentration on the threaded shield wavering. Sweat trickled down her neck.

Why are they making us wait so long? Pila said. *Have they not relayed the message?*

Oh, yes, they have. This is Salawa's message in return. She makes us wait to show us her power.

Shadows shifted at the entrance to the palace and Yeeran felt her skin pebble with trepidation as Salawa stepped out into the sunlight.

She looked just as beautiful as she had the day she'd condemned Yeeran to exile. Her braids were twisted into an intricate knot above her head, the gold beads woven into them hanging low by her ears.

Her expression was blank, devoid of any feeling as she ran her hazel gaze over Pila and Yeeran. Then her glossy lips moved as she spoke. 'So, it's really you.'

'Yes,' Yeeran replied, breathless all of a sudden. But Salawa had always been able to take Yeeran's breath away.

'You know your arrival here heralds your execution. You have breached the terms of your exile.'

Pila growled and Salawa's eyes flickered to her, a fleeting expression of surprise on her face before turning back to Yeeran.

'I know. But the news I bring is more important than my own life. Should you still wish to execute me after I have shared what I know, then so be it.'

Pila's growl intensified. *I will not let her.*

Salawa's eyes narrowed on the obeah.

Hush, Pila, Yeeran said gently. *I do not want any threat to force her hand.*

Pila snorted before letting the snarl fall from her lips.

'So will you hear what I have to say?' Yeeran pressed, drawing Salawa's attention back to her.

The chieftain considered for a moment before nodding to the guards. 'Escort her to the throne room. Remove all weapons. The obeah, I'm assuming, is an offering. Send it to the slaughterhouse.'

'No!' Yeeran shouted before the guards could move. 'The obeah stays with me, and the drum, if you look closely, is simply a drum. There is no obeah skin on it. It is also important to my tale.'

Salawa's lip curled upwards. 'You have many demands for someone who is awaiting the noose.'

'Please, Salawa,' Yeeran said softly. 'Just listen to what I have to say. I have never harmed you, and I never will.'

Salawa's expression turned hot with anger, but Yeeran staved off the fire with her next words. 'You are the fire of my heart and the beat of my drum. I am yours under moonlight. Until the rhythm sings no more.'

If Salawa could tell the lie beneath the words she didn't show it. Instead, her gaze softened and the scorn on her face abated.

'Fine. Keep the obeah and the drum.' Then she turned away, the silver train of her gown swirling after her.

Yeeran let out a breath and released the threaded shield.

The hardest part is done. Now we must let the truth speak of itself.

The throne room was colder than Yeeran remembered, the fraedia lights harsh on the gaudy drapery that hung from the windows.

Salawa was curled up on her throne. The entire dais, including the chair, was made of the bones of obeah. Yeeran had once thought it an impressive show of her power, but now her stomach curdled to see it.

Pila whined when she realised what the throne was made of, her ears going flat to her head. Yeeran sank her hand into the fur around her horns, feeling an echo of the obeah's pain.

I won't let her hurt you.

Four soldiers flanked Yeeran on either side. The one who had seen her magic at work had thankfully been left by the palace gates. So the guards here had no idea of the power Yeeran wielded.

'The news I bring is of grave importance—' Yeeran began.

Salawa held up a hand, cutting her off. 'I refuse to discuss anything with someone who wears the uniform of my enemies. Even inside out, I know the seams and the threads of those who have wronged me.'

As always, Salawa proved that she saw more than most.

The chieftain called forward a servant who left and returned with a wash bowl and plain slacks. 'Change,' Salawa said.

This too was a power play. Usually guests of the palace were given a room to make ready before attending the chieftain. But after spending time with the fae, Yeeran's modesty had been tempered. Besides, Salawa had seen her naked many times.

Yeeran stripped and washed herself with the flannel cloth. The water was lukewarm and scented with lavender. Soon it was a murky brown, and Yeeran felt immeasurably better. The slacks were loose and threadbare – another slight – but they were soft and Yeeran was grateful to be out of the dead soldier's clothes.

Salawa watched her with glittering eyes. 'I have called for refreshments. You look thinner than the last time I saw you. Exile has not taken to you well.'

Yeeran didn't reply.

'Your beast, would they like something to eat?'

Strawberries, Pila said.

'Strawberries if you have any, or fruit of any kind. And her name is Pila.'

Salawa's lips quirked in amusement. 'Indeed.'

The refreshments were cloudy water and stale bread, with unripe plums for Pila, but they would do. It was better than nothing.

Salawa sipped from her wine, a cheese platter laid across the armrests of the throne.

Finally, it seemed she had humiliated Yeeran enough for her to tell her news. She flicked her fingers in Yeeran's direction.

Yeeran took a deep breath and told her story from the beginning. She left nothing out. Well almost.

– *The feel of Furi's flushed skin beneath her fingers* –

She didn't think Salawa would be enamoured to hear about her exploits with a new lover.

But other than her adventures with Furi, Yeeran told the truth as she had lived it. Salawa asked no questions, but she leant forward a little more in her chair with each revelation.

When Yeeran had finished she leant back.

'You have spun quite a tale, Yeeran. The fae, alive and allied with Crescent, the obeah bound to them? And enough fraedia crystal to light the world? A well-told story indeed.'

Yeeran couldn't tell if she believed it or not. There was a beat of silence then Salawa reached behind the throne and withdrew her drum.

In the moment it took Yeeran to inhale, Salawa had fired a projectile of magic towards Pila.

It struck the obeah in the side.

Yeeran doubled over as she felt the resonance of Pila's pain. Again and again Salawa struck, the beats not hard enough to pierce the skin, but enough to bruise Pila's ribs.

Yeeran moved quickly, straightening despite the pain, and wove a shield in front of Pila and her. Attacking the chieftain wasn't an option. The guards were watching the exchange closely, and if for a second they thought Salawa was being hurt, then Yeeran would be dead.

The shield wove painstakingly slowly into place, stopping the onslaught on Pila's side.

Are you all right? Yeeran asked.

Pila had lowered herself to the ground, her breathing laboured. *Hurts.*

How bad?

Like when I fell out the mango tree.

Yeeran felt the tension in her shoulders loosen.

So nothing broken? Yeeran pressed.

No, I don't think so.

OK, don't move, just get back your breath.

Can I bite her now?

No, Pila.

Yeeran turned to Salawa.

'Do not do that again,' Yeeran said through gritted teeth.

Salawa chose to ignore the threat. 'So it's all true? All of it? That magic you just did is what the Crescent tribe are using?'

Yeeran nodded once. 'Yes, fae magic. Gifted to me by bonding with Pila.'

Salawa stood and walked slowly down the steps of the dais towards Yeeran until she was only a few feet from Pila.

Yeeran could smell her familiar scent: oud and cinnamon. An oil made just for her which she'd dab on her wrists and behind her ears.

Yeeran had always found it alluring, but now the smell was cloying and oppressive.

It sticks in my throat like dates left to fester, Pila said.

You always have a way with words.

Because I am clever.

Yeeran was relieved Pila was sounding more herself. Seeing her hurt was more painful than if the blows had landed on Yeeran directly.

Salawa reached out towards the shield until her fingers brushed the invisible surface.

'Incredible,' she breathed. 'I have had my research teams experimenting with obeah bones to try and replicate Crescent's new magic, but it wasn't ever the elves creating it. It was the fae.' Then Salawa cocked her head. 'Except for you. Why do you think you were chosen by this creature?'

'Pila.'

Salawa smiled as if indulging a child. 'Why do you think Pila chose you?'

Yeeran had never considered that Pila might have *chosen* her, instead she assumed their bonding was happenstance.

Did you choose me?

Pila shrugged in her mind. *I was searching, then I was Pila.*

It was the answer the obeah always gave when asked about her life before bonding with Yeeran.

'I'm not sure. She's unaware of her life before me.'

'Curious,' Salawa said, her gaze lingering greedily on Pila. 'You have given me much to think on. I will need to convey this truth to my advisors. For now, you may stay in the palace, under guard of course. We'll have to confiscate—' Salawa's breath hitched as she took in the drum by Yeeran's side properly for the first time.

It was the very same one Salawa had gifted to her, a lifetime ago.

Salawa's lips curved into a small smile and she didn't end her sentence. It seemed Yeeran would be allowed to keep the drum after all.

Then the chieftain moved backwards, as if to stretch the distance between them before more memories threatened to hold them there.

'Escort our guest to her rooms,' Salawa said, her voice once again devoid of any emotion.

But it was too late, Yeeran had seen a glimmer of the old Salawa she had known. It sent her mind into turmoil, reminding Yeeran of the life she had led here. A time when she'd been loved and loved in return. When she had fought for her tribe and her life had been full of purpose.

A time when Waning had been her home.

As she was led away from the throne room she mourned that loss, fresh as it was. Even thoughts of Furi couldn't permeate the grief that overcame her.

She glanced back at Salawa, hoping for another glimpse of her past, but the chieftain's eyes were as lifeless as stone.

But Yeeran knew beneath her stony demeanour Salawa was thinking, calculating her next move. She wouldn't show Yeeran weakness again. And love was a weakness to Salawa, it had always been.

Yeeran had done her duty by telling her the truth, but as her heart bled in her chest, she couldn't help but wonder what it had cost her.

And what it would come to cost the fae.

CHAPTER EIGHT

Lettle

It was strange walking in the sunlight again. After living beneath fray-light for nearly four months, the sun's warmth on Lettle's skin soothed much of her fear.

Golan's delight was humbling to witness. For the first few hours of their journey he said very little, his eyes wide. Then every time they stopped to rest he basked like a cat in the nearest beam of sunlight, his beautiful face tipped to the sky.

Later that day she saw him pluck a cluster of daisies to adorn his artificial leg. He sang while he did it, a small smile on his face.

This is why the curse should be broken, she thought to herself. *So every fae has the chance to sing to daisies.*

That first evening when they set up camp, Golan refused to sleep in the tent, instead choosing to sleep beneath the stars, and Lettle joined him.

'This is only the second time I've ever left Mosima,' he said quietly. So quietly, Lettle wasn't sure whether his voice had come from her dreams or from him.

She yawned and sat up as wakefulness returned to her. 'Hmm?'

'I was only six years old when the prince learned how to open the boundary. For the first few months every fae was permitted to leave Mosima. When my family's turn came, we packed a picnic and spent it in the woods south of the cavern . . .' Golan laughed.

'I think I might still recognise the tree we ate beside, as I've revisited that memory so many times.'

He was silent for a moment and Lettle relaxed back onto her sleeping mat. The full moon shone above them, a welcome sight after months of missing its silver hue.

'We were only permitted to stay a few hours. The queens were very strict about ensuring the existence of the fae was kept a secret. Then a few months later the blight began, and no one but the faeguard were allowed to leave Mosima.'

Again Lettle didn't say anything. It wasn't common knowledge that the blight had been caused by Rayan's birth. It seemed like the only fae who wasn't kept under close watch was Rayan's father, whose dalliance with an elf resulted in a baby with Jani blood.

Golan reluctantly turned away from the stars and looked at Lettle. 'Thank you for letting me come with you. This means more to me than you can realise.'

Lettle patted his hand. 'Thank you for coming with me. There is no friend I'd rather have by my side.'

Ajax, who had curled up at their feet, let out a snort.

'And you, too, Ajax,' Lettle said with a smile.

They slept peacefully until dawn when Lettle was woken by Ajax nudging her in the side.

'Ow, Ajax, stop that!' She tried to shove the beast away but he skittered backwards, throwing up fallen leaves as he did.

'Lettle?' Golan said, sitting up. 'What is it?'

'Ajax woke me up.' Lettle threw the obeah a scathing look, but something in his expression made her pause.

'It's only just dawn. I'm going back to sleep,' Golan grumbled.

'Shh.' Lettle silenced him. Then said in a whisper, 'I think Ajax might have heard something.'

Ajax bobbed his head in confirmation. Both Lettle and Golan listened to the sounds of the forest, but they couldn't hear as far as an obeah could.

'We should pack up the camp, slowly and quietly,' Lettle said.

'Whoever is out there, if we're too far away to hear them, then they're too far away to hear us.' Or so she hoped.

Ajax prowled in a circle around them as they rolled up their sleeping mats and packed their few belongings.

'Let's continue south,' Lettle said.

All of a sudden Ajax froze, his ears pinned back against his head. He dipped his horns left towards a nearby cluster of trees.

Lettle grabbed Golan and ran in the opposite direction. Ajax followed and together the three of them hid behind a grove of eucalyptus just as two shadows stretched into the clearing ahead of them.

'The note said south-west, so we'll follow the compass that way,' one of the shadows said.

'But for how long?'

The two travellers were fae, recognisable from the faeguard uniform they were wearing.

'I don't know, and I won't until we find her.'

Her. They meant Lettle. Someone in Mosima had heard Lettle was leaving and sent assassins after her. She exchanged a look with Golan.

'We need to change our course. Move into the Wasted Marshes before going south again,' Lettle mouthed.

Golan nodded.

Then Ajax scuffed the ground by their feet.

'You have a better idea?' she whispered to the obeah, wondering whether Rayan was watching behind his eyes.

Ajax dipped his head before launching into the clearing. The two fae froze as they came face to face with Ajax.

'Isn't that the king's obeah?' one of them said.

'He must be travelling with her,' the other said.

Ajax lowered himself to the ground before sprinting in the opposite direction from where Golan and Lettle were hiding.

'Follow the obeah!' the fae shouted before lurching into the undergrowth after Ajax.

'He's leading them away from us,' Lettle said. She stood, tugging on Golan's hand. 'Come on, we better move. We don't know how long Ajax can keep them occupied.'

Golan and Lettle travelled more carefully after that, each taking turns to keep watch. They didn't see Ajax again for three days as he stretched the distance between them and the assassins. Meanwhile Lettle and Golan continued south-west towards their destination.

It was only once the obeah returned that Lettle let herself relax enough to think about the implications of what had happened.

'Someone in the Royal Woodland heard where we were going. Did you recognise either of them, Golan?'

Golan shook his head. 'No, I didn't know them.' He opened his mouth to say more but closed it again.

'What?' Lettle pressed. They had been walking for four hours that day already, and she was getting a little irritable.

'Did you . . . did you notice they were Lightless?' he said softly.

'Oh.'

It was becoming more and more obvious that the assassin who poisoned Rayan wasn't working alone.

'The Lightless have much to be angry about,' Lettle continued carefully.

Golan's eyes flashed. 'They do, but that does not give them permission to launch an attack against you. Nor does it explain why they're targeting you.'

'No, I suppose not.'

A strong breeze twirled through the forest and for the first time Lettle smelled salt.

'The sea is close,' she said with a smile.

Golan's pace increased. 'The Crystal Glade won't be far away now.'

But unfortunately they lost the sunlight before they reached their destination.

'I'll take first watch,' Golan offered, then fell silent. Since their conversation about the Lightless he'd been quiet.

Ajax curled by Lettle's feet as she lay down to rest. Soon the obeah was snoring, but she couldn't sleep.

She joined Golan on the edge of their camp. For a while they sat in companiable silence, then Golan spoke.

'There wasn't always Lightless in Mosima,' he said. 'It was a few hundred years ago now, when the first fae didn't bind to an obeah.' He laughed dryly, a harsh sound that Lettle had never heard him make.

'There are records in the hospitals of the first cases, they thought it was caused by some sort of disease, a virus.' He shook his head. 'But more likely, the increased violence of the Forever War in the Elven Lands stripped the world of more and more obeah. Our soulmates were lost before we could bind.'

Guilt stayed Lettle's tongue. Not only had her father been a hunter of obeah, for years she had used obeah entrails to speak to the Fates.

'I don't mind the pity,' Golan continued. 'At least pity acknowledges the harm I suffer each and every day. It's the disgust I can't abhor, like I'm an abomination.' His voice cracked and Lettle reached for him, laying her hand on his wrist.

'Being Lightless sounds a lot like being an elf in Mosima,' she said gently.

He looked at her, but she couldn't see his expression in the darkness. 'I'm not saying that those trying to hurt you are right. Of course I don't want to see any harm come to you. But I do think the Lightless's plight has been forgotten for too long.'

Lettle thought back to the Honeypot Tavern and the anger she'd seen in the faces of its patrons.

'Rayan and Furi have a lot to put right. But they will, you have to believe that,' she said, yet in her mind she doubted her own words even as she spoke them.

With the fae on the brink of war, the Lightless will be forgotten once more.

'Perhaps,' was all Golan said.

After a few moments, Lettle changed the subject. 'When do you think we'll arrive at the Crystal Glade?'

'By midday tomorrow at the latest.'

'Why is it called the Crystal Glade?'

She heard him smile. 'Because of the trees that grow there. I've only read stories about them, but in the time before the curse the glade had been a sacred place for the fae.'

'What makes the trees so special?'

'You'll see,' he said ominously.

When Lettle eventually did go to sleep that night her dreams were plagued by nightmares of trees that shattered like glass. Each shard pierced her skin until she bled.

It took them less than an hour to reach the Crystal Glade the next day. The pine trees that had been their silent swaying companions thinned out until a clearing of spindlier trees came into view.

The trees glittered in the sunlight and for a moment Lettle thought that her dreams had been right, and the trees were indeed made of glass.

Their bark was midnight blue, their thin narrow leaves a pale green. As she got nearer she saw that they weren't beads of glass but small water droplets covering the entirety of the trunk's surface. It gave the impression that the trees were multi-faceted, like a gemstone or a crystal.

'Welcome to the Crystal Glade,' Golan said with a wide smile.

With everything she'd discovered over the last six months, from Mosima to the fae, she didn't expect anything to shock her again. 'What is this magic?'

'Not magic. You see the small veins on the bark? That's the root system.'

Lettle peered closer and could see fine white lines, like the vanes on a feather, running up and down the bark.

'They pull moisture from the air,' Golan continued. 'It's believed that the trees cannot grow anywhere else but here – it's something about the climate and the humidity.'

'They're beautiful,' Lettle breathed.

Golan didn't reply, and when she turned to look at him, his face was wet with tears.

They didn't speak for some time, each finding their own solitary path through the glittering giants.

Ajax padded by Lettle's waist, the white sand dulling the sound of his heavy paws, the noise reverberating like a heartbeat. It was a comforting reminder that a piece of Rayan was always with her.

The glade wasn't large, perhaps just a league in circumference. Waves pleated the horizon in the distance.

But there was no clear indication of where the research could be. If it was buried beneath the earth, she hoped Najma would have mentioned it – but similarly to Rayan, he exercised brevity. Like father, like son.

And now I've no idea where to look.

'Golan?' Lettle called to him and he appeared behind Ajax. 'Did you see anything that could be an old riverbed?'

Golan shook his head. His mouth moved to say 'No', but then he stopped and pointed. 'Those trees over there. Look, they're smaller than those around them.'

Lettle turned to see, Golan's meaning becoming clear. The younger trees grew in a V formation pointing towards the sea, something only noticeable at this particular angle.

Golan ran towards them, his voice excited and breathless. 'There must have been an estuary here, leading to the ocean. Perhaps it even still runs deep underground.'

Lettle jogged to keep up with him.

'Do you see anything? Maybe a mark on a tree? Or a bag tied to a branch?' she asked Golan who was still up ahead.

He turned around, and she garnered from his expression that he'd found nothing. But Lettle wasn't ready to give up on their theory.

'Keep looking,' she said, joining in the search.

They moved systematically up and down the old estuary, circling every tree. When Lettle began to retrace her steps for a third time, the sun had almost set.

'I'm losing light,' she growled.

'I think we should rest and try again in the morning, there might be another part of the glade that was once an old riverbed,' Golan said.

She knew he was right, but she couldn't help feeling dispirited.

They camped beneath the trees that night. Golan harvested some forest mushrooms which he then wrapped in seaweed and smoked over a fire for flavour.

'Who taught you how to cook?' she asked after eating her second portion.

Golan smiled. 'My uncle, he used to tell me stories as we cooked. He would say it's always best to feed the mind and the stomach at the same time.'

Lettle could tell Golan's words were tinged with an old grief. 'He's no longer with us?'

Golan shook his head, his smile falling away. 'He was the one who told me the tales of the Crystal Glade. It was why I have always wanted to visit here.'

Lettle brought her knees to her chest and wrapped her arms around them. 'Will you tell me that story now?'

For a second Golan looked like he might refuse, but when he looked back at her she noted that his demeanour had changed. His eyes had narrowed, his lips quirked playfully, ready to laugh. Here was Golan the storyteller. Lettle wondered if he bore a resemblance to his uncle.

'The Crystal Glade is no ordinary land. It was once the meeting place of the gods Bosome and Ewia. For centuries they had chased each other through the sky.' Golan looked to the moon. 'The god Bosome's silver shimmer embellished the night, while Ewia's sunrays warmed the day. Once a millennium the gods crossed paths, and during that eclipse they would meet here, on this very shore, beneath the tallest tree.'

Lettle was lulled by the rhythm of the story. Golan was doing his uncle proud.

'The lovers would only have a few moments before Ewia would have to leave to start the new day. Bosome in their grief would cry tears enough to fill a river. It is said that is why the trees here cry still and will only stop when the gods meet again in the next eclipse.'

It was a beautiful story, both heartbreaking and hopeful at the same time. But something Golan had said had made Lettle pause.

'How well-known is this story, Golan?'

He shrugged. 'Fairly well-known, a lot of people share variations of the tale about the Crystal Glade.'

'So we can assume Rayan's father had heard it too?'

'Yes, I think that's safe to assume.'

Lettle widened her eyes at him, surprised Golan wasn't yet getting it. 'You said Bosome cried enough tears to fill a river. Does that not sound similar to you?'

'"Once a river flowed",' Golan murmured the phrase from Najma's letter.

Lettle jumped up. 'You said the gods met beneath the tallest tree, right?'

'Yes, but Lettle, it's too dark to see anything.'

Golan was right. Shadows had gathered around the glade, the light from the moon only appearing in dappled patches.

Lettle couldn't wait until dawn to test her theory. She bit her cheek, impatience making the skin there itch. 'What about if we find higher ground and look at the glade from that angle?'

Golan cocked his head. 'I don't recall going past a hill, do you?'

But Lettle wasn't ready to give up. 'I can climb one of the trees. From that height, surely I'll be able to tell which is the tallest.'

Golan had the decency not to scoff. 'I'm not sure these trees are that easy to climb, Lettle.'

'Well, I have to try.'

She faced the nearest tree and wrapped her hands around the trunk. In the dark the pale green leaves looked silver.

With a grunt she attempted to scale the trunk. But the dew drops that looked so beautiful in the moonlight made the bark too slick to grasp.

'I can do this,' she muttered to herself. She lunged upwards with her good arm and for a few brief moments her hand found purchase on a gnarled part of the wood. But as soon as she lifted herself up, she found herself back on the ground again.

'Moon's mercy!' she cursed. 'Golan, come here and give me a boost, maybe I can reach the lowest branch.'

Despite the extra step Golan's cupped hands provided, Lettle was too short to reach the branches of most of the surrounding trees.

After the tenth attempt Golan begged they abandon the plight. 'My leg is aching, Lettle. I can't keep bending in this position.'

She released a sigh of frustration and looked out to the horizon. Their endeavours had led them to the edge of the beach where the sea lapped at the white sand.

Lettle paced towards the ocean. It was time to admit defeat until the morning. When her toes kissed the water, she turned back to look at Golan. 'You're right. Let's bed down for the night.'

Golan's smile was full of relief. She noticed the sheen of sweat that covered his brow. It was then that she realised it was much easier to see him on the shore where the moon's light was not obstructed by the canopy of trees.

She cast her gaze wider, her heart starting to race. From this vantage point the Crystal Glade was outlined by the moonlight, the tops of the trees gleaming silver.

'Golan, turn around. The gods have blessed this quest of ours.'

Thank you, Bosome, for sharing in your wisdom.

Her god's shimmering rays guided her to the tallest tree, north-east of her location.

'Is your leg still aching?' Lettle asked Golan with a grin.

He laughed a little manically. 'Race you there.'

Together, they lunged back into the glade, all thoughts of sleep replaced by excitement.

Shadows snatched at the moonlight as they ran beneath the canopy of the trees. Ajax pranced ahead of them snorting happily along with their breathless laughs.

They reached the tree at the same time.

From below, there was nothing out of the ordinary that would suggest this was the tallest tree in the glade. If they hadn't seen it from the beach, they would have never assumed it resided above its brethren. Its trunk was the same width as all the others, its leaves just as delicate, but when Lettle strained her neck upwards, she could see the moonlight glittering along the highest branch.

'Look.' Golan pointed to a small nook in the tree.

Lettle's hand shook as she reached in, her fingers hoping to find anything other than spiders. For a few seconds she grasped only air then her knuckles brushed something smoother than the bark of the tree.

She withdrew a wooden box and her smile grew until her cheeks hurt. 'This must be the research.'

'Open it,' Golan said, his lips trembling ever so slightly.

The lid was damp from the dew drops on the crystal tree, and as she surveyed the wood, she began to feel uneasy. The lacquer had cracked beneath the moisture, seeping into the seams of the box.

Lettle opened it with care. Her stomach sank as she saw the extent of the water damage. She pulled the contents out carefully.

'Oh, no,' she muttered. The first notebook was entirely ruined, though from the few letters she could read it looked like Najma's handwriting.

The second book was heavier and bound in leather, so it had been better protected from the water. Lettle felt a wave of relief. The pages of this book were aged and yellowed – made from a material Lettle couldn't place. The language and letters too were unfamiliar.

'Is that—' Golan asked.

'Afa's grimoire,' Lettle whispered. She couldn't believe it – she realised that in her heart she hadn't truly expected to find it. She picked up the ruined notebook again and tried to glean some of its contents.

'It looks like that part was once a glossary,' Golan said over her shoulder. As soon as he said it, she realised he was right. Though they couldn't read any of the water-damaged words, the order they'd been written in made it clear this was a key of some kind.

Some of the hope that had buoyed her deflated. They were going to have to recreate years of work to pull together another translation.

But at least it was something. Here in her hands was the answer to freeing the fae from their curse.

Her smile turned into giddy laughter and Golan joined in. The moment was a precious one, the ramifications of their journey too wild to fathom, so all they could do was laugh.

'We actually *found* the grimoire,' Lettle said, sending them into more peals of laughter. Soon she was clutching her sides, gasping for breath, and Golan's cheeks were ruddy with tears.

When they'd both cried themselves hoarse Golan said, 'It's probably time we went to bed. I'll take first watch.'

Lettle could tell from the way he said it that he desperately wanted to.

'The dew drops glitter like stars. I'd like to sit and watch them awhile,' he added.

Lettle nodded. 'Wake me when it's my turn.'

Once Lettle had settled in her bedroll she cast one last look at the glade. Golan was right: the moonlight sparkling across the forest made it look like the night sky had fallen to earth. Each dew drop twinkled with its own light.

Lettle pretended that she didn't see the tears rolling down Golan's face.

She clutched the grimoire against her chest and promised once again that she'd one day see her friend free of Mosima.

CHAPTER NINE

Furi

Furi leant forward until her lips brushed Yeeran's. The scent of her was intoxicating. Like wild sage and honey.

'Kiss me.' Furi spoke the words against Yeeran's cheek and the elf complied, taking her time to savour her.

Furi's hand ran up Yeeran's bare back, enjoying the ripple of pleasure that followed her touch.

She moved her fingers to Yeeran's chest, gliding along the warmth of her breasts to the tip of her nipple. Yeeran gasped, breaking away from their kiss, and Furi took the opportunity to run her tongue down the length of Yeeran's neck.

Yeeran's hips rocked forward, guiding Furi lower.

And lower Furi's mouth travelled until she felt the coolness of a blade at her neck.

She looked up and Yeeran held a dagger to her throat. The artery there pumped with her life's blood. From a heart that had been beating for her.

'What are you doing?' Furi asked.

Then Yeeran's blade glided across her skin in one fluid motion—

—Furi woke up gasping, her hands clawing at her neck. When she realised that Yeeran's presence had been but a nightmare she felt her heartrate slow and her eyes prickle with tears.

How dare she blight my dreams?

It is because you miss her, Amnan replied, the obeah ever the sensible one.

It had been nearly two weeks since Yeeran had left, and Furi had never been more despondent. They had parted on unsteady terms, with Yeeran returning to the ruler who held her allegiance.

I wasn't enough for her, Furi thought.

She went to save lives. Furi wasn't sure if it was her conscience or Amnan who replied. They were so often one and the same.

But whether Yeeran's reasoning was worthy or not, Furi still missed her fiercely. There was no one who had grounded her quite like Yeeran. Their love was a simple thing in a world that made things unnecessarily complex.

Furi swung her legs out of bed and began to dress.

Are you near? Furi asked Amnan.

Coming into the bedroom now. Would you like to go for a ride?

Yes, to the mango fields.

Furi had been riding to the fields every time she found herself thinking of Yeeran. It was the place she had first realised she'd had feelings for the elf.

It had been like any other day, except when Furi had arrived to work the fields Yeeran was there in a tree, her hands sticky with juice like she'd been there picking fruit for hours.

'What are you doing?' The question had come out of Furi's mouth before she could stop it.

Yeeran was startled, then she smiled when she saw it was Furi. 'I'm picking mangoes.' She'd said it nonchalantly like there was nothing remarkable about it.

'I can see that, but why are you here?'

'If you won't train me, I can at least be of help. The crops need harvesting and I have time. Watch out.' A bunch of mangoes fell from the tree.

Furi jumped back and hissed.

Why would she help harvest a home that wasn't hers?

Perhaps to impress us, Amnan replied.

Yet Yeeran had made it clear she had little respect for Furi. But the land, and the food it yielded – *that* she respected greatly.

Furi had watched how gracious Yeeran had been with her time, and how much she harvested. It was then that Furi saw beyond just the desire she felt for the elf. It was then that she knew this was someone she could one day love.

But that love had been squandered: Yeeran's loyalty to her tribe came before any love she had for Furi. And Furi would never forgive her for it.

Amnan increased his pace as they left the Royal Woodland behind, the palace now just a shadow against the cavern wall.

A trail of star gliders swirled around them. Since she'd become queen, the creatures had grown even more persistent about accompanying her everywhere, which tonight she was grateful for as they lit the path ahead of them.

Faster, Amnan.

The obeah obliged, exalting in the freedom of being outside the palace. But even that freedom was limited. When they reached the cavern walls beyond the mango fields they were forced to turn back.

If only they could travel beyond the border with ease. But Furi's connection to the curse was too strong, and if she left Mosima there'd be untold consequences. Perhaps the lakes would turn acidic, or a new blight would prevail.

As commander she'd been able to leave Mosima for up to five days at a time before the curse started punishing the land. But as queen she could leave for just a few moments. If she closed her eyes and stilled her breath, she could feel the threads of the curse wrapping around her soul. Like the hairs on her arm, she could feel the prickle of them moving like a shiver across her skin.

I'm trapped down here forever.

Not forever, Amnan chastised her. *Maybe Najma's research will glean a way out. I have seen how studiously Rayan reads his old notebooks.*

Furi laughed. *I cannot hold onto that hope, Amnan. It is a torture.*

Amnan nodded sagely. *Hope can be a torture or a balm, depending on how you accept it.*

The obeah circled back towards the Royal Woodland.

The fray was warming, bringing with it the light of day. The only people who stirred were those whose jobs required the peace of morning. She recognised one such person and dismounted from Amnan to greet him.

'Norey, how fares the woods?' she said.

The older man looked up from his weeding and smiled. 'Hello, dear queen.'

Furi cringed. 'Please do not call me queen, it sounds so strange coming from you.'

Norey was one of her father's partners and had known Furi all her life. When Norey laughed the twigs in his yellow-dyed hair quivered with him. 'Fine. Hello, dear Furi.'

She went to him and began to pluck the leaves and sticks from his hair.

'You should keep the forest in the forest,' she said fondly.

'I do try, I do try,' he said. 'Do you mind passing me the shears behind you?'

Furi did as she was bade, even offering to help Norey prune back the vines that threatened to choke an acacia tree.

As the royal horticulturist it was Norey's job to rein in the plants that threatened to overgrow the entirety of the woodland. Fed by the proximity to the Jani dynasty's magic, if the woodland grew unchecked it would outgrow its walls.

Furi and Norey worked in silence for a little while. The labour was familiar and comforting to Furi.

Norey had been a constant support when she'd been younger, listening to her childish woes and teenage arguments with her mother. Every time Norey had put her to work while she talked, distracting her mind from whatever petty fight she'd had that day.

Now he waited patiently until Furi was ready.

'I miss my childhood years sometimes,' Furi said quietly.

Norey chuckled. 'I don't. You'd chew my ear off all afternoon about why your mother wouldn't let you forge yet another sword.'

Furi smiled as she remembered that particular argument. 'Yes, my problems were much smaller back then.'

Amnan yawned and stretched on the ground by Norey's clippings – the early morning run was catching up with him already. Norey looked at him affectionately; he'd never bonded to an obeah. When Furi was young and insensitive she'd asked if Norey minded.

'The plants are my souls,' he'd replied.

Furi wondered if she'd get the same response now. Or if the years of experience she'd gained would favour her with a more truthful answer.

'So you convinced Sahar to move back into the palace,' Norey said.

'Yes, I always hated his banishment from court,' Furi said. 'It's nice to have him back. You know you are always welcome to join him.'

Norey shook his head. 'No, I cannot live where I work. I like living in the apothecary. Besides, I can't imagine the royal court would accept a Lightless living so close to the royals.'

Though Norey only teased, Furi had to look away from him. Because he spoke the truth.

There is so much I want to change about how Mosima is run.

So do it, Amnan said bluntly.

'Well, that's my work done for the day, thank you for helping, Furi. Come see me again soon, will you?' Norey said.

'I will,' Furi promised. She helped Norey pack up his things before she mounted Amnan once more.

I'm not ready to start my day yet, she said to the obeah.

The obeah sensed where she wanted to go next. He slipped through the tunnel that led them there until Furi heard the familiar sound of waves lapping against rocks.

The weapons shed in which she and Najma used to store their training tools looked so lonely on the beach.

She slipped off Amnan's back and onto the black sand of Conch Shore. She hadn't been there since she asked Yeeran to stay in Mosima as her consort.

'I want you here, by my side, always . . .'

She found herself running away from the memory until her feet met the sea.

Her sudden movement was probably what alerted the newcomer, as someone darted out from the weapons shed.

Amnan hissed and lunged after the shadow, but he had strolled too far down the beach, and by the time he reached the shed the stranger had disappeared into the Royal Woodland.

What were they doing in there? Amnan's teeth were bared in a snarl.

I don't know, but I intend to find out.

Conch Shore was a private area of Mosima only accessible via the Royal Woodland tunnels. Though land was not owned in the conventional sense, the beach had been an area only the royals visited. It was why Furi had used the waterfront to train Yeeran, away from prying eyes.

Though they had done more than just train her magic.

Her mind conjured Yeeran's maddening scent from her dream and she had to shake her head to be rid of it.

Furi entered the shed just as the fray-light had warmed to a pale orange, banishing the darkness from the corners of the building.

On the wall was Najma's sabre, a reminder of the many happy memories they'd had here. Initially the shed had been a present on her sixth nameday and Najma had filled it with toys.

Every year they'd each hide a new present somewhere in the shed's dusty alcoves. Eventually the gifts evolved from puppets to books to weapons. All of those memories lined the shelves, making the air heavy.

She steadied herself on a shelf as grief tightened her throat and riled her stomach acid.

Loss struck her in waves. Sometimes the surge could knock her down and other times it just gently lapped at the edge of her mind. But it was always there, as vast and as deep as the ocean.

As she righted herself something fell from the shelf.

A piece of paper. It said eight words:

Second assassination attempt failed. The seer still lives.

'Bring forth the servant who tried to murder Lettle.' Furi barked the command at the nearest guard as she entered the palace. 'And someone call for the king.'

'Furi, I'm here.' Rayan stood at the top of the stone staircase. On the wall behind him, carved into the cloister's alcove, was a sculpture of his father riding his obeah. It was as if Najma's spirit was haunting his shadow.

Furi had always hated the statue. With his sabre by his waist it made her brother look more violent than he actually was. Of the two of them, he had been the gentle one.

'What is that?' Rayan asked as he drew level with her.

She thrust the paper towards his outstretched hand.

He nodded, unsurprised. She noted then how sallow his dark skin was.

'What happened?' she asked.

He looked around. 'Not here.'

Her brows knotted together but she didn't question him as he led the way to the war room and closed the door behind them.

'It happened this morning,' Rayan said. 'I was just looking for you to tell you.'

'Is Lettle hale?' Though she had little regard for the elf, she was family now and that went deeper than mere regard.

'She is.' Rayan clenched his fists, the only indication that he was angry. Despite never meeting his father he was more like him than he realised. 'Ajax had them follow his trail, thankfully leading them away from Lettle and Golan. If they've returned to leave this message at least this means they've given up on finding them.' He collapsed into a chair and tipped his head to the ceiling.

'Someone knew that she was leaving Mosima. They must have heard us talking in the woodland,' Furi said. She felt her fingers tingle with magic at the thought of a spy within their household.

'It was only because I lied that they weren't able to follow her to her destination,' Rayan muttered.

Furi's gaze snapped to Rayan's. 'What do you mean, "you lied"?'

Rayan removed a letter from his breast pocket. 'Lettle wasn't taking a trip to the ocean. I sent her to collect Afa's grimoire from where my father had hidden it – in the Crystal Glade.'

Furi read Najma's final words to his son, her eyes getting hot as she recognised his handwriting.

'"I do not trust everyone here, including some of my family." Do you think he was talking about my cousin?' She wouldn't say Nerad's name out loud. Not because she cared about interrupting his eternal slumber, but because his name soured her mouth.

'Probably, but I thought secrecy was prudent,' Rayan said.

'Even from me?' Furi didn't like that Rayan had kept something from her.

Rayan met her gaze steadily. 'I was being cautious, and I'm glad I was or Lettle would now be dead.'

Furi looked away from him. There was no use picking a fight with Rayan. He wasn't the one she was mad at.

And he was right, Amnan said. *His lie saved Lettle's life.*

Sometimes Amnan's righteousness was annoying.

You know I can hear your thoughts? he replied hotly.

She scowled at him in her mind.

'I told you there'd be more of them,' Rayan muttered.

'I never said I didn't believe you, it's just that the evidence was lacking,' Furi replied.

'You know what this means?' he said.

Furi lowered herself into a chair with more care than Rayan had, though her bones felt like dead weight.

'It means they're organised,' she said. 'They're taking instructions from someone. And . . .' Furi swallowed, her mouth dry '. . . we can no longer speak freely in our own palace.'

There was a knock at the door and the guard she had spoken to earlier entered with the servant who had poisoned Lettle's mead.

Rayan sat up straight in his chair, his eyes flint thin.

'Maler O'Lightless, we have some questions for you,' Furi said.

The servant quivered, his long blond hair shimmering down his back.

'I have told you over and over again, I did not poison the mead,' Maler replied, his voice a high-pitched whine.

Rayan inhaled sharply and Furi felt the ground beneath her feet tremble from his rage.

Furi shot him a warning look. Fae life was precious and Maler would not die today, no matter the crime. But Rayan had not been raised in Mosima and the fae's ways were new to him.

'We are not interested in your falsehoods,' Furi said.

Maler opened his mouth to reply then closed it.

'Tell us who you are working with and we will lessen your sentence,' Furi continued.

'Furi—' Rayan said in alarm, but she held up her hand to quiet him. If Maler had something more to say, then this was the only way to find out.

But Maler's mouth stayed firmly shut.

'We will not offer you this clemency again,' Furi said.

'No, we will not,' Rayan added with a bite to his tone.

Still, Maler did not speak.

Rayan stood from his chair and loomed over the smaller man. 'Know this, fae life may be precious, but there are far worse things I can do to you than condemn you to servitude. I may be king of Mosima, but I was raised in the violence of the Bleeding Field.'

Maler's lip quivered but he stayed silent. When they were about to give up on him he said, 'There are too many of them. There's no way to stop it. The seer will die.'

Furi watched Rayan's eyes grow cold with fear before he turned away, and she called for a guard to have Maler removed from the room.

'If he won't speak, then what else can we do?' Rayan's question broke the silence between them.

'We need to root them out.'

Rayan began to pace. 'But how? We know so little about who these people are. We don't even know their motive.'

Furi cocked her head. 'We have to assume the motive is Lettle's race. She's an elf in the royal household, a walking target for all who have lost loved ones to the elves' massacre of the obeah.'

'I'm half-elf and I'm their king.'

'Exactly, they cannot kill you – it would endanger Mosima. But they can slight you by killing your consort.'

Rayan's eyes bored into Furi's. 'If they kill Lettle, they kill me.'

Oh, to be loved like that.

Furi reached out and squeezed his shoulder. 'We won't let them.'

He let out a slow breath. Then he frowned and picked up the letter Furi had found in the shed.

'This is in elvish – or the universal tongue or whatever you call it. Why isn't it in fae?' Rayan asked.

'The stranger must have been Lightless, like Maler. It is difficult to write fae when the language isn't gifted to you from an obeah binding. Few learn it.'

'The assassins who followed Lettle in the Wasted Marshes were Lightless too.'

They let the facts settle in their mind, but neither of them could see why the Lightless would target Lettle specifically.

'Hang on, how did the Lightless even get out of Mosima? Wouldn't they have needed to be released from the boundary by one of us?' Rayan asked.

Furi had been waiting for the question, and she tried not to look guilty. 'I released a batch of soldiers the day Lettle left, to scout the area for any signs of our troops. They returned today.'

Rayan's nostrils flared. 'You failed to mention that. Do you have the names of all the soldiers you sent out?'

The truth was Berro was usually in charge of the soldier assignments and since she was negotiating with the chieftain of Crescent, Furi hadn't been entirely organised. 'I'll get the list, though I'm less familiar with the scouts than Berro is. So even with names, I may not notice if anything is awry.'

'We can narrow it down to the Lightless, though we'll have to do it covertly of course. The people can't know we're targeting them. I also have the glimpses of memory from Ajax, so perhaps I might recognise them.'

What they would do if they caught any of them, Furi wasn't sure. If Maler didn't talk, then it was unlikely anyone else would either.

But Furi would keep searching.

'The Jani legacy must be protected at all costs,' her mother used to say. 'We are the soul of Mosima and we must be respected as such. Without us, Mosima would fail to be.'

And Lettle was part of their court now, whether Furi liked her or not.

So she'd slice away each scale of the snake until she caught the head.

CHAPTER TEN

Yeeran

Yeeran's chamber in the palace was much smaller than the rooms granted to visiting nobles. The bed was small, with sheets that scratched at her skin. The washroom was a simple chamber pot and bowl of water, instead of the pumped-in systems she was used to in Salawa's rooms. She didn't mind though; as long as she and Pila were safe, then that was all that mattered.

Yeeran slept fitfully that night despite being home. Pila had stolen the entirety of the blanket on the bed, leaving Yeeran to sleep without the comforting weight of the linen. It was similar to how she felt being home – a little cold and uncomfortable, like something was missing.

Not something, *someone*. Furi.

The fae had clawed her way into Yeeran's heart without remorse, leaving wounds of longing and fingerprints of lust.

Yeeran was still in bed when there was a knock at the door.

Pila growled and rolled out of bed, the sheets tangled in her horns.

Yeeran laughed as she walked to answer the door. *You're not as menacing as you think you look, Pila.*

She opened the door to a servant with a steaming bowl of food. The smell wafting up from the tray made her stomach instantly churn.

'The chieftain recalled that your favourite breakfast was lamb mince with garri,' the servant said. 'I have also prepared a fruit platter for your . . . companion.'

'I'll just take the fruit please. I no longer eat meat.'

The servant seemed taken aback by that. No one refused a gift from the chieftain. But Yeeran couldn't let the smell enter her rooms. Ever since bonding with Pila she couldn't stand the taste or smell of meat.

'I . . . I will return the rest to the kitchen. I was also told to inform you that the chieftain will be ready to receive you in the throne room within the hour.'

'All right. Thank you.' Yeeran closed the door and returned to bed.

Any mango? Pila asked hopefully.

No, it's not in season in Gural.

Pila's front teeth slipped out from under her top gums in an expression Yeeran had come to recognise as a scowl.

There is melon though, it is quite good, Yeeran said.

Once they'd finished breakfast Yeeran washed and dressed in the plain clothes they had left for her. She noticed for the first time how abrasive the material in Gural was compared to the cotton grown in Mosima. She hadn't realised how quickly she'd got used to the comforts there, far away from the war-torn cities in the Elven Lands.

The window in her chambers looked out on the Bleeding Field in the distance. Half a year ago the sight of the barracks would have made her heart surge with pride. Now it only left a bitter taste in her mouth.

With the fae helping Crescent many more would die on soil they didn't even know was once called the Fae Lands. She turned away from the window with tears in her eyes. Pila came and set her head in Yeeran's lap.

That was how the soldiers found them when they came to escort Yeeran to the throne room to meet Salawa.

Stay close, Yeeran warned the obeah as they were led through the tiled corridors.

Always.

The throne room was lined with more soldiers than yesterday. In addition, Salawa's advisors were in attendance. Yeeran spotted General Motogo in the sea of faces and her stomach soured. They'd been the person most gleeful about Yeeran's exile. Having Salawa's ear had often made those around Yeeran envious. But she had earned her rank, had proven it time and time again.

Until the mistake that had led to her exile.

Seek your glory in the east. That had been Lettle's prophecy. Yeeran smiled ruefully. If only she'd known that bonding to an obeah had in fact been the glory she sought, and not defeating enemies on a battlefield.

'Is something amusing, Yeeran?' Salawa asked from her throne.

She wore a pale blue dress that fell just short of her ankles where bangles jingled up to her calf.

'No, chieftain,' Yeeran replied.

Salawa seemed put out not to be included in the joke, but didn't press further.

'My advisors and I have been discussing your news. And you'll be pleased to learn that we have taken your accusations seriously. Letters have been sent to our allies in Eclipse and Waxing—'

'Allies? When did that happen?'

Salawa did not appreciate being interrupted, but Yeeran's curiosity was too strong to temper.

The last coalition between Waning, Eclipse and Waxing had been during the Two-Bladed Tyrant's reign. But the alliance had failed when Eclipse ambushed Waning's northern quarter, claiming more of the Bleeding Field.

Though they weren't in active warfare when Yeeran left, distrust between the three tribes was strong. It was General Motogo who answered Yeeran's query.

'More has changed than perhaps you have realised, Yeeran. The three tribes are united against the might of Crescent once more,' Motogo sneered.

Salawa nodded and added, 'Under my leadership.'

Yeeran tried to keep her expression clear of shock. Salawa was now in charge of all three armies? That was a change indeed. Perhaps Waning wasn't in as dire a position as Yeeran had thought.

'I am glad that my news was helpful to you. It was my intention to save lives, and to hear that the tribes now know the truth is a burden off my shoulders,' Yeeran said carefully.

Salawa raised an eyebrow. 'I can imagine so.'

'I too hope that you have implemented an immediate ban on obeah hunting,' Yeeran added firmly.

Salawa considered her before replying. 'First you tell me that the fae are fighting alongside our enemy. And then you tell me how I can kill them – and you expect me to ban obeah hunting?'

'The fae are in the process of ending their relationship with Crescent. When you kill an obeah you kill innocent people, not just soldiers.' Yeeran's voice was shaking slightly from unshed rage.

Pila growled and Salawa homed in on her. 'I wonder if my obeah is out there somewhere? If it happened to you perhaps it could happen to me,' Salawa said lightly.

'I do not think so. I'm the only elf to have ever bonded to one of them.'

Salawa's mouth turned down, then her voice went wistful. 'Do you remember that time I found a puppy in the courtyard? How I loved that thing.'

Yeeran remembered. Salawa had insisted on bringing it to the battlefield. It hadn't lived long.

Salawa turned to the carafe beside her and poured a glass of wine. 'Would you like some?' she asked Yeeran. 'It's oak barrelled, which was always your preference, if I remember?'

It seemed a test of some kind and Yeeran didn't want to fail it. 'I'd be honoured,' she replied, and Salawa poured her a glass. A servant stepped forward to bring the glass to Yeeran, but the chieftain waved her away.

'It's all right, she won't hurt me,' then she turned to Yeeran. 'You can come and get it, Yeeran.'

Yeeran looked at Pila.

Be ready for anything.

Yeeran walked up the steps to the throne and collected the drink. 'Thank you.'

She waited to see the chieftain sip from her cup before following suit. Salawa's eyes twinkled as if to say, 'Poison? How droll.'

Then as Yeeran began to retreat back to Pila she said, 'I would like to visit the fae in their home. You will take me there.'

Yeeran felt her blood go cold. 'I do not think that is a good idea, Salawa.'

'And why not?'

'Allow me to go back and seek an invitation first,' Yeeran said. Salawa would not go to Mosima with good intentions, Yeeran knew it in her gut.

'And let you leave?' Salawa's laugh was bone-chilling. 'No, Yeeran, you are not leaving my side.'

Yeeran began to swivel her drum towards her waist, ready to fire if she needed. But Salawa was faster. With a flick of her wrist a row of archers appeared on the balcony above them. The sound of bowstrings being pulled taut rippled across the room.

Yeeran's blood ran cold. She recognised the fletching on the arrows. Where Waning had perfected drumfire, Waxing had dedicated years to the refinement of obeah bone arrows. With intention, every arrow would land true.

Shhhhhuh.

Her gaze was drawn downwards towards the unmistakable sound of soldiers removing swords from their scabbards. The pommels were black, lined with obeah leather, a technique used by Eclipse to enhance their swords' blows.

To either side of Pila the Waning soldiers swung their drums to their front, their hands poised and ready to strike.

Here was the three tribes' coalition in full force. If only Yeeran were not at the receiving end of it.

She was too far away from Pila to weave a threaded cage to protect her. And as she ran forward one of the Waning soldiers released drumfire strong enough to penetrate Pila's thigh. Yeeran screamed and stumbled from the own echo of the pain in her side. She tried to run to Pila but a line of soldiers blocked her path.

'Please let me go to her,' Yeeran said through clenched teeth.

It's all right, Pila, you'll be OK.

Bleeding.

I know, don't worry. I'll take care of it.

'No, I don't think so,' Salawa said. 'Motogo, instruct the soldiers to bring in the cage.'

Yeeran felt sweat trickle down her back. Pila was snapping and growling at the soldiers who surrounded her.

'She's wounded, she needs stitches!' Yeeran shouted.

Salawa turned her gaze Yeeran's way as if she were an irritating fly. 'Tell it to calmly enter the cage and I will ensure a medic sees it.'

Pila, I need you to stop fighting them. Go in the cage they are bringing, then they will call for someone to heal you.

I don't want to go in a cage.

It won't be for long, Yeeran said. Though she had no idea what plans Salawa had for her.

Pila quietened and when the cage was brought, she limped inside it. The door closed with a bang, sealing their fates.

'Now, Yeeran. You are mine,' Salawa said with a grin. 'You will lead me to Mosima, whether you wish to or not. Otherwise . . . you meet the fate you should have met for breaching your exile. Death.'

Salawa was true to her word and had a medic stitch Pila up. The sting of the needle resonated down their connection.

It'll be over soon, Yeeran soothed, truly to keep her own frayed nerves calm.

I don't like it.

I know.

The throne room was full of people moving in and out at Salawa's behest. Yeeran was sitting as close as she was allowed to the cage door.

She'd already assessed it for any weaknesses, but Salawa had created an impenetrable iron fortress.

Fifteen soldiers had been assigned to watch her. But one would have been enough. With Pila trapped, there was nothing Yeeran could do.

What is happening? Pila asked, her voice stronger in Yeeran's mind now that the medic had finished stitching her.

They're preparing to leave. They want me to lead them to Mosima.

But you cannot, Furi would not like it.

Yeeran smiled wryly. *No, she certainly wouldn't. But I have little choice. They're threatening to hurt you.*

We can survive pain, you and I.

But not death.

No, we cannot survive death, Pila confirmed.

The sound of heavy treads grew louder until they stopped a few yards away behind Yeeran.

'It is time to leave,' Salawa said.

Yeeran turned around slowly but didn't get up from her position on the floor.

Salawa had changed into her armour. It was rare for the chieftain to be in combat wear as she so rarely attended the battlefield. It was why the black leather was so pristine, shined with oil to keep it supple, without a nick or tear in it. Silver waning moons lined the cuffs and epaulettes. The collar was obeah fur, glossy and black – from an obeah bonded to a fae.

She wore death and she sought death.

Once Yeeran would have found her beauty alluring, the outfit striking. But now Yeeran saw the ugliness of her greed and pride. It overshadowed all her comeliness.

'We will travel by camel. The obeah of course will join us via carriage. As long as you lead me to Mosima, I will free you on arrival. The obeah will not be harmed and neither will you. But if for any reason I believe you are not directing us true, I will kill you. Without hesitation.'

'Why are you doing this, Salawa?' Yeeran said softly. 'Your enemy is Crescent, the fae can do nothing for you.'

'Why?' Salawa smiled. 'Why do we fight for the Bleeding Field, Yeeran?'

Six months ago Yeeran's answer would have been righteous, her faith in the cause absolute: to mine more fraedia crystal to help feed the hungry. But now she knew the truth.

'For power.'

Salawa's eyes flickered with an ambiguous emotion: hurt? Surprise? Then her smile returned.

'Perhaps you are right. Power over our enemies but power over the land too. The fraedia mines would bring wealth back to Waning.'

Wealth not welfare.

'Do you even remember your old campaign slogan, Salawa?'

The chieftain's smile fell from her face and Yeeran continued, '"An end to war. An end to poverty. Food and peace are what we fight for."'

Salawa's lips pursed and she replied, 'Your news has already ended the war. Waning, Eclipse and Waxing have all agreed to leave the Bleeding Field—'

'Instead you take the war to Mosima's doorstep, intent on stealing the fraedia from a city whose only source of food, light and warmth comes from the crystal you want to mine.' Yeeran's voice had risen to a dangerous volume, and the soldiers around her began to shift their feet. 'Besides,' Yeeran continued more quietly. 'You cannot get into Mosima without one of the Jani dynasty letting you in.'

This time, when Salawa grinned it was full of malice. 'I have ways to get their attention. It's your job to get me there, leave the rest of the details to me.'

Then Salawa withdrew a necklace from under her collar. It was the key to Pila's cage.

She ran it through her fingers.

Yeeran could lunge for it, yank the chain from her neck and run to Pila's cage.

She'd have barely a few seconds to weave a protective barrier around her and Pila, and that would only last half an hour, at most.

The chieftain would not give up the chase on her that quickly. Now she had Yeeran, she wasn't letting her go.

Yet Salawa's eyes were daring her, as if she thought that the love they had shared protected her from Yeeran's rage.

I could strike a thread of magic to tighten around her neck, snapping the bones in the time it would take her to release her last breath.

But in that last breath she could signal for Pila's slaughter. And that wasn't a risk Yeeran was willing to take.

Salawa must have seen the defeat in Yeeran's eyes as she said triumphantly to the room, 'Let's move out.'

CHAPTER ELEVEN

Alder

'When do you want to stop for the night?' Dart asked, jogging to keep pace with Alder.

'In an hour or two. I think we'll come across a prickle bush soon where we can stock up on dessert.'

Dart nodded. He didn't question Alder's uncanny ability to know what plants were nearby.

Alder himself couldn't explain it. He just knew exactly what kind of conditions flora could grow in, and where he looked, he often found them.

It was one of the reasons he'd been nominated as Wayfarer so young. When Baba Godfi died at a hundred and nine, everyone expected Dart to take his place as Wayfarer. He was one of the oldest in the group and knew the land as well as Godfi had.

But those who had seen Alder whisper his predictions in Godfi's ear for the last two years had known that their plentiful harvest had been down to him and not the old man's experience.

When Alder had been nominated, Dart threatened to leave.

'I refuse to be led by the *den-dweller*,' he'd said the nickname with none of the affection afforded by the others. 'I will return to Crescent.' Then he looked deep into the eyes of everyone who dared match his stare and said, 'I refute the Nomad ways.'

The Nomads had gasped.

Alder felt like he was losing purchase on a slippery rope. 'Dart, you know what that means,' he said hurriedly. 'If you refute the Nomad ways, we no longer see you, we no longer hear you. Did you say this in error?' The question was a plea.

'I refute the Nomad ways,' Dart said resolutely.

The camp went silent. It was rare for a Nomad to leave; if they did, it was because they missed routine – for to be Nomad was to embrace the chaos of nature.

But the shunning was brutal and absolute. It had to be in order to protect the Nomad way of life. You either gave your all to the family or you didn't, it was as simple as that.

They had few rules out here in the wilderness, but this one was unbreakable.

The entire camp turned away from Dart. Even as he packed his things and walked away.

But that day Alder changed the Nomads' route and followed Dart at a distance. The weather had been interchangeable and there was something in his gut that said something bad was coming.

So when the rains came, Alder was prepared. The Nomads were in the mountain range in the north of the continent.

'There will be a mudslide in three days,' he had announced to the group.

And as he predicted the mudslide came, but the Nomads were protected deep within the mountain's cave network.

Dart was not.

'I'm going after him,' he'd said to Mia that night.

'You cannot, Alder, you know the penalty for refuting our ways. Besides, he is probably dead by now.' Though Mia's tone was callous, her lip wobbled. She and Dart had been close.

Despite Mia's protestations he braved the treacherous terrain. He found Dart clinging to a tree, sleep-deprived and close to death, the earth churning beneath him.

'It's not safe, Alder,' he called weakly as Alder approached.

But Alder knew where to step to prevent the mud from sliding beneath him. When he reached Dart, he guided him carefully to the ground.

'You are stronger than I thought you were,' Dart laughed weakly.

'No, you are lighter than when you left.' Alder smiled.

They exchanged a look that said more than any apology, but still Dart said it. 'I am sorry, Wayfarer, I was foolish and stubborn. My pride was hurt when the others voted for you. But I know your navigation skills are much better than mine.'

Alder nodded, there was no point being humble. It was true. 'We have camped in the caves. Come, they will require some convincing should you wish to return.'

Dart didn't hesitate. 'Yes, I do, I was rash and unthinking.'

And from that moment on Dart was one of Alder's most trusted friends. There was no one else he would rather have by his side.

'What are you thinking about?' Dart asked, drawing Alder back to the present.

'Oh, nothing much, just remembering that time you almost died.'

'When I ate the rotten thornfruit?'

'No.'

'When I got chased by the crocodile with the missing foot?'

Alder laughed. 'No, I was actually thinking about the mudslide.'

Dart's smile slipped. The ghost of guilt crossing his features. 'I will always be in debt to you for that.'

Alder waved him away. 'Don't be silly, I wanted you back in the camp.'

Dart's smile grew once more. 'Is it because you're sweet on me?'

Alder snorted. 'You wish. Besides, I think Mia would have my throat.'

Dart sobered and nodded. 'She would.'

'What is it?' Alder asked as he bent to brush away an overgrown vine from their path.

'It's Mia. She's pregnant.'

Alder turned to Dart and hugged him. 'Congratulations, another babe for the elders to fuss over. What wonderful news.'

Alder was happy for them, despite the pang of loneliness the news brought.

'Yes,' Dart said, seemingly relieved Alder now knew. 'But it means we will need to be in Caperly before winter.'

Caperly was the only village the Nomads returned to every year. It was set into the rock face of a hillside east of the Wasted Marshes. The caves held some of their supplies as well as housing the eldest and youngest who were unable to travel.

Alder rubbed his chin. 'Ah, I see. I intended to lead us to the beaches south of here for a few weeks to catch the fish migration before going north.'

'I know, that's why I wanted to tell you now so you could change the route,' Dart said.

And of course Alder would change the route. They'd had births in the forests before, but it was safer for everyone if they got to Caperly before winter.

It was a long journey. Four months if they walked directly.

He reached into his pocket and withdrew a strip of blue cloth. He waved it above his head so that the people behind him could see the change of plan.

Blue meant north-east.

'To Caperly we go,' he said to Dart.

They had been travelling north-east for nine days when Alder sleep-walked again.

He awoke waist-deep in the middle of a swamp, a cluster of water lilies floating in his palms.

Water lilies don't even grow here, the water is too acidic, he thought.

With a scowl he picked his way out of the swamp, leaving the plants to fend for themselves. It took him an hour to retrace his steps and he reminded himself to chastise whoever was on watch that night. There was no way he should have been able to leave the sky camp unnoticed.

The moon was covered in a thick icing of cloud, making shadows of most of the trees.

He moved slowly between tree roots, careful not to fall or disturb any predators in the area.

He had been walking for half an hour when he heard a sound ahead of him.

Ba-dun, ba-dun, ba-dun.

He would have known the cadence of an obeah's footfall any-where. And sure enough an obeah flew through the undergrowth, its silver eyes wide and wild. It cantered past him, its horns missing him by a hair, and was gone before he could let out a panicky breath.

The obeah had been frightened, that much was true. But what could frighten a beast that big?

There were predators in the wilderness, but few hunted game as large as obeah. And few thrived in the environment of the Wasted Marshes.

Alder slowed his pace and crept forward, retracing the obeah's footprints.

Dart always said it was his curiosity that would get him killed.

But Alder thought it was better to be curious and dead than indifferent and alive. There was no greater sin than being dull – at least in his eyes.

Half an hour on the trail and Alder heard them.

It was rare to share the forest with other elves, so it took a moment for his brain to believe what his eyes were telling him.

A retinue of soldiers riding camels moved through the woodland. At the head of the formation was a woman dressed in opulent army leathers – presumably their leader. But she wasn't who held his attention. To the leader's left was someone he recognised.

'Yeeran,' he breathed.

The elf had only been with them for a few short hours, but her stay, and her escape, hadn't been far from his thoughts.

What had she really been doing in the Wasted Marshes, and what had he said to her in his sleep to make her leave so abruptly?

Last he'd seen of her, she'd been fleeing west, into the Elven Lands. Yet here she was, seemingly directing a cohort of soldiers east.

But she wasn't in uniform, in fact she wore peasant's clothes. Simple, and a little threadbare.

Alder moved forward, disturbing some of the leaves around him. The soldier nearest him turned to the sound and Alder froze.

They inched forward searching the bushes with their hand over their drum.

Alder had never learned drumfire, or at least he didn't seem to have the talent for it – whether that was lost to his memories too, he wasn't sure.

The concept fascinated him as much as it revulsed him. Perhaps because of his affinity to the obeah, it was difficult to see them as the raw materials of a weapon.

Either way, he didn't want to be subjected to drumfire, so before the soldier parted the bushes and found him, he loped up the nearest tree.

Alder was better at climbing than walking. His calloused feet had thickened to a hard leather making it easy to climb up tree bark.

The soldier darted into the bushes, missing Alder's flight by a hair.

Please don't look up, please don't look up.

Thankfully the soldier didn't, and once their suspicions had abated, they called back, 'Clear!'

Alder was about to make his way back down the tree, when the entire procession began to move through the trail he had taken. Until they moved on, he was trapped.

CHAPTER TWELVE

Yeeran

The full extent of the party travelling to Mosima became clear to Yeeran as they began their journey east. There was the platoon of fifteen soldiers to guard Pila and Yeeran, the chieftain's quartet of personal guards, three servants, a cook and five drumbearers to man the camels.

In addition, there were two other senior officials who Yeeran didn't recognise. It was only when she caught sight of their uniforms that she realised they were ambassadors from Waxing and Eclipse.

They truly have consolidated their forces under Waning. It was almost incomprehensible to Yeeran.

Do you think one of them might free me? Pila asked hopefully.

No, Pila, Yeeran replied, trying to keep the sadness from her voice. *I think you are stuck in this carriage until we arrive in Mosima. Or until I can think of a way out.*

But when Yeeran realised they would be travelling by boat to circumvent the Crescent border, she knew there'd be no escaping.

'It is why we have not brought the full might of my army. So we can be agile and scout out this new land,' Salawa had said to Yeeran when she had asked why they were travelling by boat. She had been surprised she'd even replied; so often the chieftain had ignored Yeeran's questioning.

'But don't worry, my soldiers won't be far behind,' Salawa added, ending the conversation and leaving Yeeran chilled to the bone.

The journey by sea to the Wasted Marshes took a week. And as hours bled into days both Yeeran and Pila were feeling the constraints of their capture. Though they were together, the chieftain wouldn't let them share the same cabin.

At first Pila had been stowed with the camels in the lower decks. But Yeeran refused to cooperate, and though she had very little leverage, Salawa had agreed to move Pila to one of the cabins down from hers.

They fed and watered them both, but so much of the food that had been brought was meat-based and Pila and Yeeran suffered for it.

When they landed on the Wasted Marshes shoreline Yeeran gorged herself on the first bush of prickle berries she could find, then bundled up as many as she could in her shirt for Pila.

It was a far cry from the platters of fruit in the Royal Woodland, but it would have to do.

Her thoughts went to the fae, carefully skirting around the longing she felt for Furi, as she considered what Salawa's arrival would mean to the underground city.

Without the strength of the full Waning army, the elves would be indefensible against the faeguard. But Salawa was cunning and had always used words before weapons. Perhaps she'd offer an allyship then assassinate Furi in the night.

Yeeran's heart stuttered at the thought.

No, Salawa is underestimating the fae. Furi would not be enticed by such a ruse, should that be the chieftain's intention.

She hoped.

A wave of guilt crashed into her and she steadied herself on a tree. *Why did I ever leave Mosima?*

Because you wanted to save more of my brethren and yours. Do not forget that. The fighting on the Bleeding Field has stopped because of you. Pila's voice calmed Yeeran. *Now, are those prickle berries for me?*

Yeeran laughed and made her way back to the camp.

She approached Madu, one of the guards who surrounded Pila. 'Please, give this to her.'

Madu smiled. She had been one of the few elves who had been kind to Pila – always making sure she had enough water or enough blankets to make the pen comfortable. Madu was older than the other guards, and perhaps her experience had taught her empathy. For she saw Pila for what she was, a life to nurture.

Madu took the berries and passed them through the cage to Pila.

Thank you. They're a little sour but it is nice to fill my belly again, Pila said to Yeeran.

'Pila said thank you,' Yeeran said to Madu, who beamed.

This became their routine. Every morning Yeeran would forage and Madu would pass on a portion to Pila.

But the deeper they got into the Wasted Marshes the fewer edible plants there were and Yeeran wouldn't risk poisoning either of them.

So instead they grew weaker, surviving on the thin soup the chieftain provided while everyone else ate salted goat.

How much longer, Yeeran? Pila said from her cage one night.

I have been circling the tunnels to Mosima for three days now, Pila, hoping that a scout might see us and report our arrival to Furi and Rayan.

But no one has come.

No.

I'm hungry, I want some mangoes.

Yeeran rolled over in her pallet, disturbing the snores of her tent mate. *Me too.*

'Yeeran!' The call came from across the camp.

A few moments later Madu appeared.

'Yeeran, the chieftain is calling for you,' she whispered.

'Now?'

It must have gone midnight.

'Yes, and Yeeran,' Madu dropped her voice even more, 'I think she might have been drinking.'

It was rare that the chieftain drank to excess.

Madu escorted Yeeran across the camp to Salawa's tent.

Inside she found Salawa slumped over a map, a wine glass sloshing in her hands.

'I need you to mark our final route,' she said, with only a little bit of a slur. It was enough for Yeeran to register that she'd had too much to drink.

'I've told you, I won't be able to mark it on a map, I need to be able to recognise it,' Yeeran said. In order to keep what little leverage she had, she'd told Salawa that she would only know the route when she was on it. Which was partly true.

She'd recognised the crag that hid the tunnel to Mosima as soon as she'd seen it three days ago but hadn't wanted to reveal it.

Salawa's eyes narrowed.

'Camel shit, Yeeran. We must be close. The ambassadors are asking questions.'

Yeeran frowned. 'I thought they answered to you?'

Salawa threw her wine at Yeeran. The reaction was so excessive it made Yeeran wonder what she'd promised the ambassadors.

Yeeran ran a hand over her eyes, flicking the wine from them. 'This tantrum does not make me any more amenable to you, Salawa.'

She knew she was swimming too close to the jaws of a shark. First, by calling out her bad behaviour and then not addressing her as chieftain.

Salawa bared her teeth. 'You are lying to me, Yeeran. Based on what you told me, you travelled on foot for fifteen days after leaving the Elven Lands. We should have arrived days ago.'

'It has been difficult to recollect my path, I was tracking an obeah, like I told you.'

Salawa looked ready to throw the whole empty goblet at Yeeran and, for a moment, she thought she would. Instead, she did something wholly unexpected. Salawa began to cry.

Yeeran watched as the chieftain slumped into her chair and put her head in her hands. Tears leaked over her perfectly lacquered fingers and onto the floor.

Once Yeeran would have stooped to comfort her lover. But how could she when she'd made Yeeran's life so miserable for the last two weeks?

And she'd hurt Pila too . . .

Love and hate swirled in her chest, constricting her breathing. She stood in the flickering firelight somewhere between the past and the present, unsure what to do.

Salawa stood up from her chair, her pristine make-up smudged, her eyes wide and vulnerable.

'Yeeran,' she whispered her name, drawing out more memories of all the time they had spent together beneath blankets and sheets.

Yeeran found herself stepping forward, being once more lulled into the orbit of Salawa's love.

When the chieftain opened her arms, Yeeran stepped into them.

'I'm so sorry,' Salawa said against Yeeran's ear. 'I'm so sorry for what I've put you through. But the other tribes, they see me as a leader. They watch my every step, report back everything they see as a weakness to their chieftains.'

Salawa breathed out slowly. 'The alliance is more tenuous than I have made it seem. We lost so many soldiers there was nothing I could do but turn to our enemies. To save our people, to make sure Waning survived.'

Yeeran pushed Salawa to arm's length and surveyed her. Her eyes were red, her lips swollen from chewing them. But she looked more beautiful than ever before. This was the woman Yeeran had first come to love, the leader who had put her people first ahead of everything.

'You did what had to be done,' Yeeran said. It was not forgiveness, she wasn't sure she could forgive her for ever caging Pila, but it was understanding.

'So many nights I have thought of you,' Salawa said softly. 'When you said those words to me, in the throne room, I wanted to weep.' She cupped Yeeran's cheek and brought her closer until their foreheads brushed.

When Salawa spoke again Yeeran could taste the sweetness of the wine on her breath. 'You are the fire of my heart and the beat of my drum. I am yours under moonlight. Until the rhythm sings no more . . .'

The words were like a spell over Yeeran's sense of reason and she found herself leaning towards the shape of Salawa's lips.

The kiss was both familiar and entirely alien, as though Salawa was the same person, but Yeeran was not.

Yeeran pulled away, the spell broken.

Salawa's hand shook as she lowered it from the side of Yeeran's face. 'You do not . . . feel the same?'

Yeeran turned away and looked through the slit of the tent opening. Somewhere out there, Pila was sleeping in a cage.

So much had changed. Even if Salawa's treatment of Yeeran and Pila was all part of an act, it had stretched a canyon between them.

'You should have done this all differently, Salawa.'

The chieftain's eyes brimmed once more and she looked away from Yeeran before the tears fell.

'I know, Yeeran. From the moment I exiled you I have lived a life of solitude and sorrow. For weeks after you left, I didn't leave my bed. I regretted my actions that day, and every breath I have taken since.'

'Then why did you do it?' Yeeran cut in sharply.

Salawa recoiled, anger flashing in her eyes before cooling. But Yeeran didn't care, this reckoning had been brewing for some time.

'What else could I have done?' Salawa said. 'You went against my orders which caused the deaths of three hundred and seventy-six soldiers.'

Yeeran had always thought that Salawa should have executed her for her crimes.

But she realised now that she hadn't deserved death. Though the souls of the soldiers would forever lie heavy on her conscience, it had been the fae magic that had caused the massacre, even if Yeeran's insubordination had led them there.

'I tried to warn you about the fae magic, Salawa, even then,' Yeeran said quietly.

Salawa nodded. 'Yes, and I did not listen. But I'm listening now, Yeeran. I'm *listening*.'

But Yeeran wasn't sure what else she had to say.

'Yeeran,' Salawa said, stepping closer once more.

Yeeran looked into her former lover's hazel eyes and the years between them fell away until she was staring into the face of the woman she had first loved nearly two decades ago.

She pulled in a ragged breath, trying to resurface from the recollections that fluttered through her mind:

The first time they'd kissed on the edge of the Bleeding Field.

The quiet moments of laughter, like when Salawa tried on Yeeran's uniform and paraded around her bedroom.

Salawa's thirty-fourth nameday when they'd enjoyed a quiet celebration under the brightness of a full moon.

There were so many happy moments over the years. It was nothing like the burning fire of Furi's love; instead it simmered softly, warm and constant.

Yeeran took a step back from Salawa and the memories fell away. Looking at her now, Yeeran struggled to see beyond the broken bones of a leader in turmoil.

'I don't think I can ever forgive you for what you have done to me these last few weeks, Salawa. But we can at least take the first step.'

'You want the obeah freed,' Salawa stated, some of the warmth from her voice gone.

'Yes, you cage her, you cage a part of me.'

Salawa looked at Yeeran, her eyes searching for something, but Yeeran wasn't sure what. Then she nodded. 'I'll let the obeah go.'

Yeeran felt her shoulders droop as relief washed over her.

'But, Yeeran—'

She went tense once more. 'What?'

'You need to show me the way to Mosima, no more of this dalliance.'

'I cannot. And I will not. I can't be the catalyst that starts a new war.'

Salawa's eyebrows lifted. 'You think so little of me?'

Yeeran cocked her head. 'So, you deny you intend the fae ill-will?'

Salawa ran a hand over her brow, and when she glanced up again, she looked exhausted. 'Contrary to what you might think, I do not like violence, Yeeran. Why would I end one war to start another? No, my intention here is purely to barter. If the fae have as much fraedia as you suggest, then I'm sure we can come to a trade agreement.'

'Trade agreement?' Yeeran repeated doubtfully. 'And should the fae disagree?'

Salawa didn't speak for a moment, then she smiled. 'They won't, I can be very convincing.'

Yeeran wondered if 'convincing' meant 'threatening' in this context. But all she had to go on was Salawa's word. It had been enough for her six months ago, but now? She wasn't sure.

'We will find them eventually, with or without your help,' Salawa added gently. 'Their secret is out.'

Yeeran's chin dropped to her chest.

This was all her fault. If she hadn't gone to Salawa in the first place maybe the fae's existence could have stayed secret a little longer.

Maybe, or maybe with the fae now walking free in Crescent, Waning's spies would have eventually reported the truth.

There was no point running through possibilities, what was done was done. All she could do now was barter for Pila's freedom.

'Fine, I will show you the way once you let Pila go.'

Salawa smiled tentatively. 'Thank you, Yeeran. Will you let me do it my way? I'll not hurt her, not really, but the ambassadors cannot know that I have let the obeah go willingly.'

She looked at Salawa. The chieftain was framed by the faint moonlight of a cloud-filled sky. For the first time Yeeran saw her in her entirety, not as a lover or a ruler, but a woman whose power had isolated her from everyone she loved.

And what Yeeran felt was pity.

Her leadership must be tenuous to ask me to keep the ruse up.

'I will continue the deception of your cruelty, Salawa. But know that cruel leaders never last long.'

Salawa winced as the words hit their mark. 'I know, but for now this is the path I must continue on until Eclipse and Waxing are fully mine to control.'

Power makes pawns of us all, Yeeran thought.

'Then do what you must,' Yeeran said.

Salawa nodded and the mask of the ruler settled back onto her expression. It sharpened the lines of her smile and her eyes narrowed almost imperceptibly – but enough to make her look harsher.

The chieftain reached for her drum from beneath the table before giving Yeeran a small smile and striding outside.

Yeeran followed a pace behind.

The chieftain didn't stop until she reached Pila's cage.

'Stand aside,' Salawa told the guards around it.

Pila woke groggily from her sleep. *What's happening?*

Salawa is going to free you, don't worry, her anger is an act. We have made a deal her and I.

Salawa's orders had roused others from their slumber, and when the other two ambassadors were watching, the chieftain released drumfire at Pila's side.

Pila's yelp was entirely convincing, even though the bullet hadn't been hard enough to hurt.

'Stop!' Yeeran shouted, to add to the authenticity of the scene.

Salawa's eyes crinkled with mirth. 'Not too much, this isn't a playhouse,' she said for Yeeran's ears alone. Then she raised her voice for the rest of the camp. 'If you refuse to direct us to Mosima, then I'll be forced to kill the obeah. She will make a fine drumskin for my allied chieftains in Waxing and Eclipse.'

Yeeran saw the ambassadors nod in agreement and she had to steady her own hand from firing at them.

Pila had cornered herself in the back of the cage, her silver eyes wide and scared.

I didn't know you could act, Yeeran said to her.

I'm not acting.

That made Yeeran's heart race. Pila didn't have any history with Salawa to trust her word. The obeah felt like her life was on the line. So Yeeran cut to the chase. 'I will tell you where Mosima is. But you must let her go free.'

Salawa laughed and it carried around the clearing. 'That was not the deal we struck.'

'You of all people know that deals can be rewoven. Otherwise I would have died the day of my return to Waning.'

'I should have killed you myself,' Salawa spat. Now that Yeeran knew the character Salawa played for the alliance it was easy to see it.

'I will show you the entrance right now if you release Pila from the cage.'

'No, together you are too dangerous.'

'Release her to the north, away from the camp, I'll ensure she doesn't return.'

I'm not leaving you.

You are. You have to go to Mosima and find Furi, warn her.

You know I cannot speak to Furi like I speak to you.

You'll figure out a way, Pila.

The ambassadors approached Salawa and spoke quietly to her. Together they discussed the deal that Yeeran had already made with Salawa, but it was clever of the chieftain to make them feel like they swayed her decision making.

After a few moments, Salawa broke away from the group and said, 'Fine, we will release her outside of the camp. But if you cannot show us the entrance to Mosima in two hours, you will be killed.'

Salawa widened her eyes a little, laying bare the threat. This was one she would be forced to carry out, ruse or no ruse.

'Fine,' Yeeran said. 'That is a deal I'm willing to strike.'

Salawa withdrew the key from her bodice with a private nod to Yeeran. They had both got what they wanted.

Pila's cage was wheeled to the north side of the camp. They wouldn't let Yeeran see Pila off, but she felt the moment the obeah was released from the cage.

It was like feeling rain after a drought.

Go free, Pila. Go to Mosima. Tell the others where I am.

'Now show us the way,' Salawa said.

The camp packed up despite it being the early hours of the morning. It took a little over an hour – but Yeeran was glad of the extra time. Pila would be in Mosima by now.

Salawa approached her in her fighting leathers, a precursor to the hostility that was sure to come when she met the fae.

She stepped towards her, close enough to say under her breath, 'I'm going to have to bind your hands, the ambassadors have suggested it and I cannot refuse without betraying that I trust you.'

Yeeran didn't have time to agree before Madu came up behind her holding a chain. The soldier gave her an apologetic glance as she bound her wrists together and locked them with a padlock.

The Salawa Yeeran had once loved rippled beneath the surface of the chieftain's expression for a second and then was gone.

'Just in case you have any ideas of escaping now,' Salawa said louder for the others.

'I gave you my word,' Yeeran retorted.

Salawa held out her hand to Madu and took the end of Yeeran's chain, dragging her like a dog to the front of the procession.

'For the final time, Yeeran, lead the way. And may your compass hold true, or my drumfire will end it all.'

CHAPTER THIRTEEN

Lettle

L ettle and Golan walked in silence back the way they had come,
their footfalls heavier than they had been on the journey there.
Five days passed with nothing remarkable to note. Even the
threat of the assassins had faded like a nightmare.

Despite the earlier elation of finding the grimoire, Lettle's thoughts
were plagued with disappointment. She had soon realised how crucial
Najma's notes would have been.

'Shall we camp here for the evening?' Golan suggested. Lettle
hadn't even realised night was falling. She looked around as if for
the first time that day.

The sunset had burnished the shadows of the forest amber. The
sweet sound of bird song was quietening in the oncoming dusk.

The clearing ahead of her was small, only large enough for their
two bedrolls, meaning Ajax would steal all her side of the blanket
that night.

'Sure.'

Ajax stepped into the clearing first, his nose upturned as if
smelling something unusual. Then he whined, not a warning sound,
more a forlorn cry that made Lettle's eyes prickle.

'What is it, Ajax?' she asked.

The obeah walked forward slowly and Lettle followed.

There, cradled between a knot of tree roots, was a young obeah
cub. Froth seeped from its mouth, its eyes stared upwards unseeing.

Lettle recognised the cause of its death immediately. The purple mushrooms that sprouted by the tree's trunk had clearly been eaten.

'Poison,' Lettle said softly.

Ajax whined again.

'What is it—' Golan asked but was confronted with the answer as he looked down.

Lettle's hand went to her waist where her talismans were. It was a comforting habit but today it sparked an idea.

'I'm going to do a reading,' she said. 'With the body.'

Golan's face contorted in revulsion. 'No, that's desecrating the dead.'

'I'll be respectful, clean cuts, and bury it afterwards.'

Golan shook his head, his eyes blazing wide. 'No, Lettle.'

'The Fates haven't been speaking to me lately, maybe it's the way I'm using the tokens, I don't know. But I do know this is an opportunity I can't let pass.'

'You can and you will. It's against fae law.'

Lettle withdrew her knife. 'Well, I'm not fae.'

Golan's nostrils flared and his light brown skin became flushed with anger. But Lettle steeled her resolve and knelt beside the obeah. Ajax cocked his head at Lettle.

'Ajax, I think you should go forage for some fruit,' she said quietly. 'Avoid any mushrooms though.'

Ajax dipped his horns once before retreating.

'You too, Golan, you won't want to watch this.'

For a moment Lettle thought he'd continue to argue. But she held a knife and he didn't.

He didn't say a word as he turned on his heel and left her.

Lettle released a breath and looked up to the darkening sky. When she looked down again she became heedless, tapping into the sixth sense that allowed her to see magic.

'Hail, shining one that grants me light. Hail, shining one that guides the night,' Lettle whispered to the moon as she pierced the belly of the obeah with her knife.

The blood was warm. At the back of her mind she was pleased, the fresher the blood the more potent the telling. But some part of her was horrified by the sticky warmth that coated her fingers.

She had read the entrails of hundreds of obeah over the years. But no longer were obeah just creatures of magic, they were people with thoughts and feelings. Truth brought with it regret.

I can't stop now, she said to herself. *But what would Rayan think of this?*

This was *for* him, if only the Fates would answer.

'Hail, Bosome, give me wisdom with this sacrifice. Hail, god on high. Grant your knowledge with this here price.'

The knife sliced through the diaphragm freeing the organs of the upper cavity. The intestines spilled out across the forest floor.

'Tell me, how may I unravel the secrets of Afa's grimoire?'

The Fates didn't always answer the question asked, they had their own agendas that cared not for the whims of elves or fae.

But when Lettle looked for their response, she found it in pearls of silver moving between the organs like shooting stars.

She had not lost her magic after all. Fear shed from her soul with the motion of a waterfall, wicking off her skin and leaving only the soothing coolness of relief.

She moved systematically through each of the organs, noting the direction and movement of the magic. Each pattern formed something akin to a word in her mind. But it wasn't a language, more a knowing that she could transcribe into a sentence.

Once she had gleaned all she could she allowed awareness to flood back in as she slipped out of being heedless. She wiped her bloody hands on the warm brown fur of the obeah, before removing her prophecy journal and writing down:

In the early hours of the morrow's new day, a tree will fall by the pathway to Mosima. Seek your answers in the night, dawn will bring you peace.

A smile spread across her lips. She might be able to return with all the answers after all. But then she saw the smear of blood her nail had left on the white paper and all hope shrivelled into horror.

Tears streamed down her face as she saw the carcass for what it was. *Who* it was.

She jumped to her feet and emptied the contents of her stomach into a nearby bush.

Once Lettle was ready to walk back into the clearing, the sun had set completely. Her shoulders ached from digging the obeah's grave, but she'd needed to do it. If only to get rid of the sight of its body.

Going back to her old methods of divination had left her with a sense of longing for the world she'd left behind, and a deep feeling of revulsion caused by the world she was now in.

She thought of Shaman Imnan and the prophecy that had first led him to seek her out and train her in divination.

You will wield magic unmatched, speak prophecies unspoken. You will be the leader we seek, and the leader we are due.

At the time she had thought that had meant becoming the next shaman of Waning. A future she had fought for through study and practice. But then she'd come to Mosima and her world had changed.

Seer was not a title she was prepared for, and it had forged her a new path.

But Lettle still mourned the future she had lost, and the diviners she had left behind.

All I need to do is figure out a way to break the curse, then I can go home again, she thought fiercely, despite knowing in her gut that home could never be the same again. Not with all she had learned.

Lettle walked away from the grave of the obeah and found a nearby stream to wash. She knew her bloody state would not be tolerated by Golan and certainly not by Ajax.

When she returned to the camp, she was wet and cold. So it was a relief to see Golan had already cooked dinner.

'Is that ready?' she asked, sitting down next to the campfire.

'Yes,' he said woodenly, before ladling her a cup of soup.

They didn't speak again that night. When Ajax returned he didn't sleep curled up on Lettle's blanket and she remained cold for the rest of the night.

Sleep eluded her, so she spent the night thinking on the prophecy she had foretold. When dawn eventually broke she was ready and packed before Golan woke.

'What is it?' he said, rubbing his eyes and sitting up.

'Last night, the Fates shared their words with me: *In the early hours of the morrow's new day, a tree will fall by the pathway to Mosima. Seek your answers in the night, dawn will bring you peace,*' Lettle said. Golan looked away immediately. 'We need to get to the entrance to Mosima by midnight, something there will help us with Afa's grimoire.'

'That's a long way to travel in so short a time.' He didn't sound irritated, only tired. Sleep had not fully healed the sacrilege she had committed.

I refuse to regret something that proved useful, she thought to herself, even though she lied.

'That's what the Fates said, so I think we should get moving,' Lettle said, standing.

'Fine.'

'Fine,' Lettle retorted back.

Ajax snorted his own confirmation and both Lettle and Golan looked at him – then burst out laughing.

'To be mocked by the king's obeah . . . a new low,' Golan said, shaking his head.

'I'm sorry, Golan,' Lettle said with sincerity. 'With my inability to foretell recently, I couldn't walk away from the obeah. Back in the Elven Lands, that's how all divination is conducted.'

'I understand,' he said grimly. 'But you know better now. Obeah are a part of us.'

'Us' was tinged with a fathomless grief – laying fealty to a creature that he would never bond to.

'I didn't enjoy it. But the Fates chose to speak to me, Golan, after such a long silence.'

'I cannot say I am happy for you,' he admitted. 'Despite the prophecy, I do not condone your actions.'

Lettle tried not to grind her teeth. She understood why Golan was upset, but she was the one who had sacrificed her morals in order to unlock the secrets of the curse.

'The Fates gave me answers, so I will not lie to you and say I would not do the exact same thing again.' She raised her chin and he met her stare before shaking his head and sighing.

'Let us not dwell on it any longer,' Golan said, rising. 'We have a long walk ahead of us. We should be on guard as well. Though Ajax led the assassins away, it doesn't mean they won't have circled back.'

They arrived at the entrance to Mosima just after sunset.

Ajax hovered by the tunnel that led to the boundary. He was waiting for permission to call on Rayan. It was the only way Lettle and Golan could get back through with the human magic in place.

'Not yet, Ajax,' Lettle said.

They waited until total darkness.

'Perhaps the Fates meant for you to find whatever it is nearby?' Golan said, searching the tree line. The moon was shrouded in clouds, darkening the night further.

That was when they heard it – the sounds of boots in the distance.

'There's someone out there,' Lettle whispered.

Golan crept towards the sound. 'Not some*one*, it sounds like a group of people.'

Together they inched towards the sound, keeping themselves shrouded by the undergrowth.

Something large rushed through the trees, startling them both. The camel balked, equally as terrified of them, before cantering away.

Lettle held a hand to her beating heart. 'What is a camel doing in the middle of the Wasted Marshes?' she whispered to Golan.

His eyes were wide and glittering in the moonlight. They both turned towards the direction the camel had come from, creeping closer to the sound of people. Ajax slipped through the forest ahead of them.

When the clearing came into view Lettle couldn't help the gasp that escaped her.

'Yeeran?'

PART TWO

Afa's Grimoire

Last summer gone I met with the chieftain of the Elven Lands and the queen and king of the Fae Lands. As emperor of the fallen Human Lands, I proposed peace between all peoples.

The elves proclaimed peace had already been achieved across the continent yet 'Why,' I asked, 'was it that they use our blood and bones to speak to their god?'

The fae too sang a harmonic tune, claiming their lands were secure and free of war, but 'Why,' I queried, 'do my brethren disappear on the roads near their warrens?'

I told them then, what the elders said about the power of humans, that before our numbers diminished and our lore was stolen, we were the greatest of all beings.

The most powerful.

And I swore, we would be again.

CHAPTER FOURTEEN

Furi

'Bring in the next one,' Rayan said from the throne.

Furi rattled her fingers on the bark of her armrest. 'This is the third time we've questioned them this week, none of the soldiers noticed anything unusual on their journey topside. As each of them were paired off anyway, we have to assume the two assassins kept their true intentions a secret.'

'No, I will not give up on this, the scouting party you let out of Mosima are our only lead. That and the note in the shed,' Rayan said.

Furi scowled in frustration. 'And I caught nothing of that person's likeness.'

Amnan yawned in the branches above her.

It is dinner time, I think. Perhaps you should rest and refresh yourself, Furi?

Not yet, there are four more soldiers to question again.

Look at Rayan, his worry is making the flowers by his feet wilt. A rest will do you both good.

'Amnan says we should take a break,' Furi said.

'I think so too,' a newcomer said from the tree line. Sahar and Norey walked over hand in hand.

Furi smiled warmly. 'Hello, you two.' She went to embrace them.

'You look tired, dear Furi,' Norey said as he held her at arm's length.

'Yes, I am.'

Rayan gripped Sahar's shoulder with a tired smile of his own. 'Grandfather, it is good to see you. We missed you last night.'

Sahar returned the smile with gusto. It was so wonderful to see her father's eyes alight once more. Losing Najma had been hard on him too and getting to know Rayan had been a balm on the grief.

'That'll be my fault,' Norey said with a twinkle in his eye. 'I've made him promise to spend three nights a week with me in the apothecary.'

'The offer still stands,' Furi said. 'You will always be welcome in the palace.'

But Norey shook his head firmly. 'No, you with the Jani dynasty bloodline enjoy each other's company.' Though he said it playfully it did remind Furi that the differences between them were vast. Even Sahar was second cousin to her mother – couplings within the Jani dynasty were always encouraged to keep the blood 'pure', a practice Furi vowed to change.

'Please, Norey, stay,' Furi pressed.

Norey smiled at her a little sadly. 'I have an avocado pear that's just gone ripe, and I'm very much looking forward to it.'

Sahar's chuckle resonated around the woodland. 'He has been waiting on that pear for a week. Let him go, Furi. I'll see him tomorrow.' He stooped to kiss Norey goodbye.

Furi watched him go. 'I'm so sorry we have been taking up all your time,' she said to her father. 'If you'd prefer to live in the apothecary I would understand.'

Furi's mother and Sahar had fought terribly after he had predicted Najma's death in his talismans. Vyce could not accept the truth of it, so banished him from the palace. Furi had thought lifting his banishment had been a boon; now she wasn't sure.

Sahar patted her on the arm. 'I'm glad that I'm back. It is why I have arranged for you to have four days of my love a week and Norey only gets three.' He laughed heartily.

Furi led the way to the royal dining room, where dinner had been laid out for them for some time.

Goat's cheese covered in honey and figs were piled on a platter in the centre with breads and salads lining its periphery.

Furi reached for the flat bread, but before she could take it a servant cleared her throat.

'Queen, please allow me to taste that for you first.' The servant was small and dark-haired, her features reminded Furi of an otter.

Furi presented the flat bread to the food taster. The servant nibbled on the crust before handing it back.

After there was no reaction, Furi proceeded to eat.

She sank into a dining chair and let out a sound of contentment. She hadn't realised just how hungry she had been.

'How goes the investigation?' Sahar asked as he too tucked into his meal.

Rayan sighed. 'It's not really an investigation, we have so little to go on.' His jaw tightened, accentuating the hollows of his cheeks. Since Lettle had left Mosima, he'd retreated into himself, and his days were spent in the war room poring over the details of the scouting party or outlining possible threats.

Furi reached a hand across the table and laid it next to his. Close enough to offer support without touching him. She'd never been good at comforting people. 'We'll find out who is behind the assassination attempts, Rayan. I promise.'

He looked down at her hand next to his and smiled weakly. 'I hope so.'

'Have you been sleeping?' Sahar probed gently.

Rayan looked like he was about to say yes, but realised the bags under his eyes would give away his lie. 'No, not really. It's difficult, with Ajax and Lettle away.'

Sahar nodded. 'I understand. Why don't I make you a sleeping draught tonight? Your mind will be all the clearer for it.'

'Thank you,' Rayan said, and when he smiled it was a little surer.

Furi felt a rush of fondness for her family. Their numbers might be depleted, but she still had Rayan and Sahar by her side, and that was love aplenty.

'Enough talk of me,' Rayan said. 'Grandfather, how fares the apothecary—'

Rayan's expression went blank and for a moment Furi thought he was poisoned again. She stood from her chair and rushed towards him. Then his eyes met hers in an expression of horror.

'What is it?'

But at exactly the same time there was a sound at the window and an obeah ran through the hatch and into the room. Furi recognised her immediately.

'Pila?' Furi said as dread curdled her stomach.

The obeah began to paw the ground lurching forward as if trying to convey something, but she didn't need to. For wherever Yeeran was, Ajax too must be as the blood had drained from Rayan's face.

'The chieftain of Waning is outside Mosima, and she has Yeeran held against her will,' Rayan said.

Furi's mind went blank as fear overcame all sense of reason.

Yeeran was in *danger*.

Her thoughts went back to the last time she had seen Yeeran get hurt; how Hosta's blade had felt as if it had pierced her side as well as Yeeran's.

The flames of the anger Furi had so lovingly stoked since Yeeran had left guttered out. There would be time to spark them again in the future. But right now, the thought of saving Yeeran was more important than holding onto any quarrel between them.

Furi leapt onto Pila's back. The obeah didn't hesitate, she set off to the boundary's edge.

Amnan, where are you?

Near the mango fields. I will meet you at the boundary.

Furi had never ridden another person's obeah. Touching a faebound beast was an intimate thing. But it was so natural, as if she knew Pila's rhythm like she had known Yeeran's heartbeat.

They are one and the same, Amnan said. He sounded pleased that Pila was back. Though obeah were not bound by the love affairs of the fae, it was clear he had great affection for her.

Pila lunged up the stairs that led to the boundary's edge.

We're nearly there, Furi warned Amnan.

I'm waiting.

Furi saw Amnan's silhouette at the tunnel that led to the outside world.

Pila didn't slow as they approached.

'Aiftarri,' Furi said the word that would allow her to lift the curse.

She felt the magic that bound her to the land stretch and twist as an opening formed in the boundary ahead of her. The magic was invisible unless she looked at it through magesight – then it glowed a deep bronze, rippling with script that no one alive could read. As she crossed it and entered the tunnel she shivered.

This was her first time leaving since becoming queen. And the consequences of her rash decision would come calling.

But she couldn't let Yeeran be kept prisoner a second longer. Yeeran needed her, Pila's presence was a testament to that.

'Take me to her, Pila.'

Amnan matched the cadence of Pila's rhythm beside her as they all flew across the Wasted Marshes.

I'm coming, Yeeran.

CHAPTER FIFTEEN

Yeeran

The chain around Yeeran's wrists grew taut as she was tugged sideways.

'We've been searching for over an hour, Yeeran,' Salawa hissed from atop her camel. Yeeran was walking in the dust behind her, so that every time her camel urinated or defecated Yeeran would end up standing in it.

This façade is starting to grate on me.

When the ambassadors looked away, Yeeran said softly, 'We're close, it's just ahead of us now.'

How far away are you, Pila?

Pila didn't answer because the next second Yeeran could hear her.

The obeah charged through the forest ridden by a golden wraith.

A slow smile spread across Yeeran's face. 'Furi.'

The fae's honeyed eyes homed in on Yeeran for just a second and a shiver went through her. Then Furi looked at the chain around Yeeran's wrists and she bared her fangs in a snarl.

The chieftain's procession stopped and Salawa called out, 'Who goes there?'

They were the last three words Salawa ever said as Furi's magic lashed out and wrapped around the chieftain's throat.

'No, Furi!' Yeeran shouted, trying to stop the inevitable. She slipped into magesight and watched as Furi's magic tightened around the chieftain's throat.

Salawa's brows were knotted together in panic as her gaze sought Yeeran's. And when the warm hazel of her gaze met Yeeran's her expression turned gentle, the mask of the chieftain never to be worn again.

The years of memories shifted into sepia tones, the life of them ebbing away. Yeeran grasped for one in particular – the day Salawa had been made chieftain.

They had stood on the edge of the Bleeding Field at dawn the morning after the official celebration. Salawa was now ruler of Waning.

'We will see this war end in our lifetime,' Salawa said to her. Tribal paints still covered her body from the ceremony the night before.

'Me on the battlefield, you in the palace,' Yeeran agreed.

Salawa reached for her hand and cradled it above her heart. 'Together, the Forever War will be forever no more.'

A sound brought Yeeran back to the present. It took a moment to register what it was.

Snap.

Salawa slumped forward, the bones in her neck broken.

Yeeran choked out, 'No.' Even though she knew it was too late. The silence that followed was heavy, bleak.

Then came pandemonium.

The chain around Yeeran's wrists went slack as Salawa's body tilted forward, blood spluttered from her mouth as she fell from her mount. The camel balked and loped away from the broiling violence, causing other steeds to follow suit.

Furi had dismounted from Pila and was fighting four elves at once, her magic severing the night with sparks of light. Amnan was attacking one of the ambassadors with his horns. The smell of blood permeated the air.

Pila appeared beside Yeeran. *Can you get free from the chains?*

No, Madu has the key.

Pila looked behind Yeeran and growled. Madu was advancing towards them, her hand poised on top of her drum.

'Please, Madu, let me go,' Yeeran said. 'I won't hurt you, I promise.'

'The chieftain told me to guard you.'

'The chieftain is dead.' The words were numb on Yeeran's lips. Madu's eyes widened as if the truth were only just sinking in.

'Please, Madu.'

Madu's hand darted forward, but instead of striking her drum she removed a key from her pocket and inserted it into the padlock on Yeeran's chains.

Yeeran swung her drum in front of her chest as soon as she was free and wove a protective shield around her and Pila.

Madu misconstrued her intention and began to fire at them.

'I'm not going to hurt you!' Yeeran shouted. Pila lowered herself to lunge.

There was the cadence of more obeah joining Furi, and when Yeeran glanced around she saw Rayan enter the fight, Ajax appearing across the clearing to meet him in the middle. Together they were making quick work of the remaining elves.

Madu saw this and blanched.

'Run,' Yeeran said. The advice was her gift for letting Yeeran go. For being kind to a captive.

Madu hesitated for a moment, then spun on her heel and ran.

When Yeeran turned to join the melee, she found the ground strewn with bodies. None of the chieftain's party had survived. Furi stood in the centre of the graveyard, blood splattering her white silk dress.

Her gaze met Yeeran's.

Furi strode towards her until they stood a breath apart. They had parted in anger and were now reunited amidst violence.

'Are you hurt?' Furi asked, her voice rough.

Yeeran shook her head and the relief in Furi's expression made her smile. 'You came for me,' she said.

'You needed me,' Furi replied. Then her hand slipped up to the nape of Yeeran's neck and pulled her forward until their lips met.

Only a few hours ago it had been Salawa's mouth on hers.

Yeeran tasted something coppery on Furi's lips and recoiled.

Salawa's blood.

Furi watched Yeeran warily as she pulled away, but Yeeran wouldn't meet her eyes, instead her gaze was tugged towards a body lying in the road behind them.

'You killed the chieftain of Waning.' Grief seemed a distant thing, but it was drawing closer like a storm cloud soon to break.

Furi cocked her head in confusion. 'She had captured you.'

Yeeran shook her head, anger masking her despair. 'It was a ruse, Furi. You shouldn't have killed her.'

'What *should* I have done, Yeeran?'

'She only wanted to talk, to discuss a trade agreement.'

Furi's laugh was full of pain. 'A trade agreement? Let me guess, for our fraedia crystal? The very thing that keeps Mosima alive? Yeeran, don't be so foolish.'

Yeeran felt herself bristle with annoyance, but how could she convince Furi that she'd seen Salawa's true intentions? Furi had no reason to believe Salawa, all she was doing was protecting her people.

But now Salawa is dead . . .

'You brought them to my borders, Yeeran. You brought the person who exiled you to my *home*.' Furi's voice cracked at the end, exposing the depth of the betrayal she felt.

'She held Pila hostage,' Yeeran said breathlessly, their argument was like a sprint.

'And yet you seem convinced that she meant my people no harm. Perhaps I should have warned you before you left that your plan was folly,' Furi continued, her face flushed with anger.

'Furi—'

'Oh, that's right. I did. I told you that this would end in more violence. Look around you. You are as much to blame for their deaths as I am.'

Furi's words were a blow to Yeeran's anguished, wounded mind. It also laid bare the intensity of Furi's wrath towards her.

So many wounds to heal, Yeeran thought. *And now is not the time or place to do it.*

As she turned away from the remains of her former lover, something moved in the tree line – a silhouette of someone she knew.

'Yeeran?' Her sister stepped out of the shadows, the frown on her face enough to confirm she was still annoyed at Yeeran for leaving Mosima. Golan stood by her side.

They both took in the massacre before Lettle's gaze settled once more on Yeeran's. She strode forward.

'What do you know of Najma's research?' was the first thing Lettle said to Yeeran.

Furi snarled at Lettle for saying the prince's name out loud and thus disrupting his eternal peace.

Yeeran's mouth had fallen open in shock. 'Lettle, what are you doing here?'

'I followed a camel,' she said as if explaining herself.

'We heard fighting,' Golan added. 'And a camel came from this direction, so we followed its path. But it looks like the battle has been won.' He looked relieved and a little queasy from all the bloodshed.

'Well? What do you know of Afa's grimoire?' Lettle asked again.

Yeeran said tiredly, 'I've no idea what you're talking about.'

There was movement to Yeeran's left as Rayan walked across the clearing and embraced Lettle so fiercely that Yeeran felt an uncharacteristic stab of envy that their love could be so simple. She watched as they exchanged murmured words and a kiss before having to turn away.

Her gaze snagged on Furi beside her. 'Do you know what Lettle was talking about?' Yeeran asked her but Furi shrugged.

'No idea.' Furi looked around them. Like Yeeran, she seemed to have acknowledged that this was not the time nor place for an argument. Her voice had cooled. 'Was that all of the elves?'

'Yes,' Yeeran said, neglecting to admit Madu had got away.

'Then let us make our way back to Mosima.'

Yeeran looked back at Salawa's body. 'I would like to bury them before we go.'

Furi's face scrunched in disgust, but she didn't object as Yeeran got to work digging a grave.

Pila helped, her burrowing making quicker work than Yeeran's handiwork.

A few minutes later Rayan and Ajax, with a nod to Yeeran, began to dig too. Lettle, despite her clear grudge against Yeeran, let out a sigh and joined in as well.

It wasn't long before they had buried all the elves.

After the last bit of earth was patted onto the grave, Yeeran said some final words.

'Though our embers have faded and your drum grown silent, I will remember the tune of your song, forever more.'

Rayan saluted and Lettle bowed her head but Furi was pointedly looking the other way.

Yeeran was glad she didn't see the tears that fell to the soil in Salawa's name.

Once Yeeran had dried her cheeks, Lettle turned to Rayan and said, 'Can we go home now?'

Home.

When had Lettle's home become Mosima?

Yeeran's thoughts were interrupted as something disturbed the bough above, sending a scattering of leaves upon the graves.

Furi stepped forward, scanning the branches. 'Did one of them escape up a tree?'

Yeeran was about to explain about Madu – why the soldier would choose to climb a tree instead of running away was beyond her – when Furi went over to the tree and rattled the trunk.

The person who fell to the ground was not Madu.

The man landed on his feet, though he looked a little winded.

Furi's magic was about to lash out around him but then Yeeran recognised him. '*Alder?*'

'Hello, Yeeran.' He gave her a cheery wave and she noticed a dimple in his left cheek.

Furi sighed impatiently. 'Who is he?'

'He's one of the Nomads. And he tried to kill me in my sleep.'

'Do I have permission to kill him then?' Furi said, her words laden with mockery at Yeeran's earlier comment.

'I didn't try to kill you, I was sleepwalking,' Alder said through gritted teeth. 'And please do not kill me.'

'Sleepwalking?' Yeeran repeated.

I suppose it makes sense now why no one came after me. Though I'm not sure if I believe him.

I do, Pila replied. *He does not lie.*

Yeeran was about to ask why the obeah found him quite so trustworthy when Lettle stepped towards him, the clouds finally parting to provide more moonlight.

'Did you say his name was Alder?' Lettle asked.

'Yes,' Alder and Yeeran replied at the same time.

There was a silence as no one was sure what to do next. Then Furi said dryly, 'Well I for one would like to go to bed. So, Alder, I'm afraid we can't leave you alive. We wouldn't want what happened here today to travel to the rest of the Elven Lands. One chieftain dead by fae hands is enough for now.'

Golden threads whipped out from Furi's hands.

'Wait!' Lettle shouted. 'He's important, we can't kill him. He might be the only key to your brother's research.'

'Lettle, what are you talking about?' Yeeran asked.

'The Fates spoke to me, I asked them for help to translate the grimoire—'

'You found it?' Rayan said.

Lettle nodded.

Yeeran looked between them, uncomprehending. When she shot a questioning look Furi's way the fae shrugged like she didn't understand either.

'The Fates told me,' Lettle continued. 'That in the early hours of the morning a tree would fall by the pathway to Mosima. And his name is *Alder* . . . it must be him. Somehow, he'll help us.'

'Are you sure?' Rayan asked gently.

'Yes, you cannot hurt him.'

Yeeran recognised the look on Lettle's face. She would not budge on the matter.

Furi growled with impatience. 'Enough of this. We cannot let him go. So let us bring him with us. I'm tired and I can feel the curse calling me back to Mosima.'

With that Furi mounted Amnan. She didn't wait for Yeeran before she set off on the trail back to Mosima.

For a moment Yeeran stood between her old lover and her new. One dead, one alive.

And one weary heart.

CHAPTER SIXTEEN

Alder

Alder felt like he was sleepwalking once again.

The fae are real.

He'd been right to be curious about the riders he'd seen in the forest five years ago. They had been fae all along.

At first he'd stayed hidden in the tree for curiosity's sake, but then curiosity turned to horror as he watched the massacre play out.

He looked behind him at the mass grave and shivered. There had been something truly haunting in the way that the golden one, the one Yeeran called Furi, had watched so nonchalantly as the others buried her victims.

Then she had left on the back of an obeah.

'I'm not going with you,' he said to the others. Though his gaze caught on the beautiful fae with the long braids, he focused in on the elf who had spoken of prophecy.

'You are,' she said. 'You're too important to let go.'

'So you're taking me prisoner?' Alder said carefully. He'd rather be prisoner than dead.

'No,' Yeeran said tiredly. 'But I wouldn't bother arguing. That man standing next to her, he's the king of the fae, and if she wanted to take you as her prisoner, she could. And she would.'

Alder's mouth gaped open as the taller man – the *king* – nodded that Yeeran was right.

So they feigned choice, but there was really no choice at all. He was to go with them whether he wanted to or not. His gaze went back to the man with the long braids. They fell down one shoulder to his knee where skin blended into metal in an intricate artificial leg. He watched Alder under his eyelashes, scrutinising him in a way that made him feel naked.

The fae were everything he expected: terrifying, powerful and alluring.

If I go with them I do not know what may happen.

But the ghosts of those just passed seemed to scream at him from the shadows: *Do not resist or our fate awaits you.*

Alder tried for a smile. 'I'll go with you then.'

Something tightened against his wrists and he yelped.

'Just in case you try and flee, I'll release you when we're inside Mosima,' the king said gently. It was then that Alder realised he didn't have fangs like Furi.

Is he an elf? But surely he cannot be if he is the king of the fae.

So many questions blossomed in Alder's mind, but they were done with talking. The little group began to move out, sandwiching Alder between them, the king and the diviner up front and Yeeran behind. The other man fell into step beside Alder.

'Why don't you have any shoes?' he asked Alder. His voice was smooth and light, like a pebble skimming over water.

Alder looked down at his feet. They were mud-stained and flecked with swamp water. In comparison the fae wore black boots woven together with silver thread.

'I climb trees better without shoes,' Alder said a little self-consciously. During his time as a Nomad, he'd never felt he had to explain his clothing, or lack thereof. But there was something about this fae's inquiring eye that made him feel out of place. And he was never out of place in the forest.

'So, you climb a lot of trees?' the fae asked.

'I do.' His question didn't sound mocking but Alder was struggling to garner much from the fae's expression. 'What's your name?'

'Golan. And yours is Alder.'

'It is. Where are you taking me?'

There was a beat of silence and a small smile spread over Golan's lips. 'Mosima, it is the most beautiful of all prisons,' he said. This time Alder was sure he sounded a little mocking.

'I thought I wasn't a prisoner.'

'Oh, we all are under there. If you don't mind, I might enjoy the night sky for the last time.'

Golan tipped his head to the moon and basked in the light of the stars.

Alder followed his eyeline, though he wasn't sure what he meant. 'The Hunter,' Alder said.

'Pardon?'

'The star formation you're looking at, it's called the Hunter. The elders say that the Hunter's child asked for them to capture the tide. So the Hunter began to stalk the sea but before they could seize the tide they were cast into the sky by the moon.'

Golan's blue eyes crinkled in delight. 'What happened to the Hunter's child?'

'Well I'm glad you asked, because you see that smaller formation, with the bright star pointing east? That's the Hunter's child, known as the Hare. They tried to avenge their parent's death by cutting up the moon. For days they chipped away at it but the moon grew back, stronger than ever, and banished the child next to the Hunter.'

Golan's smile grew. 'Is that why the moon moves through phases?'

'That's the lore of the Nomad elders.'

'I like that,' Golan said.

When Golan's gaze dropped back down from the sky Alder held up his bound hands and asked, 'Is this fae magic?'

'Yes,' Golan replied. 'It is being controlled by King Rayan, the other end of it is attached to his hand. I can teach you how to see the magic if you'd like.'

Golan briefly explained the concept of magesight but after trying a few times Alder gave up.

Golan laughed at his last attempt, his nose crinkling in a charming expression of joy. 'Don't try too hard, you might burst a vein in your forehead.'

'I think this may be beyond me,' Alder admitted.

'Yes, I think so too.'

They hadn't been walking long, but the terrain had quickly changed from muddy to rocky.

'What do they want with me, Golan?' Alder asked as Furi and the obeah she rode disappeared into a tunnel ahead of them.

Golan bit his cheek before replying. 'Lettle thinks you're important in breaking the curse that keeps us all trapped in Mosima. And Queen Furi can't let you go because you could tell others what took place out here, and the relationship with the elves is already tenuous.'

'Other elves know about you?'

Golan's eyes twinkled. 'Yes, other elves know about us.'

Dart had said that there was a new magic being used in Crescent and that the townsfolk were talking of fae.

Oh, how worried he'll be when he wakes up and finds me gone.

They'd assume he sleepwalked and search for him but Alder wasn't sure how long that window of time would last before they gave up and moved on. A day or two? Maybe three if he was lucky?

I need to get back to them as soon as possible.

But Golan had spoken of a curse and a prison. Alder's mind swirled with confusion.

'Here we are,' Golan announced before he could ask more questions.

They had arrived at the end of the tunnel. Lettle and Rayan had already gone ahead.

'Without magesight it'll be dark, but just keep walking towards the light,' Golan said.

Alder stepped into the tunnel, the moonlight at his back illuminating his path until it faded completely. There was a moment when the light at the far end hadn't yet reached him and he was in total darkness.

But he wasn't afraid. Something about all this suddenly seemed right. Like the feeling he got when he knew he was on the right path to a river or an ample harvest.

So when the light eventually grew brighter he walked towards it with sure steps.

CHAPTER SEVENTEEN

Lettle

I n the early hours of the morrow's new day, a tree will fall by the pathway to Mosima. Seek your answers in the night, dawn will bring you peace.

Lettle rolled the prophecy around in her mind. So much of it still did not make sense, but she thought she'd parsed the first sentence. The fallen tree was Alder, it had to be. His name was the clue, for no other tree had fallen on the trail to Mosima.

He was important, she knew it in her gut, but she wasn't sure why.

'Are you well, Lettle?' Rayan asked by her side. He had not let her go since they had been reunited.

'Yes, I was just thinking about Alder, he's connected to the research somehow.'

They had reached the tunnel to Mosima, the damp smell a reminder of the first time Lettle had been led through here, fearful of their future – though not much had changed there.

'Aiftarri,' Furi whispered the word at the boundary and Lettle watched in magesight as the magic reacted. The script that made up the invisible curse shivered and coiled away creating an opening. They all shuffled through one at a time.

The fray-light was warming the cavern as a new day began, its colour a pale pink. Lettle cast her gaze over Mosima and gasped.

'What is it?' Rayan said. But then he saw it too.

The entirety of Mosima was covered in a white ash.

'What happened here?' Lettle said. She looked to the cavern ceiling expecting to see the remnants of a fire but there was nothing there.

She bent down and picked a leaf from a succulent that sprouted from the rocks beneath her. It was cold and stiff.

It wasn't ash, it was frost.

'Shit,' Furi said. 'This is the consequence of us leaving.'

Rayan and Furi exchanged a glance. Lettle could tell neither of them regretted their actions, but they'd have the whole of Mosima to answer to.

Yeeran joined them on the precipice and said quietly, 'You shouldn't have come.'

Furi's eyes flashed hot and Lettle knew Yeeran had angered her greatly. She marched off down the steps and into the belly of Mosima.

Rayan turned to Alder. 'Now we're in Mosima, I'll remove the magic keeping your hands bound. But I suggest you do not try to run, the boundary will not let you out.'

Lettle glanced at Alder. The elf's mouth hung open as he surveyed the extent of Mosima. Its vast green fields and pockets of woodlands sparkled with the touch of frost. Rivers, like blue threads, wound and knotted themselves through streets and tree lines. She wondered if she'd looked just as thunderstruck when she'd arrived.

'We'll find you rooms in the palace,' Lettle said to him, but he didn't seem to be listening. His eyes had grown wide, as if trying to take in the far-reaching corners of the cavern.

They made their way through Mosima slowly, Alder asking question after question of Golan who patiently answered.

But Lettle didn't eavesdrop, she was too distracted by the frost covering all the roofs. Though it had begun to melt, it would have surely damaged many of the plants.

When they reached the Royal Woodland Lettle's suspicions were confirmed. A lot of the smaller shrubs and ferns were already wilting. Whether they'd survive the day was up to the royal horticulturist.

Rayan's eyes were downcast as they reached the Tree of Souls. Though the white skeletal leaves hadn't changed, the bark seemed ashier than it had before and the plants that grew between its roots had completely withered.

He sank into his throne and pressed his hands into the earth. In seconds flowers began to bloom: white lilies and purple peonies.

The air turned sweet with the smell of nectar. Alder gasped somewhere behind them. Furi saw what Rayan was doing and lent her strength to feed to the earth too.

Lettle had once asked Rayan what it was like to be connected to Mosima. He'd said it was like the hair on his head. He didn't always feel it but he knew it was there. And if he needed to manipulate it, he could do so just by willing it, like an intricate braid.

Greenery began to bloom around them, but then Rayan fell forward, his face haggard.

'Stop, you're giving the land too much,' Lettle said, rushing towards him.

Furi was panting heavily and Yeeran went to her side, helping her to stand.

'I think perhaps we should all sleep for a few hours. You can try again later,' Yeeran said quietly.

'What about me?' Alder said behind them.

Furi's eyes were glazed and for a moment she didn't seem to recognise Alder, so Lettle said, 'I'll find him a room.'

Golan stepped forward and said in fae, 'Perhaps it might be a better idea if Alder came home with me? I have a spare room and can keep an eye on him.'

Alder looked between them, not understanding why they had switched languages.

Rayan replied before Lettle could refuse. 'I think that's a good idea. He isn't a prisoner but I wouldn't feel safe giving him access to the palace. Not with everything that's going on.'

Lettle wasn't sure what he meant, but she knew she'd find out soon enough.

'Fine, but I'll be calling on you before dinner time,' Lettle said. She desperately wanted to talk to Alder and show him the grimoire but she could see how taxing the night's activities had been on Rayan. It wasn't the time.

Alder and Golan left the woodland leaving an empty gap between Lettle and Yeeran.

There was a tense silence as their eyes met and they both began to speak.

'Lettle—' Yeeran started.

'I think—' Lettle said.

Yeeran smiled as their words ran over each other. 'You first.'

Lettle lifted her chin. 'I'm not sure why you're smiling. You were lucky Furi was able to rescue you today.'

Yeeran's smile dropped into a frown. If she'd thought Lettle had forgiven her for leaving, then she was foolish.

'Yes, I'm glad Furi was there.' Yeeran's gaze momentarily slipped to the queen's, then away.

'Did you accomplish what you sought to do in Waning?' Lettle asked, her voice laced with mockery.

Yeeran's lip trembled and Lettle knew she was thinking of Salawa. She hadn't meant to be so cruel, but her anger towards Yeeran had grown in depth during their time apart.

'Lettle, I'm tired and it's been a long day. I don't want to argue,' Yeeran said quietly.

Her stoicism only made Lettle more cross. She felt blood rush to her face as she braced herself for a heated argument.

Rayan's hand clasped hers. 'Lettle, let us go rest.'

Lettle felt all anger dissipate at his touch. Though it had only been ten days, she had missed him.

She looked away from Yeeran and the throes of their feud, and into the exhausted gaze of Rayan.

'Yes, my king, let us go to bed,' she said with a smile.

Lettle led him up the stairs to their chambers. With each step his footfalls grew surer, as if her very presence invigorated him.

As soon as they entered their bedroom, he gave her a crushing kiss.

'I missed you so much,' he whispered against her lips.

'Me too,' she said.

His kisses began to trail down her neck and she protested.

'Rayan, I haven't bathed in over a week, and besides, I thought you were tired?'

A crooked smile spread across his face as he pressed himself against her.

'Not anymore.' She felt the heat of his desire, her cheeks flushing in response.

He took her hand and led her further into their chambers where a flagstone hid the entrance to the underground bath system. He pressed down on the stone slab, and with a click it gave way to the stairs below.

'Why don't we bathe together?' he asked.

Lettle's mouth parted as she remembered the last time they'd done just that.

Instead of replying she walked down the stairs, removing her clothing as she went. When she realised he wasn't moving with quite as much haste, she turned up the staircase and said, 'Are you coming or what?'

He laughed richly. 'I was enjoying my view.'

'It's better down here.'

The gleam anemones that lined the stone ceiling and walls made the warm spring water glitter like the night sky. Lettle lowered herself into the water and groaned.

She began to massage the muscles on her arm where the wasting sickness had atrophied them. They'd grown stiff over the last few nights sleeping outside, and the water soothed them.

Fingers joined hers at her shoulder. She let out a sigh as Rayan's hands worked through the knots and pains across her muscles. Soon kisses joined his fingers and she arched her back into him, feeling the firmness of his wanting.

She tipped her head back onto his shoulder as his kisses moved to her neck and his hands moved slowly around to her chest. His caress was soft and teasing and she found herself panting in frustration.

He laughed low in his chest as he continued to toy with her. Touching her but not giving her quite enough to satisfy her need.

So she arched further forward until he was positioned just above the entrance to where the heat of her pooled. His hands stilled on her breasts, his breath hitching as he anticipated the rush of pleasure pressing down would bring. Then she drew away just as quickly.

She heard him exhale sharply and she smiled.

Two can play at this game.

'Lettle,' her name choked his throat and came out rough and raw.

She arched forward again, his hands moving to her waist, the water swirling between them.

But again she denied him. His beard scratched her neck as he bit down playfully on her shoulder.

'Do you mean to torture me forever more?' he said. 'Because you're only denying yourself too.'

His hand slipped down from her waist, his fingers circling the tip of her pleasure.

She tried to hold back a moan, she would not give him the satisfaction.

'Now?' he whispered in her ear.

She couldn't reply, only nod. Rayan kept his right hand where it was as his left lifted her up and he entered her from behind.

He moved slowly at first, matching the rhythm of his hand, coaxing the pleasure from her until she trembled around him. Then he moved quickly, his hands finding her waist again and pressing himself deeper until he stilled and shuddered, releasing a ragged breath.

'I love you,' he whispered, once the shaking in his legs had abated.

'I love you,' Lettle whispered back.

She tried not to overthink how perfect the moment was, for if she did she knew she'd realise it would never last. Not while she harboured her secret.

Rayan's lifeblood was on her hands.

CHAPTER EIGHTEEN

Alder

'So the fae language only comes to those bound to an obeah?' Alder clarified.

Golan nodded. He had been generous with Alder's queries but he could tell he was getting fatigued.

They were on their way to Golan's home where Alder was to sleep. Though all tiredness had fled his bones as soon as he'd stepped foot in Mosima.

Now he understood why Golan had said it was the most beautiful of prisons. It was spectacular. From the plants to the winding streets, everything was so perfectly made.

Since he'd been in Mosima, Alder had felt different. The hollowness in his chest that had been growing by the day seemed to abate. Like this was exactly where he was supposed to be.

I feel less lonely in this new world than I ever have among the Nomads. The thought left him wanting to learn everything he could about Mosima. What was it about the fae realm that made him feel so at home?

Perhaps it was the obeah. They roamed in abundance around the greenery and cobbled lanes.

Something ran out into the centre of the street interrupting his thoughts. It was a creature Alder had never seen before. With wide eyes and orange and white striped fur, he wasn't sure if it was a monkey or a bear cub.

'What is it?'

'It's a haba,' Golan said. 'They live in the trees mostly, but it looks like this one is carrying a message.'

Golan was right, the little creature held a scroll in its black paws. It looked at Alder curiously before sauntering off.

'The royal family use them to send letters and instructions around Mosima,' Golan continued. 'Their connection to the curse that binds them here gives them a way with the animals.'

'I don't understand,' Alder said and again Golan smiled. Alder found he liked making him smile, he just wished it wasn't because of his ignorance.

'We're here,' Golan announced, stopping in front of a red-brick house on a quiet tree-lined street. 'It's not much,' he said to Alder as they entered. 'But I have a spare room down the hall, and a pantry ahead of you if you get hungry.'

They stepped into the living quarters of the house which were richly furnished in deep reds and purples. Thick woven carpets lined the flagstone floor, and soft cream cushions embellished crimson sofas.

Alder had never seen so much vibrancy inside a room before. He was used to the beauty of nature, and though this wasn't that it came close to it.

'It is beautiful,' he said truthfully.

Golan's eyes crinkled, betraying his pleasure. 'Your room is the second door to your left. The first is the privy. If you need a bath press on the flagstone with the bubbles carved into them, it'll open to the bath network below.'

Alder's brain felt heavy with information, but he nodded. 'Thank you, Golan.'

Golan nodded. 'Now I need to take this leg off and go to bed.'

Alder looked down at the filigree metal that made up Golan's right leg. It was as beautiful and as exquisite as he was.

Just as Golan turned around to leave, Alder asked, 'Why did you offer up your home to me?'

Golan frowned. 'We don't have guests often, but they are not always treated as well as they should. The palace can be an unsettling place, especially if you are not one of the Jani dynasty. I thought you might be more comfortable here.'

Golan met his eyes and Alder could feel the sincerity in them.

'Thank you, and Golan, sleep well.'

'Sleep well.'

Though Golan's rooms were warmly furnished, Alder slept fitfully. The first hour he could not get comfortable and a sense of foreboding overcame him every time he shut his eyes. But eventually he settled and sleep took him in its grasp.

When he woke his mouth was dry and his back ached painfully. He must have forgotten to check for knots in the silkvine before lying out his bedroll last night. He opened his eyes to the brightness of the sun.

Except it wasn't the sun. It was something more misshapen and jagged.

'Mia? Dart? Where are we?' And where was his canopy? And his things?

He stood up and his memories caught up with him.

I'm trapped in the fae realm.

But he'd fallen asleep in Golan's home, not out here. He looked around him. He was at the top of the stairs that led to the tunnel he had entered from. The magical boundary that cursed the fae was ahead of him.

He had sleepwalked again.

Alder sighed and tipped his head skywards.

This is getting ridiculous. I can't even stay in bed one night.

He leaned on the cavern wall to gather his thoughts, but as his hand touched the red stone, he felt an unearthly warmth.

Curious, he ran his fingers across the boundary and through the tunnel entrance. His fingers passed through.

He drew his hands back, the skin there tingling. He tried one more time, with his whole arm this time.

Again, it passed through.

Somehow the curse did not bind him.

He looked back at Mosima then dived through.

It didn't take him long to find the Nomads. His internal compass directed him to them. They had camped west of the massacre site, far enough away to have not heard the commotion, but close enough for him to reach them in less than an hour if he jogged swiftly.

The Nomads hadn't moved the camp from where they had first erected it, six days ago. They had been waiting for him.

'Alder!' Mia shouted from the canopy above. It was clear she'd been keeping watch for him. He climbed up the nearest tree and joined her in the inner canopy.

She launched herself at him, squeezing him tight. 'We've been looking for you everywhere. Dart and the others are still out searching.'

After she gave him a good look over, she asked, 'Where in sun sins have you been?'

'I sleepwalked,' Alder said quietly.

'Again?'

'Again.'

His hands twirled a frayed piece of rope on the edge of the canopy. Without realising he was doing it, he braided it off to prevent further damage.

'Why did it take you so long to find us again? You've been gone a whole night and day.'

Alder's gaze grew distant, unsure how to explain what had happened to him.

'You can't know the path ahead before taking the first step,' Dart had always said. So he took a deep breath and recounted his tale.

'The fae? Truly you were captured by *the fae*?' From the tone in Mia's voice it sounded like she was having a hard time believing him. Even for Alder, the fae of stories were hard to equate with the people he'd just met.

He reached for Mia's shoulder and squeezed it.

'Truly, Mia. The fae are not extinct. They have been cursed to a land known as Mosima for a millennium.'

Mia swallowed loudly, the doubt from her face shedding into something akin to fear. 'The rumours from Crescent were true then,' she whispered. 'The fae have allied with them.'

'Yes, and their magic, Mia, it's like nothing I've ever seen. Strong, like iron thread and—'

'Totally invisible,' Mia finished the sentence for him. 'Dart told me what is being said on the Bleeding Field.'

'Yes and they're keeping me prisoner. They probably haven't realised I've left,' Alder admitted. 'I seem to be the only one who can pass through their boundary without the magic they conjure.'

'Well then, we need to leave before they realise. They sound dangerous.'

Alder thought of Queen Furi and nodded, but paused in the motion when his mind went to Golan. He was dangerous, but in a very different way.

'What is it?' Mia had noticed his change of expression.

'Nothing, I was just thinking about the fae.'

'We should start packing up, get you away from here as soon as possible.'

'Yes,' Alder said, but then he remembered what Lettle had said to him in the forest.

'*He's important, we can't kill him. He might be the only key to your brother's research.*'

Now he was away from Mosima, he found himself yearning to go back. His time there felt incomplete.

'Alder? Did you hear me?' He was brought out of his thoughts by Mia's question.

'No, sorry, what did you say?'

'I asked you what you were thinking, you look worried.'

Alder ran a hand through his hair. 'I'm just tired, I think. When I sleepwalk, I never feel like I've had a full night's sleep.'

'The elders in Caperly will have some sleeping tinctures that might help,' Mia said gently.

An idea struck Alder like an acorn falling from a tree. 'What if the fae can cure me of my sleepwalking? They have magic I've never seen before.'

It might be why he felt like he needed to go back there.

Mia looked dubious. 'Do you think they will?'

He looked away from Mia to the foliage below. 'I'm not sure, but I've got this feeling that Mosima is where I need to be.'

They both fell silent. Until Alder whispered, 'I can't live like this anymore. I'm becoming a liability.'

'It's not that bad,' Mia said, patting his hand.

'It is . . . Yeeran said that I tried to strike her in her sleep,' Alder admitted.

Mia's eyebrows shot up. 'Ah, makes sense now why she jumped from the canopy.'

'Yes.'

Mia bit her lip with worry. 'Are you seriously considering going back?'

'The diviner, Lettle, she seems to think I'm vital to the fae. Perhaps I can barter with them and she can help figure out my sleeping issues.'

'Are you sure?'

Alder let out an exasperated sigh. 'I don't know, I just know I can't keep going on like this.'

Mia squeezed his forearm. 'Well, at least you can always leave. We'll be here waiting.'

'Dart told me about the pregnancy. You can't wait around for me forever.'

Mia rubbed her belly and smiled. 'Not forever, no. But a few days.'

Alder nodded. 'Give me four days, and if I have found no answers by then, I will leave.'

'Four days then.'

They embraced, Mia holding onto him tightly. 'Take care of yourself and I'll see you soon.'

'Four days,' he confirmed. 'Tell Dart he's Wayfarer while I'm gone.'

Mia smiled and cradled her stomach. 'I will.'

He made his way down and across the forest back to Mosima. When he reached the boundary, he hesitated.

Was he stupid to return to the people who had captured him?

I can always leave again.

Alder passed through the boundary before he could change his mind.

He held his breath, expecting the faeguard to be waiting on the other side, but when no one arrived he released it. Despite the air being so much sweeter here, it felt artificial. Mosima was beautiful, he granted the fae that, but it felt unnatural without the sky above him.

Still, he felt immeasurably better now he'd returned.

He tried to retrace his steps back to Golan's house but wasn't sure where he was going and soon found himself lost.

Golan would have noticed him missing by now.

'Did I already walk down this street?' he mumbled to himself. The road ended abruptly, the cobbles turning into dirt. The trees here were taller and wider than any Alder had seen on this side of the continent. Except for the baobab tree in the royal courtyard. But none of the flora made sense in Mosima. Without analysing the soil conditions over a few months Alder would not be able to figure out how so many different species thrived down here.

One of the large trees had fallen across the dirt pathway ahead of him. It looked like it had died many years ago, as mushrooms and moss were growing in the grooves of the bark. When Alder drew closer to it, he could see that rot had hollowed out the inside. He dipped his head and walked through it.

Once his eyes got accustomed to the darkness he laughed in delight. Ribbon streamers hung from one side to the other. The bark was colourfully decorated in chalk, depicting child-like stick figures and animals. The trunk had become a children's playground.

He found his mind wandering to his own childhood. Had he

been a happy child? Had his parents loved him? The absence of memories made him feel as empty as the tree trunk.

Something moved in the shadows at the other end and he held his breath.

I don't even know what kind of predators live in Mosima. He knew, better than anyone, how dangerous travelling alone could be.

But then the shadows rippled and he recognised the shape of them.

'Hello there, little obeah cub.' His voice echoed through the trunk.

The obeah's ears tweaked, the stubs of its horns too small to see.

Alder crept forward, and so too did the cub.

When he was a step away, he reached out his hand. The obeah sniffed it and let out a small mewl before rubbing its cheek against Alder's leg.

Alder scratched the underside of its chin and it let out a soft purr.

He'd always had a way with obeah, his first memories were of living with them in the caves near Caperly.

'Does that feel good?' he crooned as the obeah nudged his hand for more strokes.

The obeah's ears abruptly pinned back and it raised its head.

It took Alder a few minutes longer to hear what had concerned the obeah.

'Alder?' The shout came from somewhere beyond the tree trunk. The obeah turned and sprinted away.

'Bye then,' Alder said to its retreating back before retracing his steps towards the brightness beyond.

Golan's shoulders slumped in the distance as he recognised Alder exiting the tree trunk. His cane shuffled across the leaf-strewn floor as he quickened his pace towards him.

'I've been looking for you everywhere,' Golan said. 'You're lucky I didn't inform the faeguard, I don't think the queen and king would have been happy with you wandering alone.'

Golan's brows were knotted together, Alder was sad to see it.

'Sorry, I sleepwalked and then I got lost.'

Golan's lips quirked. 'You sleepwalked?'

'Yeah, it's a thing I do,' Alder said shamefacedly.

It was clear that Golan didn't believe him.

'Lettle would have killed me if I'd lost you. She's going to be stopping by with a few questions for you.'

'And I for her,' Alder replied.

Golan gave him a curious look before nodding and leading him away.

'I can only assume you've not had anything to eat yet? Though it is long past midday.'

'No,' Alder said, realising the emptiness of his stomach. 'I am quite hungry.'

'We'll stop by the Honeypot Tavern. It's just down here.'

Golan led him to a quaint-looking building that was just on the precipice of being run-down. As it was, it looked rustic, the overgrown ivy giving it charm.

The tavern smelled of butter and something more vinegary, like Dart's moonshine – which he claimed was a delicacy, but was disgusting, though it did get you blind-faced drunk.

Several tables were full of fae eating and conversing. A few nodded to Golan as he entered, but instead of joining them he directed Alder to a quiet area at the back. He indicated that Alder should sit in the chair with his back to the room.

'Soup all right for you? Haddy does the best sweetcorn and spinach soup I've ever had. They bake the bread fresh too.'

Alder's stomach growled in response and Golan laughed. 'I'll take that as a yes.' Then he stood up and went to order at the bar that lined one wall.

While he was gone Alder looked around. Though he had seen very little of Mosima beyond the Royal Woodland and Golan's home, it was curious that there were no obeah in the tavern. According to what Golan had told him, the obeah were bonded to the fae.

When Golan returned, he asked why.

'Well,' Golan started. 'That's because no one here is bonded to an obeah. We are all Lightless.'

'What does that mean?'

Golan's mouth twitched. 'Many things, but predominantly it means we never come into our power, nor the fae language. Some, like me, have chosen to learn to speak fae. It's difficult but it is possible.'

Alder tuned into the conversations of those around them and noticed he could understand them all, unlike when the queen and king spoke to each other.

'But why have you not bonded to an obeah?'

Golan shrugged and it seemed like the weight of the world was on his shoulders. 'No one knows, perhaps our obeah were killed before they could find us, or maybe we were just not worthy of the magic—'

Alder scoffed, cutting him off. 'If there is one thing I've learned it's that worthiness is a quality made up by those who wish to justify a hierarchy.'

Golan didn't reply, but a small smile played around his full lips. 'Were you not a soldier in your Elven Lands?'

'No . . . well I don't know,' Alder said. He briefly explained to Golan his lack of memories.

'So not only do you have no family, you have no nation,' Golan said softly. Though Alder was glad to see no pity in his expression.

'I may not know who I was, but I do know who I *am*.'

Golan's smile was warm. 'That is the better way of things. Unlike some of us who are still searching.'

Before Alder could question Golan more, their food showed up.

They ate in silence for a little while, Alder savouring the soup. It was rare that the Nomads ate hot food for lunch, so he enjoyed every moment of it.

'Good?' Golan asked after Alder had groaned a second time.

'Very good.'

Golan seemed pleased. 'I thought this was the best tavern to bring you to. Few people will know you are an elf yet, and the shadows of the room hide a lot.'

Alder nodded, not having realised that there was a chance he would have been unwelcome if it was discovered he was an elf. It made sense now why Golan had chosen this table.

'The fae do not like elves?' Alder asked.

'No, the Lightless most of all. Would you like the people who killed your obeah?' Golan's tone was tinged with a bitterness of immeasurable depth.

There was a commotion at Alder's back and he turned to see a fae standing up on one of the tables in the centre of the tavern. She was being cheered on by her comrades around her.

'Why must we make do with the roles granted to us by the monarchy? Why must we, the Lightless, be deemed less than them? Now an elf resides in the palace, a seer, part of the royal household,' her voice held vitriol, 'and yet *we* are unworthy to be seen as full citizens?'

At the word 'unworthy', Alder looked to Golan. The fae's face was a mask of worry.

The woman on the table continued, emboldened by the cries of 'Speak the truth' and 'Fight for our rights.'

'They call us Lightless, not because of our condition, but because they hide our Light. They refuse to see us, so they hide us in the darkness. It is time to free the light.'

'Free the light!'

'Free the light!'

'Free the light!'

The chant caught like fire, rushing through the tavern and stifling the air.

'We need to go, now,' Golan said through tight lips.

Alder nodded and followed Golan through the cacophony. But just as they reached the door someone grabbed Alder's arm.

'I don't recognise you.' The man was clearly drunk.

Alder opened his mouth to reply before he realised his mistake.

'He's an elf!' the fae cried, noticing his flattened canines.

Golan grabbed Alder's arm and dragged him half-running through the door.

Thankfully the drunk man's cries hadn't alerted anyone else, or perhaps the fae just hadn't given any credence to them.

But Golan and Alder didn't stop running until they arrived back at his home.

Golan collapsed into one of his plush armchairs and released the catch that clipped his artificial leg in place. He lowered the leg to the floor before massaging the scar tissue just above his knee.

Alder watched him from the chair opposite, and once his breathing steadied Golan said, 'You can ask, you know. I see you watching.'

Alder frowned. 'My curiosity is never greater than someone's privacy, so no, Golan, I will not ask.'

Golan seemed surprised by the remark. 'For someone who has no recollection of your own upbringing, you are incredibly astute.'

Alder shrugged. 'I learned all I needed to from the forest and the Nomads.'

'Ah, yes, the Nomads, they are like your family?'

Alder nodded. 'The family I chose.'

Golan laughed coldly. 'Yes, there are those of us who cannot choose.'

Alder thought Golan wasn't going to continue, until he reached down into the cabinet beside him and withdrew a bottle of yellow liquid. He swigged from it before passing it to Alder.

Their hands brushed and Alder felt a jolt of warmth run up his arm at the touch. Golan's fingers were soft, but his grip on the bottle sure and firm as it changed hands. Alder looked to see if their brief touch had affected Golan too, but the fae's eyes were distant as he began to recall a memory.

'When I was twenty my father was upset that I was yet to bind to an obeah. Though there are some people who bind far later, *he* had found his precious beast at seventeen. So already I was a failure.'

Alder passed the bottle back and Golan took it gratefully before continuing.

'He believed that I needed to scale the cavern to the plains on the south side of Mosima. "Plain" is a misnomer – though the space is vast it requires a precarious climb, so is frequented by obeah more than fae. Needless to say, I fell many feet, and shattered my leg.'

Though Golan had told the story succinctly, Alder could tell there was far more pain hidden between the rhythm of his words.

The silence was filled with the sound of Golan sipping the mead, before he put the bottle down and turned to Alder with a grin.

'It was the worst and best thing to ever happen to me. Losing my leg was a difficult journey but during my recovery I learned to speak fae and began my career in beauty. Now I am the most sought-after stylist in all of Mosima.'

'And your father?' Alder asked.

'Dead. He contracted a disease not long after and refused to be seen by the Lightless healer I had called for him when I discovered how ill he had got. So he died.'

Alder felt a sense of relief. 'Good.'

Golan cocked his head. 'Perhaps, but there are many more like him.'

'So, you agree with those fae in the tavern? Free the light and all that?'

Golan's head shook back and forth. 'Yes and no. There are so many things we need to fix in Mosima, but I think so much of it stems from the curse. Without it the Jani dynasty would no longer rule the land and other kinds of leadership could be explored.'

'Lettle seemed to think there is something I can do to help.'

'Yes.' Golan frowned. 'Speaking of which I wonder where she is, she's late.'

'Well then, we might as well keep drinking. Pass me the mead.'

Golan laughed and Alder found himself closing his eyes and committing the sound to memory.

Perhaps staying here a few more days won't be so bad after all.

CHAPTER NINETEEN

Yeeran

The night following Salawa's death, Furi and Yeeran exchanged few words. It was as if they both had too much to say, so they didn't say anything at all.

Yeeran watched Lettle and Rayan head off to their royal chambers entwined in each other's arms.

Standing at the top of the steps Yeeran realised she wasn't sure where to go. Were her old rooms still available?

Furi's hand twitched by her side as if she was going to reach for Yeeran. 'You can stay with me tonight, the bed is big enough, or,' her eyes flickered cold, 'you can sleep in the living room.'

Yeeran's gaze slipped from Furi's. Grief had distorted her mind and she couldn't hold Furi's stare without seeing Salawa's dying expression reflected back at her.

First, she had been her lover, then her chieftain.

Now she was neither.

Furi seemed to sense her dark thoughts and said, 'I can find you rooms elsewhere, it is no problem.'

Yeeran shook her head. She wanted Furi close, *needed* her close, despite her actions that day. 'No, I will stay with you,' Yeeran said.

Furi's frown fell away and she smiled tentatively. 'Let us go find solace in sleep.'

Yeeran nodded, unsure whether she could ever find solace again.

'I am yours, until the rhythm sings no more . . .' Salawa whispered in her memories.

Yeeran pressed her hand to her forehead to still her roiling thoughts before following Furi.

The queen's rooms were tucked deep within the corridors of the palace. Yeeran had never been there before and wasn't sure what to expect, but nothing prepared her for what she found.

The living room was alive with plants. Some hung from the rafters and others sprouted up from the floors, the windowsill was almost completely covered in vines.

The warmth of the fire had already melted any frost on the leaves, making the air humid and sticky.

'What happened here?' Yeeran asked.

Furi looked embarrassed, an expression Yeeran had never seen on the fae's face before.

'I-I struggled to control my emotions after you left.' Her eyes were downcast. 'What you see here is me containing my feelings to my chambers.'

It tore open Yeeran's heart to imagine Furi kneeling on the cold flagstones all alone, pouring out her emotions to the land – the only being who could listen.

'I'm so sorry I left,' Yeeran said quietly. Regret was an unfamiliar feeling to her; when she made decisions, she carried them out in faith. But what had her going to Waning achieved?

A dead chieftain.

Furi dragged her gaze up from the floor and looked at Yeeran. The betrayal in her eyes was clear to see.

None of this would have happened if I had stayed.

'I wish you had not gone.' Furi said, echoing Yeeran's thoughts. Her head dipped to her chest and the plants in the room started to wilt.

And I wish you had not killed Salawa. The chieftain's death lay like a splinter between them.

But Furi was hurting, and that was difficult to ignore. So Yeeran crossed the room, stepping over a fern that grew between the flag-stones, and slipped her arms around Furi's waist, pulling her close.

'I wish I hadn't gone too, but we're together now. Because of you.' Yeeran tried to bury deep the blame she felt towards Furi for killing Salawa.

'I thought you said I shouldn't have come,' Furi said in a gently mocking tone.

'No, you shouldn't have, for the sake of Mosima. But for me? Oh, I'm so very glad that you did.'

Furi's hand travelled up Yeeran's torso until it bunched in the curls on the crown of her head. Then she pulled Yeeran's face to hers.

Despite the tautness of her hair in Furi's hand, the fae took her time to savour Yeeran. Pain and pleasure always.

The kiss was softer than Yeeran's need, but it soothed some of the tension between them.

Furi led her to her bedchamber which was sparsely decorated, but the bed was large and comfortable. Neither of them spoke as they undressed and slipped under the covers. The fray-light had grown brighter, warming the room.

'A whole night has gone,' Furi whispered. She tucked her head under Yeeran's chin.

'A whole night and a different world,' Yeeran said, looking down at where Furi's hair splayed against her chest. Gold on brown.

Furi looked up at her and frowned. Her fingers wiped across the underside of Yeeran's chin before showing her the residue on her fingertips.

'Soil,' Furi said, her voice lifeless.

Grave soil.

That was the thing with feelings you buried deep. They were always there churning beneath the surface, ready to reappear.

'She was your old lover, wasn't she?' Furi said, her voice emotionless.

'Yes,' Yeeran whispered back.

The ghost of Salawa slipped under the sheets between them, and Yeeran found herself rolling away from Furi.

Yeeran, are you well? Pila sensed her sudden sadness.

Yes, or rather, I will be. What are you doing?

Amnan and I are eating strawberries. They are a little mushy from the frost.

OK, enjoy yourself. I'm going to try and sleep now.

Yeeran thought grief would steal her sleep but surprisingly it wasn't long before her dreams pulled her under.

It was a strange thing to wake up past midday. Yeeran had done it so rarely in her life that it disorientated her. What was she to eat? Breakfast or lunch? When was she to go to bed, at sunset or sunrise?

The sheets beside her were cold and empty. Furi must have been up for some time.

Pila was curled up at the foot of the bed. She opened her eyes as Yeeran padded out of bed towards her.

You're finally awake, the obeah said.

Looks like you were asleep too, Pila.

Pila let out a snort of disbelief. *I was just resting my eyes.*

How long has Furi been up?

I'm not sure, I didn't see.

Because you were resting your eyes?

Pila smacked her lips and settled down to sleep again. *Exactly.*

Yeeran stroked her between the ears as she walked past on the way to the baths.

Once clean and dressed Yeeran made her way to the Royal Woodland, but neither Furi nor Rayan were on their thrones.

She made her way to the war room in the lower corridors of the palace. The last time she had been there was after Nerad attacked Lettle.

In her mind's eye she saw Nerad's magic tightening and tightening around Lettle's neck. The memory set her heart racing. Lettle had been so close to death.

Yeeran pushed thoughts of Nerad from her mind as she

approached the war room door. Four of the faeguard stood on either side of the doorway.

Curious, Yeeran viewed them with magesight. Her suspicions were confirmed as she saw golden threads woven around the door, barring anyone from entering.

'The security has stepped up a notch,' Yeeran commented.

The tallest of the faeguard turned to her with a bored expression. 'No one enters unless expressly invited.'

'Are Furi and Rayan in there?' Yeeran asked.

'Queen and king,' she was corrected sharply by another.

'Yes, yes, are they in there?'

'That is not information we are willing to share.'

Yeeran inhaled then shouted at the top of her lungs, 'Rayan, Furi, will you call off your overzealous guards and let me in.'

Someone cursed behind the door before it was pulled open. Furi's expression blazed like the sun. 'You didn't have to yell.'

'These fools weren't letting me in,' Yeeran explained, before crossing the now clear threshold.

She glared at the guards before closing the door.

'Hello, Yeeran.' Rayan waved from a desk in the corner.

The war room had changed considerably since Yeeran had been here last. The map in the centre was scattered with bits of notes, and the tokens of scouts and the eleven district armies were in disarray and forgotten.

'What's going on in here?' Yeeran asked.

Rayan and Furi exchanged a look.

'There's an organisation trying to target Lettle,' Furi said, sinking into a chair.

'What?'

Furi and Rayan took it in turns explaining all that had happened since Yeeran had gone, including the two assassination attempts and the note found at Conch Shore.

'Let me get this right, someone, or a group of people who are most likely Lightless, are trying to kill *my sister*?'

Furi nodded. 'We're doing everything we can to figure it out. But it's difficult, we have to assume they have more than one person working in the palace.'

'Where is Lettle now?' Yeeran asked.

'Still asleep in our chambers, guarded by people I trust,' Rayan said. His voice was clipped as if he dared Yeeran to question his ability to protect his consort.

But he'd already failed once before.

Yeeran began to pace.

'It has to be Hosta. Have you questioned them yet?'

Furi's gaze became distant, her hands balling into fists as she recalled how Hosta, a soldier in the faeguard, had ambushed Lettle and Yeeran during their first few weeks in Mosima. Hosta's prejudice against elves had led to Yeeran being stabbed and coming very close to death. Yeeran felt a rush of affection for the fierce queen.

'We have not questioned Hosta and their crew,' Rayan said, rubbing his chin. 'But I did look into them to see where their sentencing led them. All of them were assigned to the mines in the caverns to the north. I checked their worksheets and spoke to their supervisors. None of them have missed a day of work, so I'm not sure how they would have organised this.'

'I'm sure they could have figured out a way. Let us go visit Hosta, we need to speak to them,' Yeeran said.

Furi looked to Rayan and shrugged. 'We haven't got anything else, and I don't know about you but I'm getting really bored of this investigation. I have better things to be doing with my time.'

'I can't think of anything more pressing to spend your time on,' Yeeran said.

Furi's nostrils flared and she got up and stalked over to the table. With one sweep of her hands she sent the notes there flying to uncover the map beneath.

She pointed to the Elven Lands.

'Need I remind you that Berro and two hundred of the faeguard are still in Crescent trying to negotiate a peace deal?'

Then Furi pointed to Mosima.

'And if that doesn't happen then the entirety of our world is under threat. So yes, there are many pressing things I need to spend my time on.'

With that Furi stormed out of the room.

Rayan broke the silence first. 'Well, I have a feeling that there was more to that argument than there seemed to be.'

Yeeran began to pick up the papers Furi had thrown to the floor.

'Yes, things are not quite as . . . settled . . . with Furi as I would like.'

'Why?'

'There are too many unresolved matters.'

'Like you leaving?'

Like Furi killing Salawa.

'Among other things,' Yeeran said, making it clear she didn't want to talk about it.

Rayan nodded, his eyes creasing at the corners. He ran a hand through his hair, which had grown out since she'd seen him last. The black short curls were surprisingly streaked with grey.

'Are *you* all right?' Yeeran asked.

Rayan gave her a tired smile. 'You mean besides the fact my citizens are trying to kill my consort? Yes, I'm just perfect.'

Yeeran chuckled. 'Remember when we were just soldiers and the worst thing we had to worry about was our own deaths?'

Rayan's smile grew. 'Ah yes, the peace of mortal peril.'

They laughed and some of their worries fled the room.

'I've missed this,' Yeeran admitted. 'Just you and I together talking.'

Without Lettle, without Furi.

Rayan stooped over the war map in the centre of the room. Yeeran knew his mind was taking him back to the countless times he'd done the very same thing in the barracks on the Bleeding Field. 'It's been a while since it was just the two of us.'

Yeeran came to stand by his side and they both looked down at the Bleeding Field together.

'What was it like? Back in Waning?' he asked quietly.

'They lost a third of their army to Crescent and the fae.'

Rayan's eyes shuttered closed in pain. When he opened them again, the core of his brown irises blazed just like Furi's. 'Berro was meant to return a week ago. The negotiations must be taking longer than anticipated.'

Yeeran splayed her hand against the Waning district on the map. Grief blurred the edges of the border as unshed tears filled her eyes.

'Before she died, Salawa recalled the Waning army from the Bleeding Field,' Yeeran said softly.

Rayan's mouth fell open. 'Truly?'

'Yes, the war there has ended. At least until they realise Salawa is not returning from her expedition, and a new chieftain is nominated.'

Rayan whistled low. 'The Forever War ended, just like she promised.'

'Just like she promised,' Yeeran choked out.

The silence stretched as Yeeran tried to get a handle on her emotions. Rayan didn't try to comfort her, as he knew she wouldn't want it, instead he let her grieve quietly. After some time he asked, 'Shall we make a visit to Hosta?'

'Yes,' Yeeran said with relief. Though she knew the idea was a distraction, she was glad to leave the war room, the walls of which felt too close.

'Is Pila nearby?' Rayan asked.

Pila, are you still resting your eyes?

No, I'm in the woodland.

Fancy a ride?

Yes.

Yeeran turned to Rayan. 'Pila's ready.'

'Let's go.'

It was exhilarating to ride across Mosima once more. And though the frost meant the greenery was not as vibrant as it could have been, it was still so beautiful.

'How long do you think it'll take for the trees to return to normal?' Yeeran asked Rayan who cantered beside her on Ajax.

'I'm not sure. I saw Norey this morning. He's doing everything he can to preserve as many of the plants as possible. Those that don't survive can be revived by Furi and me over the coming weeks.'

It did seem like the plants around Rayan grew greener as he passed.

The curse was such a strange phenomenon, one that Yeeran did not understand. Perhaps the grimoire Lettle found could one day explain it all.

Harsh noises grew louder in the distance as they approached the coal mines. Yeeran had never been this far north in Mosima. But she had known that coal had been sourced here since the curse began.

As the fae didn't use a prison system for their criminals, all those sentenced for a crime were put into service. Some became servants, others miners.

Ajax and Pila slowed as they reached the outbuilding that oversaw the operations in the tunnels.

'This is a closed operation for the safety of all, no one is permitted here!' came the shout from one of the rooms. Then a face appeared in the doorway. Their expression was one of complete shock as they took in Rayan.

'Ah, my king, apologies I didn't realise it was you. How can I help?' The supervisor all but grovelled her way towards them.

'I was wondering if you might be able to source one of your workers for me, a fae known by the name of Hosta.'

'Hosta, my king?'

'Yes, is that a problem?'

'Not at all, not at all.' The fae bobbed her head up and down before scuttling away.

Dirty-faced fae began to peer out from the entrances of the many tunnels as news spread that the king was here. Pickaxes were paused and soon crowds began to gather.

'Perhaps we should have called Hosta to the palace,' Yeeran said dryly.

'Yes, I think you might be right,' Rayan replied.

After a few more minutes the supervisor reappeared with Hosta in tow.

Yeeran nearly didn't recognise them. Their hair was cropped short by their ears, their cheeks shallow and their lips dry. Streaks of coal coated their body which stood like a clothes hanger, barely holding their uniform up.

I had admired that they didn't have a prison system, but this is just as cruel.

To imprison someone would prevent them access to their obeah. At least those bonded can still be together, Pila replied.

Yeeran had not noticed the obeah around the mines until Pila pointed it out. Their dark fur blended in with the deposits of coal.

Hosta smiled as they recognised Yeeran. 'You've come a long way from that first day topside, elves.'

Hosta had been part of the faeguard who had captured both Rayan and Yeeran.

The supervisor hissed at hearing the king disrespected. Rayan just replied mildly, 'So have you, Hosta.'

They bared their dirty teeth. 'What can I do for you both?'

Yeeran looked to the supervisor. 'We'll need a few minutes please.'

She bobbed her head once more and retreated to her cabin.

Yeeran rounded on Hosta. 'What do you know of the assassination attempts on Lettle?'

Hosta laughed until tears streamed from their blue eyes.

'You think I had something to do with it? You know they count my shits here? They *literally* count how many shits I take a week.'

Rayan and Yeeran exchanged a glance.

'But you must have heard something at least?' Rayan pressed.

Hosta wiped their eyes, their smile turned sly. 'Perhaps I have, what would I get from it?'

'I would lower your sentence by two years,' Rayan said.

Again, Hosta laughed. 'Two years? Didn't they tell you I'm here for life? Two years is nothing. Commander Furi, or should I say Queen Furi, was very vexed with me.'

Yeeran felt the scar on her side twitch with the memory of Hosta's blade.

'We'll move you away from the mines,' Yeeran said.

Rayan gave her a warning glance. It might not be her call, but she would do anything to keep Lettle safe.

Rayan read her expression and nodded. 'We'll move you to the potato farms.'

Hosta's eyebrows shot up, giving away their surprise.

'But only if the information is worth it,' Yeeran added.

Hosta nodded and rubbed the back of their neck. 'All right, you have a deal. I'll tell you all I've heard.'

Yeeran waited expectantly.

'Their plan isn't just to kill your sister. But to bring down the entirety of the government. They want a new Mosima.'

'Who are *they*?'

'A group of Lightless, led by someone powerful. I do not know who, all I know is that they call him the "Authority".'

It wasn't a lot but it was something.

'Thank you, Hosta. Enjoy the rest of your sentence,' Yeeran said.

'What do you mean? Aren't you going to reassign me?'

Rayan looked to Yeeran and frowned.

'No,' she said. 'You deserve to rot here.'

Yeeran knew it was cruel, she had very few things in life left but her honour. But she couldn't let Hosta live an easy life, not after they had nearly killed her just for being an elf.

It was the first time that Yeeran realised that perhaps Mosima had changed her in more ways than one, and it wasn't always for the better.

CHAPTER TWENTY

Lettle

Lettle could not stop thinking about the prophecy and what it could mean. With Najma's notes completely ruined it was near impossible to translate Afa's grimoire.

But not *totally* impossible. Najma had to have started somewhere.

So that first day back in Mosima, while Rayan went about his business, she started to list the familiar letters in the hopes of ascertaining an alphabet.

It took her all day to be sure she'd found all the unique letters. And by the time she was done scouring the grimoire a headache was blossoming by her temples.

But the day wasn't over. She'd told Golan she'd stop by his house before night fell. He lived further out of the city, closer to the boundary, and it seemed a perfect opportunity to go by the Book Orchard first.

Translating the grimoire had given her a new purpose.

I need to make myself useful one way or another. Because right now, I'm a seer who cannot see the Fates.

As soon as she'd awoken that morning, she'd cast her talismans trying to read the future once more. But the Fates refused to speak. She had started to consider something might be wrong with her tokens and reminded herself to ask Sahar the next time she saw him.

Lettle opened the door to her chambers to an empty corridor. She had expected at least four guards there ready to trail her but Rayan must have dismissed them.

Perhaps he needs them for another task, the threat to me less than he'd considered.

Still, when she spotted a faeguard in the Royal Woodland, she asked him to escort her, just in case.

'The king sent a message to the barracks removing your protection, seer. Would you like me to check with him?'

Lettle looked to the fray. It was late afternoon and if she spent time double checking with Rayan she'd not get a chance to go to the Book Orchard before seeking Alder.

'Where is the king?'

'He left the woodland a few hours ago, seer. With your sister and their obeah. They departed quite swiftly. His message to release the guards instructed to watch over you came by haba not long ago.'

He must have caught the culprit behind the assassination attempts.

'Well, if he thinks the threat is over then I'll be fine.' Then Lettle smiled and, remembering what Golan had said about treating the fae kindly, added, 'Thank you anyway.'

Lettle left the Royal Woodland behind. She kept her head down as she walked, trying to avoid being recognised by any of the fae.

It didn't take her long to reach the outer rim of the city.

She turned down a cobbled road, noting the sound of merriment coming from the end of the street. As she drew closer to the building, she recognised it as the Honeypot Tavern. The last time she'd walked past she'd heard the first murmurs of rebellion from its Lightless patrons.

She pulled her shawl over her head, hiding her features as best she could, and began to quicken her pace until she saw someone who caught her eye.

Tucked into the back of the tavern, Alder and Golan sat deep in conversation.

Golan was smiling as he spoke, his expression far more carefree than usual.

She lingered by the window and watched them for a few minutes, intrigued by the spark between them.

Lettle thought of joining them, but she didn't want to disturb their peace. Besides, there'd be time to see them after her visit to the Book Orchard.

She was about to leave when she saw someone stand on a table. The chatter in the tavern died down as the fae began to speak. Lettle couldn't quite hear her, so while all eyes were on the speaker, she sneaked through the door of the tavern.

'. . . Now an elf resides in the palace, a seer, part of the royal household. And yet *we* are unworthy to be seen as full citizens?'

Lettle felt herself shrivel to half her size. The fae was talking about her.

And she was talking sense. Everyone in the room knew it, including Lettle.

Rayan may have uncovered the person behind the attempts on my life, but there are many more who might yet take their place.

'They call us Lightless, not because of our condition, but because they hide our Light. They refuse to see us, so they hide us in the darkness. It is time to free the light.'

'Free the light!'

The fae stood from their seats as the chant moved through the room, the words resonating deep within Lettle's chest.

She shivered as she felt the depth of the Lightless's struggle. All they wanted was the same rights as those faebound.

More needs to be done to bridge the gap between the two classes of fae. And Lettle realised that she was best placed to instigate such a movement.

I'll speak to Rayan tonight. Otherwise the cycle will never end, and I'll never be safe.

With a heavier heart than she'd had upon entering, Lettle left the Honeypot Tavern and made her way to the Book Orchard.

Though the library hadn't yielded many results in the past, now that she had a better grasp of the fae language she thought there might be something there to guide her in her translation of the grimoire.

The library was set deep into the cavern wall. As she walked in, she slipped into magesight, letting the glow of the boundary guide her down the tunnel.

When she reached the end, she lit a torch that was set into a cabinet just for this purpose. The amber flame banished the shadows of the vast room revealing the oak trees that had been grown into shelves, all lined with books.

The smell of stories washed over her and she released a sigh of contentment. This was her favourite place in all of Mosima. Yeeran had always had her training grounds, and Lettle had always had her books.

Not that their father had cared for either of their passions. He had died disappointed in both his daughters. Lettle hadn't become a diviner until her father passed, and she wondered what he would have thought of her new profession. Beyond seeing her consume every book she could, he had only known her as a simple nurse. One who had cared for him until her caring took a darker turn.

Though his death had been a blessing for him, it didn't alleviate the guilt she felt for killing him.

She pushed the memories of her father to the back of her mind, she didn't want them to sully this perfect place.

Afa's grimoire was heavy in her arms and she went to place it on the table that grew up from the centre of the library.

'Oh!'

The flames from her torch wavered as someone turned from their book to look at her.

'I didn't really expect to be interrupted out here,' Sahar said.

'You startled me. What are you doing here?' she asked, sitting in the chair opposite.

'I think that's a question for you, Lettle. For I have been visiting the Book Orchard for years,' Sahar said cheerfully.

'Golan showed it to me a few months back. And you're the first person I've ever seen here.'

Sahar nodded. 'Yes, I haven't been since last harvest. But I do occasionally like to sit beneath the bough of books and read. It's a shame my brethren do not do the same. They prefer the library by the university, but I like my tomes old and dusty.'

Lettle tended to agree.

'It is good to see you back in Mosima,' Sahar continued. 'My grandson was not the same since you left. How fare your travels?'

Lettle filled Sahar in on what had happened. She concluded her story by placing Afa's grimoire on the table.

'It looks familiar,' he said, closing his own book and peering over.

'I'm going through some of Najm – your son's – old work trying to translate the text.'

Sahar's brown eyes scrunched together as he tried to parse the unfamiliar words. 'What language is that?'

'It is the human language. The prince was translating it, but the key he created was damaged by water.' Lettle showed Sahar the faded pages.

'Ah, yes, I recognise it now though I must apologise, this goes a little way past my skillset,' Sahar said with a smile.

'It'll be difficult but I was hoping to read up on language structures to see if I can recreate his work.'

Sahar looked dubious. 'My son spent decades working on that and was only able to translate one word: aiftarri.'

Lettle bit her lip. 'I know, but I'm hoping I'll be able to learn more. Somehow. With the Fates once again silent, I'm not much use for anything else.'

Sahar frowned. 'What do you mean, once again? Did they come back to you?'

Lettle nodded. 'Yes, when I was topside.' She didn't elaborate on how she had used an obeah. But Sahar's eyes seemed to narrow slightly. 'I was going to ask, do you think my talismans could be faulty?'

Sahar frowned. 'Show me them.'

Lettle removed the tokens from her pouch by her waist and handed them to Sahar. He inspected them closely.

'No, I do not think so. I have never heard of talismans failing, so I suspect the Fates simply continue to be elusive.'

Lettle slumped in her chair. 'Moon's mercy, I hoped I'd figured out the issue. At least I have the one prophecy to work with.'

'What did the Fates say?' Sahar asked.

'"*In the early hours of the morrow's new day, a tree will fall by the pathway to Mosima. Seek your answers in the night, dawn will bring you peace*",' she recounted.

'The tree, that must be the elf you found, Alder. It makes sense now why you had to bring him back,' Sahar surmised quickly. 'But "*Seek your answers in the night, dawn will bring you peace*" is beyond my grasp.'

'Yes,' Lettle seethed. 'The Fates are silent for so long and then when they do speak it's in riddles.'

Sahar laughed and patted Lettle on the shoulder. 'Such is the way, my dear. Now I must beg my leave. I missed lunch and my stomach is growling something fierce.'

Lettle waved him off before returning to Afa's grimoire.

Less than an hour later her headache was worse and she had failed to parse anything.

She was about to give up when she heard a sound from the tunnel ahead. It sounded like four or five people.

Now who's here to interrupt my peace? Always the way, solitude for months and now a whole chorus.

Lettle set her scowl, ready to ward off any loud interlopers. But the scowl was replaced by an expression of fear as she watched the shadows stretch across the library.

There were five of them, all armed with swords and wearing clothes the same deep russet as the cavern, as if to better camouflage themselves.

The fingers of dread ran a course down her neck. These fae were not here to read. They were looking for someone.

Her.

But this was not the first time Lettle had been hunted in Mosima.

She had learned since her first run-in with Hosta that she should always carry a dagger.

Slowly she placed the grimoire and her journal back in her bag and pretended to search for another book while actually arming herself with the blade up her sleeve. Though part of her knew it would do nothing against five fae.

They were slipping like eels through the stacks of books, their movements synchronised and their footfalls quiet.

As they crept closer, Lettle continued to pretend to read.

Closer and closer they drew.

When they were less than a foot away, Lettle lunged, plunging her dagger into the thigh of the nearest before removing it and slashing at the face of another.

Screams cut through the air, along with blood and a fair amount of curses before Lettle was pinned down.

'Get off me,' she screamed.

A fae with long black curls appeared in her vision.

'How dare you,' the injured woman spat. Blood dribbled from her nose into her mouth where Lettle had sliced off a chunk of cartilage.

Yeeran would be proud. The thought made Lettle smile.

'You smile in the face of death? So be it. I will make the killing blow.' The woman drew back a blade to end Lettle's life.

It was only then that Lettle realised: *This is where I die.*

'No,' Lettle shouted. 'No, this is not the end.'

The woman laughed. 'Be quiet, *elf.*'

Elf, that was the reason they had targeted her.

Yet no one should be targeting her at all. If Rayan thought the threat had lessened enough to remove her guards, then who were these people?

Unless Rayan never ordered my escort to stand down.

Lettle's heart thumped loudly in her ears as she realised just how large this network must be. And all of them wanted her dead, just because she was an elf.

A lie came to her quickly.

'But I'm not fully elf, I'm part-fae too.'

The woman's arm wavered, the blade aiming for Lettle's neck. 'What are you talking about?'

'You must know of my sister, Yeeran, who bonded with an obeah. We have fae ancestry. You cannot kill me or you break your most sacred law: fae life cannot be taken.'

'I heard that you are only half-sisters and that the other had the fae heritage,' the person who had twisted Lettle's arms behind her back said.

It was true that Vyce and Chall had circulated the lie that Yeeran had fae heritage in order to reason away how she became bonded with Pila. It wasn't true – Lettle and Yeeran knew their family tree eight generations gone. But now, the seeds that the queens had sown might yet yield Lettle some fruit.

'Yes, but it is our great-grandfather who was fae,' Lettle pressed. 'If you kill me, then you are only killing one of your own.'

The woman scoffed and hawked blood on the ground. 'Nonsense.'

'It is true, why else would your king choose me as consort? Like me, he hopes my obeah will find me soon.'

Doubt crept into her attacker's brown eyes.

'Salt, what do we do?' another whispered to the woman with the cut nose. They spoke as if Lettle couldn't hear them.

'You kill her,' the woman, Salt, replied.

'No, you said you wanted to land the killing blow.'

'Yes, well, my sword hand is injured.'

'It was fine a moment ago.'

Their bickering made Lettle realise that her ruse was working. She had bought herself more time.

'We need to check this with the Authority,' the fae behind her said.

Who is this 'Authority'? Lettle thought, tucking the information away.

'But his task was clear, kill her,' Salt said, exasperated.

One of them shrugged in the corner of her vision. 'Perhaps he did not know.'

There was a silence as the assassins stood around for a few moments unsure what to do. Finally, Salt said, 'Let's take her back to base and send a message to the Authority.'

There was a collective sigh as a decision was made.

Lettle was pulled up from the ground. She reached for her bag and looped it over her head before they could stop her. There was no way she was leaving the grimoire unattended. But her sudden movements caused the fae to retaliate and they grabbed her, twisting her arm painfully behind her back once more.

'Careful, that arm is tender,' she said.

'Be quiet,' the woman snapped as they moved out towards Mosima. 'Han, Tovi, keep her silent while we walk, we don't want unwanted attention.'

Lettle resolved to keep quiet, knowing that this far out from the centre of Mosima she was unlikely to see another fae who could help. And she really didn't want to be gagged. Her voice was the only thing that had saved her so far.

The six of them walked closely together. Now they were out in the darkening fray-light, Lettle could see how their clothing really helped them to blend into the cavern walls.

They followed the curvature of the boundary until they reached a set of shallow steps in the wall. They were barely steps, more like handholds.

'Go on,' either Han or Tovi said. They released Lettle's hands and pushed her towards the ledges.

'I recommend you don't look down,' the woman said cruelly.

Lettle had very little grip in her left hand, so she was already at a disadvantage scaling the wall. But it was this or certain death, so she took her chances.

They climbed steadily, Lettle clearly the slowest of the group, her footing unsure and her grip weak.

'Where are we going?' she asked when they reached a shallow platform where they could rest a moment.

'The southern plains,' was the only reply she got.

She had thought plains would be somewhere flat on ground level, but they were already halfway up the cavern wall.

The last ascent was the hardest, but thankfully they had installed a rope to aid in their climb.

When Lettle reached the top, she gasped. The cavern flattened out into a vast outcrop before sharply connecting to the ceiling in the distance. Obeah grazed on fruit trees that looked like they'd grown there for hundreds of years. A waterfall splashed from a gap in the rock wall into a shimmering lagoon filled with lily pads and moss-covered rocks.

It was a slice of nirvana in the sky.

But Lettle was unable to appreciate it as she was dragged towards a makeshift house.

A burly man was sitting at the table when they arrived. Lettle assumed he must be the 'Authority'. If so, her life was about to be cut short.

His mouth opened in shock at seeing Lettle. 'Salt, what have you done?'

'Don't start with me, Omur,' Salt grunted. 'She says she's part-fae.'

'Surely it's a lie,' Omur replied.

'Kill her then,' Salt goaded the big man. His eyes shifted to the others and he realised that perhaps if they hadn't done it, then neither should he.

Once again Lettle had bought herself more time.

'We need to send for the Authority to verify her claims,' Salt said as she went to a drawer and removed a bandage.

Lettle's stomach sank. So Omur was not the Authority.

'He won't like that,' Omur said. 'But I agree, that's all we can do. I'll keep her tied up in the back.'

Salt nodded. 'Han, Tovi, send a message to the Authority. But remember, not the shed on Conch Shore, it's been compromised.'

The two fae slipped out.

'You need to see a healer, Salt,' Omur said.

'Yes, probably, she got my thigh too.'

'Go, I'll deal with her.'

Slowly the room emptied until it was just Lettle and Omur.

She knew she could not fight him and win.

'You don't need to lock me up, I will not flee,' Lettle said.

Omur chuckled and stroked his beard. 'I am not quite so gullible, little elf.'

Lettle smarted at being called *little*. It was one of her most hated insults.

'I promise I will not.'

'Smooth-talker, aren't you? Somehow you managed to convince those fools that you have fae blood. Now they're all frightened of killing you, and I cannot do it for they'll always wonder if I broke our most sacred law.' He laughed again. 'Clever, clever elf you are.'

Lettle lifted her chin. 'Who is this Authority?'

'Oh no, you won't get that from me. Besides, you will meet him soon enough, I'm sure. Now let's get you settled.'

He pushed her towards a back room with a bed in the centre.

'Is it just you who lives here?' she asked, genuinely curious.

Omur nodded. 'Yes, I've been here for some years now, I prefer the solitude. The perfect place to set up our base.'

'Base for what exactly?'

Omur shook his head. 'No, no, I told you, I shall not be lured into giving up my secrets. Now what's in this bag of yours?'

She tried to keep a hold of it, but Omur was too strong and he yanked it from her grasp easily.

The grimoire and her notebook spilled onto the floor.

'Please, don't take them from me, they're only books,' she pleaded.

Omur lifted her journal and flickered through it, his gaze pausing on some of the prophecies and notes.

'I heard you were a seer, shame you did not predict your own death,' he said, though his tone wasn't mocking.

'Please, if I'm to die here, let me have something to pass the time in my final hours,' Lettle said. 'There is nothing in those pages that can harm you.'

After everything she'd done to get the grimoire in the first place, she couldn't bear to let it out of her sight.

Omur met her gaze. 'I used to be like you, you know. Loved my books more than people. But the more I read, the fewer books there were to read. When I was eighteen, I finished all the tomes my family and friends owned, so I went to the university library. That was when I stopped reading.'

'Why?'

'I assumed you knew since you used the Book Orchard. A treasure of tomes but no fiction, I'm afraid.' He shook his head sadly. 'No Lightless are allowed in the university library.'

Lettle swallowed her shock. Though she had known about the university library, she hadn't realised it was only for bonded fae. When Golan had shown her the Book Orchard over the other he had said it was because the university library was too busy for her to work unnoticed.

But the truth was, she wouldn't be welcome there, because she was not faebound. The realisation left a sour taste in her mouth.

Omur handed her back the books, even letting her keep a quill and ink.

'You can spend your remaining hours reading if you'd like. But if I were you, I'd appeal to the gods. For you'll be meeting your maker soon enough.'

With that he closed the door to the room, leaving Lettle alone with her thoughts and her fears.

CHAPTER TWENTY-ONE

Furi

Furi drummed her fingers against the armrest of her throne. She was annoyed. Rayan and Yeeran had gone off to question Hosta without telling her.

You did storm out of the room, Amnan said quietly in her mind, ever her conscience.

Yeeran was frustrating me.

Amnan didn't reply, for he knew her feelings as well as she did. And he could feel how love and anger fought for purchase in her mind.

And jealousy too.

Yeeran was so willing to question her efforts in rooting out the assassin, yet it was she who had not been here. It was *she* who had left.

Furi had never felt rage like she had the moment she saw Yeeran bound in chains. And the memory of the anger still made her hot to the touch. She had sated her fury on the blood of those who had hurt Yeeran. Even killing the chieftain of Waning. She didn't regret it, and she would do it again in a second.

Even if the woman had been Yeeran's former lover.

It was only when Yeeran buried the body that Furi suspected who the woman had once been to Yeeran.

And now Furi had killed her.

Tears born of guilt seeped from her eyes and she slammed her fist on the side of the throne, intent on turning her regret into anger. The baobab, solid and unmovable, didn't quake in the face of her pitiful struggle.

Will Yeeran ever forgive me for killing Salawa?

I think the question is, do you forgive her for betraying you in the first place? If Yeeran had not led the elves to Mosima, you would not have had to defend it, Amnan replied.

Furi released her clenched fist. *She told me she didn't believe the chieftain wished to harm the fae, only to parle. And . . . I believe her. Yeeran wouldn't hurt me.*

Then why are you hurting?

Amnan was right, and she longed to hold him close. *Where are you?*

Not far, I'm returning to Mosima now.

It always made her uncomfortable when he went topside, but before she could voice her concern he said, *There's a fae messenger on the other side of the boundary. Shall I retrieve the letter?*

Yes, please. It must be from Berro.

It took Amnan less than an hour to cross Mosima with the letter in his jaw.

Thank you, Furi said as she removed it.

She let out a sigh of relief when she saw Berro's handwriting. It had been a few weeks without an update, and Furi was keen to know how talks were going, but her stomach turned to lead as she began to read.

My queen,

Talks with Crescent have gone cold. We were reaching a satisfactory solution to recall the remainder of our troops, but something has happened to stall all further progress. A messenger from another tribe arrived last night and spoke to the chieftain of Crescent until the early hours of the morning. The next day we were told that the chieftain would no longer negotiate with us. I am sending this letter ahead of our return, for I think it best that my regiment and

I come back to Mosima as soon as possible. I will try for an audi-
ence one more time, but I expect you'll be seeing me soon enough.
   Berro

'Oh, Berro.' Furi buried her head in her hands.

'Dear Furi, are you quite all right?' Norey said from across the clearing. Furi sat up and tucked the letter into her pocket.

The horticulturalist was holding a shorn branch, the leaves of which were pockmarked with frostbite.

'Yes, it's just been a long day already,' Furi admitted.

She got down from her throne and went to join Norey by the tree he was working on.

'How bad is the damage?' she asked quietly.

Norey looked at her frankly, flyaways from his knotted hair frizzed around his face. 'Bad, but it could also be worse.'

Furi put her hand to the tree bark and concentrated. In her mind's eye she could see the threads that bound her soul to it. With a bit of coaxing she could feed some of her energy down the connection; it fatigued her, but the results were worth it.

The branch that Norey had removed grew back in full health.

'Now just four thousand more plants to go,' Norey said mildly.

Furi's bones felt weak.

'Really?'

'Just in the Royal Woodland alone, but I think only the smaller ones will suffer disastrous effects, the rest simply need a little pruning.'

Norey handed her the shears and she got to work. Soon her worries ebbed away.

'Thank you, Norey.'

'Are you ready to talk about it yet?' he replied.

Furi looked around, conscious that the last time she had spoken about the assassins in the Royal Woodland someone had overheard where Lettle was going and had sent word to her would-be killers.

She thought about the secrecy that Rayan had imposed. But Norey was practically family.

Furi dropped her voice to a near-whisper and Norey gave her a bemused expression. 'The fae are targeting Lettle and our investigations are not getting very far.'

'Ah, Rayan's poisoning. Lettle was the intended victim?'

'Yes.'

'And they've tried to kill her more than once?'

Furi chewed her bottom lip and nodded.

'You have no clues, no indication as to who it could be?'

'No, we have found practically *nothing*. And I am losing my patience.'

Norey put down his shears. 'Do you know why the fae want her dead? Or why they do what they do?'

Furi plucked an errant twig from her hair and threw it to the ground. 'No, other than hatred of elves, we have no motive.'

'It may be prudent to think beyond the binary of race and consider what Lettle's death would mean to those who seek it.'

Furi began to pace back and forth thinking on what Norey had said.

'Instability? Chaos? Distraction?' Furi suggested.

'And what would that do to the court?'

'Weaken it.'

I've been thinking of this all wrong. I assumed the culprits were radicals with little to lose.

Maybe this was more complicated than she had initially thought. What if this was far more political than mere revenge on the elves?

'This is not a race war. It is a war,' she said.

Norey patted her hand. 'Maybe, and maybe not. But it is worth considering who is the real target.'

Amnan slunk out of the undergrowth and yawned. *Sahar comes from the south.*

'Hello, Father,' Furi greeted him as he rounded the nearest tree.

Sahar was lost in thought and was startled by Furi's voice.

'Oh, daughter, sorry, I was just thinking on what Lettle told me,' he said. 'I just saw her in the Book Orchard.'

It seemed that Furi wasn't the only one sharing secrets.

'Hello, Sahar,' Norey said, pecking him on the cheek.

'Busy day today, my love?' Sahar asked Norey who nodded.

'Do you mind if I have a word with Norey about our plans later, Furi?' Sahar continued.

'Not at all, but remember tonight you're dining with us,' Furi said to Sahar. She smiled as she spoke making sure Norey knew she was teasing. Though they shared her father's time, she didn't want him to feel guilty for wanting to be with his partner.

She knew what it felt like to miss the person you loved.

As she left her father and Norey and walked back to her rooms, her thoughts turned to Yeeran.

Why could they not simply love each other?

It could be because your love will always be built on the hierarchy of the throne and the throes of grief, Amnan said. *You were drawn together under instruction by the crown. And she will always be the person who killed Najma.*

And I the one who killed Salawa.

The truth of it all pierced her heart.

'Furi.' Yeeran appeared in the palace corridor ahead of her. For a moment Furi thought she'd conjured her from her mind, then she saw Rayan come up beside her.

'Furi?' Yeeran asked, stepping towards her. 'What is it?'

I'm not sure we'll ever get past the sorrow and pain that binds us together.

But Furi didn't say that, she said, 'How was your afternoon?'

It was Rayan who answered. 'Come to my rooms, I'll tell you there.'

They followed Rayan to his quarters. Furi hadn't been there since the rooms had belonged to her mother.

Another grief not yet calloused.

'The guards have gone,' Rayan muttered as they walked through the doorway.

'Did you assign them to Lettle? Maybe she went somewhere?' Yeeran said.

'Sahar said he saw her in the Book Orchard, so they must be with her there,' Furi said.

'Hmm, but surely she would have come back for dinner?' Rayan replied. He looked through the rooms, calling Lettle's name.

When she didn't reply he said, 'I'm just going to go to the garrison and check if the guards have already come back.'

Furi wondered if he was being a bit overprotective, but then she thought about what it would be like if it was Yeeran.

She'd burn down the whole palace looking for her.

As the door shut behind Rayan, Furi took a seat on the sofa opposite Yeeran. Though Rayan had rearranged the configuration, all the furniture itself was the same as her mother's.

Furi ran her hand over the fabric. The blue pattern had faded somewhat, but the feel of it was still familiar.

'I learned to walk by pulling myself up from this armrest,' Furi said, breaking the silence.

Yeeran watched her thoughtfully but didn't reply. So Furi continued, 'There's a stain on the back of this cushion from where I spilled pomegranate juice across the fabric. I tried to turn it over to hide it, but when I looked at the underside, I found that my brother had hidden a coffee stain beneath. We argued which side was worse.'

Furi shifted to point out the stain. 'I won. See here? That's the remnants of his coffee, which he was chastised for. I only found out many years later that Mother had known all about the pomegranate juice and spared me the punishment.'

Vyce had not been a loving mother, but she had loved Furi in her own way.

'She was a very great woman, your mother,' Yeeran said gravely.

'Yes, she was,' Furi replied.

What does it feel like to not grieve? She couldn't remember anymore.

'We met with Hosta,' Yeeran said after a time.

'I gathered,' Furi said.

'They said the group of Lightless is being run by someone called the "Authority". Hosta suggested Lettle's death isn't their true aim, that they seek to overthrow the government entirely.'

'I had the same thought,' Furi said. 'But you should have waited for me before going to Hosta.'

Yeeran's lips drew thin. 'You were the one who left the war room, Furi. You knew what we intended to do.'

'I was vexed with you,' Furi admitted. 'You made it seem like I wasn't taking the assassination attempts seriously.'

'Were you?' Yeeran countered. Her questioning stoked the flames of Furi's anger and she bared her fangs at Yeeran.

'Yes, I was. A slight against anyone in the court is a slight against me,' Furi said. 'And I will not have you question my loyalties to this family. I am not one to go where the wind takes me.'

Yeeran's expression went entirely blank. 'What is that supposed to mean?'

'You know exactly what I mean, Yeeran.'

The chair beneath Yeeran screeched on the flagstones as she stood up. She was not prone to fits of anger, her rage was always tightly wound close to her chest. Even now, despite standing so abruptly, her voice was steady, seemingly calm. But Furi knew the torrent of fire that burned beneath her breath.

'My allegiance was to Salawa for years. Waning was not just my tribe, it was my life's blood, and yes, I have shed more blood than you can imagine in my tribe's name.' Yeeran stepped towards Furi, looking down at her with purple shimmering eyes. 'If I had stayed without warning Salawa of the fae's involvement I would have come to resent you. Do you understand that? I left so I could come back.'

Yeeran knelt in front of Furi and reached for her hand. Her fingers were cool against the flush of Furi's skin.

'Though Waning was once my life's blood, you have become my heart.'

'You truly mean that?' Furi whispered.

'Yes, I do,' Yeeran said, bringing Furi's hands to her mouth. 'You are my starlight.'

Furi smiled. She had said the same words to Yeeran all those months ago. If she followed the star gliders' light, they'd always bring her home.

Yeeran was her home.

She was about to say as much when the door opened and Rayan strode in. Something was wrong.

'What is it?' Furi said. She pulled her hand from Yeeran's and stood.

'The faeguard assigned to Lettle said they were dismissed by me earlier this morning. They received a message in the hands of a haba.'

The creatures were what she and Rayan used to send messages across Mosima. They responded to instructions given by the Jani dynasty blood.

'And you didn't send any message?' Furi said.

'No. Lettle left the palace alone.'

Yeeran swore.

'Clever sending a haba. They must have trained it, of course the guards would think the message was from you.' If Furi hadn't been so annoyed she'd be impressed.

Amnan, where have you gone?

Near the mango fields.

Can you check the Book Orchard and see if Lettle is there?

Furi felt a prickle of apprehension. 'I've asked Amnan to check the library. I'm sure she's just got carried away with work and is safe.'

Rayan gave Furi a grateful look.

'Yes, I'm sure she's fine,' Yeeran said, though her jaw was stiff.

The three of them were standing paralysed by the unknown when there was a knock at the door.

Rayan ran to answer it. 'Yes? Oh, Golan, Alder, hello. You haven't seen Lettle, have you?'

'No, that's what I was going to ask you. She was meant to come by to question Alder on her research but she didn't show,'

Golan said. His face was flushed as if he'd had a little too much to drink.

'No, she went to the Book Orchard—' Furi replied, but then Amnan's thoughts cut her off.

She's not here. Her scent is old, maybe three or four hours. And Furi, I can smell others too, and blood. Lots of blood.

'What did Amnan find?' Rayan asked, his eyes wild.

Furi found Yeeran's gaze and held it as she relayed what Amnan had told her.

Yeeran turned grey.

'Is it her blood?' she asked weakly.

'He doesn't know.' Furi went to Yeeran and slipped her hand around her waist. Some of Yeeran's body weight transferred to her.

'But there's no body, right?' Rayan asked, his voice rolled like thunder. A storm about to break.

'No,' Furi replied.

'Then we have no time to waste, I'm calling in the faeguard to search the area near the Book Orchard.'

'Wait,' Furi said before Rayan could leave the room. 'We don't want this news to get out. If we tell the faeguard then it'll spread through the city in hours. It could cause her abductors to retaliate or move location.'

'But we have to look for her.' Rayan's voice was strained.

'We will, but we should restrict it to the people in this room.'

Yeeran nodded her agreement. 'It makes sense, Rayan.'

'We should ask Sahar and Norey too,' Rayan said, still unhappy. 'But if we don't find her soon, I'm bringing in the full might of the faeguard.'

'Agreed,' Furi said.

Rayan's expression turned determined and he strode from the room.

Yeeran was about to do the same, but Furi caught her hand. She brought her fingers up to her lips and kissed them.

'We'll find her, Yeeran.'

Yeeran didn't smile, though she squeezed Furi's hand back before nodding. 'We'll find her,' she said grimly.

Neither of them acknowledged that she might not be alive when they did.

CHAPTER TWENTY-TWO

Lettle

Lettle was bored. The room she'd been locked in had quickly become stuffy, but she'd managed to jam open one of the windows. She leaned her shoulder against the windowsill and breathed in the air that flowed through the gap.

She'd contemplated attempting to break it and climb out, but the house backed onto the cliffs. And there'd be no surviving that fall.

I refuse to die today.

Through the crack in the window, she could see the entirety of Mosima. It looked like a picture-perfect paradise from this height.

But I'm still a prisoner whether I'm up here or down there.

She had started to hope again that one day she and Rayan would leave this place. With Alder's arrival and the Fates speaking to her once again it seemed that might come true. But since returning back to Mosima her dreams seemed more distant than before.

Especially now she was trapped in a house that no one would care to look in.

I will probably die up here. Once the Authority arrived and rooted out her lie, the ruse would be over.

The grimoire lay open on the bed. Thankfully Omur had not taken it away from her. Not that it had done anything more than distract her for a few hours.

She had started writing out similar words to see if she could translate their meaning. But she was not a linguist, and had soon got irritated.

Then she'd turned to her talismans. Casting the tokens to read the Fates had become such a familiar disappointment. But she tried, again and again.

She'd noticed that the edges of one of her tokens – the lungs – had been worn smooth from all the throwing. So she'd stopped in case she damaged the others too.

A whole night had passed and she dipped in and out of sleep. But when the fray heralded dawn she'd already been up for hours.

Though she'd found a flask of water by the chamber pot, she'd been offered no food. Lettle was used to hunger pains; even if she hadn't had to suffer in recent years, the memory of the feeling had never fully abated.

Where is this Authority? Let's get this over with.

She looked around the room once more for anything to eat, but there was little in here except a bed and a few personal items clearly belonging to Omur. She spotted a plant growing through the corner of the far wall where the foundations of the shack met soil. She went over to inspect it to see if it was edible.

The plants in Mosima were often different to those found in the Elven Lands. But she recognised this one, it was called a flutterlily because of its long petals that moved in the breeze.

Unfortunately for Lettle it wasn't edible – the leaves were bitter and would give you a sharp belly cramp. She knew from experience, having tried to eat it as a child when their food had run low.

Flutterlilies grew in abundance around their old home and 'flutter races' had provided Yeeran and Lettle with endless joy.

'See how the petals fold in just so? Then you can spin it. Look how far it flies,' Yeeran had said, her teenage face already fore-shadowing the striking features that adulthood would bring.

She bent a flower to Lettle's height. 'You try.'

Lettle's face pinched with concentration as she folded the purple petals inwards, just like Yeeran taught her. The first flower failed, but the second managed to catch the wind and spin even further than Yeeran's.

'Let's have a flutter race!' Yeeran said.

And just like that, hours of fun were had.

Now, Lettle plucked a few of the flowers and began to fold them, her fingers remembering the shape and creases to obtain optimum distance.

The trick was leaving one of the petals down so that it acted like a propeller. She'd been proud of her invention and Yeeran had spent years trying to work out her folds, to no avail.

A laugh escaped Lettle's lips as she plucked another flower.

Oh, Yeeran, how silly all our fights seem now.

Her fingers kept working as her mind wandered down the lanes of her memories.

Though Lettle was disappointed that Yeeran always put her career ahead of her, thinking back it was clear Yeeran had always been there when Lettle needed her most.

Not that Lettle would ever admit that. No, if she got out of here, she'd harbour her anger for a little longer, even if it had lost its edge.

She smiled as she walked to the window. She had made a handful of little folded flutterlilies. Peering through the gap, she pushed them through and watched as they rained down on Mosima.

They looked so beautiful against the warm fray-light but she didn't get a chance to appreciate the sight for the door to her prison opened.

Omur stood there, his eyes downcast. 'The Authority is unable to visit until tomorrow, maybe not until the day after.'

Lettle looked past him to see a bonded obeah leaving through the door. An open letter lay on the table.

Interesting, the Authority is not Lightless.

Lettle looked back to the obeah to try to ascertain any distinguishing features but it was already on its way out. She did, however, notice it had a white patch on its hindquarters and committed the detail to memory.

'If I'm to stay that long, do you have anything I can eat?' Lettle asked. If these were to be her last few hours on earth then she'd like to be full when she went.

Omur nodded. 'I was just making jollof rice. Would you like some of that?'

Lettle's eyes must have widened as Omur laughed and said, 'I take that as a yes.'

'Please,' she said.

'I'll bring it through.'

A few moments later Omur brought through the food. She was surprised to see that he carried a plate for himself too.

She sat on the floor and began to eat while he sat on the bed.

'You were hungry,' he stated after she had finished and he'd barely begun.

'I learned to eat fast when I was younger. It was the only way to ensure your food stayed yours.' She wiped her lips.

He looked thoughtful but didn't ask any more questions.

'Why do you want to kill me?' Lettle asked.

Omur shook his head, refusing to answer. His generosity didn't extend beyond the borders of her prison, it seemed.

'If I'm going to die anyway, you might as well tell me,' Lettle said.

Omur set down his fork and sighed. 'Some of the Lightless have been organising for a few years. It started off small – a book club if you'll believe it.' When he smiled, Lettle knew he'd been one of the founding members. 'Like I told you, books are hard to come by if you're not allowed access to the university library. So we met intermittently, swapping stories and novels that had been kept in the family.' He looked out the window, his gaze going distant.

'But the more we read, the more we questioned. And soon we realised that the villains in all our books sounded very similar to the Jani dynasty. For years we petitioned and debated with the court for better rights. But there always seemed something more important to contend with. At first it was the boundary opening. Then it was the blight. And then . . .' he looked to Lettle pointedly.

'Me and my sister,' she finished for him. Lettle had always hated the way she was treated in Mosima and she thought she understood where the anger came from – elves had been killing obeah for millennia. But this perspective, that her very presence directed the Jani dynasty's attention away from matters within Mosima, was new.

'And what about the Authority?' she probed.

'He is a relatively new figure within the organisation.' Omur's lip curled and Lettle realised he didn't really respect the Authority's authority.

'But he has supplies and contacts that have changed our fortunes,' Omur continued. 'He has promised a new government if you are killed.'

This was invaluable information if Lettle got out.

Lettle shivered. 'Why does killing me help you?'

'We cannot kill the king or queen or Mosima will fall. You, however, will destabilise the king and make sure we're seen seriously,' Omur said.

'But surely keeping me alive as ransom to meet your demands will be a better way of doing things?' Lettle said.

Omur frowned, thinking it through, then he shrugged. 'Maybe, but the Authority has the ear of my people, and this is what he wants.'

Lettle shook her head. 'You know none of this matters if war comes to the boundary's walls. Crescent are likely to retaliate for Komi's death.'

Omur tipped his head to the side. 'We care not for the elves. They cannot get in here, and we cannot get to them, not without the king and queen, who will soon be our pawns.'

Lettle started to laugh. She had thought this organisation sophisticated, people she could reason with, even support in the future. But now she realised how naïve they were.

'You are all being played for fools. This "Authority" cares nothing for the Lightless or he would not be putting such a target on your backs. You think once the population knows you've killed the king's consort things will get *better* for you?' Lettle snorted. 'No, you are just as dead as I am.'

Omur's face flushed and he stood. But he didn't contradict her.

'You know, don't you?' she continued. 'That your comrades have sold their lives away. Is that why you live up here?'

Again, Omur didn't answer, but the plate in his hand shook a little.

'Let me tell you, it doesn't matter how far in the sky you hide, when Rayan finds you, he'll make you pay.'

Omur picked up her empty plate and retreated from the room, Lettle's laughter echoing out after him.

Lettle woke up with a start. A whole night and day had passed and she was still a prisoner.

She looked to the slip of sky outside. It must have been past sunset and she had fallen asleep with her face in the grimoire. She'd left a smear of drool over the pages and she wiped at it with her sleeve.

A book that's a thousand years old and I go and get my saliva on it.

Then she registered what the sound had been that had woken her up.

There were voices in the room beyond.

The Authority was here.

Her heart started to thump against her ribs as she crept towards the door to listen in.

'The search party was too close to the trail so I had to wait until they passed,' the newcomer said. It was a voice Lettle thought she recognised but couldn't place.

'When will they give up looking?' Omur replied.

'When there's a body.'

Lettle's skin rippled with goosebumps.

'I had to partake in some of the efforts last night, just to put them off the scent,' the Authority continued.

'I understand.'

'And we also had to spend the better part of the day trying to convince everyone she does not have fae blood,' they said.

Omur chuckled. 'It was a clever ruse. She has a sharp mind.'

'Oh, yes?' the other said. 'Too sharp to slaughter?'

'That's not what I said.'

'You could have done it, you know. I wouldn't have minded, we could have dispelled the rumours she started after.'

Omur sounded like he had got up from his seat. 'Maybe, but I thought it best to wait for your word.'

'Oh yes, my word. You may have it. Kill her.'

Omur inhaled sharply. 'If you wish.'

'I do.'

Lettle backed away from the door as she heard Omur's footsteps approach it.

She looked behind her trying desperately to find somewhere to hide. But there was nowhere except the window, which would have been certain death.

Is it better to face the afterlife on your own terms? The thought struck her between the eyes and she lunged for the window with her fist held high, intending to break the glass.

But Omur caught her before she could reach it. She kicked and bucked in his grasp, trying everything in her power to get free.

'I will not let you kill me, I will not!' she screamed.

'I'm sorry, Lettle,' he whispered in her ear, and to his credit, he did sound sorry.

But she didn't care. She sank her teeth into Omur's forearm.

He cursed and relaxed his grip for a second.

A second too long.

Lettle lurched out of the bedroom and into the kitchen area beyond.

Then she stopped, her feet frozen in place as she came face to face with the Authority.

'Hello, Lettle,' Norey said.

PART THREE

❧✥

Afa's Grimoire

I once thought power was measurable, that it had limits. But the pages in your hands show you the extent of a human's power, and it is vast.

We are made of the essence of the earth. We are the bones and breath of a god. We do not deserve to cower or hide.

I have spent years reclaiming the lore of my forefathers stolen by the elves and fae.

The fae stole the language of rocks and made a crystal like no other. Fraedia, they call it, to mimic the rays of their god in their warrens beneath the earth.

The elves stole the language of the skies calling the moon to a day-time sky, eclipsing the sun so their divination was more potent.

I found the words they used and destroyed what was left of their textbooks and notes. The human magic is for us alone.

The elves speak of a prophecy:

Forever the war will rage, until united, the three shall die.
Humans made low, then fae made lower,
Then elves in ignorance, gone is their power,
Cursed to endure, cursed to survive.
All shall perish lest all three thrive.

But I asked myself, is it better to survive cursed or to die free?

Perhaps, reader, your answer was different to mine, and if so, I only ask for forgiveness.

What I did was for the sake of humanity. Remember that in the end.

CHAPTER TWENTY-THREE

Alder

Alder was getting to see more of Mosima than he had before. Though the search for Lettle was a serious one, he couldn't help but enjoy himself as he discovered new pockets of beauty in every corner.

Mosima was a big place to scour and the search party was moving through it in segments.

'Furi, you and Yeeran search east of the Book Orchard, Grandfather and Norey will search west. Golan, Alder, start moving south towards the inner city. I'll do another sweep of the library and see if Ajax can pick up her scent. Look in abandoned houses, forests, gardens. Knock on doors—'

'Why should we say we're knocking?' Alder asked. All eyes turned to him and he immediately regretted speaking. He was the odd one out from the group – the only one who wasn't family or a close friend to Lettle.

'Tell them you're looking for a lost kid. If they look suspicious, report back to us,' Furi grunted.

Alder nodded, biting his cheek before he asked more questions that set the fae looking at him again.

'We'll meet back in this orchard in six hours, unless you learn something before then,' Rayan continued.

The group started to move out but Alder lingered next to Rayan.

He felt more comfortable around the king than the rest of the fae. Perhaps because he'd been raised an elf.

Rayan looked sallow, the skin under his eyes gathering shadows. Though Alder had no cause to feel sympathy towards the king – he was after all keeping him prisoner – Alder couldn't help but empathise. Rayan had been kind, if not as friendly as Golan, and it was strange not to see him smiling.

Alder stepped towards him with an urge to comfort him. 'Once, one of my companions, Damal, went missing,' Alder said to Rayan. The king looked up as Alder spoke, not realising he was still standing beside him.

'I feared the worst. We were on the southern isles where the tide is quick, and the native animals quicker. The search party lasted five days but we found no trace of Damal. The likelihood of finding her alive was dwindling by the day. Then one morning, a week after she went missing, she was sighted. She'd got stuck on a cliffside and required rescuing, but otherwise Damal was completely hale'

'She was truly unharmed?' Rayan asked.

'Yes, she'd survived without food or shelter for longer than seemed possible. What I'm saying is, do not underestimate Lettle's will to live. And do not give up hope,' Alder said.

'But Damal wasn't being targeted by people who wanted to kill her,' Rayan said bleakly.

Alder dipped his head, conceding to the facts. 'No, but Lettle is hardy, like a winter cactus, she can weather anything. Spikey too.'

Rayan tried to smile but failed. Though he did stand a little straighter than he had a few moments ago. As if the invisible ache in his chest had eased somewhat.

'Thank you for telling me that story, Alder. I know Lettle will fight with everything she has.' Rayan rested his hand on Alder's shoulder. 'And thank you for joining the search. I know you didn't quite expect your life to take this turn, willingly or not.'

Alder laughed ruefully. 'No, a few days ago I didn't know the fae existed.'

'Once we find Lettle I'll discuss your release with Furi. There's no reason to keep you trapped down here longer than necessary. The curse is for the fae alone . . . and the people who love them.' Rayan's voice petered off into a rasp. Then he nodded to Golan once before heading off towards his assigned search area.

Alder watched him go, his obeah joining him. They walked in sync, their footfalls heavy with worry.

When Alder turned to join Golan, he found the fae watching him curiously.

'That was well done, Alder,' he said. 'Few can talk to the king so candidly.'

Alder shrugged. 'He's not my king.'

'Indeed, he is not.'

They spent the whole night and the following day moving south systematically knocking on doors and checking empty houses. But they found nothing amiss.

Every few hours they would return to the orchard to discuss their progress. Each time Rayan and Yeeran would appear more haggard and worried than before.

Twenty-four hours after they had first started searching for Lettle, Golan and Alder returned to the meeting point. They were the first to return.

'Rayan will want to call in the faeguard. It's been too long and we've found no trace of her,' Golan said, the bags under his eyes heavy with worry.

Alder nodded, and as he did so his stomach growled. They had missed yet another meal. He reached up into the bough of the nearest tree and plucked an apple. Its skin was a glossy golden colour, like fresh honey, and the flesh proved just as saccharine.

'These apples are delicious, have you tried one? I don't think I've ever eaten a sweeter fruit,' Alder said. He picked one for Golan and handed it to him. 'Here.'

Golan's smile was a little strained but he took the fruit from his outstretched hand and bit into it. Alder had noticed his concern for Lettle had suppressed his appetite.

Golan's wan skin turned a little warmer as he chewed on the apple. 'It's good.' Abruptly his expression changed and he started to cough.

Alder's blood ran cold and he was plunged into the freezing water of a memory.

He and Livy had stumbled across the lake late in the day. They had sneaked away from the Nomads just before dinner time to go for a swim.

'Race you to the shore,' she chimed. Her voice was like music, her auburn hair trailing behind her like a symphony on the breeze.

Alder let her win. Partly because he knew she'd be pleased and partly because he liked the view from behind. Livy was Alder's first love.

At twenty-five he thought she was to be his only love, and maybe that would have been the case if she hadn't died that day.

It wasn't the water that took her, though cold and rough that it was. It was the berries they had found by the shore.

'These are so tasty, try some.' She plucked some of the juicier berries and placed them on his tongue.

'Delicious,' he agreed. Juice ran down his chin and she leaned forward, darting her tongue out to lick it off. The smile she gave him was salacious.

He laughed and pulled her close. Her bare skin was still wet from the lake water and she shivered.

'Let me get the towels,' he said.

She pouted but didn't object, so he knew she must have been very cold indeed.

He didn't have to go far and when he returned, he was surprised to see she had given up picking berries already and was lying on the ground.

'That was a small harvest,' he said as he threw her a towel. It was then that he heard a rasping, squeaking noise, and realised it was coming from her.

She was choking.

'Livy!'

Her lips had turned blue, her eyelids were fluttering open and shut.

Alder threw the rest of their belongings to the ground and went to her.

In his panic he began to shout for help, before he remembered what to do.

But by the time he started thumping her back it was too late. She had already died.

Of all the memories Alder had accrued since being with the Nomads, this was by far the worst. If only it too had been lost to him.

And here was Golan choking. This time Alder would not react slowly. He ran to the man's side and began to beat his back.

'Breathe, Golan. Breathe.'

'I am breathing!' Golan managed to get out, ducking from Alder's next onslaught of blows. Alder stopped and Golan moved out of reach of his arm.

It seemed Alder might be the one not breathing. He let out a shaky breath.

'I thought you were choking,' Alder said, his eyes wide and wild.

'I did, but just for a second.'

'I thought you were choking,' Alder repeated. His memories still haunting his mind.

Golan took a hesitant step towards Alder. 'I'm fine, see?' He reached out a hand and laid it on Alder's forearm.

Alder's skin warmed where Golan touched it and he felt the chill of Livy's ghost abate somewhat.

'I'm sorry,' Alder said after a few moments. 'A . . . friend of mine died choking many years ago. I-I—'

'It's all right, you don't need to say anything more.' Golan's gentleness brought tears to Alder's eyes and he dashed them away with the heel of his hand.

At some point during the excitement they had both dropped their apples. Golan noticed him looking at the cores on the ground and reached up to the bough to pick them another.

'Oh,' Golan let out a startled sound. 'Hello there.'

A couple of young obeah were lounging in the tree above. Alder had seen them earlier but hadn't thought to remark on it.

'It's rare to see such young ones around people. They tend to prefer each other's company until the moment they bond,' Golan said, smiling up at them.

'Really? I see them all the time.'

Golan's eyebrows shot up as one jumped down and trotted over to Alder.

He held out his hand and the obeah sniffed it before rubbing against his leg. 'I've always had a way with obeah. Ever since the Nomads found me living with them. I think they sense my kinship.' The second obeah was shyer than the first, and much younger. But after some coaxing it too joined Alder.

'Remarkable,' Golan breathed.

There was a sound in the distance and the two obeah's ears pinned to the backs of their heads. The sound got louder and then they bolted.

'Well, it was nice while it lasted. Shall we go see what the commotion is?' Golan said before leading the way back to the road.

Yeeran was running towards them, her hand out as she cried, 'I found something.'

She held up a purple flower.

'What is it?' Golan asked.

'A flutterlily.' Yeeran's smile was triumphant. 'When we were younger I made up this game called flutter races. We had no money for toys and it would distract Lettle from her hunger.'

Alder was surprised to learn that the sisters had been through such hardship.

'You see the way it's folded, that's definitely Lettle. I've found three so far, all north of here.'

It wasn't long before Rayan and Furi joined them at the meeting point.

'Where are Sahar and Norey?' Yeeran asked, impatient to direct everyone towards the site where she'd found the flowers.

'I saw them earlier. They hadn't finished their search area, so are going to continue into the night,' Rayan said. 'Take us to where you found the flutterlilies.'

Golan and Alder jogged beside Rayan, Yeeran and Furi who had mounted their obeah. Thankfully the spot wasn't far from the apple orchard as another day gone without a full night's rest had taken its toll on Alder's stamina.

'There's more over here!' Yeeran shouted, stooping down to pick up a purple flower.

Soon all the group were looking. They found twenty all told.

'She must have passed through here,' Rayan said.

'Yes,' Yeeran nodded.

Alder threw one of the flowers into the air to get a sense of the distance it could travel. 'But you see the way the flutterlily moves laterally? It would be odd for her to have thrown these in this formation unless she was zig-zagging through the terrain.'

Golan frowned but nodded. 'You're right. And I guess it wouldn't make sense if she just made them and dropped them on the route as they'd be in a clearer formation.'

Yeeran frowned. 'But this must be Lettle, there's no one else who would know of this game.'

Alder looked up. 'I think she must be throwing them from a height.'

Yeeran shook her head. 'How? They can't have camped out on the ceiling.'

Golan looked skywards. 'No, but the southern plains are not far from here.'

'Those routes have been closed since your accident,' Furi said to Golan quietly.

'Exactly. It would be the perfect place to hide someone,' Golan said.

'What are the southern plains?' Yeeran asked.

'A rocky outcrop halfway up the cavern's walls. It is a haven for the obeah and was often used as pilgrimage for those wanting to bond to one. It's a difficult and risky hike.'

'And you think they took Lettle up there?' Yeeran said softly.

'Potentially,' Furi replied.

'Well then, let's go,' Yeeran said.

'I . . . I don't know the trail,' Furi admitted.

Golan stiffened beside Alder, but he didn't speak.

Not knowing the way didn't seem to faze Yeeran as she and Rayan had made up their minds. They began to walk determinedly to the boundary.

'You're going the wrong way,' Golan said tiredly.

Furi looked to him. 'Would you be able to guide us? I know that is asking a lot.'

From the shadow that crossed Golan's features, Alder thought that perhaps it would require too much of his new friend. Alder stepped closer to Golan, letting him know that he had support if he needed it.

After a quiet sigh, Golan said, 'If it means we get Lettle back, then I will show you the way.'

Getting Lettle back meant Alder would be one step closer to figuring out what was happening to him.

'I'll come with you,' Alder said softly enough for only Golan to hear. The fae gave him a grateful smile and it sent a thrill into the depth of Alder's stomach.

The journey up the cavern was a treacherous one. But Alder was used to climbing. Unlike the others, he walked without shoes, preferring the grip that his leather-like soles gave him.

Halfway up they paused on one of the wider ledges.

'You look happy up here,' Golan said to Alder. 'More free.'

Alder laughed. 'There is nothing better than feeling the earth beneath my feet.'

Golan was out of breath, and sweat coated his top lip, smearing some of the beard hair he'd drawn there. Like many of the elves that Alder knew, Golan presented his gender without the need for hormone tinctures. The precision with which his beard had been drawn on looked even more alluring now it was smudged with perspiration. But Golan hadn't asked for help once and kept a steady pace. It couldn't be easy for him, especially with Yeeran and Rayan at his back.

They had both been quiet since they had started climbing, each holding a silent tension that made Alder think they were getting battle-ready. Their obeah had joined them and were prancing about on the trail in precarious positions that only someone like Alder would attempt.

Furi stood a little further away, her gaze cast down on the city below.

'We should continue on,' Golan said. But Alder could see he was still fatigued.

'Yes, before we lose more of the day,' Yeeran said.

'I could do with a couple minutes more rest,' Alder said.

Yeeran looked like she was going to respond, her mouth opening and closing with impatience. But then she seemed to notice how tired Golan was and decided against it.

Good, no one should rush into a battle.

Not that Alder had ever been in a battle in his life – that he could remember anyway. Though he was all sinew and muscle it was because the land had made him that way. Fights in the Nomads were rare and often subdued with a good meal of redred stew.

Alder's mouth salivated as he thought of his favourite dish. The beans flavoured with palm oil and tomatoes were a delicacy he missed.

Three more days, then he would be reunited with the Nomads. Three more days to get answers.

'The next part is the steepest bit,' Golan said quietly, cutting through Alder's thoughts. 'It was where I fell, last time.'

Golan's jaw quivered ever so slightly as he added, 'I'm not sure I can do it.' His words were for Alder alone.

Alder stepped even closer to Golan. 'The trick is keeping your core centre as close to the ground as possible.' He touched Golan's lower back and eased him into the right position. 'Keep your knees loose.'

'My artificial leg—' Golan began to say, his eyes widening in panic.

'Will be fine.' Alder kept his voice firm and calm. 'The hinge on your knee moves with your thigh, so the principle still applies. I will walk on your right side, by the ledge. I'll keep you safe.' He slipped his hand in Golan's.

The fae's mouth parted at the touch and he looked like he was going to say something before abandoning the thought and simply nodding his thanks.

Alder raised his voice and said to the others, 'I'm ready, let's move on.'

The rest of the journey up the cavern wall was done in silence. Everyone was too preoccupied with watching their footfalls.

All of a sudden Golan's false leg slipped out from under him and he wavered a step ahead of Alder.

Alder caught him just before he fell.

'I have you,' he said gently.

Golan's blue eyes were full of fear. His lips trembled and Alder had the urge to run his thumb over the swell of the soft skin.

'I have you,' Alder repeated, drawing him close until both feet were firmly planted back on the ground.

Golan let out a slow breath, his hands gripping Alder's forearms so tightly it almost hurt.

'Thank you,' Golan said, and Alder felt the depth of his gratitude.

Golan moved more slowly after that, but it wasn't long before they reached the plains.

Alder wasn't sure what he expected, but a waterfall that fed into a turquoise lagoon was not it.

Fruit trees of all kinds were growing wild and free in the fertile soil provided by the soft rock of the cavern and the lagoon. Young obeah pranced from tree to tree, casting dark shadows on the wildflowers that sprouted from the ground.

Even the frost that had harmed the leaves of the land had barely affected the foliage here, though Alder could tell they weren't in full bloom.

At the far end of the plains was a house.

'That wasn't there before,' Golan said carefully.

Rayan and Furi had already begun stalking towards it. Yeeran's hands were poised above her drum, whereas Rayan's were held aloft. Alder had learned that Rayan didn't need a drum to access his magic like Yeeran did.

But it was Furi who raced forward on her obeah and broke down the door. Rayan and Yeeran followed her into the house.

A scream split the air, sending the young obeah in the clearing scattering.

Golan and Alder exchanged a glance before joining the others inside.

CHAPTER TWENTY-FOUR

Lettle

'It was *you?*' Lettle said to Norey. 'All this time, it was you?'

Norey smiled. 'I have been involved in this organisation for some time. Years before you arrived, Lettle.'

'But you are Sahar's partner.'

'And best placed to see how poorly equipped the Jani dynasty is at ruling the fae,' Norey said.

Omur came up behind Lettle and she sprang forward away from his grasp. She reached the door before Norey could get up to stop her.

The light breeze was a welcome relief, even if she knew it wouldn't last long. She couldn't outrun Omur.

She dashed towards the trail that led down into the belly of Mosima, but as she got to the edge Omur pulled her back.

'Please, Lettle, don't make this harder than it is,' Omur said. His face was flushed, his breath coming fast.

'What? I should just roll over and let you slit my throat?' she growled.

'Peace, Lettle,' Norey said, sauntering over. 'There is no use struggling, there is no one who will come save you up here.'

But instead of making her despair, Norey's words had ignited something in her.

She didn't need anyone to save her. She could save herself, she just had to be smart about it.

'That's it, let Omur lead you back inside. I'd rather not soil the plants out here with your blood,' Norey said.

Lettle relaxed her hands by her sides and Omur led her by the elbow of her weakened arm. It gave her full mobility in her right hand, not that she was sure what she was going to do with it.

'Omur, you don't have to do this,' Lettle said quietly.

'I have no choice, Lettle, I have nothing left to live for,' Omur replied. She looked up at his face and it was fixed in a determined expression.

'You are a pawn and you know it,' she said.

Omur didn't reply.

As they were nearing the house again Lettle stumbled.

'Are you hurt?' Omur asked almost as a reflex.

Lettle laughed. 'You're about to kill me and you ask if I hurt myself from falling?'

Omur's lips thinned and he looked away. In that moment she slipped the rock she had lunged for under her sleeve. Whether she'd have an opportunity to use it before she was murdered was yet to be determined.

Norey had returned to his seat in the kitchen, his eyes glittering as Omur brought her forward.

Omur pulled out a blade from his waist and turned to press it against Lettle's neck.

'Wait,' Lettle said, panic rising from her stomach. This was not how it was supposed to go. She had to keep them talking. 'Before you kill me, can you tell me why you want me dead?'

Norey sighed before nodding to Omur who dropped the blade to his side. 'That's a complicated answer, Lettle.'

'Good job we've got time,' she replied.

Norey laughed. 'Do we?'

'Yes,' she replied steadily.

I will not die today. The words had become her daily mantra.

She shifted the rock from her sleeve to her hand.

'Things need to change,' Norey said simply. The answer

dumbfounded Lettle and she found herself delaying her plan to engage with him.

'But death never leads to change, just look at the Forever War.'

'No, not death, but you are just the pebble, Lettle. It is the ripples upon the water that we seek.'

She scoffed. 'Furi is going to be devastated to learn of your treachery. She sees you as family.'

'What I do, I do for her family.'

Lettle shook her head, she'd heard enough of his lies. She lunged forward bringing the rock down on Norey's head.

His eyes widened in shock as blood began to dye his yellow hair red and he slumped backwards.

Lettle had expected Omur to have grabbed her by now, but when she turned around, he stood rooted to the ground, his eyes glued to Norey's as blood trickled to the floor.

'He's not dead,' Lettle said. 'But he will be soon.'

Her voice snapped Omur from his daze, but he still stood paralysed.

'If you want to save him, you need to take him to a healer, now,' Lettle continued. She stood with her back to the door, ready to flee. Omur was still armed, and though the rock had worked on Norey, she doubted she could get away with it twice since Omur knew what was coming.

Norey began to fit, his chest constricting as more and more blood gushed from the wound.

Omur's mouth opened and closed, but no sound came out.

He is letting him die.

Norey's breath hissed out in the silence, and then he was still.

Lettle had become a murderer once again. But this time, she felt no guilt.

She was about to turn and leave when the front door opened with a bang.

An ear-splitting scream cut through the room. A scream Lettle recognised.

Furi.

The queen stood in the doorway, framed by the dimming embers of the fray-light, it was as if fire lit her silhouette. Lettle didn't need to check magesight to confirm she wielded threads of golden magic at her side.

Furi's mouth hung open in horror as she recognised Norey's body.

But then Rayan stepped into the space beside her and all of Lettle's focus turned to him. He took in the room regimentally, noting the exits, weapons and assailants.

His jaw was set in a deadly expression that, despite Lettle's circumstances, still gave her quite a thrill.

Rayan swept past Furi, his hands held out as he wove a binding around Omur.

'Are there more of them?' he asked Lettle and she shook her head.

Only then did he come to her, sweeping her off the ground in a crushing embrace. She buried her head into the crook of his neck and inhaled his familiar scent: sage and bergamot.

'I'm so glad you're OK,' Rayan said. His voice was muffled against her hair but she heard the hitch in it.

'I am,' Lettle said, holding onto him tighter.

'Tell me this is some mistake,' Furi said behind them.

Rayan set Lettle back on the ground.

'No mistake, Furi, he just ordered Omur to kill me,' Lettle said.

Omur's gaze snapped up at being addressed, only just registering what was happening.

Someone hesitated on the threshold to the room, Lettle recognised the shape of their shadow before they stepped into the light.

Yeeran crossed the room to Lettle.

'Are you hurt?' Yeeran asked. She looked hesitant, her eyes downcast.

Lettle slipped her hand out of Rayan's grasp and stepped towards Yeeran.

'I'm fine, sister.' Then she embraced her. For despite the shards of friction between them, this was a moment of reconciliation, even if the embrace hurt a little.

Yeeran's muscular build softened as she wrapped her arms around Lettle. It was enough for Lettle to know how much she appreciated the touch.

As they separated, Lettle realised she still held the bloodied rock in her hand. She dropped it and a thud resonated across the room.

Furi's eyes narrowed on her murder weapon. 'You killed him?'

Lettle looked to Omur before replying. 'I did.'

Furi shook her head, tears dashing across her face. 'No, no, no, no. You must have misunderstood, Norey wouldn't be part of this.'

'He was at the very heart of the organisation,' Lettle said as gently as she could. She knew her words would hurt Furi.

'I don't believe it.' Furi shook her head once more.

'Lettle speaks the truth.' Omur spoke for the first time. 'Like me, Norey's mission here was to kill Lettle.'

Furi's expression turned haggard, as if the truth had stripped her of all vibrancy.

'What is your name?'

'Omur O'Lightless, my queen.'

Furi snorted. 'It truly is a mockery to be called queen in the house of a traitor. Why do you seek to bring down the Jani dynasty?'

'Something needs to change,' Omur said simply.

The answer did not satisfy the queen and her magic whipped around his throat.

Lettle stepped forward. Omur hadn't been exactly *kind* to her but he had fed her when he could have left her to starve.

'He's not the one making the orders, he was only the one carrying them out,' Lettle said.

Furi twisted her hands, the threads around Omur tightened and he began to choke.

'She's going to kill him,' Lettle whispered in horror.

He would have been complicit in your murder, her conscience said.

And yet, she couldn't let Furi break the most sacred rule in Mosima, all because of her.

'Furi, stop,' Rayan said.

Furi acted like she hadn't heard him and Lettle cast a pleading glance Yeeran's way.

Her sister nodded sharply and went over to Furi. As soon as Yeeran stepped into the queen's eyeline her entire demeanour changed. Gone was the hardened royal, in her place stood a woman in pain.

Furi's face crumpled and the magic around Omur's neck released. Yeeran folded her into her arms and led her outside, murmuring gently in her ear.

When they were gone Omur said quietly, 'Thank you, Lettle. You didn't have to speak up for me.'

'No, I didn't. You will serve your penance, not at the hands of vengeance but justice,' Lettle said.

It was then that Lettle noticed Golan and Alder standing in the glade beyond the open door.

Golan gave her a small wave that was full of relief and love. Alder nodded in her direction. She noted how closely he stood to Golan, their hands brushing against each other's.

'Perhaps we should return to the palace and continue our interrogation there. I'm sure you're eager to get back,' Rayan said. His hand went to her left shoulder and soothed the aching muscles there.

He always knew what she needed. She gave him a grateful smile and leaned into him.

'A full meal and a familiar bed sounds like the perfect evening.'

Alder cleared his throat and everyone looked to him. 'The trail is too dangerous to walk at night, I recommend we wait until dawn.'

His gaze flickered to Golan, and Lettle wondered if his concern was mainly for him.

Lettle looked at Norey's body and felt her stomach churn with the realisation that she had taken another life.

At least it wasn't Rayan's. The thought was bleak.

'I need to get out of here,' she said to Rayan before striding out into the darkening night.

Yeeran and Furi stood at the cliffside of the plains talking quietly to each other. Lettle gave them their privacy and lingered by the lagoon.

'The way you dealt justice, Lettle, you were born to be royalty,' Golan said behind her.

She turned to him. 'I don't think Omur really wanted to kill me,' Lettle admitted.

'Oh? Was that not a dagger in his hand?'

'Yes,' she said, turning her gaze back to the lagoon. 'But he was just doing what Norey told him to. And Norey believed my death would have brought change.'

'The only thing your death would have brought is vengeance upon the Lightless. This group is a small percentage of the people I know and love—'

'I went to the Honeypot Tavern, I saw how angry the Lightless are. They may not all be actively involved in the plot to kill me, but they all feel the bloodlust.'

Golan shook his head. 'Only because of people like Norey, who made it seem like your death was the only solution.'

Maybe it is. Maybe vengeance would have come first, but the ripple of change would have happened later.

'Things can't go on like this, Golan. I didn't see it before, but I do now. Furi and Rayan are ignoring the plight of those not faebound. I want to work with the Lightless to make changes in Mosima.'

Golan looked out across the water, contemplating. Then he let out a small laugh. 'Few would be rescued from captivity and want to parle with their capturers, Lettle.'

Lettle lowered herself to the rocks by the water's edge and washed the blood off her hands. 'I had a lot of time to think and I think a partnership with the court and the Lightless is the only way things will improve. Will you help me lead it?'

Golan joined her by the lagoon, removing his metal leg before dipping his own toes in the cool water.

'I wasn't born to be a leader, Lettle.'

'Exactly, that's what makes you the perfect candidate. It has to be you, Golan, I can't do it alone. You have both the respect of those faebound *and* you are Lightless.'

He looked unconvinced.

Lettle released a slow breath and said quietly, 'I want to call it the "Free the Light Initiative".'

Golan scrutinised her, his blue eyes narrowing. 'Clever. You're taking the very phrase they are using to stoke the flames of rebellion to further your cause. You're stripping the words of power.'

Lettle shook her head. 'No, I'm *giving* them power. For the first time the Lightless will be a part of the court. We can change it all, Golan.'

His gaze grew wistful and she knew she had him. 'Tell me you'll do it.'

'I'll do it,' he said with a shy smile but when he turned to her, his expression grew more serious. 'Let's change the world.'

'Let's change the world.'

Lettle felt something loosen in her mind. Like a thread unwinding, tugging her down a path she had not considered before.

Politics.

Though the thought scared her, it excited her too. Change didn't just have to come from prophecy, she could still forge her own path in the present.

Alder hovered a few paces away. Lettle dipped her head in his direction. 'New bodyguard, I see?'

Golan didn't say anything for some time, but his smile was shy.

Lettle's hand trailed in the water, her fingers skittering along lily pads as she waited for him to speak.

'He's different,' were the two words Golan settled on.

Lettle gave him a frank look that said, 'You've got to give me more than that.'

'I don't know, he's protective, kind. But also there's a hardness to him—'

'I bet.'

Golan didn't laugh and his gaze turned distant. 'Like he's seen the entirety of the world and understands his place in it. He has *endured.*'

Lettle wasn't sure what Golan meant, but she let him daydream for a moment before asking, 'Have you learned anything about him that could help me figure out Afa's grimoire?'

Golan shook his head. 'No. He knows nothing of the fae, and even less about humans.'

Lettle threw a pebble into the lagoon, scaring some of the birds who were drinking at the far end.

'The Fates said he was important. So, he must be.'

Golan looked sceptical but was clever enough not to voice his thoughts in front of her.

'We'll take it in turns to keep watch tonight in case any more traitors show up. Someone will also have to keep an eye on the prisoners,' Yeeran said behind them. She was holding Furi's hand tightly in her grip while a family of star gliders spun around them.

Lettle stood up from the lagoon and retied her sandals. She knew it was the right thing to stay, but she had been looking forward to sleeping in her own bed that night.

'I'll go see what Omur has left for us to eat,' she said.

When she entered the shack again, Rayan was sitting opposite Omur at the table.

Norey's body had been moved to the back room and the blood cleaned up.

Both of them were silent and the air was charged with a tension that left her skin prickling. A quick look into magesight confirmed that Rayan still held the threads that bound Omur's hands.

'The plan is to wait for dawn before we go back down,' Lettle informed him.

'All right.' His voice was cold as he stared down Omur.

Lettle came up behind him and wrapped her hands around his shoulders.

'He could have hurt me, Rayan, but he chose not to. He gave me food and a blanket when others would not have been so kind.'

Her words were like hot water over ice and she felt his muscles relax.

'He didn't hurt me,' she said again. He pulled her onto his lap, still not taking his eyes off Omur as he held her against his chest.

'I was so worried.' His voice rumbled against her neck. 'I couldn't imagine losing you. Life would have no meaning without you, Lettle.'

'I know.'

She also knew that he would never have to live in a world without her, for he would die first. By her hands. She squeezed him a little tighter, her eyes growing hot.

'Thank you for fighting back, for surviving,' he said.

'I will always fight for you,' she said, knowing he would never truly understand her meaning.

He pushed her to arm's length. 'Are you sure you're all right?'

'I'm fine. But I am a bit hungry. Do you remember when we were travelling in the Wasted Marshes and you made that purple potato stew?'

He smiled. 'Yes, you told me it was the most disgusting thing you'd ever eaten.'

Lettle's eyes twinkled. 'I lied.'

He laughed. 'I figured after you filled up your bowl for the third time.'

'There are some growing near the lagoon. Do you think you could make it again?'

Rayan nodded. He was probably aware that it was a distraction, but Furi and Rayan were too emotionally invested to be trusted with Omur's welfare.

'We can lock Omur in the bedroom. There's no escaping there, I tried many times.'

Rayan's smile slipped, but he agreed and let her move the older man into the back room.

Norey's body was covered with a blanket in the corner. Lettle's eyes skittered over it.

'Thank you, Lettle,' Omur said quietly.

'Don't thank me yet, we're all stuck up here for the next twelve hours so just hope that the fray warms before Furi or Rayan lose their temper,' she said before closing the door.

This time when it locked, she was the one holding the key.

After the fray dimmed its light for the evening, the group bedded down for the night. There wasn't much room in the small kitchen, so they all decided to sleep outside.

Yeeran led the decision and Lettle wondered if it was because she sensed Lettle's trepidation about spending another minute under the roof that had been her prison for two days.

They lit no fire, the temperature was mild, like it always was in Mosima. And they had no need for light as the royals attracted the glowing orbs of star gliders. Even here the little flying lizards had found them.

Rayan was snoring softly beside Lettle. Though the meadow wasn't entirely comfortable, his shoulder was better than any bed.

But she wasn't tired.

She sat up and looked around. The rest of the group were asleep, except Yeeran who was taking first watch.

Lettle untangled herself from Rayan's arms and padded over to Yeeran. Pila was dozing by her feet and looked up as Lettle sat down, then settled back to sleep again.

'I wish I could sleep that easily,' Lettle said quietly.

Yeeran smiled fondly and rubbed the underside of Pila's chin. 'She can sleep anywhere, any time.'

'Do they dream? Or have nightmares?'

Yeeran's brows knotted together. 'I'm not sure. I'll ask her.'

There was a silence as Yeeran spoke to Pila down their connection.

Yeeran cocked her head. 'She says yes, she dreams of her time before she was Pila.'

'What does that mean?'

'I'm not sure, she told me to leave her alone now.' Yeeran laughed, and Lettle was sure that she was missing some part of a joke.

The silence was interrupted with the soft sounds of sleep.

'How did you know where to find me?' Lettle asked, disturbing the babbling of slumber.

Yeeran reached into her pocket and pulled out one of the flutter-lilies Lettle had been throwing out the window.

'Only you could fold them to travel as far as they did,' Yeeran said.

Lettle laughed. 'Yes, you hated that I always beat you. But it's all in that first fold.'

'Are you finally going to show me how you do it?' Yeeran asked, her eyes twinkling.

Lettle reached for the flower and carefully unfolded each petal.

'See, this petal here, that one should be pointed, I use it as a little propeller.'

Yeeran watched before carefully recreating it at Lettle's direction. Then she launched the flutterlily into the air, so it floated upwards and over the cliff to the city of Mosima below.

'Twenty years and I finally have the secret. I knew I'd get it out of you eventually,' Yeeran said beaming.

Lettle smiled back and for a brief moment she felt seven years old again. The joy of besting her sister the sweetest feeling in the world, sweet enough to numb the feelings of the gnawing hunger in her belly.

'Thank you for rescuing me,' Lettle said softly.

'You know I'll always come for you, sister,' Yeeran said, and Lettle nodded.

'Yes, I do. I realised you might not always be around when I want you, but you are when I need you.'

Yeeran shook her head. 'Not always, I failed you with Father.'

Lettle shut her eyes as she felt her blood surge in her veins as her heart began to beat faster and faster.

She didn't want to talk about Father. Though she had lanced some of the grief once she had confessed to his death, the wound still bled.

'I wish you had told me what was happening,' Yeeran continued. 'I would have—'

'What, Yeeran? You would have stopped me from killing him?' Hot tears fell down Lettle's cheeks.

'No, that's not what I said.'

'It doesn't matter, what is done is done. And though I wanted you there, Yeeran, I didn't need you then either. I dealt with the situation as best I could. Like I did today.'

Yeeran reached out and squeezed Lettle's hand. 'It was mercy. Father was a proud man, he wouldn't have wanted to live like that.'

Lettle felt the wound of grief close a little more at Yeeran's words.

She didn't trust herself to speak again so instead she laid her head on the soft grass. With her older sister watching on, sleep soon found her.

CHAPTER TWENTY-FIVE

Yeeran

When Yeeran's watch was over, she woke Rayan and he took over.

Furi looked to be asleep by the lagoon, a little way away from the main group. But when Yeeran returned to her she saw that her eyes were open, glittering with star glider light.

'Father will be devastated,' she said quietly as Yeeran laid down and pulled Furi towards her chest.

'You need to try and sleep,' Yeeran said.

Furi sat up and tucked her knees against her chin. 'I can't stop thinking about what he will say. I'm not sure what will hurt more, Norey's betrayal or his death.'

Despite Yeeran's exhaustion, she sat up and placed a soothing hand on Furi's back. 'It's a problem for tomorrow. Now you should sleep or it'll make the next day infinitely harder.'

'I don't want to sleep,' Furi snapped back, then she let out a breath. 'Sorry, I'm just finding it hard. He was like family.'

But not family enough to be allowed into the fae court.

Yeeran didn't voice her thoughts to anyone but herself. Though what Norey had done was a betrayal of the deepest kind, Yeeran had been starting to notice how different life was for the Lightless in Mosima. Even she seemed to have more rights.

'Would you like something to eat or drink? I can check the kitchen for more food?' Yeeran asked.

Furi shook her head, her gaze going to the lagoon. 'I think I'd like to go for a swim.'

Oh, how desperately Yeeran wanted to sleep.

'Swim?'

'Yes.' Furi stood and began to remove her clothing. First she removed her boots before slipping out of her trousers and blouse. The lace of her undergarments were woven so finely that they hid nothing beneath. They were shed a moment later. Finally, she released the clip that kept her curls tucked into her neck, and her golden hair fell down her back following the curvature of her spine.

Star gliders spun around her, lighting her bronze skin a golden umber.

'Are you coming?' she said with a small smile.

All of a sudden Yeeran's tiredness seemed a thing of the past.

'Absolutely.'

The water was colder than Yeeran expected and she regretted removing all her clothing. In the daylight the lagoon had looked turquoise, but now it had turned an inky black.

Yeeran waded in, surprised at how deep the water went, and soon she was swimming to keep up with Furi's strokes ahead of her.

It looked like Furi was aiming for the waterfall and Yeeran's regret deepened.

This is the last time I let a beautiful woman coax me away from sleep.

Then she laughed, because she knew it wasn't true. She'd follow Furi anywhere.

The water grew shallow again near the edge of the lagoon where the waterfall ran into the rocks below. Furi sat beneath the gentle running of the water.

'Nice shower?' Yeeran asked as she reached Furi.

Furi smiled. 'Yes, refreshing. You should try it.'

'I think I'll enjoy the view.'

'Scared to get your hair wet?'

Yeeran's eyebrows shot up. 'Yes actually, I just washed it yesterday morning.'

Furi's smile turned mischievous.

'Furi, whatever you're thinking, don't do it.'

The queen laughed then skimmed her hand across the water, splashing Yeeran in the face.

'Hey! Stop that.' Yeeran began to splash her back using her legs to surge up a wave.

Furi slipped and fell backwards. When she didn't immediately reappear, Yeeran called out, 'Are you lying in wait back there? Because I won't fall for an ambush.'

When there was no answer, Yeeran cursed and followed Furi behind the waterfall. Even though she knew the splash would come, it was still a relief to feel it and know Furi wasn't hurt.

Yeeran flicked water from her eyes. 'That was a dirty trick, I thought you might have hurt yourself.'

Furi laughed all the harder. It was nice to see a lightness in her eyes even if Yeeran knew it would be brief.

Yeeran looked around for the first time. They were in a cave hidden behind the waterfall. The walls were lined with vines, and the shallow water at their feet turned into moss the deeper she walked in. She slipped into magesight to see how far the cave went. The glow from the curse stopped twenty feet away, a small cave then, but a beautiful one.

'Did you know this was here?' Yeeran asked.

'No, I've never been to the southern plains before. The trail has been closed for some time.'

Yeeran's toes sank delightfully into the moss. She lay down on it and looked towards the cave's entrance.

Everything beyond was obscured by the fall of the water. They were in their own private room.

Yeeran held out her hand to Furi who grasped it with a smile before joining Yeeran on the moss.

'It's so comfortable,' Furi said.

'It is.' Yeeran leant on her side and Furi did the same, their noses almost touching.

'When I was captured by Salawa I used to dream of you under star glider light. Just like this, so beautiful, so perfect,' Yeeran whispered.

For the first time, Salawa's name didn't invoke any resentment towards Furi.

'No one is perfect, Yeeran. Take you for example, you cannot get your hair wet.' Furi smiled at her own joke before adding, 'But you are very nearly close to it.'

Then she crossed the small distance between their lips and kissed her.

Yeeran's hands needed no map to chart the curves and pleasures of Furi's body. She knew her body intimately, knew that if she nipped at Furi's neck she would gasp and if she sucked at Furi's nipple she would arch her back.

Down she travelled, towards the warmth that gathered between her legs. Softly she caressed the hair there, teasing her fingers along the sensitive bit of skin that made Furi shudder.

Yeeran pressed a smile to Furi's navel before her lips joined her fingers, coaxing sounds of rapture from Furi's throat.

First, she explored her lazily, her tongue circling while her fingers roamed deeper. But then Furi's need overcame Yeeran's rhythm and she began to arch towards her mouth, faster and faster.

Yeeran obliged and met the speed at which Furi's pleasure reached its zenith. She cried out once before tightening her hands in Yeeran's hair. Then her legs trembled and she collapsed back onto the ground.

There was no more satisfying sight than seeing Furi spent and flushed with the aftershocks of bliss.

Yeeran watched her for a minute. Then Furi, feeling her eyes on her, pushed herself to her elbows. 'I'm not sure what you're waiting for, I've got a hundred more things I'd like to do and the first one is savouring *you.'*

Yeeran's laugh was cut short as Furi was true to her word.

Though they didn't quite reach the hundred mark, that night they did give it a very good try.

CHAPTER TWENTY-SIX

Lettle

'He's going to jump!' The shout pulled Lettle from her sleep and she sat upright.

The fray was lit in the colours of early morning. But something wasn't right.

What had woken her up?

'Stop him, Lettle!'

She turned to the sound of the shouting. Golan was sitting up, his hands frantically pointing at a figure behind her. Lettle followed the path of his gaze and saw Alder standing by the cliff's edge.

The others were being roused from their slumber, but Lettle was the closest. She jumped up and ran towards Alder.

'Alder, what are you doing, you're going to fall.' She grabbed his shoulders and pulled him backwards. Though he was tall and strongly built, he was lighter than she expected, as if he had the hollow bones of a bird.

He fell to the ground.

'What is wrong with you?' she chastised him.

It was then that she realised he wasn't fully there. His eyes rolled back in his head and his mouth frothed with saliva.

'Laqid har alwaqar litahhiq elnugu'a,' he murmured.

The nonsense words seemed familiar to Lettle.

'He's sleepwalking,' Golan said as he joined them. He shook him by the shoulders, but it didn't work.

Furi appeared with a mug full of water and emptied the contents on Alder's face.

He spluttered awake.

'That's for waking me up before I was done sleeping,' she said, before sauntering away again.

Alder's face was a mask of bewilderment. 'What happened? Why am I wet?'

'Furi,' Lettle and Golan said at the same time.

'You were sleepwalking,' Golan explained.

Alder rubbed his face and flicked away the water from his hair. Lettle noted how Golan's eyes lingered on the droplet that had made its way down his open collar.

'Again?' Alder said as he sat up tiredly. 'They're getting worse and more frequent.'

'It happens to you often?' Lettle asked.

'Yes. What did I do this time?'

'You tried to jump off the cliff. And you were making sounds, almost like a language.'

'Ah yes, Mia calls it my "nightmare tongue",' Alder laughed bitterly.

'Yes, it did seem like you were having a nightmare,' Lettle said.

'How are you feeling now?' Golan asked, his face pinched with concern.

'Fine, just groggy.'

'Same,' Furi said from across the meadow, her voice laced with sarcasm.

'I shouldn't have taken my leg off while on watch,' Golan said, shaking his head.

'Don't worry about it, it worked out in the end,' Alder said. 'Not dead yet.'

Yeeran wandered over with a cup of coffee in her hand. 'Did I miss something?'

Lettle laughed. 'No, Alder was just sleepwalking.'

Yeeran looked at him curiously. 'So you really do sleepwalk.'

Alder gave her a rueful smile. 'I tried to tell you. I really wasn't trying to hurt you that night.'

Yeeran shrugged, the matter forgotten. 'Coffee's on the stove.'

Rayan was in the kitchen when Lettle entered.

'You look well-rested,' she commented, circling her arms around his waist.

Rayan let out a small laugh. 'It's surprising how capturing the person trying to kill your lover does that to you. I slept better than I have in weeks.'

Lettle smiled against his chest. 'I did miss our bed though.'

Rayan's torso hummed beneath her cheek as he made a content sound. His hands rested on her lower back, though she could tell they wanted to wander further.

'At least now we can get back to a normal routine,' he said.

Lettle looked up at him. 'Nothing about our time here has been normal, Rayan.'

He chuckled. 'True. But now we can get back to figuring out a way to break the curse.'

Lettle chewed her lip. *He makes it sound so easy.*

She untangled herself from his embrace and walked to the stove. 'Has anyone offered Omur something to drink?' she asked him. 'I doubt it.'

Lettle exhaled through her nose and poured Omur a mug of coffee. She unlocked the door to the room beyond and was confronted with a familiar smell.

Sweet and cloying, with a rotten undertone that she'd recognise anywhere. It was the smell of death.

Norey's body had already started to decompose.

She located Omur in the corner of the room, as far away from the corpse as he could get. He looked up at her as she entered.

'I've brought you coffee,' she said.

He took the mug from her outstretched hand. 'Thank you.'

She turned to leave, her duty of care complete. Then she noticed the grimoire open on the floor next to him.

'You were reading my book?'

He gave her a rueful smile. 'Well, I needed . . . distracting. I realised you were trying to translate it, so I had a go.'

She picked up the notes he had added to her journal.

'I figured that some of the singular letters were either "i" or "a". Then I looked at familiar subjects of the sentence to deduce whether there were similarities. For example, I suspect this phrase is "I am" because it follows a similar pattern here and here.'

Omur had done more in one night than Lettle had in days.

Perhaps that was what the prophecy meant – that Omur would be the one to seek answers in the night?

But she couldn't trust him alone with Afa's words, so she packed up her books and said, 'Now the fray-light is bright enough, we'll be leaving shortly.'

She locked the door behind her and went back out to the plains.

Everyone was slowly waking up and getting ready for the descent. Alder was leaning against the cavern wall, seemingly recovered from his night terror.

Her mind went back to the prophecy, the grimoire heavy in her hands.

What am I missing?

Rayan slipped his hands around her waist, making her jump.

'What are you thinking about?' he asked by her ear.

'Alder.'

Rayan quirked a brow. 'Should I be jealous?' His tone was playful and she rolled her eyes at him.

'He's different to other elves, don't you think?'

'Yes, he's a Nomad.'

'No, it's more than that. Why else would the Fates guide me to him?'

Rayan shrugged. 'Are you sure the prophecy was about him?'

'Yes, it has to be, unless I missed something else that night . . .' The bitterness of disappointment made her nostrils flare.

The first time the Fates speak to me and I fail them.

'I'm sure you're right, Lettle,' Rayan said soothingly.

But what if she wasn't?

She watched as an obeah cub jumped down from a tree and approached Alder. He bent down to scratch its chin.

She entered magesight out of curiosity.

Like all living things he had a core spark of light, though his was burnished a darker colour than the gold of the fae, or the silver tones of the elves.

He rested his back against the cavern wall and something interesting happened. The bronze scripture that made up the magic of the boundary parted where his body brushed the rock. A halo of magic sparked along his skin making his silhouette difficult to look at.

Lettle stepped closer, her mouth agape. 'What in the name of all three gods is happening to you?' she whispered, but the sound carried to Alder.

'What is it?' he said, his expression concerned.

'Lettle?' Rayan said to her left, immediately looking for the threat.

'Look at Alder in magesight,' Lettle said.

Curiosity called the others and gasps rippled across the group.

'Will someone tell me what is happening?' Alder said.

It was Golan who answered, his eyes wide with wonder. 'The boundary doesn't hold you.'

'Oh, that.' Alder relaxed.

'You knew?' Lettle said.

Alder looked a little sheepish as he nodded. 'Yes, I figured it out the first night in Mosima. I sleepwalked to the boundary and found I could pass through.'

Golan frowned. 'Why did you bother coming back?'

Alder looked to Lettle. 'Something here feels unfinished. Like I'm meant to be here. I also thought maybe you might be able to cure my sleepwalking.'

Something was unravelling in Lettle's mind, the facts of which were just out of reach.

She took out her prophecy journal and looked at the scrawl she had written.

In the early hours of the morrow's new day, a tree will fall by the pathway to Mosima. Seek your answers in the night, dawn will bring you peace.

Seek your answers in the night. She had assumed that was the time in which she had to read the grimoire, but perhaps all she had to do was listen.

'Alder, who were your parents?' Lettle asked gently.

The man gave a nonchalant shake of the head. 'Not sure. I lost my memories when I was eighteen. The Nomads found me in the mountains east of here.'

Lettle stepped closer and peered at his ears in a new light. Like the other elves she had assumed that he was dismissed by the Crescent army whose practice was to slice off the tip of the ear.

But now she looked more closely, there was no scar damage there, the ears were perfectly round.

'Lettle, what are you thinking?' Yeeran asked. Of course she would have seen the revelation roiling across Lettle's expression.

Lettle felt breathless, her heart beating faster than her body could comprehend. But she had to be sure.

She removed the grimoire from her bag and thrust it in front of Alder's face.

'Can you read that?' she asked, a hint of desperation making her voice shake.

He shook his head and her stomach sank, but it didn't disprove her theory entirely. Though it would have made her life a whole lot easier.

She started to pack the book away but Alder stopped her.

'Wait.' His hand hovered above the page. 'Laqid har alwaqar litahhiq elnugu'a. I recognise that sentence, how do I recognise that?'

Lettle smiled triumphantly. 'Because you spoke those words last night. Alder, I think you might be a descendant of humans.'

Someone scoffed behind Lettle, it sounded like Furi. So Lettle laid out the facts.

'You're able to pass through the boundary – magic put in place by humans. And your ears, I can see why you would have assumed you were a Crescent deserter, but I do not think they have been cut.'

Furi stepped closer to Alder and inspected his ears, but Lettle wasn't yet done.

'The Fates told me to seek my answers during the night. I think that when you sleepwalk, you're accessing your old memories, and the "nightmare tongue" you speak is actually the human language.'

Alder's mouth fell open, but then he closed it with a laugh. 'Humans haven't been seen for a thousand years.'

'That's what we thought of the fae,' Yeeran said. Her eyes were wide with shock, immediately believing Lettle's theory. Furi on the other hand still looked sceptical.

'Are you really suggesting Alder is part-human?' Furi said.

Lettle put her hands on her hips. 'Yes.'

Alder was shaking his head. 'How can I be related to a human? I have never met one in my life.'

That was where Lettle's logic ran out.

'I don't know,' she admitted. 'But I know I'm right. How else would you know the words you've just read?'

Alder looked at Golan and then back at Lettle. A little crease formed between his eyebrows.

'I . . . I . . . I'm not sure.'

The doubt in Furi's face had lessened. Lettle smiled, unable to keep the excitement from her voice. 'If we can tap into your sleeping mind, we might be able to fully translate the grimoire. We might be able to break the curse completely.'

There was a silence as the truth permeated the air and shock turned into realisation.

Rayan started laughing, and it was so infectious Yeeran and Lettle joined in too.

'We can go *home* again,' Lettle said. Yeeran's grin slipped and

Lettle wondered if her sister was questioning what home would look like without Salawa.

Then Furi's dry voice cut through the joy of the moment. 'Let's not get ahead of ourselves. Though it does seem plausible Alder is likely descended from humans, he still cannot speak or read human and, until that happens, I will not let hope mar my judgement. For now, let us return to the palace.'

Furi's words didn't impact Lettle's excitement and she was about to tell her as much when there was a new voice on the plain.

'Rayan, Furi.' Sahar appeared at the top of the trail. 'A package has arrived, you're needed at the palace.'

CHAPTER TWENTY-SEVEN

Furi

Furi's stomach sank as her father walked towards her. Not because of the news he brought, but because of the news she was about to tell him.

His face was lightly peppered with sweat though his breathing was steady. He'd always kept up with his fitness in his later years, though it would have been an arduous journey for anyone.

'Father you shouldn't have come, you could have sent a soldier,' Furi said.

And we could have this conversation in the comfort of our rooms, she thought.

This conversation will be hard anywhere, Furi, Amnan said. He felt far away.

Where are you?

Conch Shore with Pila, she wanted to chase the waves.

She felt the warmth of Pila's companionship across their connection and Furi's eyes slipped to Yeeran's. So many threads bound them together.

'I assumed that you must have found Lettle and since you didn't want any of the faeguard involved I thought it best if I came alone. Took me all night to figure out where you'd gone. Thankfully a farmhand spotted you going up the trail last night.'

'Still, you could have sent your obeah. It would have been an

easier trek for Cori,' Rayan said, guiding him to a raised section of
rock where he could rest his feet.

'Grandson, are you implying I'm not fit?' Sahar said with a fond
smile.

'No, Father, but the trail was closed for a reason,' Furi said.

'Well then, we better get back down it before more people spot
us breaking the law,' he said laughing.

Furi didn't smile. How could she when she was about to break
his heart?

She handed him the rest of her coffee, delaying the inevitable.
'What's this about a package?'

Sahar looked at her and swallowed. 'It arrived this morning on
the other side of the boundary addressed to the king and queen. I
let in a scouting party, who carried it to the palace for you.'

'Thank you, Father. I'm sorry we weren't there to let them in.'
Furi often forgot that his Jani blood, though weak, allowed him to
open the boundary too.

'No bother, but perhaps it would be prudent to return as soon as
possible – Lettle!' Sahar exclaimed as he noticed her on the edge of
the group. He opened his arms to hug her and she went to him.

'I'm so glad you're safe,' he said.

'I am, thanks to them,' Lettle said, pointing to the group.

'Actually, you seemed to have handled your enemies well without
us,' Furi muttered.

Lettle's eyes narrowed but she didn't respond.

*Amnan, will you return to the southern plains with Pila? Yeeran and
I will need to return to the palace soon. A package has arrived for me
and Rayan.*

*You haven't told your father that Norey's body lies fifty feet from him
yet?*

Furi inhaled sharply. *No, I'm getting to it.*

Sahar looked to the house at the end of the plains. 'Did you
capture them? The people trying to hurt Lettle?'

Rayan and Furi exchanged a look.

'Father, why don't you come with me a moment? We can talk over here in private.'

Sahar frowned but he nodded. 'If you wish.'

She led him away from the group, towards the house. He whistled softly beside her. 'It really is beautiful up here, we should look into getting the trail made safer.' He laughed. 'But I suppose if everyone could come up here it would no longer be peaceful.'

They entered the shack. Furi's heart twisted with the hurt she was about to inflict.

'Father, when we arrived there were two people keeping Lettle hostage. One was a man called Omur, and the other was your lover.'

She would not disturb Norey's infinite slumber by calling on his name, despite his betrayal.

'Norey?' Sahar said with surprise, believing him still alive. 'He's with one of our suppliers for the apothecary, he went last night after we finished searching our segment of Mosima . . .'

Furi tried to swallow the sob that lurched up her throat but her words still came out thick with grief. 'He ordered Omur to kill Lettle, and . . . and in self-defence Lettle struck him with a rock. He died, Father. He's dead.'

All blood ran from Sahar's face. 'No, I don't believe it.'

'Father . . .' Furi's voice cracked.

A low groan emanated from Sahar's throat and he began to rock back and forth on his heels.

'No, I don't think so. I don't think so, daughter.'

Furi met his eyes. 'His body is in the next room should you wish to see it.'

Sahar's mouth opened in a silent cry, then his shoulders began to shake as a sob took a hold of his whole body.

'This can't be true,' he wept.

Furi's own tears wet her cheeks. 'It is, Father. His betrayal was absolute.'

Sahar inhaled slowly then took shaking steps towards the door. The key was in the lock and he turned it with trembling hands.

'Be mindful, the other prisoner is very much alive,' Furi said quietly.

Sahar's hand paused on the door handle. He nodded once as if to steel his resolve before pushing it open.

Furi watched as he crossed the room to the shrouded body. He peeled back the covering over Norey's face and let out a haunting cry.

'Oh my love, I am so sorry. I am so very sorry,' Sahar said. He laid the cloth back over his partner's face before turning to Omur. His eyes narrowed until they were flint thin as he scrutinised the traitor. 'You.' His voice was taut with tension as he pointed to Omur. 'You let this happen.'

Omur's eyes widened at the accusation and the big man seemed to shrivel in on himself. 'No, it was Lettle—'

'Do not speak to me, I will not listen to the voice of a traitor.' Sahar's voice rose in volume. Furi was surprised at the strength of his rage, but grief did strange things to gentle people.

Furi stepped in between them.

'Omur wasn't the one giving orders, Father.' She pointed to Norey's body. 'He was known to the organisation as the "Authority".'

Sahar stilled. 'I don't understand. None of this makes sense.'

'Omur will be punished, but for now, let us return to the palace. I will have some of the faeguard come to retrieve his body later.'

Sahar looked at her and said miserably, 'I don't want him to be left alone.'

It seemed like Norey's betrayal hadn't tarnished Sahar's love for his former partner.

'If you wish to stay here, then you can. We'll escort Omur back to the palace with us.'

Sahar nodded. 'I will stay.'

Furi didn't like leaving her father up here grieving alone, but time with his thoughts was perhaps what he needed to come to terms with Norey's treachery.

And despite the grief that hung heavy in her mind, she was curious about the package left for her at the boundary's edge.

Berro may have sent something with one of her faeguard, she thought. *But why would the messenger not stay to make sure I retrieved it?*

These questions could only be answered by returning to the palace.

'Omur, please hold out your hands,' she said.

He did as she asked, and she wrapped a thread of magic around his wrists before tugging him forward.

'Come along, time to return to the palace and your sentencing,' she said. 'Father, I will see you soon.'

But Sahar wasn't listening, he was kneeling by Norey's body with tears falling down his face.

The rest of the party were ready and waiting by the trail's edge.

'How did it go?' Yeeran asked quietly.

'He's staying until I send the faeguard to retrieve the body,' Furi replied.

'Was he angry?'

'And heartbroken.'

Yeeran's fingers brushed away an errant tear that had slipped from Furi's eyes. 'I'm sorry,' she said. But they were only words, and words could do nothing for Furi right now.

Furi started down the trail.

'I called on Amnan, he was with Pila so they'll both be at the bottom of the trail when we arrive.'

'Thank you.'

They journeyed down from the plains slowly, everyone taking their time. Omur stumbled more than once as having his hands bound made it difficult to keep his balance.

After Lettle appealed for him a fifth time Furi agreed to remove the thread as the only way was down – dead or alive.

Alder was the only one of the group who seemed confident on the steep slopes, his tree-bark worn soles gripping the ground with ease. He walked as lightly as the obeah who pranced from rock to rock, and it felt as though, given the chance, he'd be doing that too.

A human descendant among us. Furi shook her head in disbelief. Though he was never far from Golan to help guide him down the steeper slopes.

He always smelled like kin to me, Amnan said.

He was found surrounded by obeah, perhaps he was raised by them too.

That would make sense, he agreed. *It's like he's one of us.*

We're nearly at the bottom of the trail.

We're waiting.

'Rayan, I'll go ahead with Yeeran, I suspect the package is from Berro. Keep our prisoner close. I'll see you back at the palace.'

Rayan nodded, his hand tightly entwined with Lettle's as he helped her down the last few steps.

Amnan loped towards Furi and she mounted him in one quick motion. Yeeran did the same with Pila.

Furi looked at Yeeran who was smiling.

'Want to race?' Yeeran said.

Furi laughed and instead of responding she said to Amnan, *Show Pila why you're the fastest obeah to have ever lived.*

They arrived back at the palace breathless and smiling. Yeeran was so good at distracting Furi from her worries, she wondered if she'd learned it growing up with Lettle.

Yeeran jumped down from Pila's back when they reached the Tree of Souls.

'You cheated, you took a shortcut,' Yeeran teased.

Furi shrugged. 'A race is a race, it's your fault you don't know the city as well as I.'

Yeeran stuck her tongue out at Furi and she was reminded of all the ways they had put it to good use last night. Yeeran saw her expression change and stepped closer to her. She tilted her head to the side before pressing a kiss against her neck.

'Hmm, though I'd very much like to continue, I should probably find out what Berro wants first,' Furi said.

Yeeran pulled away with a smile. 'Fine, pressing matters first . . . then me second.'

Furi pecked a kiss onto her cheek. 'You're never second, Yeeran, not in my eyes.'

The look Yeeran gave her was full of tenderness and it made Furi's throat hitch.

'My queen, did Sahar find you?' A faeguard appeared behind them.

Furi turned to them with an arched brow. 'Yes, where is the package?'

'By the throne.' They saluted and stepped away, their duty done.

Furi looked past Yeeran to the Tree of Souls and saw a wooden box set on the dais by the trunk. She strode towards it.

To the king and queen of the fae, the words said on the box's lid.

'This doesn't look like Berro, she would have written to me in fae, not the universal tongue,' Furi said frowning.

She removed the wax seal that secured the lid and opened it.

Nothing could have prepared her for the empty eyes that stared back at her. Cushioned against silk was Berro's head.

Furi felt herself go numb.

'What is it?' Yeeran said, stepping closer.

But Furi had no more words left.

'No, that cannot be, oh three gods, Furi, I'm so sorry.' Yeeran's arms circled Furi's shoulders, but she couldn't feel them.

Her hands shook as she removed the letter sealed into the underside of the lid.

To the king and queen of the fae,

United we stand, all four districts of the Elven Lands against your tyranny. First you claimed Akomido's death – a grave slight against Crescent. And now we have discovered you have slaughtered the chieftain of Waning and the ambassadors for Waxing and

Eclipse. We will not tolerate these hostilities any longer and have proclaimed them as an act of war. We will retaliate in kind.

Signed: Chieftain Motogo of Waning, Chieftain Kojo of Waxing, Chieftain Yao of Eclipse and Chieftain Waksa of Crescent

Yeeran read over her shoulder and gasped. 'United? This has never happened before. They're all abandoning the Bleeding Field . . . for the fae.'

Furi looked at Yeeran and said, 'How did they know about the others? How did they know I killed the chieftain of Waning? No one survived.'

Yeeran opened her mouth to agree, then closed it. And in that hesitation Furi knew there was something she wasn't telling her.

'Tell me,' Furi said.

Yeeran met her gaze. 'There was a soldier, Madu she was called, she'd been kind to Pila and I. She was the only reason we survived the journey because all Salawa had for us was salted meat. Madu let me forage for berries.' Yeeran swallowed and ran her hand through her hair. 'I let her go, I had to let her go, Furi.'

Furi kicked the box containing Berro's head and it toppled down the dais until Berro's unblinking eyes rested between Yeeran and her.

Furi's rage left her as quickly as it came. What was the point? She could not change anything. Yeeran had done what she had done, and so had Furi.

It had been Furi who had slaughtered the elves. And she knew she'd do it all again to save Yeeran.

'You know, Amnan once said that our love is bound by grief. But I think it's murder that binds us, Yeeran. No matter how hard we try all we do is kill the people we love.' And with that Furi stepped down from the throne and walked away from the only woman she'd ever truly loved.

CHAPTER TWENTY-EIGHT

Alder

Alder was quiet on their way back to the palace. The revelation of the day stilled his tongue.

I am human.

How was it possible? He wasn't sure, but the more Lettle spoke, the more it seemed true. How else could he explain the language of his dreams, or his ability to walk through the boundary?

Even his affinity to the forest made sense. Though he knew very little about humans, he'd heard the lore from the elders in Caperly: humans were made by the Earth god, Asase.

Alder held out his hands in front of him. His freckled skin looked the same as it had a few hours ago, but he knew the blood running in his veins was different to that of anyone else he had known.

The hollow pit of loneliness he had harboured in his stomach grew ever greater.

He'd thought the depthless abyss had been caused by his lack of memories, or the absence of a lover, perhaps even the lack of bonding to an obeah, but now he knew what his body had always known. He was not like the others.

He was human.

'Alder? Did you hear me?' Golan's soft voice drew him out of his morose thoughts.

'No, sorry, what did you say?'

'I asked if you were feeling all right.'

Alder looked at the fae. All of the make-up that usually glazed his face had gone. Without his lotions and tinctures to maintain them, Golan was bare-faced in front of Alder for the first time.

His skin was pale brown, his cheeks gently blushing from the exertion of the descent. His blue eyes, which were filled with concern, looked wider without the golden shadow that usually lined them. Even his two braids had come loose and his dark hair ran down his back in delicate waves.

He was the image of beauty.

'What are you looking at?' Golan said self-consciously.

Alder shook his head, smiling. 'No, nothing at all. I was just thinking how comely you look this morning.'

Golan's blush deepened but his eyes danced playfully. 'So I take it you're feeling well then?'

Alder looked away from him, the brief moment of flirtation gone as he went back to his troubled thoughts.

'I . . . I'm not sure. I suppose I've never felt fully elf, I always thought that the emptiness was my lack of memories, but now I wonder if it isn't something more than that.'

Golan tilted his head and gave him an encouraging nod for him to go on.

'I've always been a little different, I guess? The forest speaks to me in a way that comes naturally. Like I'll always know where a plant would flourish best, or where to forage come harvest time. So I think Lettle's right. Everything points to the conclusion that I'm part-human.'

They were nearly at the Royal Woodland. Lettle and Rayan walked ahead with Omur in tow. As they crossed a stream, Alder looked over the bridge to see a school of fish dart out of the shallows.

'It feels like all my life I've been trying to swim with the fish, but I've actually been a newt this whole time,' Alder said.

Golan reached for Alder's hand, stopping him in his tracks. 'But look,' he said, pointing to a creature on the shore of the river. 'Newts can still swim.'

Alder didn't want to contradict Golan to point out that what he was looking at was actually a baby salamander – because the sentiment still stood. And it was worth biting his tongue while Golan still held his hand.

'Yes, they can,' Alder agreed.

'You are still the same Alder you were a few hours ago. Only now you have some answers to the things happening to you.'

It was true, he had sought answers and he'd been given them.

'Lettle seems so sure that I'll be able to harness my ancestors' magic and somehow break the curse,' Alder said. The weight of that responsibility felt heavy on his back.

'Yes, but don't let her eagerness overcome you. Lettle is my greatest friend, but sometimes her ambition comes at the sake of others.'

'What I don't understand is how I exist at all. I've travelled the breadth of the continent and never met a human before.'

Golan's smile was sly. 'But remember neither had you met me.'

Could it be possible that the Nomads had not noticed an entire civilisation somewhere? It stood to reason that if the fae could hide from them, then humans could too.

He rubbed his brow. 'I may have some answers but in turn I have more questions.'

Two more days. He'd told the Nomads that he'd return to them in *more two days*.

I could just leave now. The thought held no conviction, he knew his business was still unfinished here.

Golan's thumb circled the hand he was holding in a gentle caress. 'We'll figure out the answers to those questions too.'

Alder nodded once.

'Come on, we had better catch up to the others,' Golan said, dropping Alder's hand.

They walked the rest of the way in silence.

When they arrived in the Royal Woodland Yeeran was alone sitting by the foot of the thrones with a closed box held between her hands. Unshed tears gathered in her eyes.

'Yeeran are you well?' Golan asked. But just as he voiced the question, Furi appeared behind them, and it was clear where the source of Yeeran's misery was.

Though the frost had long gone from the leaves of the plants, an iciness had settled in the air between Furi and Yeeran. The queen strode past Yeeran, her gaze sliding away from the box she held.

Something had happened in the hour they had been apart.

Alder watched Rayan approach the Tree of Souls and for the first time he spotted words engraved in the bark above their seats.

'What does that say?' Alder asked Golan.

It was Lettle who replied. *"Cursed to endure, cursed to survive. All shall perish lest all three thrive."* They are the words of a prophecy linked to the fae's imprisonment.'

'But why were they imprisoned?' Alder asked.

Lettle met his gaze. 'The only person who could tell us, is you.'

Alder frowned and looked back to the thrones. Rayan and Furi were speaking quietly to each other in fae while Omur knelt in front of the dais.

'What are they talking about?' Alder asked Golan.

'Omur's sentencing. Accused are sentenced quickly around here. And because there is no need for witness testimony, given Lettle and the royals were there, this will be quick.'

This new world was so different to everything Alder had ever known. For someone to have this much power over another's life was difficult for him to comprehend. Though he had a semblance of leadership over the Nomads as their Wayfarer, he had no authority over their lives beyond the direction of their feet.

'As he is Lightless, you will be able to understand the sentencing as they'll speak it in the universal tongue.'

Mosima was also a world separated by languages. Those with a grasp of both flowed between one into the other so seamlessly Alder wondered how they kept up. But to him, and to the Lightless who hadn't learned fae, he was only ever in half of the conversation.

Rayan and Furi appeared to come to an agreement quickly.

'What do you think it'll be?' Lettle said to Golan's left.

'I'm not sure, the mines maybe?' he said.

'Maybe,' Lettle said. She was watching Rayan closely, but Alder's gaze was drawn to Furi's. Her eyes were red, her hair in disarray. It was as if the grief of yesterday had returned tenfold. It once again made Alder question what had happened between Furi and Yeeran, and what was in the box that neither of them would look at.

'Omur O'Lightless,' Furi said, her face passive. 'You stand accused of attempted murder and treason. We are in the process of uncovering your accomplices under the name of Salt, Han and Tovi. This is your opportunity to share all you know of your mission, it may result in a lesser sentence.'

Omur hung his head but did not speak.

'You refuse to cooperate?' Rayan said, his expression harsh. He had always seemed so gentle to Alder, but there was a violence there that he was ready to call upon when needed. It was why Alder found him the more fearsome of the two monarchs. His rage was quiet, deadly and unexpected, whereas Furi wore her anger as proudly as her clothing, it cloaked her like armour.

Omur looked up and said, 'I will tell you nothing, there is no use interrogating me. Let us be done with this.'

Furi's lips quirked as if this was the outcome she had wanted. 'As you wish. You are sentenced to forty years of labour.'

Golan winced. 'Forty years, that's a lot.'

Lettle looked troubled but said nothing.

'Where are you to send me?' Omur said, his voice devoid of emotion.

'The aqueducts. You will be our new cleaner.'

Omur slumped to the ground.

Golan gasped but Lettle and Alder didn't understand the gravity of the situation.

Golan held a hand to his mouth. 'He is being sent to clean the bath network beneath the city. It is the most dangerous task in Mosima, as the spring water ebbs and flows – floods in the tunnels happen often. Aqueduct cleaners aren't expected to survive long.'

'It's a death sentence,' Alder surmised.

Golan nodded. 'It is the worst sentence anyone can be given.'

Furi called forward the faeguard who escorted Omur away.

'I asked Rayan for mercy,' Lettle said quietly. Her brows knitted together. Then her face set into a determined expression.

'Lettle . . .' Golan had noticed her change in demeanour, but it was no use warning her.

'Come see me in the morning?' she said to Alder. 'I'll be in the royal chambers.' Then she dashed off after Omur.

Alder watched as the royals left the courtyard. Furi walked as if someone held a knife to her back, Yeeran a step behind her, equally uncomfortable. She still held the box cradled against her chest.

Rayan kept looking to where Lettle had followed the faeguard, and he hesitated, seemingly ready to go after her. But then he thought better of it and trailed after Furi and Yeeran instead.

Cracks in the Jani dynasty were forming – and from what Alder understood, this was what their dissenters had wanted.

'I'm not sure about you, but I could do with a rest,' Golan said.

'And some food,' Alder added.

Golan chuckled. 'Yes, that too. Why don't we break our fast in the obeah orchard?'

'The obeah orchard?'

Golan's smile was mischievous. 'I think you'll like it very much. This way.'

They crossed the woodland, moving behind the Tree of Souls. Alder looked up as they passed, marvelling at the expanse of the tree up close.

Mosima truly is a wonder, he thought. *The Nomads would love it here.*

But he knew the Nomads would never truly settle anywhere. It was what he loved most about his family. They moved like leaves on the breeze, only staying in one place for no longer than a season.

Golan led him through an archway in the red brickwork of the palace wall. It fronted a tunnel that opened out to a courtyard at the far end.

The courtyard was enclosed by the palace building, so would not be obvious to those who didn't know where to find it.

Alder's mouth hung open as they stepped into the garden. The trees and shrubbery had all been landscaped in a spiral, the largest of which grew along the circumference whereas the smaller plants took residency in the middle.

'Pear, apple, peaches, mango, strawberry . . .' Alder let out a slow breath. It was a forager's dream.

'Feel free to pick any of it,' Golan said.

Alder could barely contain his joy. He walked in a daze through the branches of fruit. A shadow jumped out in the path ahead of him and he let out a startled cry.

'This is where the palace obeah graze. One of the Jani ancestors grew this for them around three hundred years ago,' Golan explained. 'Hence it is called the obeah orchard.'

Now Golan pointed it out, Alder could see the creatures prowling among the branches and lingering in the strawberry bushes.

'Gooseberries!' He spotted the spiky plant growing in the distance and rushed to it. There was something about the tart leathery skin and the sweet innards that had always appealed to him.

He plucked a few and popped them in his mouth. As suspected, they were the most delicious gooseberries he'd ever had.

'How could this be so sweet, especially after the frost they had?'

'The orchard was one of the first areas Furi restored with her power. It's been a solace for the creatures bound to the fae of the palace for so long.'

Alder groaned as another gooseberry burst on his tongue. 'I'm just not sure how you could ever do anything other than eat,' he said, turning to Golan with his mouth full.

Golan chuckled and raised his hand to Alder's mouth.

Alder froze, unsure what was about to happen. He could feel his heartbeat in his throat as Golan's fingers brushed his jaw. The moment was brief, too brief.

'Gooseberry juice,' Golan said by way of explanation, but the touch had affected him too. Alder could tell by the way he looked away shyly.

Say something. Say anything! his mind screamed, but he couldn't put into words what he wanted to express.

Golan, I would like to kiss you? Who asks that? Besides, Alder was just a temporary guest in Mosima. He'd be on the road again with the Nomads soon enough.

Alder regretted letting the moment pass him by as he went back to picking gooseberries.

'Why don't you try the blueberries.' Golan's voice was a little rough and he cleared his throat before continuing. 'I've been told this year's batch are particularly sweet. They're over here.'

Alder's tongue was still locked so he just nodded and let himself be led away.

CHAPTER TWENTY-NINE

Lettle

L ettle was furious with Rayan. She'd asked for clemency when he sentenced Omur and he'd given him exactly the opposite. This was the issue with Mosima – they doled out justice but never explored the root cause. Rayan's vengeance had swayed his hand.

'Omur!' Lettle called. Omur looked back at Lettle with a vacant expression. The faeguard escorting him turned around.

'Seer, we're taking him to the aqueducts as instructed,' one of the guards said.

'Give me a minute with him, please.'

The faeguard hesitated.

Lettle let out an exasperated sigh. 'You can watch from the tree line over there. His hands are still bound so I doubt very much he will do anything.'

The faeguard exchanged a glance, and Lettle was about to put on her more regal voice when they nodded and moved to the side of the path.

When they had gone, Omur said tiredly, 'What do you want, Lettle?'

'I want you to tell me why you didn't cooperate.'

Omur shrugged. 'There is no point. Even if I gave you the names of everyone I knew in the organisation you cannot stop the branches of change. More rebellions will grow from the stems you cut away.'

His words felt like a prophecy, and her hands went to the talismans in her pocket.

'Why? Why rebel? Why not work with the court to make it better?'

Omur shook his head and looked at Lettle as if she were a child.

'You are more naïve than perhaps I was. Do you know why our book club started out so small? Because only those who can read fae can read books. There is no longer a printing press in the whole of Mosima that caters to the Lightless – and yet we are not taught the fae language in schools. It is kept from us, deemed too difficult to master unless bonded to an obeah.'

But I managed to learn it, Lettle thought. *I'm not very proficient in speaking it, but at least I can understand it.*

'The very foundations of Mosima society have been built to keep the Lightless in the dark,' Omur continued.

And Lettle had to agree. The injustice of it all made her lips curl up in a scowl.

'I'm going to help change it,' she said with finality. 'Without violence.'

Omur's gaze moved lazily to Lettle's throat. 'You know I could still kill you with my hands tied?' Though his words were a threat, Lettle didn't feel threatened.

'But you won't.'

'That's your problem, you see the good in people, Lettle. Even when there's no good in them left.'

Lettle took a step back out of precaution and Omur's eyes danced as he said, 'You think I'm talking about me, but I was referring to the Jani dynasty. They are corrupt to their core.'

Lettle shook her head violently. 'No, you're wrong.'

He looked thoughtful for a moment, then he said, 'Do you ever wonder why the Jani family are our rulers?'

'They are tied to this land. It makes sense.'

'Does it? Just because they are bound to the Tree of Souls does not mean they should be our rulers.'

Lettle looked up as the breeze shook some of the leaves from the canopy. She noticed how half of them were brown and blistered from the frost.

But even with the damage they had done they were the only family that *could* rule Mosima.

'I have seen Rayan turn a man to stone by calling forth the ground beneath his feet. I have watched Furi make the wind howl and grow ferns from the flagstones of her bedroom floor. Their connection to Mosima runs deep. I see no one else who could be more worthy of protecting it.'

'Protecting the land is one thing, but they have failed their people. The Lightless have been forgotten for too long,' Omur said. 'We grow tired of being second-class citizens for an affliction we cannot change. I will never bond with an obeah, but that does not mean I should not be allowed to work where I want to work—'

'You can work where you want to,' Lettle protested.

'You think I always wanted to be a carpenter? No, I dreamed of being a healer, a doctor at that. But Lightless are not allowed to work in the infirmary.'

Lettle was about to protest again, but then she remembered Jay, the healer who had helped her sister all those months ago. Jay hadn't been allowed to work in the hospital either. Yet Furi had believed she was the best healer around.

'Furi and Rayan have no prejudice against the Lightless, you must *know* that,' she said.

'And yet, nothing changes.'

Lettle wanted to say that they'd been a bit busy, but she knew it would sound like an excuse. For the average Lightless, they didn't care what was happening beyond Mosima's walls. Their life and home were here.

'But you could have worked with them, cooperated to instigate change. With the Authority now gone—'

Omur frowned, almost imperceptibly.

'What?' she said.

He released a slow breath, his eyes darting to the faeguard and back to Lettle, but he didn't reply.

She felt a sense of trepidation run across her skin like the fingers of a ghost. 'Norey *was* the Authority, wasn't he?'

But Omur's lips were pressed into a thin line, an impenetrable defence.

Lettle thought back to everything that had transpired. How could she have forgotten the obeah delivering the note? Even Omur's words from two nights before had come back to her: the Authority 'is a relatively new figure in the organisation'. And yet Norey had said he'd been a part of it for years.

Here they were thinking they'd caught the spider in the centre of the web, but all they had done was get caught up in the net.

Lettle nodded to the faeguard and Omur was led away. Then she set her shoulders and strode off towards the war room.

The air was tense and stifling as Lettle entered. Rayan, Yeeran and Furi were standing over a box in the centre of the table. But whatever it was, it wasn't as important as her news.

'Norey wasn't the Authority. Whoever he is, he's still out there,' Lettle announced.

Furi was the first to turn around, and Lettle was surprised to see she was crying. She wiped the tears from her eyes with a scowl. 'What did you say?'

'The Authority, he's still free.'

Furi tipped her head to the ceiling and said to the gods, 'Can this day not end, please?'

Lettle rounded the table to sit in a nearby seat when she caught sight of what was in the now open box.

'Shit, is that *Berro*?'

Yeeran winced at her callousness, but Lettle couldn't pretend she'd held any affection for Furi's second-in-command.

Still, she listened as Yeeran explained what had happened.

'All districts, united as one?' Lettle breathed. 'That is a lot of soldiers.'

'Yes,' Rayan nodded.

'And is what you mean to tell us, Lettle, that not only have we failed to stop the war with Crescent, we have failed to stop the rebellion in Mosima too?' Furi asked, though she sounded like she didn't want an answer.

Lettle nodded and explained what she'd discovered.

There was an awful silence after she'd spoken. It was the type of silence that brewed from everyone in the room thinking dark thoughts.

'But maybe,' Lettle said with a cheerfulness she didn't feel – anything to banish the haunting quiet, 'Alder will be able to help us end the curse.'

'We don't want to end the curse,' Furi growled. 'Not now, not while the boundary is the only thing protecting us from the army that's coming to our door.'

Yeeran looked thoughtful. 'Unlocking the grimoire's secrets will result in more than just breaking the curse. We may be able to tap into human magic – which could sway the war.'

Of course, Yeeran would look to weaponise Alder. It left a sour taste in Lettle's mouth.

'That's not the point—'

'Yeeran's right,' Rayan interrupted her. 'Human magic could be our answer in fighting the elves.'

Lettle shot him a dark look. 'Do we have to resort to war?'

Rayan met her eyes. 'War is coming, Lettle, whether we want it to or not. I for one would like to come out unscathed.'

Furi nodded slowly. 'All right, continue your research with Alder. I hope you are able to unlock the grimoire's magic, Lettle. For all our sakes.'

It sounded like a dismissal, and though Lettle was keen to return to her work, she wasn't yet finished.

'I want to set up a new partnership with the Lightless – the Free the Light Initiative. A group dedicated to improving the rights of the Lightless. And make it a part of the court.'

Furi snorted. 'What?'

'You'll never end the dissent with the Lightless until you actively try to fix the problem. The Lightless are second-class citizens, and they shouldn't be. Golan's already agreed to lead it with me.'

Furi rubbed her brow and said, a little too patronisingly in Lettle's view, 'I don't think now is exactly the time to make significant changes within the court.'

'It is exactly the *right* time. Otherwise, this rebellion will continue on.' Lettle looked to Rayan but it was Yeeran who came to her defence.

'Lettle's right. We need to start making changes to the way the Lightless are treated. If not, you'll end this organisation and they will become martyrs for another.'

Lettle gave her sister a grateful nod.

Furi opened her mouth to argue, but Rayan cut her off.

'Let us discuss it. Change may be slow in Mosima, but if the fae can accept me as their king, then this will be far easier,' Rayan said.

Lettle narrowed her eyes. It wasn't the blind commitment she was hoping for, but it would have to do.

'I'll leave you now to discuss. But there's only one answer I'll accept,' she said tartly before leaving them to their planning of bloodshed and war.

CHAPTER THIRTY

Yeeran

After her argument with Furi, Yeeran felt wretched. Time and time again, Furi's words were never far from her mind.

'I think it's murder that binds us, Yeeran. No matter how hard we try all we do is kill the people we love.'

And Yeeran knew why she couldn't move on from those words – because they rang of truth.

Berro's head was heavy in her hands. After Furi had left the woodland, she had gently returned the fae's remains back into the box it had come in. But she found herself unable to let go of it.

She had watched as Furi had handed out justice to Omur, swift and sure. That was thing with Furi – she knew her mind and it was difficult to sway her from it.

But Yeeran refused to give up on her, on them. They had so much more than death between them. They had love and companionship and . . .

Her thoughts shuttered to a stop. Was that all they shared between them?

But love was enough, it had to be.

Love can be enough, Pila responded. *But only if the other person chooses it too.*

Once again Pila proved to be the wisest of them both.

I am wise, the obeah confirmed. *Would you like to come swimming with me later?*

Maybe, but there's so much going on here I don't know if I'll be able to get away.

Politics are boring, Pila declared. Again, a sage observation.

The sentencing was brief and when it was over, Yeeran watched as Lettle dashed after Omur. Golan and Alder went in the opposite direction towards the obeah orchard.

With nowhere else to go, Yeeran followed Furi.

'You do not need to come with me everywhere,' Furi muttered. 'I am not a vase about to break.'

Yeeran paused, unsure whether to go on. 'But I like to be near you,' she said.

Furi looked at her, then her gaze dropped to the package in her hands and all fight left her. 'Bring her to the war room,' she said softly.

Yeeran followed Furi with heavy steps. When they entered the war room, she placed Berro's remains on the table in the centre. Though small, it was as if the box was a ravine that separated her and Furi.

Rayan walked into the tense silence. 'What's that?' he asked. He started to open it before Yeeran could warn him.

'I wouldn't . . .'

'Three gods . . .' he breathed.

Seeing Berro's severed head once more seemed to suck all the air from Furi's lungs and Yeeran jumped forward to catch her as she lost her balance.

'Here, sit in a chair.' Yeeran set Furi down and the queen gave her a grateful nod.

Rayan was reading the letter that came with Berro's remains, the veins in his neck bulging.

'How did this happen?' Rayan asked.

Furi looked to Yeeran before she replied. 'Does it matter? Either way the elves found out about the massacre, and now we must pay the price.'

Rayan's head shook back and forth. 'I thought talks with Berro were going well . . . For Crescent to join the fight . . .' his voice faded into obscurity.

Furi riffled through some letters on the table and withdrew the one she was looking for. 'This came from her a few days ago.'

Yeeran read some of it over her shoulder.

. . . A messenger from another tribe arrived last night and spoke to the chieftain of Crescent until the early hours of the morning. The next day we were told that the chieftain would no longer negotiate with us . . .

'Why didn't you tell me this had come?' Rayan asked, a knot between his brows. Yeeran had been about to ask the same.

'I'm not sure if you've noticed, but there have been other things on my mind,' Furi said sarcastically.

The air in the room crackled with an unpleasant pressure.

All of a sudden there was a sound at the door and Lettle strode in.

'Norey wasn't the Authority. Whoever he is, he's still out there,' she declared.

Her words set off a chain of events that strained the tension in the room even more.

When Lettle left, Yeeran said to Rayan, 'If the Authority is still out there, you should probably have more of the faeguard follow her.'

'And this time, tell them they can only be dismissed by either the king or queen,' Furi added.

Rayan's eyes narrowed. 'Yes, Lettle is not to be out of sight by the faeguard under any circumstances.'

He slipped out of the room to implement the orders.

'How do you fare?' Yeeran asked Furi once he'd gone.

Furi's grin was mocking. 'My father's partner is dead and is currently being brought down from the plains, the rebellion I thought I'd quashed is actually still in full formation, and oh, all the elves in the world will be knocking on our door to kill us all.'

Yeeran grimaced. 'Listed out, it does sound dire.'

She wanted to go to her and comfort her, but wasn't sure she knew how. For the first time, she didn't know what Furi wanted.

There was a knock at the door. Yeeran went to answer it. On the other side of the threshold was a young woman holding a tray.

'I've brought refreshments from the kitchens,' she said.

Yeeran let her in and she set the tray down on the table. When the servant didn't leave immediately Yeeran frowned.

'Is there something else you need?'

'She's the food taster, Yeeran. She needs to taste everything we eat in case it has poison in,' Furi said. 'Your name is Anyah, right?'

Anyah nodded before getting to her task.

'What a wonderful job,' Yeeran said dryly.

Suddenly Anyah choked and Yeeran and Furi turned to look at her, their eyes wide. But Anyah wasn't coughing from poison, she had just noticed Berro's head.

Tears sprang to the servant's eyes and she wiped them away with the back of her hand. 'I'm so sorry. It's just that . . . she was someone I looked up to. Before my time here I had wanted to be in the faeguard . . .' Her voice trailed off with a hiccup.

'Tell no one of what you have seen here,' Furi said, her voice like stone. 'You may leave us now.'

As Anyah slipped away, Yeeran realised how much Berro's death would affect more than the people who had known her. She was Furi's second-in-command, and with her dead the queen was even more vulnerable.

'The news will get out soon enough, we already know the woodland is compromised,' Yeeran said.

Furi closed her eyes and when she opened them the golden core of them blazed hot with pain. 'If no one knows, then perhaps this is all just a nightmare.'

Yeeran kneeled by Furi's chair and reached for her hand. It was cold, but her grip was firm.

'We will get through this. And when we do, we'll make time to mourn the dead.'

But how many more will there be? The unspoken question crept up from the corners of Yeeran's mind.

It was then that Rayan returned, his expression bleak. 'So while Lettle works with Alder, what do we intend to do?'

'We cannot have our focus split across the threats within Mosima and those beyond our borders, but both are a problem,' Furi said quietly.

Despair thickened like a fog and only Yeeran could see through the haze of it. But she was battle-worn in ways the other two weren't. She'd been in rooms just like this for years.

She stood up and straightened her shoulders. 'Perhaps splitting our focus is exactly what we should be doing. Furi, you can begin to prepare the barracks for war, and Rayan, you can concentrate on rooting out the Authority.'

Rayan looked up, and though there was more light in his brown eyes, he didn't look determined – and determination was the only thing they had against an unknown threat.

'How though? Furi and I have been at this for weeks.'

Yeeran chewed her lip, shifting through the strategies she'd implemented during the Forever War.

Then an idea came to her. 'Do you remember when we ambushed Crescent's infantry? It was a few years ago, but we lured them out by seeding rumours that we would be conducting a training routine on the eastern bank. We made ourselves look weak, easy pickings. Then brought the full might of our regiment once we'd got them in position.'

'Yes, I remember,' Rayan said.

'We need to do the same here, lure them out. Seed rumours that we believe we've found the Authority. Make ourselves look weak—'

Furi scoffed. 'We cannot look weak. We'll lose even more support.'

'Perhaps not weak,' Yeeran continued carefully. 'But preoccupied. Put on a banquet, invite everyone of import. Lettle said the Authority had an obeah, they must be close to the palace somehow. We make

Lettle look vulnerable, perhaps lead her off somewhere on her own. But ensure we have enough faeguard waiting in ambush.'

Rayan's hands clenched by his sides. 'I won't put Lettle in danger again, I can't.'

'That's the thing, she won't be. We'll orchestrate the whole thing, ensure the faeguard are lying in wait.'

Rayan rubbed his stubbled chin, still concerned. 'Can we use someone else for the bait?'

Yeeran shook her head. 'You know we can't, they want Lettle, and so it must be her.'

He let out a heavy sigh but didn't contradict her, because he knew the plan made sense.

'So you're suggesting a trap?' Furi said. 'How would we hide a regiment of faeguard among the people?'

'Dress them in formal wear, swap their swords for hidden daggers,' Yeeran said.

'A lot of the faeguard's faces are known, especially the ones we trust the most,' Furi said.

'Then we make it a masked banquet,' Rayan said.

Yeeran nodded enthusiastically. 'Perfect.'

Furi was still frowning but Yeeran could see she was coming round to the idea. 'We'll need a reason to host it.'

Yeeran cleared her throat. 'Lettle just gave us the reason. Why don't we announce her new initiative? We can even get her up on the stage to promote it, furthering the target on her back.' She felt a little guilty for using Lettle's noble pursuit so brazenly. And though she agreed with her sister's notion, catching the Authority was more important right now.

Furi and Rayan exchanged a look.

'This could work,' Furi said. 'I did wonder why you were so quick to support her.'

'I think Lettle's idea is a sound one, but she is not used to the bureaucracy of a government and by the time any changes are made, the Authority may have already taken her life,' Yeeran said.

Rayan's jaw clenched and Yeeran was sure she heard him grind his teeth, before he said, 'I will not let that happen.'

'We could also announce Alder as human,' Furi added. 'He is the first person of human heritage we've ever known and the news could prove a good distraction for our gambit. It could also strengthen our alliance with him.'

Though Furi didn't say it, they were all thinking it: if Lettle was able to unlock the power in Afa's grimoire, then there was no telling how valuable Alder could prove to be.

'The Royal Woodland is too risky though, there are so many exits and tunnels that we'd be spreading ourselves too thin,' Rayan said.

Yeeran realised he was right. She thought through the configuration of the palace and her mind went to the obeah orchard she'd seen Alder and Golan heading towards.

'What about the courtyard where the obeah graze?' Yeeran asked. 'It's enclosed within the palace walls so we could position the faeguard along balconies as well as in the party itself. There's also only one exit.'

Furi considered it. 'We've never hosted a party there before, but it could work.'

'Yes,' Rayan said resolutely. 'Leave the planning to me, you concentrate on preparing the barracks for battle.' Then he added gently, 'As commander and queen, you'll need a new number two, so perhaps now is the time to consider one.'

Grief robbed all hope from Furi's face and she nodded.

'We cannot tell anyone the true purpose of this venture,' Yeeran said. 'Not even Lettle. She must be ignorant of it, for as much as I love my sister, she does not know how to hide her true purpose. If she knew she was bait, she'd be looking in the tree line for every guard hiding there.'

Rayan hesitated, but eventually he agreed. 'All right, let's set a trap.'

CHAPTER THIRTY-ONE

Alder

Alder's blood fizzed with anticipation as he and Golan made their way to Lettle the following morning. He had slept fitfully and woke still exhausted. But thankfully he hadn't sleepwalked.

The royal chambers were as opulent as they sounded. Every piece of furniture was velvet and the walls were mounted with beautiful depictions of plants and flowers. Lettle was sitting at a desk in the living room when Alder and Golan entered. She saw Alder looking at one of the paintings in particular and grimaced.

'I didn't choose any of them, they were Queen Vyce's. I just haven't had a chance to rip them down.'

Alder laughed politely. Lettle still made him feel a bit on edge, perhaps because she was always assessing him, waiting for him to do something unusual. And when he did, he felt like he was an experiment that had just proved her hypothesis. It made him feel . . . isolated. As if her eyes saw only a product and not a person.

Is this what it is like to feel human?

He pushed his thoughts aside and lowered himself into one of the chairs. As he did, Lettle threw a book at him. He caught it instinctively and the little smile she gave him made him feel like he'd completed a trick.

'The book is called *The Story of the Wheat, the Bat, and the Water.*

It talks about the origins of the three beings and touches on an important prophecy. I think you should read it,' Lettle said.

Alder glanced over the gold-embossed spine. 'It's in fae.'

'Golan can read it to you,' she said. 'But maybe later. Right now I want to see if you recognise any other words in the grimoire. Perhaps looking at it will unlock your memories.'

It seemed worth a try, and so he went over to her desk and did as she bade.

At some point after the first hour lunch was brought in. Alder was glad, but Lettle hadn't wanted to stop while they ate, though she was *very* strict about crumbs near the books.

By the second hour Alder had a terrible headache and was struggling to focus on anything.

'It's not working. Other than that first sentence, I don't recognise a thing.'

'Let's try meditating next, has Golan taught you magesight? No? Moon's mercy, we'll have to start from scratch. Here's a technique I learned as a diviner . . .'

And on it went, for another two hours. When magesight still seemed beyond him they moved to different techniques of meditation. Though it wasn't especially hard, Alder struggled to clear his mind in order to explore what Lettle called 'the hidden pockets of his brain'.

Again, another two hours passed.

Alder found himself getting fed up as the sky darkened outside. He was about to suppress another sigh when Golan said, 'I think that's enough, Lettle.'

Lettle looked sharply over at Golan. For a moment it looked like she was about to protest but then she glanced at Alder and took in the exhaustion on his face.

'Fine. But you need to sleep here tonight. I want to record everything you say and do in the night.'

'Is that necessary?' Golan said before Alder could protest.

'Well, someone has to,' Lettle said. There was a small smile playing on her lips but Alder didn't quite understand why.

'I'll do it,' Golan said. 'At least Alder is comfortable at my house. There's no need to bring him here.'

Lettle's smile grew and Alder finally caught onto her meaning. Golan's face flushed a warm peach colour.

Alder coughed into the awkward silence. 'Well then, perhaps we should—'

To Alder's relief the doors to the royal chambers opened and Rayan strode in, looking as tired as Alder felt.

'Oh,' he said in surprise. 'I didn't know you were all here.' Rayan's voice was tinged with the type of disappointment that only unexpected visitors can conjure.

'We're just leaving,' Alder said.

Rayan smiled weakly. 'You don't have to leave on my account.'

'No, Lettle's been working Alder to the bone, I think it is time to rest,' Golan said quickly.

Rayan went over to Lettle and pressed a kiss to her forehead. 'How has it been going?'

When they were apart, Alder couldn't imagine a more unlikely couple. Rayan calm and gentle, more prone to smiling than frowning. And then there was Lettle with her sharp scowls and inquisitive eyes. But together, they fit so perfectly. Like Mia and Dart, their love was palpable to the lucky few who got to witness it.

Lettle closed her journal with a sigh. 'No progress. But tomorrow is another day.'

Rayan winced and rubbed his eyes. 'There's something happening tomorrow that might hamper your plans.'

'What is it?' Lettle asked.

Golan and Alder lingered by the doors to the royal chambers, waiting to hear what Rayan had to say.

'We're throwing a banquet and the three of you will be the guests of honour,' Rayan said, swinging his gaze between Lettle, Golan and Alder.

'*What?*' Alder said.

'We'll be announcing a new initiative that will see the Lightless inducted into the fae court for the first time. Lettle and Golan will be spearheading this new partnership. Furi and I also think it'll be a good opportunity to announce that humans walk among us once more. It may ease some of the tension in the city.'

Lettle's eyebrows shot up at the same time as Alder's stomach was sinking.

'My notion has been approved? Truly?' she asked.

'Yes, we've invited both the Lightless and the court to the banquet.'

Alder looked to Golan, whose eyes had started to shimmer with tears. Alder rested his hand on the fae's shoulder and Golan turned to look at him.

'The Lightless invited to a royal banquet? That's never happened before,' he said softly.

'I said we'd change things,' Lettle said from across the room. 'This is only the start.'

Golan nodded, and the movement caused an unshed tear to fall. Alder wanted nothing more than to brush it away and hold Golan close. But then Lettle spoke again.

'The banquet to celebrate is tomorrow?' Lettle frowned. 'That's quick, Golan and I haven't even sat down to discuss how the organisation will run.'

Rayan's mouth worked for a second before he simply said, 'The plans have been made, that's what I've been working on all afternoon. It's to be a masked banquet so the Lightless feel less exposed.'

Alder suddenly felt too hot. 'What do I have to do during this banquet exactly?'

'Oh, nothing,' Rayan said. 'It's just an opportunity for the court to eat and drink as much as they can.'

Panic had started to make his belly churn, but Golan on the other hand, his eyes were sparkling with excitement.

'It's been a long time since we've had a banquet. You'll love it,' Golan promised, but Alder wasn't quite sure.

The two of them waved goodnight to Lettle and Rayan before

leaving the palace. The walk to Golan's home wasn't a long one but Alder appreciated the cool air and the quiet.

Well, not entirely quiet. Golan was running through all the outfit options he had for Alder.

'I think silver, silver will suit you. The warmth of your skin and your grey eyes, oh wait, no, maybe sapphire. I have the most gorgeous sapphire cape . . .'

Alder let him continue on, the joy in Golan's face eliciting a smile on his.

A full day had almost passed again and the countdown to leave with the Nomads was getting closer minute by minute.

'No, I know, red, red to bring out the strawberry colours of your hair . . .' Golan was still going as they walked into the warmth of his home.

The fire was lit and the torches burned brightly. Alder realised Golan must have a servant of some kind but he hadn't yet seen them.

Golan hesitated on the threshold of the house.

'I . . . I'll bring in a pallet and sleep on the floor of your room if that's all right? I'll keep a notebook and pen beside me in case anything happens.'

Alder shook his head. 'No, I don't mind staying in your room with the bigger bed. It's probably a good idea we share anyway, because last time you didn't notice me sleepwalking. At least this time you'll feel the mattress move.'

'We should tie you up,' Golan said laughing. Then he realised what he'd said and looked stricken.

Instead of waving away the awkwardness, Alder chuckled and said, 'Maybe, one day.'

The air in the room sparked with anticipation. Golan's full lips parted and he said a little breathlessly, 'To my room it is then.'

The fifteen paces across the corridor felt like drawing back an arrow in a bow. The tension was tightening with each step, and when they crossed the doorway Alder let the arrow fly.

His hands swept up from Golan's lower back to the nape of his neck as he drew him towards his lips.

At first Golan reciprocated slowly, the kiss soft and tender. But then the passion between them grew hungry and Alder pressed his body closer to Golan's until there was no space between them.

Golan made a small sound in the back of his throat as he felt Alder's thigh touch his. The sound was enough to send all his blood rushing to one place. He deepened the kiss once more before drawing away and pressing his lips against Golan's jaw and neck.

'Alder,' Golan said. It sounded like a command, and it drew Alder's attention back to his lips which were pink and parted. 'Undress me,' he continued.

Alder had never been so willing to meet a demand. He took his time pressing each button through the hole of his shirt before turning to his trousers.

He knew he was moving agonisingly slow, but he wanted to relish the feeling where cloth turned to skin – to appreciate every bit of Golan's body.

When he reached his upper thigh he asked, 'Do you mind?'

Golan shook his head, giving him permission to remove the artificial leg. Alder always noticed as the day drew on, Golan would begin to favour his right leg. And for what he had in mind, he wanted Golan to be comfortable.

The silver metal slid away and Golan relaxed backwards on the bed. His sheets were silk and the sheen of them reflected the firelight of the torches. He glittered like a god.

'You look otherworldly,' Alder breathed.

Golan laughed. 'You're the one who's human.'

Alder's smile faltered. He didn't want to be reminded of that fact at this moment.

'Does it bother you?' Alder asked quietly.

Golan frowned, then laughed. 'Of course not, you're Alder. That's all that matters.'

He beckoned him to the bed but Alder suddenly felt self-conscious.

'Come here,' Golan said softly. The dangerous edge was back in his voice and it stoked the flames of Alder's desire once more.

Alder went to lie beside him.

Golan's muscles rippled as he used his arms to sit up before straddling Alder, who was still fully clothed.

He lowered himself down until their chests were touching and then he whispered, 'You are Alder. That is all that matters. Not the shape of your ears,' his tongue glided along their rounded edge, 'nor the blood in your veins,' further down he trailed, across his neck towards his navel, undressing him as he went.

Golan's hands glided over Alder's bare chest, his lips resting above his heart. 'All that matters is what's in there.'

Then he continued his exploration, his hands working down towards the swell in his trousers, until they were dispensed of too.

'Golan,' Alder said as his mouth teased around his hipbones before moving towards the aching part of him.

Golan looked up, his smile soft and mischievous. 'Do you want me to stop?'

Alder could feel Golan's breath travel down the length of him. He didn't trust himself to speak so he shook his head.

Golan's mouth encased him and he let out a groan. His hands went to the back of Golan's head as he set out a rhythm of pleasure that had Alder's blood singing.

He moved slowly at first, his hand guiding him up with the movement as his tongue swirled and his mouth sucked.

Then he moved faster, taking him deeper, until Alder was at the brink.

'I'm close,' he gasped.

Golan's eyes were alight with arousal as he watched Alder writhe beneath his touch.

'Golan . . .' His name was like a key and it unlocked the door to oblivion.

Stars danced across his vision as he shuddered through the echoes of completion. It felt like hours, it felt like seconds.

Golan sat up, a satisfied smile spreading across his lips.

Alder watched him for a moment, enjoying the flush that travelled up his chest and the light sheen of sweat that shimmered across his neck.

Then he placed his hands on Golan's hips and guided him back down on the bed.

'I think it might be your turn,' Alder said. Golan's eyes began to burn hotter as Alder's hands began to explore the warmth of his desire.

When they eventually went to sleep that night, it was the early hours of the morning. And for the first time in a long time, Alder didn't dream.

CHAPTER THIRTY-TWO

Lettle

Golan strode into Lettle's chambers with a lightness to his expression that she had never seen before.

'Good night?' she asked carefully.

Golan shot her a knowing look. 'Yes, thank you.'

'Have any notes for me?'

'He didn't sleepwalk last night.'

Lettle sighed. 'Did you have to tire him out?'

Golan laughed and it cut through her irritation. 'How did you know?'

'It's obvious from the way he looks at you. I'm glad you've finally succumbed. Where is he anyway?'

'I left him to dress for the banquet, which *you* should be doing, seer.' He pulled out his cloth bag which was always filled with make-up and trinkets.

Lettle looked down at her notebook. She was slowly trying to translate the sounds Alder had made from memory using some of the ciphers Omur had suggested.

It was not going well.

'I'm not attending tonight,' Lettle said. She'd had time to think about it, and though she appreciated Rayan and Furi's faith in her idea, the pageantry of the banquet seemed at odds with her plans for the initiative.

Let them celebrate while I begin the true work behind closed doors.

'I don't think it's optional, Lettle,' Golan said.

She didn't look up from her notes before replying, 'I'm the seer and the consort to the king. I think I can do what I want. Besides, you're a better public representative of the initiative. You're Lightless, plus they don't want to kill you.'

Rayan strode in from their bedroom dressed in a long violet cape decked with gemstones and a loose-fitting cream shirt and trousers. Lettle's eyes lingered where the buttons of his shirt revealed the slip of dark skin of his chest.

In his hand he held a cream mask lined with lavender flowers.

'You look wonderful, Rayan,' Lettle said.

'Indeed, a well-put-together outfit,' Golan added.

Rayan gave him a lopsided grin. 'That is high praise from you. Thank you.' Then he looked at Lettle and said, 'You're going to be late, you know.'

She waved a hand over her work and said, 'I'm not going.'

Rayan's lips drew into a line before saying, 'You *have* to come.'

'Why? I hate small talk. And the Lightless I'll want to be working with won't be the people you invited. So I don't really see the point.'

'Lettle . . .' he frowned as if considering his next words carefully. 'I think it'll be good for Mosima to see the Jani dynasty united as one. Besides, I would like it to get back to the Authority that you are hale and whole.'

Lettle couldn't understand it. 'But surely I'm safer here, there are more guards than I can count surrounding our rooms.'

Rayan shook his head. 'You are never safer than by my side. Please, Lettle. I want you with me tonight. I even had a matching mask made, it's on the bed.'

She considered for a moment, but there was no hesitation really. If Rayan wanted her there, then she'd be there, for that was the partnership they had.

'Fine,' she said. 'Golan, we've got a lot of work to do in a very short space of time.'

* * *

Lettle walked over to the obeah orchard with sullen steps. Golan had chosen a lilac gown to match the purple tones of her and Rayan's masks. Though she noticed hers was barely a slip of fabric that just spanned her eyes. She'd hoped for more of a covert mask so she could have hidden on the sidelines of the party.

The dress felt like water on her skin as she moved. The sheer fabric ended at her ankles, showing off the crystal-adorned sandals she wore. It revealed an ample amount of cleavage, but she'd become used to the less modest cuts the fae wore during her months here. Now she couldn't imagine wearing the restrictive clothes she'd worn before.

Golan led the way down the tunnel to the obeah orchard. The sound of party-goers and music got louder as they approached.

When they stepped into the orchard Lettle was dumbfounded with the transformation.

Colourful silks hung from the balconies all around the courtyard. Star gliders glittered like fallen stars, some fluttering in spirals among the dancers. Candles had been placed in the trees, scenting the already fragrant plants with honey and roses.

Servants moved between the masked people, each holding a tray of food or drink. Lettle spotted Anyah in the periphery of her vision, ready to taste test anything she reached for.

'This is marvellous, perhaps Rayan should plan all the banquets. Just look at the flowers he's grown around the dance floor,' Golan said.

But Lettle was no longer looking at the decorations. Her attention was entirely consumed by the fae who lingered at the edges of the orchard.

Despite their masks Lettle could tell they were Lightless. Though she couldn't see their expressions it was clear they were uncomfortable and finding solace among their kind. Whereas those faebound were dancing merrily, obeah weaving around their legs.

The differences didn't end there. The Lightless's clothes were less opulent, less vibrant. Their masks looked homemade, while those in the royal court wore extravagant face coverings peppered with jewels.

It was as if an invisible fence ran around the periphery of the party separating the Lightless from the rest of the fae.

Lettle shook her head.

This was a terrible idea. The Lightless don't feel welcome here, it just highlights more of Mosima's division.

And would in turn incite more anger towards her – an elf dressed in finery, more comfortable than they were among the ruling class.

Lettle shivered and tried to bring her mask lower on her face. None of them had noticed her yet, but she still felt the weight of their hatred.

I would hate me too, she thought glumly.

'Oh look, there's Alder,' Golan said, pointing to a lonely figure picking raspberries from a nearby bush. 'I knew the green would suit him,' he continued triumphantly.

Alder wore a corseted jacket of deep forest green that flared along the sleeves. His trousers were a rich earthy brown ending in black boots. Lettle and Golan strode towards him.

'Sorry we're late, Lettle was acting like a child,' Golan said.

Lettle swatted at his arm. 'I was not, I just didn't want to come.'

Alder grimaced. 'I didn't want to come either,' he admitted. 'Golan made me wear *boots*.'

Lettle laughed. 'They do look good though.'

'There you are,' Rayan said, appearing in front of her. 'Oh good, and you're with Alder and Golan. All of you, come with me please.'

Rayan seemed jittery and Lettle slipped a hand around his waist. She was surprised when her arm touched something cold beneath his shirt.

'Are you wearing a dagger?' she asked as he began to lead her towards a raised platform in the centre of the party.

He wrapped an arm around her shoulders as they moved through the crowd. 'Yes,' he said. 'Remember, the Authority hasn't been caught yet.'

Lettle hadn't forgotten, especially surrounded by the glittering eyes of the Lightless.

The band was in full swing, playing a jaunty melody that kept the dance floor alive with spritely dance moves. It was at odds with Lettle's mood and she found herself turning back to look at the Lightless who were watching the band from the edges of the orchard. None of them looked happy to be there.

'Who are all these people?' Alder asked as he and Golan followed Rayan and Lettle through the crowd of dancers.

'The royal court. Those in charge of agriculture, housing, waterways, mines . . .' Golan listed off the most important people, but Lettle stopped listening. She'd met them before and only remembered a handful of names.

'Rayan, where are you taking us?' Lettle asked as she spotted a dais had been erected in an area in front of the band. Next to it was the basin of fire that was usually placed in front of the thrones in the royal courtyard. It was the first time Lettle had seen it lit since the night the queens had died. The chalice, filled with wine that the king and queen would sip from before dousing the fire at the end of the evening, stood on a precipice beside it.

She'd be watching Anyah to make sure there was no poison in it tonight.

'It's time to announce the initiative to the court, and introduce Alder too,' he said grimly.

Lettle's chest constricted with panic. 'What? Now? Oh, do we have to? I don't want to stand up in front of all these people. I don't know if you've noticed but the Lightless don't exactly look like they're having a good time.'

'That's only because they don't know why they're here. Only a few hundred accepted our invite, and I think it was mainly out of curiosity.' Rayan turned to her and smiled. 'And now it's time to give them hope.'

Lettle swallowed her nerves and nodded back at him. 'OK.'

He squeezed her shoulder before ushering her onto the dais. Golan and Alder were a step behind.

Furi, dressed head to toe in burnt copper silk, took to the stage from the other side. She tipped her head in Lettle's direction.

Although Furi hadn't initially been supportive of Lettle's idea, she was glad she'd agreed to it. The welfare of *all* her citizens was just as important as trying to protect Mosima from war.

And where Furi was, Lettle knew Yeeran wouldn't be far behind. And sure enough, there was her sister, dressed in a leather doublet and a chainmail veil standing a few paces away from the dais.

'Golan, why are we standing on the stage? Everyone is looking at me,' Alder whispered. Golan quietened him by slipping his hand into his.

The band's music faded away until silence swept through the party. Lettle watched as the Lightless drew nearer to the stage, closing the space between those bound and not.

When Furi spoke, it was in the universal tongue. 'Welcome, all, to the obeah orchard. A sacred place blessed by my ancestors as a haven for the court's companions. You may all be wondering why you have been invited here, those bound and unbound together.'

It was a cue for Rayan to speak. Lettle was surprised they had organised this so thoughtfully, it solidified her faith that change was possible.

'We acknowledge that there is an imbalance in the rights of those deemed Lightless and those faebound. Responsibility lies with the Jani dynasty for allowing this segregation to fester and grow, and it is now time for us to put it right.'

Furi stiffened beside Rayan and Lettle wondered if he'd added the part about it being the Jani's fault.

'You may be wondering who these masked individuals are beside me. Some may recognise Seer Lettle, an elf whose experience in Mosima has ignited tensions in the city, bringing to light more problems than even I had considered. Next to her is Golan O'Lightless, a trusted advisor to the court, whose support in this matter has been unrelenting.'

Rayan took a deep breath before continuing. 'Together they will be launching the Free the Light Initiative within the royal court that will see the Lightless become a part of our governing body. The voice of the Lightless has been silenced for too long, and the queen and I seek to right the wrongs of injustice and inequality among *all* of our people.'

Murmurings began in the crowd, the faebound of the royal court were frowning – unhappy with the change in status quo. But Lettle didn't care about them, she was watching the Lightless.

Their masks hid most of their expressions, but what she could glean from their demeanour suggested they were less than impressed. Many had folded their arms, and some were even leaving the orchard. Their chatter increased in volume and Lettle could hear the dissent in their tone.

Furi fought to be heard. 'Tonight is a celebration of this new initiative. A much-needed change within Mosima.'

Her words were drowned out by the noise, and she looked to Rayan. He shook his head, unsure what to do.

Lettle stepped forward and Golan gave her an encouraging nod. 'I know most of you hate me,' she shouted. It took a moment, but the crowd began to quieten. 'I'm an elf accepted among the royal court and consort to your king. I have more rights than you.' Mutterings from the Lightless began to grow again but she stopped them with a raised hand. 'And that is *not right*. It is time things changed. Though Golan and I will be leaders of this new venture, we will be truly led by *you*, by your experiences and your wishes. To make Mosima a better place for all. When I say "free the light", I mean it. It's time for the Lightless to come out of the dark.'

Lettle felt the atmosphere shift among the Lightless. It was only slight, but the scales had tipped from hostility to curiosity.

Rayan beamed beside her. 'That was well done,' he said under his breath.

Even Furi was gazing out at the crowd with awe and Lettle had to wonder whether she'd ever seen this many Lightless in one place.

Lettle stepped backwards, done with being in the spotlight. But the royals were not yet finished with their introductions.

'There is one more surprise for you tonight,' Rayan said. 'The third and final person we'd like to draw your attention to is Alder. Our guest and the first descendant of humans seen in a millennium.'

Shock rippled out across the orchard.

'We will be working with him on learning more about the curse that binds us here,' Furi said. 'We cannot promise our efforts will be successful but know that we try.'

There was a moment of stunned disbelief, then someone shouted, 'You mean there might come a time when we are free?'

Furi nodded. 'That is our goal.'

The hope that swept the orchard was universal, whether they were faebound or not.

Someone gasped, then another let out an elated cry. Soon a cheer spread through the crowd, the wave of joy made Lettle smile.

This simple act of unity was the first step forward for her initiative.

The band began to play again and this time when Lettle looked to the dance floor it was as if the party had transformed. The Lightless hadn't fully integrated, but the hope that the two announcements had brought had done more to break the boundaries between the two groups than Lettle could have imagined.

The five of them walked off stage. Rayan murmured his apologies that he had to check on something before disappearing into the crowd.

'Well, I'm glad that's over,' Alder said. He looked visibly shaken by the ordeal. Lettle doubted he'd ever had so many eyes on him at once.

'Why don't we dance?' Golan said. He held out his hand and guided Alder to a corner of the dance floor where they wouldn't be bothered.

The band's melody took a more sombre note, shifting to a haunting ballad that had Alder and Golan moving closer to each other.

She watched them dance for a little while, Golan so careful and tender while Alder was simply adoring.

'You did well, Lettle,' Furi said behind her.

Lettle turned and smiled. Though deep down she was annoyed at how good Furi's approval felt.

'I just told them what they wanted to hear. That I would be someone who listened instead of ruled.'

'Listening? I don't remember that being within your skillset growing up,' Yeeran said, joining them.

Lettle gave Yeeran a sardonic grin. 'People change.'

'And so do places,' Furi said thoughtfully as she looked out across the orchard.

'You should go and mingle, meet some of the Lightless,' Furi encouraged Lettle.

'Mingling' was the last thing Lettle wanted to do. She'd rather go back to her chambers and begin outlining the aims for the initiative. But she knew Furi spoke sense.

She drifted through the party, nodding at anyone who looked her way. She was aware she didn't have an approachable demeanour, so she tried to loosen her stance and painted a smile on her face as she walked.

'Is the party over yet?' a voice said to her right.

Lettle recognised Sahar beneath the plain strip of fabric that covered his eyes. The mask did nothing to hide the dark bags that gathered there and she knew Norey wasn't far from his thoughts.

The funeral had been carried out last night, but Lettle didn't attend. Rayan had thought it a good idea that the murderer not be present at the victim's funeral.

'I'm surprised you're here,' she said carefully. Together they walked to the edges of the orchard where they could talk more freely.

They had not spoken since he had discovered Norey's betrayal, and her part in his death.

'I don't blame you, Lettle. Not for his death,' Sahar said.

Lettle felt herself relax in relief. 'I would understand if you did though.'

'I know. You're understanding like that. But it wasn't your fault.

It was mine.' Sahar's speech was a little slurred, and as a tray of mead passed by, he took two glasses and handed one to her.

'It wasn't your fault, Sahar. No one knew about his true intentions, he hid them well.'

Lettle jumped as someone tapped her on the back. It was Anyah. 'May I?' she asked.

Lettle handed her the drink with a scowl. 'I can't wait to be able to eat and drink again without someone breathing down my neck.'

Anyah didn't twitch at Lettle's surly mood. She just did her duty as usual.

'How goes your divination?' Sahar asked over the rim of his glass. 'Have the Fates spoken to you again?'

Lettle shook her head. 'No, I've given up trying for now.'

'You cannot give up, Lettle. You cannot be a seer without seeing things.'

'I know that,' she snapped back, more harshly than she intended. The old man smiled sadly and she felt dreadful.

'I'm sorry,' she said. 'I'm just frustrated.'

'Do you have your talismans with you now?'

She nodded. She never went anywhere without them.

'Why don't we find a quiet spot and give it a go together? Perhaps there is something you're doing wrong.'

Lettle wanted to say that there was no use, but it was an excuse to slip away from the party. It unnerved her that everyone here knew who she was, but she had no idea who they were beneath their masks.

'All right.'

A tray of breadcrumbed mushrooms passed just before they left, and Lettle grabbed the whole platter before following Sahar.

Sahar led her deeper into the Royal Woodland until they reached the pathway to Conch Shore. The sounds of the waves soothed her as they got closer.

She rarely came here. It had been where Furi had trained Yeeran and that somehow made her feel like she was trespassing in a way she felt nowhere else in the palace.

The fray was setting from deep red to the colour of a purple bruise with the oncoming night.

'Here will do,' Sahar said, sitting on the soft sand with ease. He always seemed so frail, but she was consistently surprised at his suppleness.

Lettle set the tray of mushrooms to the side and took out her talismans. 'When I was on the plains I noticed that one of them had grown more smooth than the others. Do you think that could have something to do with it?'

She held it out to Sahar who scrutinised it in the fading light. 'No, I don't think so. Try casting them.'

Lettle was about to throw them when she saw something move near the shoreline. As it came closer she realised it was an obeah.

'Ah, it's Cori.' Sahar beckoned his obeah closer. As she drew nearer Lettle felt unease prickle up her spine.

She'd seen his obeah many times before, but there was something in the way she moved that was setting alarm bells off in her mind.

'Cast the tokens, Lettle,' Sahar said, drawing her away from her thoughts.

She nodded and threw the talismans across the sand. But Cori caught her attention as she stood and turned, facing something she heard behind them.

It was then that Lettle saw the patch of white fur on the back of her leg.

Her blood ran cold and she froze.

Sahar was the Authority.

No, he can't be, her mind screamed back at her. It wouldn't make sense.

'Now enter magesight. And tell me what do you see?' he said by her side. For now, he hadn't noticed anything amiss, so she pretended to do as he said and looked down at the tokens while keeping him in her peripheral vision.

Please, Sahar, let it not be you.

'I see . . .' she started, but her voice trailed off into nothingness as she saw the glint of a blade as Sahar slowly removed it from its sheath.

He thought she was in magesight, unable to see the shapes of things not alive.

'What do you see?' he prompted.

She tensed her muscles, getting ready to run, but then Cori whined beside them.

Sahar jumped up and spun around.

Someone threw themselves at Sahar, pinning him to the ground. It took a moment for Lettle to recognise Anyah, the taste tester.

The servant grappled with Sahar, kicking the dagger from his hand, but not before he nicked her wrist with the blade. Crimson blood sprayed across the sand and she cried out.

'Anyah!' Lettle ran forward but Cori locked her horns over Anyah's body, preventing her from moving.

The dagger glinted on the sand a foot away from both Lettle and Sahar.

Lettle lunged but the older man was too quick.

Before Lettle could scream, Sahar was holding the blade to her throat.

'Sahar, put down the dagger,' Rayan said coldly.

Lettle felt Sahar's grip tighten as he whirled them both around.

Rayan stood there surrounded by party-goers, all brandishing their own blades. But then Lettle looked more closely and she realised they weren't part of the court – they were faeguard.

She didn't need to look with magesight to know they all wielded magic along with their swords.

'Grandson . . . you don't understand . . .' Sahar stammered.

'Drop it,' Rayan said.

The blade began to press down on Lettle's neck and she cried out as she felt her blood trickle down her skin.

There was some commotion as someone joined the soldiers and worked their way up to the front of the formation.

'Father?' Furi had never looked more heartbroken. 'No, it cannot be.'

Sahar took in a ragged breath. 'Furi, my daughter, listen to me, this is not what you think.'

'Are you the Authority?' she asked, tears running down her face.

Sahar's shoulders slumped and the dagger fell to the ground. 'Yes.'

'Lettle,' Rayan called her over. She felt immediately safer by his side – the faeguard at her back helped too.

'Rayan, help Anyah,' Lettle said. 'She saved me.'

Rayan looked to where Cori still held Anyah captive beneath her horns.

'Call off your obeah, Grandfather.'

Cori moved back, and Anyah scuttled away towards safety. She held a hand over the wound at her wrist.

'Go to the palace healers,' Lettle said to her quietly. 'You'll need stitches.'

Anyah met her gaze and nodded once, but just as she turned away Lettle said, 'Thank you.'

'You would have done the same for me,' Anyah said with a shrug.

Lettle felt Anyah's trust emanate from her words. Perhaps because not everyone in Mosima would have tried to save Anyah if their roles were reversed, as being Lightless made Anyah less important in their eyes. If there was one good thing to come out of tonight, it was this – the faith she had started to garner among the community.

Once she was gone, Lettle turned back to Sahar.

'Why?' Furi asked him, her voice cracking as she spoke.

Sahar looked at Lettle. 'Do you want to tell them, or should I?'

Lettle's brows knotted together as everyone turned to look at her. 'I've no idea what he's talking about.'

Sahar looked around at the blades pointed at him and saw there was no way out other than speaking the truth. He took a step towards Rayan.

'A couple of months ago the Fates spoke to me of you.' Sahar's lip began to shake and his eyes filled with tears. 'Losing my son was more difficult than I could have ever imagined. He was my confidant, my friend. And then the gods gifted me you. Such a sweet boy, like he was, but hardened by the world in ways my son had never been. Rayan, you brought me back to life.'

Rayan was crying now, his heart breaking as his grandfather laid bare his betrayal.

'I saw how Vyce was tortured by the truth of prophecy, and I told myself I would never deny it, like she did. But . . . but, Grandson, when the Fates spoke to me of your murder . . .'

Lettle heard ringing in her ears as her heart began to pump faster and faster.

'. . . I could not let that happen. I fell prey to the very same trap Vyce did . . . but I could not . . . I could *not* let another one of my family go. So when I learned of my love's betrayal, instead of turning him in, I joined them in the hopes of ridding me of further grief. But it did not work . . . and I lost him as I will one day lose you.'

Sahar's words disappeared into sobs.

Rayan shook his head. 'I don't understand, the Fates have spoken of my murder?'

Lettle tugged on Rayan's sleeve, panic surging up her throat. 'I think we should give him a little time, maybe?'

She would do anything for this truth not to be spoken.

But Furi pressed Sahar further. 'What did the Fates say, Father?'

Sahar took in a shuddering breath before pointing to Lettle. 'One day, she will kill Rayan.'

Lettle's world came crashing down around her.

CHAPTER THIRTY-THREE

Alder

Alder eased into the music slowly. He'd never been a dancer – even during the harvest festivals the Nomads held, he'd needed a lot of rum before being lured to the dance floor.

But he wanted to be close to him and Golan wanted to dance, so Alder danced.

'You move so well,' Alder commented as Golan pivoted on his artificial leg in an elaborate swirl.

Golan's eyes twinkled from the compliment. 'I've always loved dancing,' he said. 'I find it soothes me in ways other exercise cannot.'

He grasped Alder's hands and pulled him closer. 'Apart from one other thing.'

Alder chuckled and drew him close enough to nip the pointed tip of his ear.

Golan shuddered slightly before whirling away.

They danced like that for some time, as playful as they were sensual. It was as if no one else mattered.

And no one else did. Even when the band paused for a break, they didn't stop. Instead, they continued dancing to the song only the two of them could hear.

Tonight, I have to leave with the Nomads. The thought was brittle against the warmth of the moment.

But did he *have* to leave? Though he knew his night terrors were linked to being human, he had no idea what caused them or how to control them.

And the curse on the fae, Lettle believed he was the answer to breaking it. Could he really walk away and leave the fae to their fate?

Alder looked around and wondered if he could live here indefinitely. With star gliders twirling around him and the warmth in his belly from mead he thought there were worse places to be.

'What are you frowning about?' Golan asked.

'I was just thinking about the curse, and why you are all so desperate to break it. It's a paradise down here.'

Golan's hips stopped swaying and he let out a sigh. 'Yes, it is a paradise, but it's still a prison. It removes our ability to choose and over time that becomes a choker around our neck.'

Golan pointed to the frostbitten leaves that had fallen around them. New shoots were growing, but the orchard wasn't as fruitful as it could have been.

'We are also tied to the Jani dynasty line. They control the world we live in, and that volatility is hard to ignore.'

Alder nodded, but he didn't really understand it for he had lived without rules his whole life. Except the rules of nature.

That was the one thing that unsettled him about Mosima: nothing grew here like it was supposed to. Influenced by the Jani's magic, plants could grow at whim ignoring the rules of seasons. It didn't feel wrong exactly, just strange. He missed the cyclical routine of the surface.

'The Nomads are waiting for me. I have to go to them tonight,' Alder admitted.

All expression fell from Golan's face. 'You're leaving?'

'No . . . well, I don't think so. Maybe . . . I'm not sure.'

Golan stepped off the dance floor towards the thicker foliage around the edge of the clearing.

Alder followed him. 'Golan, where are you going?'

Golan turned. 'You need to decide, Alder. And to do that, you need to go see the Nomads. I'll walk with you to the boundary.'

Alder hesitated. He knew he had to go, that the night was wearing on and that they would be waiting on him.

But he wasn't sure what he was going to do. Alder and Golan walked to the boundary in silence, each immersed in their own thoughts.

When they reached the tunnel to the outside world Alder couldn't help thinking: *This cannot be the last time I see Golan.*

He looked at him, but Golan's face was impassive.

'What would you do if you were me?' Alder asked.

Golan considered him for a moment. 'I have never had the family that you have with the Nomads, so I cannot fathom what it would be like to abandon them. But neither do I want you to leave, not just for me, but for the people of Mosima. You could change our future.'

'Do you really think so? Because I'm not sure.' He couldn't spend the next few months or years meditating with Lettle in the hopes that somehow, they might figure out how to speak human.

And then there was the war. He had no experience of war and wanted no part in the bloodshed.

But Golan . . .

'I don't want to leave you,' Alder whispered.

Golan looked into his eyes and said simply, 'I won't ask you to stay.'

'Why not?'

'Because like I said, I value choice, and though I do not choose to live down here – I would never ask someone to bind themselves to a prison.'

'You are a far greater man than I deserve, Golan.'

Golan's laugh tinkled across the gap between them. Alder closed it, wanted to be nearer to the sound, to his smile.

He kissed him slowly, not like a goodbye, but like the beginning of something more.

Golan broke away first and said against Alder's lips, 'Go now, and maybe I'll see you again.'

Alder closed his eyes, breathing in the warmth of Golan's scent before turning and leaving Mosima behind.

Alder followed the trail until he saw the signs of the Nomads' canopies in the bough above him. He trilled out a warning call before climbing the nearest tree.

'Is that you, Alder?' Mia was bounding from canopy to canopy, leaving disgruntled Nomads in her wake. A slower, bulkier shadow followed her.

'Hello, Mia, Dart,' Alder said, taking a seat in the nearest hammock.

Mia launched herself at him, squeezing his lungs of air. 'We thought you were dead!'

'I said I'd be back in four days,' Alder choked out. When she released him, he took in a deep breath.

'You really waited until the last minute,' Dart said, nodding a greeting before sitting opposite him.

'I've been a little preoccupied . . .' Alder said before launching into the story of what had transpired over the last few days.

'You're *human*?' Mia exclaimed when he'd finished.

'I think so,' Alder said.

'But what does that mean?'

'I'm not sure, but apparently I speak the human tongue in my sleep.'

Mia clapped her hand to her mouth. 'The nightmare tongue!'

'Exactly, somehow it's all linked to my sleepwalking.'

Dart was frowning. 'Maybe when we get to Caperly we can ask the elders a bit more about how they found you. I'm sure they'll know more.'

Alder didn't reply straight away.

'You *are* coming with us to Caperly, aren't you?' Mia asked, her hand hovering over her belly where the slightest hint of a swell could be seen.

'I'm not sure I can, there's so much I could still learn. Besides, I might be able to help break the curse on the fae.'

'So what? Who are the fae to you?' Dart said. 'Nobody.'

Golan's face flashed beneath Alder's eyelids.

'If I can help, I don't see why I shouldn't.'

Mia nodded. 'That's fine, we can stay out here for another month, give you some time—'

Alder shook his head. 'No, war is coming, these forests won't be safe for much longer. Besides, you need to get to Caperly before you're too far along.'

'Alder, we're not leaving you.' Dart's voice was firm.

'You have to.' The decision came easy to him now he'd said it out loud. Of course he couldn't leave Mosima behind. Not yet.

'We'll wait for you, at least a few more weeks,' Mia said, her eyes beginning to swell with tears.

'No, Mia,' Alder said gently. 'Dart, you are now the Wayfarer of the group. Please get them safely to Caperly.'

Dart's hand reached out and rested on Alder's knee. 'Alder, you can't do this. You know the Nomads will not accept a new Wayfarer unless illness or age robs you of your ability.'

'There is one other way, Dart,' Alder said sadly.

Dart shook his head and his voice cracked as he said, 'Don't.'

'I refute the Nomad ways,' Alder said softly.

It was like an ice storm had swept through their conversation. Both Dart and Mia's faces turned cold as they looked past him as if he no longer existed.

'I love you both dearly. Know that if I can, I will one day find you again,' Alder said, his throat thick and hoarse.

Dart's eyes flickered to his for a final time and he nodded almost imperceptibly.

Climbing down from the safety of the Nomads' home was the hardest thing Alder had ever done.

When Alder returned to Mosima the fray was dark. He stumbled over what he thought was a rock.

'Ouch.' The rock spoke.

'Golan?'

'The very same.'

Alder reached for him, wrapping his arms around him. 'You waited.'

'I wasn't sure you'd come back,' Golan said into his shoulder. 'But I hoped, I really hoped.'

Golan trembled with relief beneath Alder's embrace.

How could I have considered leaving him?

Alder pulled him tighter, inhaling the sweetness of his perfume. Then he released him and brought his hands to either side of Golan's face. He finished the kiss he had started earlier.

When he was thoroughly satisfied, Alder broke away and said, 'I had so much more to do here.'

Golan laughed. 'Evidently.'

Alder ran his thumb along Golan's jaw. The creases of worry that had marred Golan's face before he left had gone.

'Thank you for waiting. For trusting I would come back to you,' Alder said softly.

Golan laid a hand above Alder's heart. 'I know you, Alder. Even if you don't know yourself.'

Alder had never felt more seen, more vulnerable, than he did in that moment. Of course Golan had known what his decision would be.

He slipped his hand into Golan's and together they walked back to the palace.

'Do you think the party will still be going on?' Alder asked.

'I doubt it. They will have doused the fire by now.'

'Then why are we going back?'

Golan squeezed his hand. 'Because that's the best bit. It's in the darkness where the true party begins.'

Alder felt his skin tingle with anticipation. But when they reached the obeah orchard, the flame was still burning and there were no guests to be seen.

Rayan sat on the ground by the fire, his head in his hands. He looked up as Alder and Golan walked over.

'What happened?' Golan asked.

Rayan looked wretched as he said, 'Sahar was the Authority.'

'What?' both Golan and Alder said at once.

'Yes, he was the one who poisoned the mead. And let out the assassins who tracked Lettle. He funded the rebellion in exchange for them killing her. All because of a prophecy.' Rayan dropped his head into his hands once more.

Alder was trying to follow, but half of what Rayan said hadn't made sense to him. From Golan's wide eyes, though, it seemed that something was slotting into place.

'Where is he now? And Lettle?' Golan asked.

'He's locked in the war room. Furi couldn't bear to sentence him, and truth be told neither can I. As for Lettle, I'm not sure. I . . . we . . . fought.'

Golan exchanged a worried look with Alder. That did not bode well.

Rayan stood up from the ground and looked left and right as if unsure where he was going. Then he mumbled something about food and wandered off.

'We missed a lot,' Alder said.

Golan frowned. 'Yes. I'm worried about Lettle. Let's go and find her.'

They walked the halls of the palace until they reached the royal chambers. When Golan knocked it was answered immediately.

'Oh, it's you,' Yeeran said.

Alder raised an eyebrow.

'Sorry, I thought you were Lettle,' she said.

They stepped into the room and Golan said, 'So she's not here then?'

'No, she walked off saying she needed some time alone.' Yeeran chewed her bottom lip.

'We've just seen Rayan,' Golan said.

Yeeran winced. 'It's all such a mess.'

'What happened exactly?' Alder asked.

Yeeran explained it all in detail, the ambush they had laid and the trap Sahar had sprung.

'And now Lettle's mad at me, Rayan's mad at her, and Furi's mad at everyone,' Yeeran finished.

Golan's eyes flashed with anger. 'I think Lettle has a right to her anger. You used us as bait to lure in the Lightless?'

Yeeran had the decency to look ashamed. 'Yes, but we had to keep our intentions secret . . .'

Golan began to pace. 'Do the king and queen even support the initiative?'

'They do,' Yeeran said hurriedly. 'This party was just an opportunity we could not pass by.'

Alder could feel the heat of Golan's anger. He'd never seen the fae so incensed before. A part of him enjoyed the flush that ran up Golan's neck and longed to caress it. But the severity of the situation stayed his hand.

Golan stopped pacing and dropped into a sofa with a heavy sigh. 'The initiative is meant to be based on open communication between the faebound and the Lightless. What you did undermined everything we're aiming to do.'

'I know. And I also know we owe you more than just an apology. What can I do?' Yeeran asked.

Golan's expression turned haggard. Alder sat beside him on the couch and leant his head on his shoulder.

'First we can start by sitting down together, all of us, and discussing the expectations that Lettle and I have within the royal court.'

'That's doable.'

Golan began to outline more changes he would like to see. His voice vibrating in his chest beneath Alder's ear.

Alder felt his eyelids grow heavy as Golan and Yeeran spoke. He hadn't had much sleep the night before and the activities of the day had exhausted him.

It wasn't long before he fell into a fitful sleep.

CHAPTER THIRTY-FOUR

Yeeran

Yeeran watched as Alder twitched in his sleep.

'Maybe he'll sleep talk,' she said quietly.

'Maybe,' Golan replied. 'We should write down what he says for Lettle.'

Lettle. Her name felt so fraught in her mind. She couldn't imagine how her sister was feeling. To know that she would be the death of the person she loved?

Yeeran shook her head, it was an unfathomable torment. If only Lettle had shared the load of it, they might not have missed the signs in Sahar.

Do not feel guilty, Yeeran, Pila said, coming to sit by her. *No one knew it was him.*

I know, but it's just . . . hard to accept that I didn't do enough. If we had at least told Lettle of the ambush this might not have gone so wrong.

If you had done that, then Sahar might not have been caught.

Yeeran rubbed her eyes and Pila put her head in Yeeran's lap, mewling softly. Yeeran scratched the underside of her chin. *Is Amnan with Furi?*

Yes, he comforts her, like I comfort you. I do comfort you, yes?

Yeeran smiled. *Yes.*

Furi had been distraught when she told Yeeran they had caught the Authority. She almost couldn't get the words out.

'It was F-Father,' she had said bitterly. Tears ran down her face but it was as if she couldn't feel them. 'He was the one who let the assassins out the boundary, he was the one who sent the haba to dismiss the guards at Lettle's door . . . he had known about the plains because he was going there as the Authority . . .'

They stood together in the empty orchard. Yeeran had made quick work of emptying it of all guests. The orchard felt eerie with just the remnants of the party left. Some of the streamers had fallen from their balconies and empty glasses littered the ground.

Yeeran stepped towards Furi to give her comfort. But for a second she wasn't sure Furi would go to her open arms.

When Furi did Yeeran let out a sigh of relief. 'I'm so sorry, Furi. I can't imagine how you must be feeling.'

'I'm not sure how to feel either,' Furi admitted.

'Where is Sahar now?' Yeeran asked, her lips against Furi's hair.

'He's being guarded in the war room. I couldn't sentence him tonight.'

'No, I understand.'

Furi pushed her out of the embrace and said, 'There's more.'

As Furi explained Lettle's part in it all Yeeran felt the urge to run to her sister.

'And Lettle? Is she with Rayan?' she asked.

'Yes, I left them together on the beach.'

Yeeran let out a sigh of relief. Hopefully the two of them would make it through this.

Furi looked around the orchard. 'Look at the remains of my court, Yeeran. Who can I ever trust again?'

Yeeran's hand went to Furi's waist and she brought her back into her embrace.

'You can trust me, you can *always* trust me.'

Furi abruptly pushed Yeeran away again, as if she was suffocating her. 'It's all too much, Yeeran.'

'Where are you going?' Yeeran called out as Furi began to stride away. 'Furi!'

The queen paused, waiting for Yeeran to catch up, then set off again.

'Furi? Where are we going?' Yeeran pressed, but the fae's lips were firm.

Eventually Yeeran realised their destination. White stones lined in mounds surrounded them.

None of the graves were named, for the fae believed names drew the souls back to earth, but Yeeran had been here before, so she recognised some of them. Furi stopped by the row at the edge and pointed to each grave in turn. Yeeran didn't need Furi to name them for her to know who they were.

Najma . . . Vyce . . . Chall . . . Nerad . . . Norey.

And Yeeran added her own names to the list too – Komi, Salawa.

'Soon Rayan, too?' Furi said. Her eyes burned red but she no longer cried. 'Death is all around us, Yeeran.' As she turned to walk away Yeeran caught her hand.

'But we, Furi, are *alive*. Don't walk away from me now. As long as you're willing to fight for the love we have, I'll be here, by your side.'

Furi looked at Yeeran's hand in hers and she said weakly, 'I'm so tired of fighting.' Then she slipped out of Yeeran's grasp and was gone.

A sob started in the back of Yeeran's throat as a chasm of emptiness opened beneath her. It threatened to swallow her whole but she wouldn't let it. Not here, in this haunted place.

She stilled her heart and settled her breath.

Something brushed past her leg and for an absurd minute she thought one of the ghosts had risen from their grave to taunt her. She jumped back only to realise it was Pila weaving between the tombs.

Always here, always yours, Pila said and it felt like the warmest of embraces.

Thank you, Pila. Let's leave this place. I have worried about the dead for long enough. It is time to make my peace with the living.

Together they walked to Conch Shore to check on Lettle, but the conversation with her sister hadn't been successful either.

A sound at the window shocked Yeeran from her memories and she was brought back to the present. It was a familiar noise, but one she had never heard in Mosima.

She went to the window and marvelled at the droplets on it.

'It's raining,' Yeeran said.

'It can't be.' Golan joined her at the window and looked out. Then he let out a long sigh. 'The Jani family are hurting.'

Yeeran wondered who had caused the rainfall, Furi or Rayan.

'Laqid har alwaqar litahhiq elnugu'a,' Alder murmured, and both Yeeran and Golan went to his side.

'Did you get that?' Yeeran asked and Golan nodded, already jotting it down in a notebook.

Pila had sat up and was watching Alder.

What is it? Yeeran asked.

Alder suddenly stood up from the chair, his eyes glazed and half-open.

'Laqid har alwaqar litahhiq elnugu'a,' he said in Pila's direction.

Golan looked between the obeah and Alder.

Pila? Yeeran asked as the beast's ears pinned back.

I . . . I can understand him, Pila said.

What do you mean, you can understand him? Yeeran asked.

It is easy, like breathing. I hear his words as if you have spoken them.

'What is happening?' Golan asked, having noticed Yeeran's silence.

Yeeran swung wide eyes to Golan. 'Pila says she can understand him.'

'What? What is he saying?'

Pila translated and Yeeran repeated it. 'He just said: "The time for the curse to end is fast approaching."'

CHAPTER THIRTY-FIVE

Lettle

Lettle had stood in front of a dagger, drum, arrow, even a sword, and had never felt as much fear as she had beneath Sahar's pointing finger.

Then he condemned her with his words: 'One day, she will kill Rayan.'

The silence was all-encompassing, closing in on her like darkness – until Rayan's laugh broke it.

'What? That can't be true.'

Sahar looked to Lettle. 'Tell him.'

Lettle dragged her gaze up to where it had sunk to the ground. When she met Rayan's eyes, they pleaded for her to tell him it wasn't true.

'Rayan,' in his name she hid a thousand apologies.

Rayan's mouth went slack with shock.

She could see his trust in her fracturing, each word a shard that made her wince. 'Why didn't you tell me?'

'I-I couldn't.'

Furi looked between them then back at Sahar. 'Look what lies have done to our family.'

The condemnation was bleak against the crashing waves of the sea.

'Father, I cannot sentence you tonight,' she continued. 'I need to sit with my grief. Some may think it weak, but I cannot in good faith be impartial.'

Rayan was still looking at Lettle like she already held a dagger above his heart. This was what she'd been afraid of.

Furi indicated for the faeguard to lead Sahar away before trailing the procession with heavy steps.

It left just Lettle and Rayan on the beach.

'When did you first foretell my death?' Rayan asked.

Lettle swallowed and stepped towards him. Not close enough to feel his heat, but enough for her to fill his field of vision.

'Five months ago, when we were on our way to Mosima.'

He inhaled sharply but let her go on.

'Remember what I told you, that the Fates said a person born from a storm's mist will be my beloved?'

He nodded and she took a deep breath before saying, 'The second part of it was: *But when the waning moon turns, you will grant them their death.*'

He took a step back from her as if struck by drumfire. His expression turned guarded, bringing tears to Lettle's eyes.

'That is why I didn't want to tell you. You think I intend to hurt you.'

'Lettle, I am not mad because the Fates have told you of my death at your hands. What I have learned from prophecy, from you, is that we cannot predict how and what it might mean. Perhaps you trip me up in my old age, or maybe I catch a flu from you. It does not worry me that you will be the death of me as I know you will never intend to kill me. But, Lettle . . . you hid something from me, something that was used against me and my family. I . . . I don't know if I can forgive that.'

Rayan turned away and, in that moment, Lettle knew what death would be like, for it felt like her heart had stopped. She reached for him, holding onto his shirt with a desperation she'd never experienced before.

'No, you don't get to walk away from me. You lied to me, too, don't forget. You hid Ajax from me!' she shouted.

Rayan's hand went to her neck where the necklace he had made for her lay. His fingers ran along the different beads and stones representing so many memories.

'I did lie to you, Lettle, though at the time I thought I was doing the right thing. And since then I have regretted it deeply. But perhaps you're right, I too am to blame for all this. We might love each other, Lettle, but without trust we cannot live for each other.'

Then his hands dropped to his sides. Lettle grabbed the necklace and wrenched it off her neck.

'So one lie and you abandon everything?' she said, holding the beads aloft.

Rayan didn't reply so she turned to the sea and threw the necklace into it.

When she looked back, he was gone.

She fell to the ground and cried until she had nothing left.

Lettle wasn't sure how much time had passed when Yeeran found her on the beach. The fray was dark and the torch Yeeran held made the waves glitter with sparks.

'Lettle?'

Lettle looked up, her eyes blurry.

'I've spoken to Furi. She told me what happened,' Yeeran continued.

When Lettle didn't get up, Yeeran knelt in the sand and wrapped her arms around her. But Lettle felt hollow, like she wasn't fully present.

'Lettle, why are you wet?'

'I went swimming, tried to get back my necklace,' Lettle said. Though it felt she answered from a great distance away.

Yeeran only held her tighter.

'I'm so sorry about it all,' Yeeran said softly into her hair. 'When we laid the trap we had no idea it would be Sahar.'

It took Lettle a moment to hear her words and when she did, she pushed Yeeran away so she could see her expression in the firelight.

'What trap?'

Yeeran's brows knotted together. 'Oh, I thought Rayan would have told you by now. The party, it was to lure out the Authority.'

Lettle felt her despair crystallise into rage. '*What?*'

'Don't be vexed with him. I insisted we keep it secret from you, I knew you wouldn't be able to keep it from your face if you knew you were bait.'

Yeeran said it so matter-of-factly that Lettle wanted to claw the passive expression off her face.

'You used me as bait and *no one told me?*'

'Sorry, Lettle.' Yeeran had the sense to look a little more abashed.

'And the initiative, do they even intend to let me run it?'

Yeeran nodded. 'Yes, the timeline to instigate it was just brought forward to allow for the ambush.'

Lettle was beyond furious. She stood up and began to walk away, unable to abide Yeeran's presence any longer.

'Where are you going?' Yeeran called after her.

'Away from you. All of you. Don't follow me.'

'Lettle, be careful, just because we caught Sahar doesn't mean there's no more danger.'

'If you cared about putting me in danger you wouldn't have used me as bait,' Lettle shouted back.

Rayan didn't tell her about the trap either. His earlier words were given new meaning: 'We might love each other, Lettle, but without trust we cannot live for each other.'

He was right, she thought bitterly.

She let her anger lead her wherever it willed. At first she was just determined to get away from the palace, her feet pounding the ground in frustration.

Part of her thought about leaving Mosima altogether. At least in Waning she'd have her diviners to comfort her. But then she realised she couldn't leave even if she wanted to. She didn't have Jani blood.

For the first time in a long while Mosima truly felt like a prison. She looked up and realised where her rage had her taken her. Sahar's apothecary.

The shop was dark. Lettle tried the handle, it was unlocked as she suspected.

No need for security in paradise, she thought ironically.

The smell of spices and herbs wafted across the doorway as she stepped into the cool room. She found a torch by the door and lit it, setting the shelves of jars twinkling.

One jar stood out in particular. The label read 'teqan root'.

It was the poison Sahar had used to lace Lettle's drink.

How had she been so blind?

But Sahar had been cunning, even in the moments while Rayan lay dying he pretended not to know the antidote. She wondered now whether the dose had been lethal enough for Rayan's size, as she doubted Sahar would have hesitated if Rayan was close to death.

No, the poison had been measured for her alone.

Lettle took down the jar and smashed it on the floor, then ground the glass into the teqan root with her heel so it would be unusable.

She moved into the back room where Sahar and Norey slept, but she realised that too had been a lie. Dust lined the headboard of the bed, and the contents of a glass of some sort of juice had gone mouldy on the bedside table. The nights away from the palace must have been spent on the southern plains.

The only thing that wasn't covered in dust was the desk in the corner.

She went to it and threw open the drawers. There was nothing of note in the papers she found, which were predominantly stock lists. As her anger cooled, she wondered what she was even doing here.

Sahar had admitted to his deeds, anything else would be for the faeguard to find.

But then she saw it, his prophecy tokens tucked away in a glass jar at the back.

Sahar had always stressed how important it was always to have your talismans with you. Why would he hide them away?

She opened the jar and spilled the tokens out onto the desk. The wood, having been carved many decades before hers, had grown smoother with handling. She ran her hands over them, wondering why Sahar no longer kept them with him.

'Ouch.' She recoiled as one of the tokens nicked her skin. She picked up the offending piece. It was the lungs, the only talisman that had resisted the grinding of age. She held it up to the firelight. It also appeared to be slightly more rudimentary than Sahar's other pieces.

A thought occurred to her.

'No, he wouldn't . . .' she whispered her denial to herself while simultaneously withdrawing the proof from her pocket.

She removed the lungs from her set of talismans to compare.

The wood was smooth and intricately drawn.

Sahar swapped the pieces.

She stood there in shock for a minute piecing it all together. Talismans only worked for those who carved them.

Why else would Sahar not bother carrying his unless he had rendered them unusable too?

She thought back to when Sahar could have had the opportunity to swap them. Then it dawned on her: a few days after Yeeran had left, Lettle had called at the apothecary and Sahar had gone to the back to oil her pieces. Soon after, the Fates stopped speaking to her.

It must have been then. But what did he get out of this?

She tried to imagine Sahar sitting here, reading his own prophecy that proclaimed Lettle would one day kill Rayan. Already grief-stricken from the loss of his son and nephew, Sahar would not have been able to cope with more death.

Besides, Lettle knew what it felt like to try to deny a prophecy.

But it always came true. *Always.*

Her throat constricted, making her breath uneven as she conjured Sahar at this very desk hatching a plan to kill Lettle. And the prophecy tokens?

How better to hide his intent than to take away her ability to foresee it?

His denial turned to madness.

'Oh, Sahar, you fool.'

She swapped back her talisman and balled all her tokens in her fist. Then she cast them out across the floor.

As soon as she slipped into magesight she saw the silver glow of prophecy. She sagged with relief, dropping to her knees as she began to read the future.

The stomach blossomed with a string of magic, the trail of which ran across the floor towards the lungs, indicating the end of something old, something binding. The lungs on the other hand were twisted upwards with a pearl of magic pointing east, suggesting that this prophecy would soon come to pass. The intestines had taken on a curious shape of magic, one that Lettle had never translated before, but she recognised the symbol from her studies – this foretelling was about humans.

She worked her way through the rest of the swirls and shapes until a sentence formed in her mind. When she had parsed the nature of the prophecy in full, she adjusted her eyes back to the torch-lit room.

She spoke the prophecy out loud, the words given meaning as she said them, '*Enslaved then bound, lost then found. Humans made low no longer. Cursebound to centuries on four fleet feet but soon their freedom beckons.*'

Lettle tilted her head trying to understand it, but the words were nonsense to her.

'Humans made low no longer?' she whispered. The words were reminiscent of the prophecy told a thousand years ago:

Forever the war will rage, until united, the three shall die.

Humans made low, then fae made lower,

Then elves in ignorance, gone is their power,

Cursed to endure, cursed to survive.

All shall perish lest all three thrive.

But Lettle didn't understand how they could be related.

'Four fleet feet?' Again, Lettle shook her head.

She scooped up her talismans before taking Sahar's too and strode out of the apothecary.

An obeah bounded past her and she jumped out of the way.

'Watch out . . .' her shout trailed to a whisper.

Four fleet feet.

She turned to magesight to confirm the thought that had struck her. The obeah's core of light was bronze, something she'd noticed before but had never questioned.

She'd only seen the same hue on one other – Alder.

Obeah were once humans.

EPILOGUE

Furi

Furi sat on her throne watching as the leaves around her began to wilt. Laden with fat droplets from the rain shower, they fell quickly to the ground. Puddles pockmarked the oversaturated soil, unused to rainfall. She watched as two of them combined into a small stream that weaved through the undergrowth, uprooting some of the ferns and shrubbery.

But there was nothing she could do to stop the destruction her connection to the land was causing. Her grief had eclipsed her mind so completely.

She'd lost too much too fast.

Furi, you have to fight this despair, Amnan urged as the grass around them turned brown and the colour began to spread.

What's the point? she said back to him. *There's nothing good left in Mosima.*

What about me? he said.

When Furi didn't respond something sharp pierced her arm and she looked down to find Amnan's jaw locked around her wrist.

You're not pleading your case very well, she said. But the pain had brought her out of her haze and she was able to stop the rain.

This wallowing is not you, Furi, you have to resist it.

She nodded, but tears leaked from her eyes.

All of a sudden, a sharp breeze ran through the woodland, stronger than anything she'd ever felt in Mosima.

This is what they want, Amnan continued. *To break you so much that Mosima suffers. Do not give them what they want.*

Furi nodded and attempted to get a grip of the wind that howled through the trees. She tried to clear her mind of the horrors of the day. It was hard, the burden so difficult, but eventually the wind stopped and she opened her eyes.

Someone moved in the forest ahead. Using magesight Furi confirmed that they were Lightless. Furi got up from her throne intent on following them – for why would someone be walking through the Royal Woodland on their own so late at night?

She recognised who they were as she got nearer.

'Anyah?' she called out.

The food taster turned around at her name and dipped her head in a bow.

'My queen.'

'What are you doing? It's late to be out.'

'I went to see the royal healer.' She held out her wrist, brandishing the stitches there.

'I don't suppose anyone has thanked you for saving Lettle?'

Anyah smiled ruefully. 'It was no problem, I'm just glad I was there. It was only because I'd seen her leave with a tray of food I hadn't yet tasted.'

Furi laughed. 'That is lucky indeed, that you take your job so seriously.'

Anyah looked up at her frankly. 'I have no choice, my queen. If I let the seer die, then my sentence would be extended.'

'True, but you didn't need to jump in front of a blade for her.'

'No, but it was that or let her die,' Anyah said. Her honesty was refreshing.

'From what I heard, you fought well. Where did you learn?'

Anyah smiled again, this time a little playfully. 'I have four older brothers.'

Furi's thoughts went to Najma.

'Did I say something wrong?' Anyah asked, stepping forward.

'No, not at all, I was just thinking of my own brother. He taught me how to fight too.'

Anyah nodded.

'Why were you sentenced to servitude in the palace, Anyah?' Furi asked.

'I enrolled in the faeguard two years before my eighteenth birthday. I didn't get to training before they found out I had lied about my age.'

'And you were sentenced here? For how long?'

'Your mother thought it prudent that I learn patience, so I am in my fifth and final year.'

Five years. That was a lot for such a small lie.

An idea came to Furi. A rash one, and probably something she would regret but there were so few people she could trust.

'You once said that you looked up to my former second-in-command. How would you like that role?'

By saving Lettle, Anyah had proved she wasn't part of Sahar's organisation. And perhaps having a Lightless as her number two would help her fix some of the wrongs of the past.

Anyah's eyes widened to globes. 'But I know nothing. Less than nothing. I only had a couple of hours' training—'

'None of that matters – only that I trust you. Training can come after. What do you think?'

Anyah didn't hesitate. 'Yes, absolutely, yes.'

'Then Anyah, would you like to come with me topside? There's something I want to see.'

When Furi thought Anyah's eyes couldn't get any wider, they did.

'Yes,' she said breathlessly.

Together they walked the length of Mosima, star gliders trailing in their wake until they reached the boundary.

'Aiftarri,' Furi said and the magic parted to let them through.

'Now I can't be long, a few minutes at the most,' Furi said.

'What are we doing?'

'Climbing trees.'

Anyah must have thought Furi had lost her mind, but when they exited the tunnel into the moonlight Furi ran to the nearest tree and started to climb.

'Come on.'

Anyah needed no further encouragement. The woman was sprightly, her muscles supple from kitchen work as she followed Furi up the tree.

When they crested the canopy, Furi looked out towards the Elven Lands.

At first her eyes didn't see anything amiss, but then she saw them, like fireflies in the distance, torches danced along the dark horizon. And though she couldn't hear them, she imagined the footfalls of their boots thrumming out towards the forest like a battle drum.

'What is it?' Anyah asked.

'That is war.'

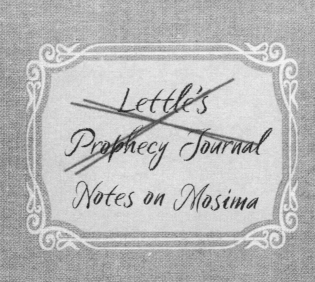

~~Lettie's~~
~~Prophecy Journal~~

Notes on Mosima

Colonel no longer – Y

❧ ELVES ❧

YEERAN ~~Colonel~~ of the Waning Army. *She/her*

LETTLE Diviner pledged to the Gural diviners, and sister of Yeeran. *She/her*

And now Royal Seer of the fae and consort to the King – L

King of the fae and son of Najma – R

RAYAN ~~Captain~~ in the Waning Army, defected from Crescent as a child. *He/him*

KOMI Elf captured by the fae ten years ago and kept prisoner in Mosima. *He/they*

AKA Chieftain Akomido of Crescent, the Two-Bladed Tyrant. Deceased – L

SALAWA Chieftain to the Waning tribe, and Yeeran's lover. *She/they*

IMNA A Gural diviner who now resides in the infirmary due to illness of the mind. *He/him*

MOTOGO General of the Waning Army. *They/them*

MADU Soldier in the Waning Army, only survivor of those who captured Yeeran. *She/her*

'Guest' is a stretch. Lettle won't let him leave until she figures out the prophecy he relates to – Y

ALDER One of the Nomads who was found by the trail to Mosima. A guest of the fae. *He/him*

❧ FAE ❧

FURI ~~Commander~~ of the faeguard and daughter of Queen Vyce of Mosima. *She/they*

NERAD Prince of the Jani dynasty, son of Queen Chall. *He/him*
Betrayed the fae and killed his mother and aunt. Now dead – L

VYCE Queen of the fae, ruling in tandem with her sister Chall. *She/her*
Deceased. Murdered by Nerad – Y

CHALL Queen of the fae, ruling in tandem with her sister Vyce. *She/her*

GOLAN Stylist to the fae's elite. *He/they*

HOSTA One of the faeguard who escorted the elves from the Wasted Marshes. *They/them*
Sentenced to the mines for crimes against us – R

BERRO Faeguard. Furi's second-in-command. *She/they*

SAHAR Former seer in the fae court. Father of Furi. *He/him*

NOREY Sahar's partner and Royal Horticulturist. Lightless. *He/him*

And my father - R

NAJMA Prince of the Jani dynasty killed by Yeeran. *He/him*

∽ OBEAH ∾

PILA Bonded to Yeeran. *She/they*

XOSA Bonded to Nerad. *She/they*

AMNAN Bonded to Furi. *He/they*

HUDAN Bonded to Najma. *He/they*

SANQ Bonded to Berro. *She/they*

MERI Bonded to Chall. *She/they*

ONYA Bonded to Vyce. *She/they*

CORI Bonded to Sahar. *She/they*

Pila once again would like to reiterate that she is not only the cleverest of all the obeah but the fastest too – Y

✇ HUMANS ✇

AFA Name attributed by the fae to the last living human. Believed to have cursed the fae to Mosima. *He/him*

Also known as the 'Wandering Human' in elven lore – R

✇ GODS ✇

ASASE The earth god who came into being as a grain of wheat. Created humans and bestowed on them the magical language of the rocks and trees. *They/them*

EWIA The sun god born as a bat with two heads. Created the fae and granted them the gift of sunlight magic. *They/them*

BOSOME The moon god, who resides as a drop of water in the sky. Created the elves with the power to read the Fates. *They/them*

Praise merciful one – L

❧ TERMS ❧

BINDING BANQUET A party that marks the binding of a fae to their obeah. It includes drinking, dancing, and merriment.

CAPERLY A mountain village where those too elderly and too young to travel with the Nomads reside.

CONCH SHORE A beach that runs the length of the bay situated west of the Royal Woodland. It is fed by an estuary on the eastern coast of the continent.

Accessed by the people trying to kill Lettle. I have stationed more guards at the entrance in case they return – R

CRYSTAL GLADE A forest south-west of Mosima. The trees there are uniquely covered in dew drops.

DRUMFIRE The magic predominately used by the Waning tribe in warfare. Obeah skin is used to adorn drums, which is then harnessed to create magical projectiles.

FAEGUARD The soldiers who protect and police the citizens of Mosima. The faeguard ranking system is numerical ranging from one to three, except the commander who exists outside and above the ranks.

FRAEDIA A crystal that mimics the properties of sunlight which can be used to grow plants and warm homes. The most valuable elven commodity.

FRAY The fray is a cluster of fraedia crystal that grows from the ceiling of the Mosima cavern.

FREE THE LIGHT INITIATIVE A new venture run by Lettle and Golan to improve the Lightless' rights in Mosima.

For the first time the Lightless will be a part of the governing of Mosima - L

FAE MAGIC The fae can summon a magical thread, only seen through magesight. It can only extend as far as the height of the fae who wields it. Strength and duration varies per person.

*They are treated poorly in Mosima, as
if they are not whole - L*

LIGHTLESS Those unbound to an obeah.

LORHAN Capital of the Fae Lands that used to reside on the Bleeding Field.

MAGESIGHT The ability to see magic through a sixth sense. Diviners call this 'becoming heedless'.

*It only took Rayan a few
minutes to learn it, and Yeeran
a week - L*

*It didn't take me a
week, Lettle. Just a
few days - Y*

MOSIMA The underground cavern where the fae have been cursed to live.

SOUTHERN PLAINS An outcrop halfway up the cavern wall in Mosima. The trail was closed after Golan lost his leg falling from the cliff's edge.

FAE LANGUAGE The fae language comes fully formed to those who become faebound. The sounds are difficult to master if you are Lightless. Therefore, all fae are first taught the universal tongue, that elves refer to as elvish.

THE FATES The Fates allow diviners to parse the future. They are believed to be part of the god Bosome's many influences in the world.

The prophecy I read in my most recent research rings of truth, I cannot shake it from my mind.

Forever the war will rage, until united, the three shall die.
Humans made low, then fae made lower,
Then elves in ignorance, gone is their power,
Cursed to endure, cursed to survive.
All shall perish lest all three thrive
— L

The Fates have not been forthcoming recently, though I managed to glean the following that relates to Alder:

In the early hours of the morrow's new day, a tree will fall by the pathway to Mosima. Seek your answers in the night, dawn will bring you peace — L

OBEAH Creatures that bind to fae, enabling them to come into both the fae language and fae magic. They are beasts of magic, which has made them vulnerable to overhunting by elves.

No one knows how or why obeah choose the people they do. I often wonder why Pila chose me, an elf who has murdered her kin. Though I am grateful – Y

THE BLIGHT A large agricultural district, three fields wide, that has been pockmarked by acidic soil.

Caused by me being born outside of Mosima – R

STAR GLIDERS Small lizards with translucent scaled wings. Often seen around those with Jani blood. Their bulbous heads are bioluminescent and light up the Royal Woodland at night.

ACKNOWLEDGEMENTS

Book twos in trilogies are notoriously hard, and I wasn't sure I could do it again. But there is something about the Faebound world that drew me in, despite my trepidation. As soon as my fingers touched the keyboard, new characters and settings poured forth – and it's only because of the people around me who foster this creativity that *Cursebound* is now in your hands.

Thank you to my incomparable agent, Juliet Mushens and the whole team, Kiya, Liza, Alba, Catriona, Rachel and Emma. The team isn't complete without my wonderful US agent, Ginger Clark – thank you.

To the editing team: Rachel Winterbottom and Tricia Narwani – the guidance you provide is invaluable. You are my guiding lights among the darkness of my blank screen.

Thank you to the wider teams whose hard work turns my words into stories.

From the Del Rey team: Ayesha Shibli, Keith Clayton, Scott Shannon, Julie Leung, Marcelle Iten Busto, Alex Larned, David Moench, Jordan Pace, Angie Campusano, Ada Maduka, Ashleigh Heaton, Tori Henson, Sabrina Shen, Kay Popple and Regina Flath.

And the Voyager UK team: Catherine Perks, Emily Chan, Terence Caven, Susanna Peden, Sian Richefond, Leah Woods, Holly Martin and Rosie Hawkins.

Thank you to illustrator Joe Wilson and designer Ellie Game. *Cursebound* is somehow even more beautiful that *Faebound*!

Endless gratitude to the booksellers and the retailers: Waterstones, Goldsboro, FairyLoot – thank you for your continued faith and support (and those *stunning* editions).

To my family: the El-Arifis and Dinsdales, thank you for everything you do. Shout out to Rachel Bell to whom this book is dedicated. Though we may not be sisters by blood, we're pretty close to it.

To the gays and gals: Karin, Sam, Tasha, Hannah, Lizzie and Amy. Thank you for keeping me sane(ish). And to my guys, Laurie and Jim, who make each day better than the last.

Finally, as always, my last words belong to you, dear readers. I will always be grateful for our journeys together through words and ink. May it continue.

FOR REBELLION TO IGNITE, SOMETHING MUST BURN

Discover Saara El-Arifi's *Sunday Times* bestselling The Ending Fire Trilogy.

Available now.

HARPER
Voyager